The Borders

Revell Cornell

This one is for my wife,
Liz,
who sat night after night,
probably bored out of her mind,
as I sat tapping away at the keys

Chapter One

Monday. 2 a.m.

The streets were empty as the two policemen continued their slow exterior inspection of shops and stores in the city centre. The police car they rode in crawled along, its pace being hindered by wind that was increasing in strength, and rain that was hammering out a tattoo on the roof of their vehicle. The swishing wipers were just about coping with the torrent of water that ran down the windscreen.

Pubs that just over an hour ago were teeming with alcohol fuelled life, now stood silent. The last bus had left the station an hour ago, and the imbibers who lived out of town were now probably dead to the world between duvet and mattress. Others who lived local had long since cleared the lively nightlife area that was the Newcastle upon Tyne Bigg Market; 'Bigg' being the olde English word for Barley

To the right and left of the car that was decaled in Northumbria Police colours, retail outlets, restaurants and cafés that hours ago glowed and glittered, were now steeped in darkness. All were given a long slow look by the driver of the car and his partner. Visibility was reasonably good, but a flashlight was still being used to enable the officers to inspect dark corners more closely.

Constable John Gibson, the older of the two policemen, twisted on his seat and aimed the flashlight down the alley to his left.

"Whoa!" he exclaimed.

His partner, Tim Johnson, stepped on the brake and moved the automatic gear shift into P. He looked in the direction of John's stare, and then leaned across the centre console to get a better look.

"See it? Under the waste bin?" said John.

Tim leaned more, eyes strained for a moment, then said, "Be easier with the window down."

John hit the button on the door to his left powering down the window to just below eye level. Raindrops splashed on his face.

"It's just a dummy isn't it? From the dress shop." said Tim.

John watched for a moment, then said, "What, a shop dummy with trousers and shoes on?"

John held the flashlight steady, pointing the beam of light to underneath a large waste container.

"Well it's not moving that's for sure." He thought for a moment, then said, "Swing the front end around. Put the headlights on him."

Tim groaned. "Ah, man! If it's not a dummy, it's a bloody tramp. Just leave it."

Tim sat back in his seat, raised his left arm off the steering wheel, eased back the sleeve of his black uniform jacket, and checked the illuminated dial on his watch.

"Look, we're finished in just over an hour," he said, "Let's not spoil it, eh?"

John turned and looked at his partner as he thought on the suggestion.

The weather was atrocious, vicious, and the wind was increasing in strength by the minute, howling, and rocking the car. The rain, blown up the River Tyne by a strong easterly wind, was now pebble-dashing the blue and white chequered car with raindrops the size of pea-gravel. John turned again and peered through the gap between the glass window and the top of the door. The prone figure was just distinguishable amongst the rubbish that had been piled up against the overfull commercial bin.

Doubt set in. John began to wonder if the figure was indeed an out of fashion mannequin thrown out by a local store. The human form lay part underneath the bin, with only the lower body parts projecting into the direct path of the torrential downpour. The bin stood on twelve-inch wheels, and John guessed that the person, if it was a person, had tried to scramble underneath for what little protection it offered.

He watched for a few seconds more, watching, hoping for movement. Nothing, then, suddenly, a gust of wind lifted cartons and empty boxes and swirled them around the dead end that was the alley. John pushed his door open.

"*That* isn't a shop dummy. And tramp or not, no one could sleep through this racket," he said.

Tim growled as John stepped out of the vehicle and let the wind slam the door behind him. Tim reached for the gear shift, then stopped, listening for a moment as a message came through on the police radio. Satisfied that the subject of the message was of no interest to him or his partner, he reversed a car's length, eased forward again, and then did a ninety-degree left hander. The full beam of the headlights shone on his partner's back, and John's shadow loomed large on the wall at the far end of the alley. The teeming rain sparkled like a million needles in the spread of light projecting from the car.

Tim hunched over the steering wheel and looked beyond the sweeping wiper blades that were now barely coping with the incessant run of water. He saw his partner crouch down on the wet, glistening cobbles, drag the figure out from under the bin, and then flick an over- the-shoulder beckoning hand. Tim groaned again, placed his flat cap on his head, and then pushed open the driver's door. He dashed around the front of the car toward John, hand on cap, leaning into the wind, and leaping over the streams of water that ran between the cobbles. He stopped beyond his partner and looked down on the figure that he could now see was indeed a man. He braced his feet and leaned against the force of the wind on his back.

"And?" Tim shouted.

John looked up, eyes narrowed against the stinging rain. The noise of the downpour lashing and rattling against the bin all but drowned out his voice.

"He's still got a pulse," he said with raised voice.

Water streamed down the peak of John's cap and onto his nose. He shook his head, dispersing most of the rain from his face, and then wiped off what remained with his right hand. He shouted up to Tim.

"Come on, man. Ambulance! While he's still got life in him."

John turned to the man again, and eased him onto his back. He stopped short of turning his head away as he winced.

"Jesus Christ!" he said.

Tim looked down and then gently wiped the man's face.

"Fuck! That's one hell of a beating."

*

Seventy-five minutes later, the two constables sat patiently outside a cubicle, in a corridor, in the A&E department of the Newcastle upon Tyne R.V.I. hospital. They had played the whole incident by the book – clear concise reporting, no ambiguities, no grey areas - so, John figured, they would be relieved shortly, and allowed to end their shift.

He stood, and then paced back and forth. His wet trousers clung to his legs. He idly spun his damp cap around on his left fist. He'd just about read the print off the various notices and information leaflets that were pinned to the cream walls of the corridor. Boredom was imminent.

John wasn't an impatient man, he could wait, he could pass time, but he couldn't sit still. His wife's comment on the day he'd switched to traffic was, 'You'll last a week. Sitting in a car will drive you up the wall.' That was nearly ten years ago. Sure, one of John's problems was his low boredom threshold, but, life in traffic was never boring. For all that, a detective's position was John's dream.

He walked back to the A&E reception area. For a city centre hospital, it was relatively quiet. To his right, in an office set behind a waist-high, green

Formica counter and a glass screen, a middle-aged lady in a light blue uniform, stood tap-tapping at a computer keyboard. Beyond the lady in blue, a young girl in denim jeans, and a grey short sleeved, round neck top, busied herself in the depths of a filing cabinet drawer.

The patients awaiting attention were indeed patient – and quiet. A woman, possibly mid-thirties, and dressed in jeans and a short cream jacket, sat with a young boy of middle-school age. She looked at him tenderly as he held a hand to his right ear. He winced now and then, and twitched occasionally, in response to the sharp sudden stabs of pain. Each time he twitched, the woman, gently caressed his shoulder and looked on sympathetically. She leaned toward him, gently eased his hand down, and looked into his ear. She studied what evidence she saw, and then smiled at the boy kindly.

The only other people waiting, a young couple, an elderly man, and a young Asian lad, continually looked around at the four blank walls, the clock on the wall in front of them, and, occasionally, to the office. John turned and headed back to where he'd been seated outside the cubicle.

A nurse passed by and gave John an unseen admiring glance. She saw a man who was maybe forty-five years old, brown hair, a touch over six-feet tall, a lean, muscular, broad shouldered frame, and a face with kind green eyes. The she saw the ring on his wedding finger.

When shifts allowed, John and his wife Lynn spent one of their two free days working with under-privileged kids. They'd given up on all the tests, drugs, rhythm patterns, specialists in the U.K and Europe, homeopathic suggestions, and even some of the whacko suggestions on the internet. After twenty years, and as many false alarms, they decided it was just not meant to be. Lynn could not conceive, but they kept on trying, and Lynn said that working with the kids kept her hormones in place.

The curtains around the cubicle parted, and the stinging scent of antiseptic drifted out. John turned to face the duty doctor.

"Anything worth noting, Doctor?"

The doctor, tall, just this side of skinny, early thirties, with already thinning fair hair and a face that said he was getting the shit end of the stick, sank his hands into the pockets of his open white coat. He smiled wanly, but only for a split second, and then shook his head.

"He'll live," he said. "There's nothing broken, but, as you saw, he's very badly beaten around the face and head."

He indicated behind him with a backward nod.

"I continually think that I've seen about as much a beating as a man can take, then…." He shook his head, pausing for a moment, and then said, "So, I guess he holds the record - for this week anyway."

He took a deep breath, and then released it with a slight growl. He shook his head, slowly. "'Do no harm'. I made that promise within the Hippocratic Oath, but by God if I could get my eyes on some of the people who perpetrate violence like this I would…"

John sized the doctor up again, and doubted very much if the doctor could, or even would, do anything.

The doctor spoke resigned, matter-of-factly. "His eyes may be of some use to him – once the swelling goes down. We'll know better when we can get to them without causing damage; maybe tomorrow."

"Is he conscious? Can I talk to him?" said John.

The doctor edged past John, and walked off. He spoke without turning.

"He's sleeping, but you can see him if you really need to. Tell the nurse I said it was okay."

He paused, maybe mulling on his words, then walked on again, mumbling. John was sure he heard the words 'bloody alcohol'. He wondered if the doctor should see someone about possible depression

John eased between the rustling plastic curtains of the cubicle. The nurse, maybe five-feet two, chubby, and short dark hair, turned to face him. She spoke softly.

"I heard. You need to be quick though. He's being transferred to a ward as soon as the porter can find a trolley."

She turned back to adjusting the flow from a bag of liquid something hanging from a portable stand. The business end of the drip was in the back of the injured man's left hand.

John squeezed between the nurse and the bed, stooped, and studied the man's face – all yellow ointment and bandages. John looked to the nurse

11

"Anything serious or just cosmetics…" He checked the name tag on her uniform; "… Nurse Carter?"

Her eyes opened wide in mock surprise.

"Cosmetics? That's a new one." She thought for a moment. "You heard the doctor. His heart's beating strongly. He's breathing, and the tidying up, and stemming of further damage has been done. When he comes around…"

John interrupted. "No 'if' about it? He'll definitely regain consciousness? He's been out a long time."

She looked at the patient again.

"His blood tests show that he's three times over the drink driving limit. So, is he unconscious because of his injuries, or has he just passed out? Maybe he …"

A head poked through the cubicle curtains, and said, "Trolley's here, Jill."

Jill looked up and saw a hospital porter. She nodded to the porter and then turned to John again.

"Anyway, his vitals will be checked regularly, and when he comes around we'll examine him again. Now, if you're finished ...?"

John held up his palms as Jill pulled the curtains fully open, exposing the side of the bed.

"Sure, sure. Just carry on," he said.

He bent over a chair where the man's clothes lay folded, and began to examine them. He started with the jacket.

"No wallet, money bag, purse …?" he asked, as he lifted the garment.

Nurse Carter shrugged. "What he had when you brought him in is all on that chair. His boots are under the bed"

She helped the porter as he paralleled the trolley. Then, simply and quickly, they took the weight, and then pulled the sheet that the man lay on from the bed to the trolley. The man came with it.

"Right," said Jill, "I'll be back for his clothes in a minute. Okay?"

She turned away from John, and then turned back.

"Oh, and Doctor Clarke thinks the patient is aged around thirty, thirty-five, if that's any help to you."

John's brow furrowed as he examined the man's black, trousers.

"Oh, aye, thanks. Look, I'll probably not be here when you come back, but chances are the C.I.D. will be. Catch you later, eh? Oh, and they may want to see his clothes again. Would you store them somewhere safe please?"

He continued examining the man's still wet trousers, as the mystery man was wheeled away to a ward. He startled as Tim crept up behind him and tapped him on the shoulder.

Tim grinned, "Nervous, are we?"

John ignored the friendly jibe.

"Look at this," he said, "Real James Bond stuff. Not one label or logo on his clothes. We've got the man from nowhere."

Tim looked over John's shoulder.

"See. No wallet, no money, nothing," said John.

"So he was robbed," said Tim, "It happens."

John faced his partner.

"What, they took the tags out of his trousers, and his shirt? And look, no label on the inside pocket of his jacket. Muggers are doing that now are they?"

Tim frowned. "Look, maybe this one is a bit out of our league, mate. Let's just leave things alone, eh?" He shook his head. "This is a job for the suits, John."

John stood up from where he crouched over the chair. He grinned at his colleague.

"I love puzzles, me"

Chapter Two

Monday. Late morning.

The specially adapted Renault Traffic Master edged forward at the traffic lights. George Thompson, the driver of the vehicle, checked in his wing-mirrors, then spoke to his co-driver, Prison Officer Kenny McDonald. Both men wore full prison officer's uniform.

"She's still there. Still up my arse."

The lights changed from red and amber, to green alone, and George moved off across the junction, still with an eye on the silver Peugeot 307 behind him. Kenny, six feet two inches, and one of Pharaoh's lean cattle, leaned forward, and peered into the mirror on his side of the prisoner transport van – the P.T.V.

"I see her," he said, "What do you think? You worried?"

George slowed, and flipped up the sun visor, as a bus pulled out in front of him and blocked the glare of the early morning summer sun.

"I'm not sure. This is an A road, so it could just be…and she's on her own… but why the fuck doesn't she overtake?" said George.

He thought for a moment.

"It's been nearly two miles now," he said.

He followed the bus, stuck in its wake in the busy high street as pedestrians darted between gaps in the traffic. This wasn't going to be a fast ride.

Kenny spoke as he studied the reflection of the car.

"Y'know, some people have a phobia about overtaking any sort of Police vehicle. They've got a guilt complex. Y'know, like, have I taxed the car, are the tyres legal? That sort o' thing." He reflected for a moment, "It wouldn't do any harm to ring it in, I suppose."

George took his eye off the bus in front, checked in his mirror again, and then nodded.

"Yeah, better safe than…" he said, "Jot her number down will you? I think its S60 KAT. Can you see it?"

"Yeah, brand new model, private number plate. Some fucker with money."

Kenny undid a second button on his Government Issue blue shirt, reached for the police standard radio handset as he spoke, and then hit the single button that put him in touch with the Prisoner Movement Department, the P.M.D., at Northumbria Police Headquarters. In less than a minute, he had identified their vehicle as P.T.V. 39 on route to Durham Prison, carrying three prisoners from the Newcastle Quayside Law Courts. His message of being concerned at a following vehicle was taken, and a course of action initiated.

*

John Gibson reversed slowly down the sloping tarmac drive of his three-bed semi, as his wife, Lynn, walked gingerly alongside the car. John had a foot clearance on the left of the car where the grass of the front lawn seemed to grow faster than he could cut it and another foot on his right where the roots of the Acer trees were beginning to show. His wife, Lynn, stooped her five-feet, nine-inch frame down to the open driver's window. Her long, auburn hair tumbled over her face, and the unzipped jacket of her black tracksuit fell open.

"Did you hear me?" said Lynn

Lynn's voice was a little raised, a little threatening, as she spoke. She tried her best stern expression, but still John smiled.

"Yes, love, I heard you. And, like the weak willed husband that I am, I will obey you without question."

The suppressed grin on his face widened. He gave in, stopped the car, knocked it out of gear, and snatched on the handbrake. He laughed out long and loud; and then he sighed.

"Ah, Lynn, you're lovely, and funny, and…"

Lynn's anger subsided – marginally.

"Okay, okay, but promise me you'll be there. I mean it, John. I want a holiday before the summer's over."

John nodded emphatically, and slapped both hands on the steering wheel.

"Yes, yes. I promise you. I'll be out of the hospital just after eleven, and I'll be at the travel agents long before twelve. There, are you happy now?"

"Half happy, but I still don't understand why you have to see the hospital mystery man. And I'm still not sure that you getting involved is a good thing. Why are you doing it?"

"Lynn, love, I feel sorry for him. He looked pathetic, and his face… I don't know, I just want to make sure he's alright. I'm curious. Okay?" He grinned. "Have I got your permission?"

"I… oh, yes. Go on. Get yourself away before I change my mind."

Lynn slapped the flat of her hand on top of the saloon car, and edged away from it, backing up the drive. John put the gear stick into reverse gear again, and began steering the car out on to the road.

"You're in the wrong job," Lynn shouted. "I think what you're looking for is Social work."

She smiled, and then waved John off.

*

As the Low Fell high street disappeared behind him, George watched the blue lights set in the grille of the trailing unmarked police car flash into life. It pulled out from where it had settled itself five minutes earlier, five cars behind him, and the two lanes of opposing traffic parted to allow it through.

George put his foot down. His speed crept up to fifty miles an hour, and the gap between him and the following Peugeot opened up to sixty metres. Within seconds the unmarked car had pulled alongside the car that was the source of George's concern. He watched in the exterior rear-view mirror, as the police driver indicated to the Peugeot to pull to the left hand side of the road, and then pulled ahead into the gap created by George. That's it, he thought, the Peugeot was out of it.

George did not see the black Mondeo; the same Mondeo that had always been there since he'd pulled away from the Law Courts. Still six cars behind, it followed the six cars in front as they overtook the now parked police car.

George hated his job, but what else could he do? He'd left a secondary modern school in 1970-something with no qualifications whatsoever, and laboured on building sites for nearly twenty years. His assets then had been his endearing boyish grin, his cute unruly mop of raven black hair, and his muscles. Steroid free muscle that he'd added to his six-foot frame was the result of hard, back-breaking jobs where the only requirement was strength. It had been when he'd hit thirty-something that he had decided he needed a job with prospects; prospects in George's case meant security of work, and maybe a pension. He was big, strong, subservient to anyone in a suit, and desperate for stability in his income. The prison service grabbed him, and moulded him. George had found the stability he sought; stability for his wife, his kids, and the safety of a regular income – as meagre as it was.

George was not high security. He'd never get anywhere near murderers, terrorists, child abusers, rapists, or even violent gangsters. For all his size and strength, George was docile, facile, and malleable, but his presence made any prisoner think twice. So, George spent his prison career with young men, young men who'd served their apprenticeship in young offender's camps, and then worked their way up the ladder to the real thing. At each correction centre they would learn a new skill. They would enter the system as shoplifters, car thieves, or D&D's, and graduate as safebreakers, forgers, bank robbers, or maybe, if they had really impressed someone, leave prison with an introductory password to their local drug dealer.

George should not have been in the prison van that day. Usual story; man rings in sick, staff shortages, holidays, and George finds himself doing the court run. He'd get extra pay, and, with early starts and late finishes, there'd even be a little overtime which would all help to pay for the little extras that made life in the technological age bearable.

George settled back, checking his rear-view mirror once more. He saw the stationary police car, lights still flashing, and the suspicious Peugeot, both parked up way behind him now. The journey continued in peace. Kenny twisted open his Thermos and filled a mug. George drank from the flask top, and drove with one hand.

The blockage on the A1M was the last thing that the two prison officers wanted on what was quickly becoming a very hot day. Just south of the Birtley service station, was a hired articulated lorry spread across the two south-bound lanes of the motorway. Vehicles were backed up for nearly a mile. From his vantage point where the motorway crested a hill, Kenny remarked that it looked odd, the way the lorry was at a near perfect right-angle to the flow of the traffic – as though parked. He studied the lanes of stationary cars, vans, wagons, lorries and buses, and then spotted the sign showing a turn-off just this side of the jack-knifed lorry. He shrugged, reached for the radio mic and reported the incident to the P.M.D. He informed them that he was heading for the Chester-le-Street turn off, by means of the inside lane, and would then continue on the old A1 trunk road, to Durham. He was given the go-ahead after thirty seconds of consultation between the P.M.D. and Durham Prison. George relaxed again, switched on the A.C. and thought of how he was going to enjoy the summer sun after the previous week of constant rain.

As George began his manoeuvring to take him over to the inside lane, the driver of the following Mondeo, a man of Asian origin, reached for his cell phone lying on the dashboard.

*

John Gibson sat opposite the mystery man, listening to his story. The man had gained consciousness early that morning. He had been discovered wandering around the adjacent ward, barefooted, with outdoor clothing in his arms. Only after ardent pleading by Nurse Carter's shift replacement, had the man conceded to wait until he'd had a few X-Rays taken. He was now sitting up in bed, sheets tucked in tightly around him, in pyjamas provided by the hospital. His bandages had been removed showing a gaunt but handsome face, still smeared with a yellow coloured cream. His eyes were slits only identifiable by the light they reflected. His skin was bruised, shiny and taught with the swelling resultant from the injuries.

The conversation was not going as John had hoped.

"Okay, okay, no problem. I understand," he said, "but, when the duty lads come in, you're gonna have to give them some details anyway. They'll be doing it officially."

The man shook his head slowly, held his arms tightly against his sides, and sighed noisily

21

through fat, swollen lips. For all the swelling and bruising, the man's words were reasonably distinct. His accent was Home Counties, maybe even London.

"I've done nothing," the man blubbered. "I didn't ask for your help. What is there to tell?"

"Come on, mate, get real. If they think there's something suspicious about you they can always find a charge to hold you on. And let's be honest, you say you weren't robbed, but you cut the tags off your clothing, and who the hell cuts out the label from the inside pocket of their jacket? Is that not suspicious? And you don't carry any I.D.! Nothing. What's all that about?"

John studied the man for a moment.

"Look," he said, "I'm simply asking who you are, and is there anyone you want me to contact? Mother, father, wife…?"

The man hung his head, and then slowly looked sideways. John studied him. Was the man thinking, playing for time, or exercising his neck?

"I'm a free-agent," the man said. "Okay, a bum if you like. I don't draw dole money, or any other government hand-out."

He'd sprayed spittle when he'd said the word 'bum'. He wiped a dribble of saliva from the corner of his mouth with the back of his right hand. John stored that fact in his memory bank – possibly right handed.

"So where'd you get the money for booze?" asked John. "You were reeking of it last night, and even now you still smell a bit fruity."

The man sighed again, and then rolled his eyes behind his puffed up cheeks. He spoke as if counting, pausing between each sentence.

"Odd jobs. Dish washing. Tidy-up gardens. Give window cleaners a hand, emergency labour on building sites, serve in chip-shops. I get by. I get paid out of petty-cash, back pockets."

John hunched forward in his chair, the beginning of a smile on his face.

"But what about washing your clothes, how the hell do you smarten up for serving in chip-shops, as you say? And why won't you give a name? You could be lying." John shook his head and said, "Hell's teeth, the lads are going to have a field day with you."

The man stretched toward a box of tissues on the bedside cabinet. John stood, reached over the bed for the box, and passed it to him. The man pulled a tissue from the box, again with his right hand, and wiped his mouth. John sat again, and waited. Was the man playing for time, making up his story?

The man groaned, and then looked around his bed.

"Where's my bag, my back-pack?"

John followed where the man had looked, then shrugged.

"There wasn't one at the spot where we found you" He grimaced. "Does that mean you *were* robbed?"

The man nodded slowly, delicately, and spluttered slightly as he spoke.

"Guess so, but it was only my change of clothes. My paper money, what little there is, is in my boots, and… "

John held up a palm to the man.

"Okay, look, it's obvious you're not a bum in the true sense of the word. So what is it? Down on your luck, out of work, left home, done a runner… what? And what's your name? Eh? Why won't you tell me?"

John watched as the man stared ahead. Then, slowly, a tear rolled up over his lower eye lid, balanced, than ran down his right cheek. Unable to control the tears now, he shrugged, resigned, gulping back the sobs.

"Okay. My name is Stephen Donnelly, I'm a recovering alcoholic… and… I… I killed my wife."

Chapter Three

Monday. Mid-day.

Kenny drained his cup of coffee, and then reached across the cab to take the flask top from George. George released the top as he studied the road ahead, and then dropped his free hand onto the gear lever. Kenny nodded in the direction of a vehicle joining the trunk road from a farm track on his left.

"Look at that idiot! Watch him, George."

George looked ahead, across the fields at the side of the road, and saw a large truck bumping and charging over the rutted dirt road towards a field gate that the P.T.V. would pass very soon

George eased off the accelerator fractionally and looked on as the truck - a yellow recovery vehicle, complete with jib, cable, and hook - bounced along towards where he would be in less than a minute. The truck slowed as the driver looked in George's direction, took in what was happening, and then stopped at the junction.

As the prison van passed, the truck driver acknowledged his reckless speed to George by holding up a gloved hand up in front of him. George in turn raised his hand, thanking the driver. The van sped on, and the truck pulled out behind it, spraying grass and dirt as its spinning back wheels fought to gain a grip with the high revving low gear. As soon as the tyres of the recovery truck did grip the tarmac, its speed increased, and the gap between the speeding prison van, and the rapidly accelerating truck closed. Then, as both vehicles approached a stretch of dual carriageway, the truck pulled out to pass. The gentleman that George was, he slowed down to facilitate the truck passing him.

As the truck cruised alongside, the passenger in the truck held up a gloved hand, again acknowledging George's kindness. George glanced sideways and saw that again, the hand hid the passenger's face. The truck edged ahead, its four litre engine effortlessly eating up the miles.

Kenny pointed at the vehicle as it sped past.

"Not much of a businessman is he?" he said.

"Eh? How do you mean?"

Kenny sat back in his seat and folded his arms. He spoke derisively.

"The paintwork's shit. No name, no telephone... *whoa!*"

Kenny threw up his hands in front of his face.

Both prison officers would later describe the light as blinding.

The truck had swerved violently in front of the prison van, leaving a gap of less than three metres between the two vehicles. As the truck straightened out, the driver had jammed on the brakes, while in turn his passenger tripped a switch that connected four throbbing generators bolted to the bed of the truck to sixteen large floodlights strapped across the back of the cab. The light was indeed blinding. The blue smoke thrown up by the squealing tyres filled the space between the truck and the van, as George stood on the brake pedal of the P.T.V. For all George's knee-jerk reaction, he could not prevent his van slamming into the extended, reinforced rear bumper of the truck;

26

scalding hot water and steam from the van's radiator squirted and hissed into the air. The engine of the prison van clanked as it idled. Only then were the sixteen floodlights switched off. Instinctively, George knocked the gear stick into neutral.

In the time it took George to gather his senses, glance sideways to check on Kenny, and then look ahead again, two men had appeared on the bed of the truck. Both men, one of them well over six feet tall while the other would struggle to reach six feet, wore red overalls, black balaclavas, and each held a sawn-off shotgun.

The taller man yelled, screamed, "Don't touch the phone! Don't touch the fucking phone!"

The other man then jumped down from the recovery truck and levelled his gun at the bottom of the driver's door.

His first shot blew a ragged hole in the outer skin of the door, at the lower left hand corner. George turned sideways, wide-eyed, to look down on the man. George was not yet terrified, but he was past nervous. The man pointed the gun up to him.

"Open the door!" he roared, "Open the fucking door!"

George froze, and the man fired again; another hole in the door, just above the previous one.

"I promise you, the next one will take your fucking feet off" the man shouted.

And still George sat, frozen to the spot. The man snapped the gun, and inserted two more cartridges into the shotgun. He pulled back on the hammers.

He shouted again. "You've got three, mate. One, two…"

George pulled back on the door release and the door clicked, then eased an inch. His attacker yanked the door open wide, reached up, grabbed the sleeve of George's uniform jacket, and pulled him sideways. George tumbled down, reaching out to grasp the handle of the door to help soften his fall – he missed. He landed head first, his outstretched arms broke his fall, but the backward over-bend of his hands broke the scaphoid bone in each wrist.

The tall man on the truck jumped down. He ran to Kenny's side of the van, and pointed his gun.

Kenny was no hero. He shouted, "Wait! Wait!"

He pulled the handle on the inside of his door and pushed. The door swung open and the man aimed the gun at Kenny's face. With his head, he indicated the side door which would slide back to reveal the prisoner's area of the van.

"Open it - now! Move you cunt, fucking move!"

Kenny pressed a switch on the dash, then dropped down to the road and opened the side door on the van. He remembered later that he'd thought, 'Burglars? Three fucking burglars? What the fuck does he want with them?'

Two of the three shackled prisoners, all still in civilian clothes, sat bemused, squinting, in the sudden bright light. The other prisoner, a young Asian man, stood defiant. No one moved. The gunman looked in to the mobile cell, and then prodded Kenny with the shotgun. He shouted just as the overheated clanking, banging engine of the prison van ground to a halt.

"Unlock them. Set them loose."

Kenny shrugged, apologetically, pleading. 'I don't have them. The driver. He always has the keys.'

The gunman growled, and then again prodded the two barrels into Kenny's chest, "So get them of your mate, you fucking idiot."

Thirty seconds had passed since the time of the collision.

On the driver's side of the vehicle the mangled door had now been slammed shut, and Kenny saw George hunched, crouched, against the front tyre, with a shotgun aimed at his face. George held his wrists up, in front of him. His chin lay on his chest, and he groaned deep in his throat.

The man who had pulled him from the cab was screaming at him.

"Stand up, you fucker! Stand up"

Kenny recognised the man's accent as Yorkshire. He tried to remember which of his prisoners, if any, was from Yorkshire. He looked ahead and saw a Vauxhall Vectra slow, pull on to the grass verge that ran alongside the dual carriageway, and then stop fifty yards ahead of the recovery truck. The hijacker who was hovering over George followed Kenny's gaze, then turned toward the Vectra, pointing his gun. The Vectra lurched forward and then stalled. The unseen driver started the engine again, slewed on the grass as he let the clutch out achingly slow, and then screamed away, crunching each gear change.

Kenny pointed to George, with an open hand, and spoke to the man who stood over him.

"He can't move. He can't put weight on his wrists. Look they're fucking swelling."

For his concern, Kenny got the butt of the shotgun rammed into his stomach.

"Lift him! C'mon, get him on his fucking feet. Hurry up, you cunt!"

Kenny placed himself between George and the hijacker. He reached forward, placed his wrists under George's arm pits, and then lifted. George shuffled on his knees, and then stood.

Forty-five seconds had passed. Another saloon car slowed, stared, and then screamed off.

After sixty seconds, Kenny was cuffed to an overhead steel bar in the security area of the van, and George was cuffed to Kenny ankle to ankle. The three prisoners, two white men and the one black man, were free of their con-joined handcuffs. All three were still in civilian clothes. Before the door was shut on him and George, Kenny saw the hijackers pull the tallest of the burglars, a long lean white man, toward them. The short vicious hijacker then pointed his shotgun at the other two.

"You've got seconds to piss off, or we blow your fucking legs away," he shouted.

The captive burglar looked alarmed. He looked from one to the other of the hi-jackers. He protested loudly.

"Hang on, lads. You've got the wrong one. I didn't organise this. You're making a mistake. It's not me you want."

The more aggressive of the hi-jackers, the shorter one, pushed his shotgun under the burglar's chin.

He growled, menacingly. "How the fuck do you know who we want?"

He swung his gun back to the other two prisoners.

"Go! Fucking go!"

From where he was now cuffed to the inside of the cell, Kenny saw both the other burglars head off across the fields. The white youth headed east, while the Asian lad began jogging towards the north. Then the door was slammed shut.

Kenny looked to George, still holding up his swelling wrists.

Seventy-five seconds had passed.

What Kenny did not see was the Mondeo that had previously overtaken the unmarked police car come screaming alongside and then skid to a rubber-burning stop. The male driver revved the engine as the two hijackers shoved their captive onto the floor in the rear of the car and then sat either side of him. The car roared away. The incident had lasted eighty-three seconds.

*

John Gibson pulled the chair closer to the hospital bed, and then checked over his shoulder; no one watched from outside the room. He saw the notice on the corridor wall requesting that everyone sanitize their hands on entering and leaving the ward. He promised himself to do it on the way out.

Stephen sobbed pitifully. John reached up and gripped his shoulder.

31

"Hey, hey, come on, mate, calm down. Tell me about it – get it off your chest, eh? Come on, Stephen. What is it? How did you kill your wife? What was her name?"

The sobbing died between sniffles. Stephen gently wiped the bruised skin around his swollen eyes with a tissue, threw the tissue into a waste-bin to his left, and then tentatively drew his hands down over his face. He gulped, head bowed.

"Sue… I stabbed her," he said. "We argued, she shouted… I shouted back, she pushed, I pushed, then… the knife… I grabbed it and… she's dead."

He lifted his hands in a 'that's it' manner, and then the tears flowed again.

John studied Stephen. He waited a moment before speaking.

"Where Stephen? Where did all this happen?"

Stephen stared ahead, into nowhere.

"Did you hear me, Stephen?"

Stephen nodded.

"Kitchen. It was morning, a real bad day. I really needed a drink. She talked to me, trying to calm me, then… a shout, a push, and… that was it."

He took another tissue from the box that was now on his lap. He wiped the saliva from his bottom lip.

"And you live where?" said Stephen.

"London. Highams Park."

John nodded. "So you stabbed your wife, Stephen. Then what?"

Stephen squeezed his eyes tight shut, opened them to the slits that they were, and then shrugged.

"I ran. I just left her. I Left her lying on the floor, blood pouring from her chest. I was frightened. I ran."

John thought for a moment, and then reached to the bedside cabinet for a piece of paper. He emptied what he took to be painkillers out of a small box, then ripped the box open. He placed the unprinted internal part of the box face up on his knee. He pulled a pen from his inside jacket pocket, and sat poised.

"What's your home phone number, Stephen?"

As he wrote the number down, a voice behind John turned him.

"Jesus, you're bloody keen, aren't you?"

John stood. The speaker was D.C. Keith Matthews, casually dressed in a charcoal grey suit, blue open neck shirt, and highly polished black shoes.

"Come on then," he said, "what gives? If I remember correctly, it's your day off."

"Just trying to be a Good Samaritan, Keith."

John half turned and looked over his shoulder. He saw Stephen struggling to get his thoughts in order. Tears were flowing again. John thought for a moment, then turned back to Keith.

"Can I see you outside a minute, mate?" said John.

John gripped Keith's elbow and manoeuvred him out of the room.

In the corridor, Keith jerked his arm free and said, "I'll let you off with that bit of man-handling, just this once though. What the hell was that all about?"

"You're going to get nowhere with the mugging aspect of this. He was drunk. He'll not remember a thing. What you need to…" John thought for a moment. "Look, keep an eye on him for five minutes will you. I need to make a phone call, and then I'll give you all I've got. It might save us all a lot of paperwork in the long run. Okay?"

Keith shrugged, "Yeah, okay, no problem. Just get a move on will you. I'd like to get this sorted, or shifted, today."

John knew that 'sorted, or shifted' meant either case closed, or progressed upwards. He looked along the corridor and spotted a payphone on a wall, opposite a small cafeteria.

"Back in a minute," said John.

John's phone call took seven minutes; he returned to find Keith sitting next to an empty bed.

"And he's where?" said John.

"Toilet. Getting changed. Back in a minute," said Keith, languidly. .

"Fuck! Jesus, Keith. I asked you to keep an eye on him. How the …?"

John looked both ways along the corridor and saw the toilet, ten feet away to his right. He dashed to it, opened the door, and looked into an empty room.

"Shit! Shit shit shit," he exclaimed, thumping on the door.

Keith caught up with John and looked past him.

"Ah, fuck. I thought... anyway, he's not even a suspect is he? He's just another mugging victim."

John rubbed his brow with the flat of his hand, exasperated at Keith's laid back attitude.

"Look. He's not just a mugging victim. He thinks he murdered his wife. He's distraught; he thinks he's on the run. He's nearly a fucking basket case, we..."

John paused for a moment, thinking. He checked his watch, and then decided.

"Right. It's all yours. Ring it in. Get your note book out."

Keith snapped back as he retrieved his note book from an inside pocket. "Whoa. Less of the orders, eh? And ring what in?"

John pointed to the notebook.

"Just get this down, will you? His name is Stephen Donnelly. He thinks he murdered his wife, but he didn't, she's fine. She said she stabbed herself accidentally – believe that if you like. She's worried sick. He's a recovering alcoholic, and was once treated for depression. He's... he's..."

John paused, and then looked directly at Keith.

"Listen. We've got to get him. His wife said he could be suicidal."

"Again, whoa, and calm down, mate. He can't be far."

John pointed to the set of pyjamas lying next to the toilet bowl.

"He's had most of the night to get this arranged," he said.

John pushed past Keith and walked back to the hospital room; Keith followed. John paced the floor for a few seconds.

"Just ring it in, eh?" he said. "What else can we do? Just give them the whole story, and… well, I don't think there's a charge to face is there? His wife says she accidently stabbed herself; though how the hell do you stab yourself in the clavicle is beyond me. Anyway, no complaint has been made, and all I did was find him unconscious in an alley."

Keith grimaced. "Yeah, maybe, but I'll bet we're both up in front of Bellamy before the weeks out."

"So what? Stephen Donnelly is out there thinking he's on the run, and his head is not exactly all together, is it?"

Keith did not answer.

"Sod this," said John, "I'm gonna see Bellamy now and put him in the picture. We don't want a suicide that could have been prevented, do we.'

"Hang on, hang on; just calm down for a second, there's an easier way than that. Just get his wife to report him mentally ill, missing from home, and last seen in the Tyneside area. Missing person. Simple"

John looked at Keith with an 'are you stupid?' expression.

"Are you fucking serious? I'm traffic; speeding, car crashes, mangled bodies, no tax disc. For all that I love my job. I'm not going to jeopardise that by lying to an inspector. Jesus!"

As John turned to walk away, he faced a nurse coming up behind him.

"Excuse me, gentlemen, but we need your assistance. Mr Golightly in Ward seven had his clothes stolen during the night."

Chapter Four

Matty Williams was a reluctant escapee. He knew he was in Leeds; he'd deducted that from the skyline, and the motorway road signs he could see below. He'd also been to Leeds many years previously when their football team and Newcastle United had been in the same league.

Matty's captors hadn't hooded him, but, on his being taken from the prison van, he'd been made to lie on the floor of the Mondeo. He hadn't a clue as to where he'd been, or which route had been taken. Whenever he had attempted to speak, they had stamped on his legs.

His captors had switched cars approximately six miles - eleven minutes - south of Durham. Within thirty-five minutes of the release of the prisoners, the car driver had swung off the old A1 trunk road, cut across to the A19, done a few lefts and rights, and then pulled up on an Industrial Estate just north of Middlesbrough. Inside another few minutes the car had been torched, and the group had split up. The driver had then driven off in a Ford Focus, as Matty was being squeezed into the hardwood box on the top of the white Transit van. The box had then been ratchet strapped down to the roof rack, along with metal slats of the type used on roller shutters.

Once the van had reached its destination, Matty had been pulled out of the box by his feet, rolled off the roof of the van, pulled to his feet, and then slammed up against the side wall of the building. His head was twisted to face right and his left cheek brushed up against rough brickwork. He watched as one of his captors unlocked a side door. Once through the open doorway, kicks and punches guided Matty up the stairs of the empty office block. That had been hours ago.

Matty had given up on thinking 'why'; now was now thinking rationally on his future, even tentatively wondering if he could escape. He calculated that he must be on the tenth or eleventh floor. All the windows in the room were intact, but covered in a light film of dust. Everything pointed to the fact that it had been a long time since this office had seen activity. The room was about one hundred feet long and maybe twenty-five feet wide. A4 sheets of paper and other office consumables littered the floor; the latest dated piece of paper he could find showed fourteenth October 2010. The double glazed windows were locked and, Matty figured, they would be about twenty-four millimetres thick, and that included the twelve millimetre air gap.

Matty had been a glazier in a previous life. He rued the day he'd gotten involved in crime, especially today. Fuck, he didn't want to escape. He'd only been given a twelve-month sentence, and that meant he could have been out in six. In addition to a short sentence, he'd had himself declared bankrupt before he'd been judged, hence all his debt would be wiped out, and the cause of his turning to crime would be non-existent when he came out.

Matty walked to the door of the office, placed his left cheek against the wired glass panel in the steel door, and looked to his right. His captors stood at the far end of a corridor, talking animatedly between themselves. He wished he could hear what they were saying, or that they would maybe say who they were, or why they had made him a prisoner on the run.

All Matty wanted to do was go back to prison.

*

Just over one hundred and twenty miles to the northeast of where Matty was being held, Balvindar Barianna walked through the backstreets of a small seaport town. She paused a second. The doors to a mosque, one hundred yards ahead of her on the left, were being closed. After another minute, Balvindar walked to the Victorian building, which adjoined the mosque, and knocked on the front door. A huge man dressed in a brown jacket, black tracksuit bottoms and brown sandals, opened the door. His white open-neck shirt showed dirt around the collar. He stepped aside, not speaking, and Balvindar entered.

Balvindar was second generation Pakistani, but Balvindar was also a local lass, Newcastle bred and born, and schooled privately on Tyneside. Her accented English was as natural as any Geordie's, but she could also speak Urdu, as and when, gratifying the wish of her mother and father.

Balvindar was dressed western style; tight, figure hugging blue denim jeans, a black, hooded tracksuit top and white Asics trainers. The make-up she normally wore had been removed in deference to the man who had summoned her. Balvindar followed the man who'd opened the door through the building to an office at the back. The man knocked on the office door, announced himself and Balvindar, and then entered. He stood to one side of the door and indicated for Balvindar to sit down on a chair in front of an old wooden desk. He then turned and left the room.

The office was grubby and, apart from the desk and chairs, empty - bare floors, bare walls and a naked light bulb. Everything said cheap. The light emanating from the bulb could not have come from anything larger than a sixty-watt source. The only item on the desk was a copy of the Quran.

On the opposite side of the desk, an elderly man sat in traditional Pakistani imam dress. He sat hunched forward. He wore traditional black headwear, and his face was weather beaten and lined with deep furrows across his forehead and down his cheeks and mouth. His facial hair, full beard set, was grey, and his nose was hooked. His robes hung loosely on his thin frame. He stared at Balvindar.

The man was the imam Nasr, the elected leader of the mosque. Balvindar did not like Nasr, did not trust Nasr, and would not be here today if it had not been for Sanjar. Nasr sat behind the desk with his back to a window. The window was covered in newspaper, thereby preventing the curious seeing into the room. Beyond the paper-covered glass was a back yard not visible to Balvindar. The yard was littered with old papers, a bike frame, a battered and rusting pram, a broken set of wooden ladders, and empty paint tins. Balvindar looked around the room and thought poverty.

Nasr smiled, nodded slowly, and spoke in Urdu. "How are you my child?"

Balvindar's throat was dry, her voice near rasping. "I miss him. I will miss him for a year, but I will wait for Sanjar."

The imam smiled sourly at Balvindar's naiveté. He knew for a fact that if certain conditions prevailed, she would never see her boyfriend again.

Balvindar looked away. In her heart of hearts, despite what Sanjar had told her, she could not bring herself to like the man who expected to be obeyed.

"I have news for you, Balvindar. There has been… an incident, an incident which allowed Sanjar to escape from the van that was taking him to prison."

Balvindar stared at him, wide-eyed. Her lips parted, but no words came. She looked down to her left, thinking. The imam watched her closely. She looked up again, at the imam.

"But… are you sure? He hasn't contacted me. Surely he would have made his way to me. Has he spoken to you… or…?"

She looked down again, lost in thought.

Nasr studied her, watching, waiting for more words as she struggled to make sense of the news. None came.

"We must speak with him, child. The need to speak with him is very important. If he does contact you, you must tell him to make contact with me. Do you understand?"

Balvindar did not respond.

Nasr thought for a moment, then pressed the wi-fi bell push underneath his desk; seconds later the man who had let Balvindar into the building returned. Until that day, Balvindar had never seen the man before. Her heart skipped a beat, the stranger looked evil.

Nasr said, "Hameed. Please tell Balvindar where Sanjar is."

Hameed looked puzzled for a moment. Then he stared at Balvindar, his angry eyes challenging her. He also spoke in Urdu. "We do not know." He paused for a beat, and then said, "He has disappeared."

Balvindar instinctively covered her mouth to stifle the cry she needed to utter. Was Hameed lying? She knew that these were violent men, killers, and that they would not hesitate to murder Sanjar if he became a danger to them. Then rationale kicked in, they needed her boyfriend, he was critical to their plans, they could not afford to kill him. Then she thought again - no one is indispensable.

The imam studied Balvindar. He saw genuine shock. He nodded, satisfied. He made eye contact with his aide, and then spoke to Balvindar.

"I see you are perhaps worried. We need to find Sanjar, child. At the very least we need to know why he has not contacted us. If he had been captured, we would know, so, where is he? Do you have any idea where he may have gone? Maybe he is a little nervous, and is hiding somewhere, with someone, a friend, a relative, we need to know."

He looked to Hameed again, but continued speaking to Balvindar.

"Do you have your mobile phone with you, child?" he said.

Balvindar nodded. "Yes," she said.

"Good. I would like you to sit with Hameed for a while, and think. You must think where Sanjar may be. Hameed will do his best to help you remember. Who knows, maybe Sanjar will ring you. I will return later. Do you understand?"

Balvindar understood. She understood that, if they deemed it necessary, she would be held and questioned, until Sanjar surfaced. Only now did it finally hit home as to how important Sanjar was. And there was only one way a Muslim graduate in chemistry could be important to these people.

*

The sound of the ringing cell phone alerted Matty's captors. Guard duty was not their speciality, and increasingly they were becoming bored. The taller of the two men, Jamal Hakim, second generation Pakistani, born in Bradford, reached into the inside pocket of his leather blouson, pulled out the phone and held up a hand.

"It's him," he said.

He hit the green button on his Samsung.

"Yes, Hameed?" he said.

"We lost him."

Jamal's jaw dropped. He stared at his partner.

Hameed snapped angrily, "Do you understand?"

"Yes, I fucking understand, and I've got a million questions, but they'll have to wait, won't they. So, what's plan B?" he said.

The voice was terse. "At the minute, just hold on to him. And when this is over, we need to talk, Jamal. Understood?"

Jamal spoke, resigned. "Aye, yes. Understood."

Hameed ended the call, and Jamal held the silent phone to his ear for a second, thinking. He turned to his partner, Gurp Sahid, again second generation Pakistani, born in Wakefield, as he put the phone back into his pocket.

"Sanjar's gone awol!" he said.

"Who's Sanjar?"

"The fucking prisoner we released when we took that idiot along the corridor. Y'know, the whole fucking purpose of the plan."

"Fuck off." Gurp's words accompanied a scornful look.

"Like I'm gonna joke about it!"

The two men stared at each other - incredulous. Jamal broke the silence.

"And we've got to hang on to Mr. Fucking 'what's it all about, mate', until we're relieved."

He nodded in the direction of where Matty was imprisoned.

Gurp said, "What's the point of that? We don't need him anymore. Sanjar has been released. This lad is excess baggage now."

Jamal thought for a moment. "I dunno. I suppose we need to know Sanjar is back in view, before we get rid of him, I think, maybe - I dunno."

Gurp threw up his hands. "This is bloody stupid. Just dump him. Blindfold him, put him out in the streets, and leave him. It's up to him after that. He's a con, he won't squeal, he won't identify us."

Jamal put his phone back into his pocket. "Nah, fuck that, we do as we're told. And I'm fucking hungry, so let's just leave the decision making to some bugger else."

Chapter Five

John Gibson checked the room again. The highly polished, dark wood dining table was set with two single yellow candles in twisted ornate silver candelabras, silver cutlery laid out with parade ground precision, and napkins rolled and presented in silver holders. To the left side of the dining table stood a small side-table set with condiments, a corkscrew, matches, and a wine-chiller. The wine in the chiller was the last bottle of four cases that John and Lynn had brought back from France the year before.

Beyond the table, the French doors leading out into the garden were open. Hanging in front of the doors, a full-length net curtain moved gently in the warm evening breeze and, beyond the doors, the garden presented itself in full bloom. The kidney shaped lawn, surrounded by annuals and bedding plants, showed saturated colours in the last light of the setting sun.

John checked his watch - eight-thirty. He mulled over the day's events, and wondered where Stephen was now. Had John's fellow officers managed to spot Stephen? He knew they would keep an eye out for him. A favour for a colleague that helped pass the time more quickly during quiet periods was always welcome

Stephen needed help, John knew that. He'd seen what alcohol could do to a family. His mother had suffered his dad for years. Then when his youngest brother, the last to leave home, had

47

married, his mother had upped sticks and left his dad – as clinically cold and as simple as that. No afterthought, no regrets, she had planned it for years. Get the kids up, see them married and settled down, salt a few quid away, then, and only then, think of yourself and get your life back together.

John's dad had tried to make it up. He had tried with flowers, chocolates, cards, and incessant phone calls, to make up for nearly thirty years of misery that he'd inflicted on a good wife and mother. He'd failed, because, when it came down to the wire, when a final choice had to be made, John's dad would choose the bottle above everything else - every time.

Lynn got home a few minutes before nine. John backed into the dining room, leading eyes-closed Lynn by the hand. She saw what she saw, and was overjoyed. She kissed John, then he kissed her, then their kisses became passionate. Lynn needed to shower; John said he'd join her. They got as far as the landing at the top of the stairs before they stripped each other, and made love as if for the last time – then they showered. Minutes later, refreshed, dressed, and hungry, they raced, laughing like children, to the dining room, hurriedly sat down to dinner and ate ravenously.

The meal was more than passable, and John could not remember when he had tasted wine as good as this - it made up for his efforts at the baked salmon. They did not rush the evening, but, as soon as John had cleared the almost licked-clean crockery of the desserts, they moved out on to the patio - Lynn with a glass of wine and John with a Bacardi and coke. They talked and watched as the shadows of the Acers stretched across the garden, before melting into the ground. And they talked on and on; Lynn sitting on a plastic garden seat, and John on a bleached, dried out log that he'd dragged up from South Shields beach, too long ago to remember when.

Breaking a warm silence, Lynn said, "You know, you're not bad for a copper."

John's eyebrows rose, and Lynn smiled.

"No, I mean, you're not grab 'em, try 'em and fry 'em, are you?"

John laughed lazily, his stomach jumping as he smiled tight lipped and his eyes creased.

"There's good in everyone, Lynn."

Lynn opened her mouth, about to protest.

"I know, I know," said John. "There's the real bad guys, the killers, the abusers, but... It's the 'never had a chance' brigade, that needs help. The young 'uns without a home life or a family set up, and the ones with no education. Once they're involved with crime they haven't got a chance, have they? I know, I know, you've heard it all before." He smiled. "You know, only you would listen to me spout off like this."

Lynn waved her empty glass and John picked up the wine bottle resting on the rusting barbeque. He stood and spoke casually as he poured.

"I think I'll have a run up the A68 tomorrow; have a little look for Stephen - Stephen Donnelly. Remember, the lad we found last night? D'you mind?"

Lynn shook her head and grinned.

"I just *knew* you couldn't let that go. I would have bet on it. Why?"

John shrugged. "I feel sorry for him. He has a wife who is breaking her heart worrying about him, and, well, the bloke has a problem." John paused. "A problem I've seen before."

"You think he's heading for the Borders?"

John nodded, "Well he's come this far north; my guess is he's heading for Scotland. Then, I reckon he'll try to lose himself in the Highlands or at the very least somewhere north of Edinburgh."

"John, the Borders covers an area of thousands of square miles. And at this time of the year it's going to be tourists from Morpeth to Melrose. Between the three fishing rivers alone, there's what, sixty miles as the crow flies?"

"And I know that, but I thought… well, I don't know what I thought, but maybe I can track him somehow."

He mused for a moment.

"I tell you what, I'll go up the old drover's road, take my time, mooch around a few villages, ask a few farmers, then I'll come back on the A roads."

Lynn stood, and put her arms around her John's neck.

"Way to go, Hiawatha. You can do it." She snuggled into this neck. "Now, take me to your wigwam, Chief."

*

Thirty-eight miles northwest of where John and Lynn settled down for the night, Stephen stuck his head into the rush of water for the third time. He lasted seven seconds, surfaced, shook the water from his head, and then rolled over and lay on his back by the side of the stream. He sucked in air. His face still ached, but the pain was easing.

He looked skywards. How many years had it been since he'd seen stars like he could see tonight? He touched his still swollen eyes. He felt good; frightened, but good. The city provided walls, boxed alleyways, hot air outlets and, always somewhere, a roof over his head. Nothing was weather-tight in the hills, but still he had a good feeling.

The night was warm, even without the necessary low cloud cover to hold the heat of the day down. He half sat up, resting back on his elbows. Straight ahead, in the gloom across the stream, he could see the edge of the Keilder Forest. He remembered the facts he'd read on one of the many tourist leaflets he'd picked up that day; over two-hundred and fifty square miles of Scots pine, larch, and Douglas fir, amongst other genus of trees. Further up stream to his right, just before the flow of icy water slowed in its tumbling down toward the Reiver River, smooth boulders loomed either threatening or protecting, depending on your nature. To his left, down stream, the forest ended abruptly and he could see the white wool of sheep as they grazed in the moonlight. He cocked his head. The only sound to be heard was that of the dancing, dashing water, bouncing over rocks and landing with a splash. The silver spray sparkled in the moonlight.

He sat up, swivelled on his backside and looked down stream. The rush of water followed the gentle gradient to the vale below. About three miles to the north, on the other side of the river that the stream flowed into, he could see the lights of what he reckoned to be a farmhouse. The temptation of a night in a barn was intense, but, the last thing Stephen wanted was to be stumbling around a farmyard at midnight, and setting a guard dog off barking.

He hung his head, thinking of Sue. It had crossed his mind that she may have lived. His spirits rose when he thought of that possibility. And then again, what if she had died? He had to think that was the case. He'd hung onto his pay-as-you-go mobile phone for three days; she had not contacted him. After the third day, the battery had run down simply because he'd had the phone switched on continuously, hoping Sue would contact him. Stephen had thrown the phone away, just south of Durham City.

He thought of the copper in the hospital. Sure, he'd report to his superiors, and sure, they'd be searching for him, but where would they start? Maybe, hopefully, the coastal route to Edinburgh. But, then again, surely they'd put out his face, or at least a verbal description, on the television?

He felt thirsty again. He stood and walked to the tree line. He reached down into the backpack that he'd bought as soon as he'd cleared the hospital, and pulled out his last bottle of carbonated spring water. He drank, gulping great mouthfuls, until the bottle was now less than half full. He belched as he screwed the top back on the bottle. This time he was going to do it. Cold turkey, drying out, whatever you wanted to call it; Stephen was once again adamant that he could, and would, knock his drink problem on the head.

He checked the backpack again; sandwiches, crisps, chicken legs from a fast-food joint, bananas, soap and a towel, and, the three items he'd struggled to find on his route - a pouched knife with a serrated blade, a wind-up torch, and a compass. A B&Q store on the outskirts of Newcastle had satisfied his needs in that department, just before he crossed the City boundary. The paper money once safely stored in his shoes was now down to pound coins in his pocket.

He needed to sleep. When he slept, time passed. The more time that passed, the greater the odds became in his favour. But, Stephen could not summon instant sleep. The craving filled his troubled mind; sleep did not come that easy. He needed to occupy his mind, his body, tire himself out, focus ahead, keep looking ahead, and keep moving; anything to keep his mind off alcohol.

He'd walked and trotted for most of the day, but ran when the gradient was with him, for nearly thirty-two miles. He'd repeated his mantra continuously, 'Just look ahead, move your legs, focus on a point in the distance, keep going, concentrate on standing upright and moving.' He'd targeted one chicken leg every ninety minutes, and had averaged six miles per chicken leg, before resting for a brief spell.

He'd reached the edge of the forest at nine-o-clock that evening, found a sheltered spot beneath a tree, and lain down. He drifted in and out of sleep for an hour. When he awoke from his snoozing, he'd sat on the parka he'd stolen and laid back against the trunk of the tree. Minute particles of bark pushed through the grubby T-shirt he'd also stolen from the hospital and scratched the skin around his shoulder blades. Stephen's wanting eased as he watched and focused on the colours of the sun set. Then, when the sky had turned black, the craving had returned; he found solace, distraction, by dipping his head in the rushing water of the stream. When the craving returned again, he gripped clumps of grass, describing the feel of the grass with his inner voice. When he'd gotten as much time out of the grass as he could, he picked up on a twig and began the thought process again. Anything to take his mind off alcohol.

He reached down into the backpack again, and pulled out the torch and one of the leaflets that had a small map of the area printed on the reverse side. He thought of tomorrow, and where he would go. He figured the police would reckon on him doing, what, maybe fifteen miles a day? So, maybe he had a little start on them. If the map was to any scale, he estimated the distance to Jedburgh to be maybe twenty-five or thirty miles. He set that as his target for the next day.

The craving hit him again. He gripped his stomach with his right hand, and then checked his watch – five after midnight. He'd gone just over twenty-four hours without an alcoholic drink. He looked at the watch once more. It was a cheap Timex, a present from his son. He had two children, one of each. He thought to himself, 'How would they feel? Their dad had murdered their mum.'

54

Stephen wondered, 'Why hadn't the muggers taken his watch?', and then he smiled - and winced with the pain. He nodded to himself, thinking, 'No self-respecting mugger would steal a Timex.' He looked to his watch, now sad again, and saw that his attackers had cracked the glass covering the bezel. He groaned, barely audible.

He put the map and torch back into his pack, then dropped to his knees. He stretched out on his stomach, then slowly raised himself on his hands, shoulder width apart, and began. Up – down, up…

Stephen prepared himself for a long night. He needed to tire himself out; so tired that he would not be able to think.

Chapter Six

Twelve miles to the southeast of Stephen's position, Sanjar Khan covered himself with more straw, and then pulled the arms of his sweatshirt over his hands and gripped the cuffs. Satisfied that he was fully covered, he shuffled back into the corner of the stall, away from the pile of horse dung in the centre aisle of the stables. The smell attacked the back of his throat.

Sanjar lay in the middle stall of a row of five. He thanked Allah for the summer's night, the shafts of moonlight slicing through the gaps in the wooden walls, and the fact that all except one stall was empty. The horse in that stall, a chestnut mare that looked as though she was in foal, had not given him a second glance as he'd tiptoed into the stable. He tried to remember how many horses were in the field that he'd just skirted; the number of horses was irrelevant, but the exercise passed time. His mind drifted back to Balvindar. He wondered how she had coped with imam Nazr.

Sanjar had no doubt that she would have been questioned. Where would he go, Balvindar? Why has he not contacted you, Balvindar? You must help us find him, Balvindar. Sanjar thought of his mother and father, and their consistent warnings to stay away from the 'bloody Yorkshireman', the imam, the Leader. They had repeated the same word over and over again – 'wicked'. Not bad, not dangerous, not sly, not malevolent, not scheming; just wicked, plain and simple.

Sanjar had never gone against his father. Like his older brother and two sisters, again both older than him, he'd obeyed his father to the letter. His obedience was born not out of fear, or respect for elders - although respect for elders was paramount - he had obeyed his father out of love, and an admiration for what his father had done with his life.

Sanjar's father, Asad, had left Iran in the eighties. He had come to Britain with his wife and three young children. In the early years, before Sanjar's birth, he'd been unable to follow his profession as an architect. Recognising pride as a sin, Asad had accepted all that was offered him by the British government; the flat in the east end of the city of Newcastle upon Tyne, the few sticks of furniture, the meagre but sufficient benefit allowance, and the first job – warehouseman in a D.I.Y store. He had suffered the job for three months.

Asad had left the D.I.Y. store not because he felt it was beneath him, but because the hours of the job, and the constraints attached, did not allow him time to seek out contacts in his chosen career. To further himself, and in a plan to provide more adequately for his family, Asad had bought a bicycle, a ladder, a bucket, a rubber squeegee and three wash-leathers, then headed for the money part of town – the Jesmond and Gosforth area to the north of the city. He had knocked on doors, put introductory letters through letterboxes advertising his architectural skills while building up his window-cleaning round, and worked from sunrise to sunset. It had taken over three months, but eventually he had made a contact, an architect employed by the city council who had put Asad in touch with a firm working on the new Metro Centre. It was the chance Asad had been waiting for.

From the design and drawing of independent staircases, car parks, security out-houses and other apprentice tasks, he'd gradually proven himself while studying for English architecture exams. Sanjar had been born one year after passing the final exam.

Sanjar stiffened. Someone was in the stables. He heard footsteps, light footsteps, a woman, he was certain. He tried to squeeze himself further back into the darkness of the corner, against the split wooden boards of the stall. He silently cursed the moonlight that he had been thankful for moments earlier. He breathed through his mouth, silently, just as they had taught him. He covered his nose and mouth to deaden the sound as he gulped. The footsteps stopped for a moment. Had someone come to check out the horse in foal? He heard shuffling and kind words. The footsteps came towards him; then they stopped again.

"Right! I've got a shotgun, so don't even think of trying anything."

It was a female voice.

The footsteps came nearer. Dressed in denim jeans, cowboy boots, and a grubby, brick-red T-shirt, a woman appeared at the entrance to the stall. She was not lying about the shotgun. She indicated to him with the weapon.

"Stand up, but stay where you are."

Sanjar nodded, as he surfaced from beneath the straw. The woman saw a young man, clean shaven, slim, height just below six foot, and muscular.

"Now, listen, and do nothing."

Again, Sanjar nodded. He guessed that the woman was maybe five-foot six inches tall, and a few years older than his twenty-four years. She was slim, but curvy. She flicked her long auburn hair with a jerk of her head. The shotgun remained levelled at him.

"As well as this gun…" she whistled, "I also have Kai here to protect me."

She clicked the fingers of her left hand, still holding the gun with her right, and a large German Shepherd dog trotted to alongside her. Kai spotted Sanjar, and growled. The girl paused, studying Sanjar in the moonlight.

"Well I never! What are you? Indian? Pakistani? An Asian tramp. That's a first – for me anyway." She narrowed her eyes. "But you're not a tramp, are you? Designer sweater, Nike trainers, and what, Gucci jeans?"

She leaned forward, her eyes narrowing as she inspected Sanjar.

"No, you're too light for the sub-continent. What are you? What nationality are you?"

"English," Sanjar said softly.

The girl smiled. "I guess I asked for that, eh?"

Again she indicated with the shotgun.

"Stand up and move toward that shaft of light, slowly."

As Sanjar stood, she pulled an iPhone out of the rear left hand back pocket of her jeans.

"Please," said Sanjar, "I've done nothing wrong. I just want somewhere to sleep for the night. An arranged marriage, I'm running away from an arranged marriage."

The girl smiled, "I'll bet you are. I thought it was the women who protested. Smile."

She held up her phone, pointed it at Sanjar, and dazzled him with the flash of the camera. Sanjar watched as she checked the photograph.

"Good," she said

Then, with one eye on him, the girl hit a number of buttons, waited a second, nodded to her self, and then put the phone back into her pocket. She looked to Sanjar.

"That's better, I can see you now."

Sanjar spoke quickly. "I've done nothing wrong; I promise you."

The girl continued to stare at him.

"I'm making a protest. I'm English. I want to choose who I marry."

Still the girl remained silent. Sanjar hung his head.

The girl said, "You look worried. Now, why would you look worried, because you also look sensible? And, if you are sensible, you must realise that I'm not going to shoot you without a good reason. For example, if we stood here all night, and you didn't make a move on me, I wouldn't shoot you. If you did make a move on me, first of all I'd sic Kai on you, and then, if he could not pull you down, and I was still in danger, I'd shoot you. Probably blow your head clean off."

She watched Sanjar shuffling his feet.

"But, I've also taken the precaution of sending the photograph of you to my friend, along with the message 'See what I've found in the Stables.'."

She took a deep breath.

"So, all in all I guess you'd be pretty stupid to try anything, wouldn't you?"

Sanjar tried again. He said, "Please. All I want is a night's sleep. I'll be gone at sun-up, before you wake. I promise."

"Swear to God, or Allah, or whoever you believe in?" the girl mocked.

Sanjar's expression hardened.

"I can't do that," he said. "Even you as a Christian must not use your Lord's name in vain."

The girl nodded. "*My* Lord's name in vain, eh. So, you're what, a Muslim? Hindu?"

"Muslim. My father and mother are from Iran. I have followed their faith."

"Yeah, whatever. Any identification on you?" the girl asked.

Sanjar shook his head.

"Right, my name is Abigail and…"

Abigail's phone ping-pinged. She took it from her pocket again, read the message and smiled.

She said, "My friend says you look shaggable."

She clicked the phone, then put it back into her pocket.

"Please," said Sanjar, "it is not nice to speak like that."

He looked Abigail straight in the eye. She returned the stare.

"You know, if you'd given me any other reply than that, I may have telephoned the police. You've just gained yourself some brownie points… What's your name?"

Sanjar thought for a moment. Her friend had the photograph, lying was pointless.

"Sanjar," he said.

"Okay, Sanjar, here's what I'm going to do. As mad as I must be, I believe you, and-"

"Would you be mad to believe me if I was white?"

Abigail snapped back. "Oh for fuck's sake, don't start that pathetic crap!" She sighed. "Now shut up, and listen. You can stay here the night. In a moment, I'll give you the keys for that box," she indicated with her head, "and you can get yourself a horse blanket. Okay? Now, give me ten minutes start, then you can come over to the house, and I'll have tea and sandwich for you. I'll also have the gun with me, all the time. When you've been fed, you can come back here. You should know that I set the alarms on the house. Okay?"

Sanjar said, "Yes."

"Good, and if you're still here when I wake up tomorrow, you're welcome to another cuppa and a sandwich. Deal?"

Sanjar smiled. "Deal."

Chapter Seven

The sun rising over his right shoulder gave John Gibson clear vision over the valley below him. So far this year, and for all the recent rain, the summer had been a record breaker as far as temperatures were concerned. John had taken the time to do a few calculations the night before. If he had assessed the situation correctly, Stephen was either somewhere down there, maybe, or, maybe, eight miles to the west, just over the hills on his left.

John did a sweep of the valley for as far as he could see, from right to left. Apart from the animals in the field, nothing moved. He admitted to himself that only the most ardent hikers would follow the roads snaking out below.

He checked his watch. He'd set his alarm for thirty minutes before sunrise. Lynne had grunted, and turned over at the incessant beeping of the alarm clock at four in the morning. It was now just six-forty, and John figured that maybe Stephen was still asleep somewhere – a hedge, a barn, or maybe the back of a trailer which was maybe hitched up to a tractor. He sat down on a rotten tree stump, and poured hot unsweetened black tea into his flask top.

John watched as the countryside awoke. He'd heard the dawn chorus as he'd prepared his flask at home, in the kitchen. On the journey to where he sat now, he'd watched the sky brighten in the east through the car's rear-view mirror.

Just left of centre down in the valley, he spotted movement. It was a vehicle. John knew it

63

could not be Stephen driving. He picked up his binoculars anyway, lined-up his vision with the vehicle, and then focused in. It was an A.T.V., much loved by shepherds and cowherds. The driver, a short, stocky man, was wearing what looked like a green corduroy cap, checked shirt with sleeves rolled up and a baggy 'brace and bib'. John watched as the man slowed beside a gate leading into a field stocked with sheep. Within a minute, the man had locked the gate behind him, and was circling the field scattering what John figured to be nuggets of food additives. John lowered his binoculars, then scanned the rest of the valley again as he reached down blindly for his coffee.

The sun rose, and the shadows shortened as the valley came to life. A tractor moved diagonally from bottom left to top right across John's vision, then disappeared behind a wood. Just after seven-thirty, a woman and a child walked what John judged to be a quarter of a mile from their home to the east, beyond the woods, to a minor road. The child boarded a school bus five minutes later. As the bus disappeared from view to the south, a woodpecker began its rat-a-tat-tat behind him, and John smiled. On days like this, there was no place more beautiful than the Borders.

At ten minutes past eight, John stood. He figured that with Stephen's problems, there was no way he would sleep beyond seven-thirty; therefore it was probably safe to assume that he wasn't in this valley. The likelihood was that Stephen probably had a head start on him, over in the next valley.

John took the Ordnance Survey map from his bag and unfolded it on top of the tree stump he'd used as a seat. He traced his finger to the northwest of his position. He checked the contours, and the scale. His eyes darted back and forth across the map, and then settled on a point seven miles north of the next valley. The centre of the contours, at eight hundred feet above sea level, would give him a near three-sixty viewpoint of the minor roads around him. He tapped the point on the map.

"Aye, that's it," he said.

He folded the map and headed for his car.

*

To the east, in the farmhouse, Sanjar drained his cup, and then thanked Abigail.

"You're welcome," she replied. "So, what now? It seems a bit childish. You know, forced marriages, running away from home. Don't you think you should just go back and stand your ground?"

Sanjar shrugged. "Don't know. It's trying to balance two cultures. I…" He thought for a moment. "You're right. It's crazy, isn't it?" Another thoughtful moment, then, "I'm going home."

He smiled and stood.

Abigail grinned. "That's my boy, and hey, if it's any good to you, I'm heading toward Newcastle in about an hour. You're welcome to a lift."

Sanjar raised a palm toward her.

"No, no. I'll be fine. It's a lovely day, I'll get a lift sooner or later; but, if you see me, please don't pass me by." He held out his hand. "Once again, thanks a lot."

Abigail shook his hand, and wagged a finger of her left hand at him.

"And get that chip off your shoulder, eh?" she said. "All that black white crap. Yes?"

Sanjar nodded, grinned, and released her hand. Abigail picked up the dirty plates and cups from the table, and turned toward the sink. Behind her, Sanjar reached forward and gently picked up the serrated bread knife from the kitchen table.

*

A further three hundred miles away to the south, in an office that overlooked Pall Mall, London, Commander Clive Brasher recently of M.I 5 and now without portfolio, sat silently at his desk and listened to the not so good news from the police officer sitting opposite him. The officer, Chief Inspector Alex Taylor, five–feet ten-inches of solid muscle, finished reading his notes aloud, and shrugged.

"Bad luck or good planning, sir?"

Brasher and Taylor were the temporary officers in charge of a hastily formed group of professionals, with the sole purpose of identifying potential terrorist gangs forming on mainland Britain. Brasher's group had no peers; neither were they part of a hierarchy. Their chain of command, line of command, was as intricate as the worldwide web. Brasher could call on any person, personnel, whether military or civilian, and use all and any necessary equipment to safeguard the people of Britain. Brasher's team were simply called Rangers.

The office was a room on the first floor of a building with an original Georgian façade, which today was bathed in sunshine. Tall sash windows faced south, and Brasher's desk backed onto one of the windows. Blackout blinds were pulled halfway down, shielding the two men from the glare of a sun heading toward its zenith. To the right of where Brasher sat, ubiquitous filing cabinets stood either side of the door leading into the office. To the left, a fitted bookshelf ran the length and height of the wall. The floor was covered in brown chequered linoleum, which Taylor figured must have been laid at least forty years previous. Brasher's desk, his chair, and the chair that Taylor sat on, were on an island of carpet set just off centre on the lino.

Brasher tightened his lips, shook his head.

"All right, let's go over the obvious, Alex."

He paused, letting his words sink in, then continued.

"He's done a bloody runner, hasn't he? Why? What the hell is he playing at? Do we have any clues?"

Taylor took a deep breath, puffed out his cheeks and exhaled through pouting lips.

Brasher continued. "Don't answer that, Alex. It was rhetorical." He shook his head.

"And why the hell would a terror merchant get himself arrested doing a stupid burglary? Why would he put his whole crew at risk for... what, a bloody shopkeeper's computer? And how the hell was he sent down for his first offence? Who the hell supervised that case?"

Taylor grimaced, and shrugged.

"Can't answer that, sir, but maybe he needed the electrical components?"

Brasher scowled, "Come on, Alex. You don't believe that. They've probably got electrical components coming out of their ears."

"But from a stolen computer they'd be untraceable, sir."

"Alex!"

Brasher reached forward, and picked up his pipe. He stood as he tampered the contents down into the pipe bowl, and then walked to the shaded window. He raised the lower sash to chest height, and then raised his pipe to Alex.

"Do you mind?"

He lit his pipe without waiting for an answer.

Alex shuffled on his seat, uncomfortable with the silence. He was also uncomfortable with his dress. His dark blue lounge suit was not meant for a summer's day. He loosened the top button of his white shirt behind his blue tie.

"Sanjar was last seen heading north, sir," he said.

"Where north? Be specific, man."

Alex sat forward in his chair.

"I would surmise Newcastle, sir."

Brasher ummed, nodding, and then carried on smoking. He stooped his six-feet, four inch, slim frame, and looked out under the blind, onto the street below. His grey, thinning hair flopped over his brow.

"North, eh? Back to his family? No, of course not. To his friends? Possibly."

He turned to Alex.

"Any activity with regard to said friends?"

Alex massaged his brow, and opened his eyes wide, blinking.

"His girlfriend, Balvindar, she made her way to the mosque yesterday, and, as of ten minutes before I came in here, she was still there."

Brasher spun around sharply. Alex nodded.

"Yes, exactly," he said. "Maybe slapping her around a little, probably a lot, trying to get something out of her that in fact she isn't aware of. Or, maybe just waiting for her to answer a call from Sanjar, if it comes."

Brasher paced the room, smoke flowing behind him. Alex turned away, a look of annoyance on his face.

Brasher said, "Okay, again. From the top. Tell me about Sanjar."

Alex took a deep breath, held it for a moment, and then exhaled, noisily.

"Okay. Solid English education. All private schools, then on to university to study chemistry. Mixed in well at all his schools, was well liked, and made friends easy. And, as far as we can gather, sir, Sanjar never came up against discrimination of any kind - racial, colour, or whatever."

Alex turned on his seat to face Brasher, who was now leaning against a filing cabinet. Brasher nodded.

Alex said, "The father speaks passionately about his hate for the Sunni, and the Shiite, and all the other fractions."

He paused, then nodded, confirming to himself.

"Maybe his father's hate for the fundamentalists drove Sanjar into looking into them. You know, tell a child not to do something and, without a reasonable explanation, he'll want to find out why for himself."

Brasher opened his arms to Alex.

"Certainly," he said. "Find out why. But why, for what reason, would he get mixed up with militants?"

"Why do any of them, sir? Brainwashed, idealists, fed up with what they see as un-equality, no hope in the world they live in."

Brasher pushed himself off the filing cabinets and, holding his pipe by the bowl, waved it airily as he paced in thought.

"Yes, yes, but heavens, this Sanjar had it on a plate. What turned him?"

He sat back at his desk and tapped his pipe into an old brass ashtray.

"Anyway, let's push on. Where are we at in the search?"

Alex massaged his brow again. "Well," he said, "the local boys in blue are obviously looking for him. If they do manage to pick him up, we ourselves can then arrange for him to escape again, but this time we'll have a drone on him. However, in the mean time, all commanding officers are aware that if captured, Sanjar is not to be left alone until one of our chaps has had a word with him."

"How far could he have gone in the time he's been free?" asked Brasher.

"With a lift from a passing vehicle, he could be anywhere between Newcastle, and John

O'Groats. But, we feel he's going to stay local, and try to contact the people at the mosque again."

Brasher cupped his chin, with his right hand, then rubbed his lips with his index finger as he mulled over Alex's words.

"Look," he said. "What if he went deep, and then waited for the others to go to him? What if he felt that we were on to him, and that he may be taking trouble to their door if he made the mosque his bolt-hole?"

He nodded to himself, then continued. "On the other hand, what if we can safely presume that none of them are aware that we are onto them with regard to terrorism activity and that they believe it's only Sanjar's burglary that the police are interested in?"

Alex made as if to speak, but Brasher held up a palm. His eyes narrowed.

"How do you leave a terrorist organisation, Alex? How do you tell them you've had enough, and you're leaving, thank you very much?"

"With great difficulty I would imagine, sir; if you could get out alive anyway."

Brasher grimaced. "Of course. Now, let me see," he said. He stood, circled his desk, and stopped in front of Alex. "Right. First of all, I want your best men onto Sanjar's girlfriend twenty-four hours a day. He'll ring her sooner or later, so we are on to the phone lines, aren't we? Landline and mobile?"

Alex spread his hands, "Of course, sir, and we are already tracking his girlfriend."

"Good. And I do mean your best men, Alex. She's going to be the link. Secondly, contact

Northumbria Police, and double check their chopper is up for it with regard to heat sensors and thermal imaging."

Alex stood, gathered up his briefcase and walked toward the office door. His cell phone vibrated as he reached for the door handle.

"Excuse me, sir."

Alex tapped the receive button.

"Go ahead."

He listened for a while, and then said, "Excellent, you know what to do. I'll be in contact again shortly."

Alex turned to Brasher.

"Possibly news we're waiting for, sir. Northumbria Police have had a report of a young Asian tramp, supposedly a tramp or vagrant, stealing a bread knife from a farmhouse just northwest of Newcastle. And, believe it or not, he gave his name as Sanjar."

Brasher brightened, his eyes widening. He indicated Alex's vacated chair.

"Well, well. Do tell."

Alex sat, recited verbatim his previous cell phone call, and Brasher listened without interruption. Alex finished his recitation and waited.

Brasher nodded, as he moved to a map on the wall above the filing cabinets. He traced his right index finger across Northumberland.

"Fine, fine," he said. "Now, when you do speak with the Northumbrian police, kindly inform them that they need to square the area between Hadrian's Wall, Housesteads, the east coast, and as far north in the Borders region as they can go. I doubt very much if they'll have much success during the day, but at night, with a heat-seeker, infrared, maybe. They need to scan farms, outhouses hedges…"

"They'll have a devil of a job, sir. Animals in the field, in barns…"

Brasher flipped his hand dismissively.

"So, they'll have a few problems. Better that than another bloody bomb brigade up and running. Anyway, I'll make inroads at the M.O.D. The R.A.F. Boulmer search and rescue chopper could half the task if we could utilise that. Oh, and the Air Ambulance, use that whenever we can. I'll authorize the forms to kit it out with necessary cameras."

Brasher stood up, and Alex took it as his signal that the meeting was over.

"Oh, and remember, Alex, we tell the uniform boys absolutely nothing. It's all on a need to know basis. I'll contact the chief constable of Northumbria."

Brasher turned back to the window, and looked down on the Pall Mall.

Chapter Eight

Balvindar checked her cell phone again – nothing; no missed calls, no unread texts. Where was he, where was Sanjar? She looked over her shoulder, again, but, again, no one in the busy street even resembled what she considered to be a tail. Just ahead of her she could see a newsstand. She slowed, checked out the headlines on all the displayed newspapers, but nothing sprang out from the front page. She picked up the early edition of the *Newcastle Evening Chronicle*, handed over money and walked off without her change.

She folded the newspaper and scanned the street again. Her pinched expression reflected the stress that was building inside her, and with Balvindar's stress came hunger. She checked out her position in relation to the local McDonald's. Hell, she'd used the fast food outlet for as long as she could remember; where was it? She blinked, shook her head angrily, then looked again – she spotted the yellow arch a further one hundred yards along the busy high street.

Seated at a window seat, drinking black coffee, Balvindar checked the street again – nothing. She opened the newspaper and methodically scrutinised every column inch. She shook her head - not one mention of what was surely a major news item. Had the police not made it public? Had someone put a D notice on the story? If so, why? The only cases in court on the day before were Sanjar for that stupid burglary, and a group of three other small time crooks, which consisted of one repeat offender on a charge of petty theft and another two lads, like Sanjar, on a burglary charge.

She folded the newspaper, put it to one side, then stood and left her half finished coffee. As she stepped out onto the pavement, she checked her phone again; and again – nothing.

Along the street to her left, the man behind the wheel of the lone Skoda on the taxi rank dismissed the objections of the passenger trying to get him to drive to Newcastle Central Station. The driver was slim, clean-shaven, his skin shone, and his hair was in the style of a fifties crew cut. He wore a green T-shirt, and brown coloured cargoes. The whipcord muscles of his arms tensed on the steering wheel.

"Well, is this a taxi or what?" the would-be passenger shouted.

"Or what! Now fuck off," was the reply.

The driver spoke without looking at the man. He watched as Balvindar exited McDonald's and headed off again. The would-be passenger picked up on the driver's southern accent.

"Cockney bastard!"

The driver spun and glared at the man; the man turned and hurried away. The physical size of the driver had not scared the man, more the look in the man's eyes, the wide-eyed killer look, the 'get in my way and you die' look. The driver turned his attention back to Balvindar, and crawled along the street in first gear.

Ahead of Balvindar, a man sitting on a parked scooter tracked her in his rear-view mirror.

He saw her turn down a side street, after she had once again checked that she was not being followed. He revved up the engine, and the automatic gearbox engaged. Making a u-turn in between the sparse traffic, he sped back to where he'd last seen Balvindar. He flashed his headlights at the taxi as he turned into the side street. The driver acknowledged the man on the scooter with an upraised palm, and then slowed to a stop.

Even at that early hour of the day, the heat was stifling. People walked slowly and not a breath of wind stirred. The man on the scooter saw Balvindar ahead of him and slowed. He watched as she entered the code into the digital lock on the entrance door of a block of privately owned flats. Less than a minute later he watched as she drew the curtains on the bedroom window of her apartment. He guessed that she had probably been questioned from the time she entered the mosque annex until the time she'd left.

The heat was getting to the man. He removed his helmet, and loosened the buttons on his green N.A.T.O. jacket. He hooked the chinstrap of his helmet on one side of the handlebars. The taxi appeared across the entrance at the top of the street. The scooter driver interlocked the fingers of his hands, reversed them, then held them above his head as if stretching. The taxi-driver acknowledged the signal, looked around him, and then drove forward to a gap in the parked traffic, fifty yards ahead, on double yellow lines. He cut the engine, and snatched on his handbrake as he spotted a telephone box at the entrance to the bus station opposite.

Leaving the taxi with its hazard lights flashing, the driver dashed across the road, into the phone box, then dialled an inner London number. The number was a direct line to Brasher's office. Brasher answered on the second ring.

"It's Compton, sir," said the taxi driver. "I was told to ring you directly today."

"Ah, Compton. Yes, indeed. Good news, I hope. Just one moment, please."

Brasher pressed a button on the top of the receiver, waited two seconds until a green icon on the receiver glowed, then spoke again.

"Okay, you can speak freely now. Carry on."

"It is news, sir, but we're not moving forward as it were."

"Go on," said Brasher.

"She left the building next door to the mosque this morning, sir, around about nine-fifteen, sat in a local park for nearly fifteen minutes, then headed off again. I took over from Jameson approximately twenty-five minutes ago and followed her into town. She stopped at a newsstand, scanned the nationals, and then bought a copy of the local *Chronicle*."

"What do you mean, 'scanned the nationals'? Why? Why would she do that?"

Compton began to speak, but Brasher interrupted.

"No, sorry, don't answer that. I was thinking out loud. Go on."

Compton thought that for someone in the spook business, Brasher did a lot of thinking out loud.

"Yes, sir. She went into a McDonald's, sat for ten minutes reading the newspaper from front to back, then left and returned to her flat. Wilkinson is with her now. He's out in the street, probably got his scooter stripped again."

"Stripped?"

"Well, not stripped. He's got it down to a fine art, sir. Takes off cosmetic bits and fannies on with the plugs or the carb. He can be off again within seconds if need be."

Brasher smiled. Sometimes, but not often, he missed the street work, with its odd moments of humour and the comradeship. Compton interrupted his thoughts.

"Sir?"

"Yes, yes, fine. Look, you park up somewhere close at hand, relieve Wilkinson, and get back in touch as soon as she moves. Do you understand? As soon as she moves. Oh, and Alex should be contactable again within an hour. Okay? Thank you. Bye. "

Brasher put the receiver down without hearing Compton's response. He pressed the secrecy button and the glowing icon dulled. Next, he pressed the intercom button and held it down. His secretary, Alice, in the adjacent office, responded instantly.

"Yes, sir"

Brasher paused a moment, nodding. A physical display of his arguing a point subconsciously.

"Sir?"

"Alice, have you any idea where Alex Taylor is at present? I know he's not to be contacted for an hour, but…"

Alice knew, and she also knew that Brasher knew she knew; but ever the gentleman, he never presumed.

"Yes sir, he's-"

"Ah, good. Would you mind contacting him and asking him to contact me immediately? Thank you."

Brasher released the intercom button - a button that could not be left in the on position. He reached for his pipe, emptied the bowl, and then re-filled with fresh shag. He lit the pipe as he walked to the window, still open from his previous smoke less than thirty minutes earlier.

He thought on Balvindar's actions, her scanning the newsstand, selecting a local edition, then speed-reading it from front to back. It was obvious - she had not heard from Sanjar. The tap they had on Balvindar's cell phone had shown nothing since Sanjar's escape. She was looking for news in whatever form.

So, why had Sanjar not contacted his co-conspirators? What was the point? Was it possible that Sanjar was wise enough to believe he'd been discovered, and the last thing he wanted was to leave a trail back to his cohorts in terrorism? Or, did he want to be re-captured as a simple burglar? If so, why not give yourself up?"

The phone on Brasher's desk rang. He turned, still puffing, and picked up the receiver. Alex Taylor's voice came through loud and clear, but panting. Brasher pressed his finger on the secrecy button. He informed Alex about his thoughts on Balvindar's action, and Sanjar's disappearance.

"Sounds plausible, and highly likely, sir," he said.

Alex thought for a moment.

He continued. "Am I right, sir, when I say that I believe we're simply waiting until we capture Sanjar, before pulling in as many as we can with regard to this little escapade?"

Brasher pondered for a moment.

He said, "I don't think he is going to lead us to anyone new, so, first of all he will be arrested as an escaped prisoner. Once he's inside, we'll plant someone on his landing who will hopefully gain Sanjar's confidence. Then, we'll do as we always do, Alex. We'll pull them all in but one, then follow the surviving rat as he heads off towards another pack that he thinks of as being sympathetic to his cause."

Brasher tapped his pipe against the ashtray, and wiped his lips with a handkerchief.

"Right, Alex. You're camping out tonight. Flights will be booked, and an old buddy of yours will pick you up at Newcastle airport. You need to get a move on. Speak to Alice, she has all the details."

Alex took a deep breath, and then replied after a meaningful second, "Of course, sir."

Basher was brusque in his response. "Don't get petulant on me, Alex. Believe me, I would not have actioned your pitching camp on Tyneside unless the situation deemed it necessary; not least because I am keenly aware of the additional cost, and the resultant pressures from bloody government ministers. Now, let's get the job done without the huffing, puffing, and sighing."

Alex's response was immediate. "Of course, sir, of course."

Brasher wondered if he'd gone too far in his reprimand. Maybe his choice of words was not what he should have used on a man with Alex's credentials. He spat out his response to his unspoken thoughts, "Fuck it, man. I should not have to talk like that. Not to you. No more, eh?"

No quarter was given by allowing Alex to reply; Brasher steamed on. "Right, we have that other helicopter. Necessary additional equipment for the North East Air Ambulance chopper will be in Tyneside today; it will be fitted today, and will be used tonight. The Boulmer air-sea rescue chopper is out of commission for six hours – unavoidable maintenance; but, I'm assured by the R.A.F. chaps that we will have it in time to ride in parallel tomorrow night. Right, keep in touch."

He allowed Alex the time to acknowledge his instructions, and then hung up.

Chapter Nine

Stephen paused, cocked his head slightly, and strained to hear; a car behind him, or simply a tractor in a field? He was on one of the many C roads that criss-crossed the Border region, a road that would have been last on the county council's maintenance list. Green, lush grass was gradually reclaiming the tarmac, sprouting from the abundant holes and cracks in the road. Stephen figured that maybe the true edge of the road was at least a foot back from the edge of the grass. The dense, leafy hedgerows, no longer trimmed unless reported by road users or caring farmers, stood one-foot above him.

He stood motionless. He felt the savage heat of the July sun on the back of his neck. He moved his head fractionally, lining his ear up with the road he'd travelled. The engine sound was smooth, and soft; it had to be a car. He pushed through a small gap in the hedge to his left, keeping the branches away from his face, and carried on walking. A driver in a speeding car would not see him beyond the full summer bloom of the shrubs and trees.

The car, a Mercedes estate, sped by without slowing. Stephen carried on walking along the edge of a cornfield until the sound of the car's engine was no more. Once again, he stood for a moment and listened. Satisfied, he began to push his way through the hedge, then stopped, startled at the sound of the voice behind him.

"It's easier to walk on the right-hand side of the road," said the voice. "You can see the traffic coming toward you. Except on right-hand bends, of course."

Stephen turned, nervous. He saw a man standing in the field of golden corn, about twenty-feet away. The man was dressed in a tan T-shirt that had seen better days, and what looked like ex-army issue fatigues. The man's brown hair, touched with grey, was shoulder length, wavy, but unkempt, and the skin that showed was the colour of shiny brown leather. He was unkempt. Not Hollywood unkempt or designer unkempt, just plain old bedraggled, with what looked like a three-day growth of grey stubble. The man smiled, and glanced over his left shoulder. That was when Stephen saw what looked like an English longbow in his right hand.

The corn came up to the top of the man's thighs, nearly waist height. Stephen strained to see a quiver of some sort on the man's back. It wasn't hanging on the stranger's back; it was attached to a wide leather belt that girdled the man's waist. The man appeared to glide through the crop. Hardly an ear of corn moved as he sidestepped and manoeuvred his way toward Stephen.

The bowman switched the bow to his left hand, and then held out his right hand; it was covered with an adapted glove that fit over two fingers only – the index finger, and the middle finger.

"Hello, I'm Billy. And if you lived around here, depending on your outlook on life, you'd know me as either Silly Billy, or Billy the Bow."

Close up now, Stephen saw more grey hairs and guessed Billy would be in his mid-forties. He was a handsome man, clear green eyes, muscular, but lithe, with a complexion that many endeavoured to emulate with a spray can.

Stephen replied without thinking.

"And hello to you, I'm Stephen, Stephen Donnelly."

He shook hands with Billy, and then gathered his thoughts.

"You gave me a bit of a shock there. I didn't see you."

Billy said, "Doubt if you'd see much through those eyes anyway. What happened? Accident?"

"Yeah, something like that."

Billy smiled. "I was hiding, trying to use that car that passed. What was it? A Merc?"

Stephen spluttered through his still swollen lips. "Yeah, a Merc." He shrugged. "You've lost me. Why were you hiding, why did you need to use the car?"

The smile stayed fixed on Billy's face, as Stephen gently massaged his lips.

"Old injun trick," said Billy. "Wait until a car comes by and the partridges, for some reason best known to themselves, take flight either towards me, in this field, or away from me, in the other field. If they come toward me, I eat like a king, if not, it's bloody rabbit again."

And Stephen felt himself smile for the first time in days – and his face hurt. He pointed to the bow.

"You're that good, eh?"

Billy smiled, and shrugged. Stephen carried on the conversation.

"Are you local, do you live around here?" he said.

Stephen swept his right arm out front and away to his right. Billy looked around, and then turned back to Stephen.

"More local than you I guess. Originally I'm from just south of Sunderland, but you I think are maybe from London itself, or Essex maybe. Yes?"

Stephen smiled and nodded an acknowledgement of Billy's knowledge of accents.

"So, how come you're stalking the fields for partridges? Shit food at your hotel is it?"

Billy laughed heartily.

"Aye, something like that," he said.

He looked Stephen in the eye, deciding. He looked over his right shoulder at the sun, and then turned back to Stephen.

"Look, it's nearly mid-day. Do you fancy a bite to eat? My tent is just beyond that copse. I wouldn't mind a bit of company."

He turned and walked away, the sun now on his left.

Stephen hesitated for a moment, then thought, yeah, why not?

Stephen felt a cramp in his stomach. He mumbled his mantra. "Keep talking, keep moving, and keep your mind off it." He nonchalantly rubbed the spot where the cramp had surfaced and said, "Yeah, what's on offer? Fried fox, marinated magpie? And don't tell me you can tell the time by looking at the sun. I saw *Crocodile Dundee*. Where have you got the watch hidden?"

Billy laughed again, and Stephen envied how Billy laughed so easily.

"No, no, slightly more technical than that. See that tree at the edge of the field, and see where the sun is? Well in that position, in summer, I know it's nearly mid-day. In winter, the sun, looking from here, would be about two fence posts along to your right, at this time of day."

Stephen stopped dead.

"In winter!" he said. "Are you serious? You live here – in a tent?"

Saliva ran down Stephen's chin as he spoke.

Billy didn't break step. Stephen upped the pace as the gap between them increased.

"Deadly serious. I'm here until they put me six foot under, or whatever they'll be doing with bodies by then," he shouted.

After nearly ten minutes of stumbling over rutted fields, and a few minutes striding through the thin end of a copse, they came out into an open grass area which sloped only slightly up toward the west, and Stephen gasped.

"Jesus. What the fuck!"

And Billy laughed again.

"Aye, that's the usual reaction," he said.

Stephen walked around the structure open mouthed. He spluttered.

"I don't believe it. It's bloody amazing. It's even beautiful. Where the hell did you get if from? Is it real? Did you make it?"

Stephen watched as Billy took in every inch of his home.

"I went to America, what, about ten years ago? I had a holiday on a dude ranch, and, while I was there, we had a day trip arranged to meet a group of Sioux Indians, or Native Americans if you like, and that was it. I was hooked. I went back to visit them nearly every day for the rest of my holiday and, apart from other things, came away with the skills necessary to build a tepee."

Stephen shook his head, slowly, a smile spreading across his face. His gums behind his swollen lips still showed blood leaking.

"It's massive. Where did you get the skins? Is it waterproof? Whose land is it?"

Then a cramp hit him, and he grabbed his stomach.

Billy watched as Stephen nearly doubled over. He stood silently, waiting for Stephen to stand up straight. Stephen smiled weakly.

"Phew, that hurt," he said.

Billy stopped smiling.

"As much as your face does? You're not going to start rattling are you?"

"What? Rattling? What do you mean?" said Stephen.

Billy stood for a few seconds, not speaking, staring at Stephen.

"No," he said, "I don't suppose you are, otherwise you'd have known, wouldn't you."

He watched as Stephen uncoiled.

"Better?" Billy asked.

Stephen nodded. Billy waited a moment.

"So, what is it? Grumbling appendix? Too much warm water? A bad take-away last night?"

Stephen delayed, groaning and rubbing his stomach, as he thought of what might be an acceptable lie. He looked at the solemn face of Billy and realised there'd be no fooling him; not that it mattered, Stephen would be on his way in a few minutes, and Billy would never see him again.

Then Billy said it for Stephen. "It's booze, isn't it? Or it was. You're on the wagon, aren't you? And it must have been bad, eh?"

Billy studied Stephen with an open, peaceful expression.

"Is that why you're on the back roads?" said Billy.

Stephen straightened up completely, and exhaled noisily.

"Eh?"

"You're trying to avoid people; and pubs, and supermarkets, off-licences, hotels, wine shops, and every corner shop that has a licence to sell alcohol. Amazing, isn't it? It's easier to buy alcohol than it is to buy fruit and veg."

"You're not helping, mate," Stephen said.

Stephen rubbed his eyes, gently. Billy turned away and stepped into the tent, the flap closing behind him. Stephen heard him shout.

"No one can help you, no one. Anyone tells you different – they're lying."

Stephen looked down at his feet, thinking. He knew Billy was right, and that the yearning would always be there, as would the memory of murdering of his wife.

Billy stuck his head out of the tent.

"Fancy a boiled egg salad?" he said. "Lettuce, carrots, spring onions, mushrooms, wild rocket, and good old boiled eggs, sliced. Oh, and a dessert of strawberries with full cream milk. Yeah?" And then, as an afterthought, "All grown in the Borders."

Stephen looked up. "Huh?"

Billy pushed through the flap, carrying a plastic dish in one hand, a plastic jug in the other, and went toe to toe with Stephen.

"Look. From the time you wake, all through the long drawn out day, you're wishing, hurrying, the hours away. Over and over you're saying to yourself, 'I wish it was ten-o-clock, I wish it was mid-day, I wish it was four-o-clock, I wish it was bed-time.' Anything, just to get another day over, and diminish the longing for the drink."

Billy held his head perfectly still as a butterfly passed in front of him. His eyes locked on the insect, following it across his line of sight. Then he turned back to Stephen.

"But it's not the passing of time that's important, Stephen. It's erasing the memory. It's making alcohol the last thing you think of at anytime at all, until, you hope, it never crosses your mind."

He thrust the dish into Stephen's hand, smiling.

"So, here, make yourself busy sunshine, take your mind off it. Vegetables are hanging in that aluminium foil sack..." He pointed to a tree to his left. "All you have to do is top, tail and peel. I'll sort out the eggs and strawberries."

Stephen took it all in as he looked around.

"And the milk?" he said.

Billy pointed to a herd of cows grazing on the other side of the stream that ran by his camp. The stream was maybe thirty-feet away from Billy's tepee, and maybe twenty-five feet wide.

"Back in a minute," he said.

Billy turned to go, but Stephen grabbed his arm.

"Look, how come you know so much about-?"

"That's a campfire story, Stephen. You know, when everyone's receptive, relaxed, not competitive; ready to listen, and learn from the mistakes of others."

Chapter Ten

Sanjar figured that if he couldn't see over the top of a hill, then obviously he was not on the skyline. He had travelled in that fashion for nearly five hours now; along the side of a hill or fell, then, when he had to cross a road or track, look for shrubbery or woodland which touched the path he intended to cross, wait for a few moments listening for traffic, then dart across. The crest of a hill presented a similar problem – he could not afford to be seen - therefore he could not walk along the skyline.

He calculated that he was still making nearly five miles an hour; a rate that he knew was good in the present terrain. He stopped for a moment, suddenly realising his shadow was at times in front of him or to the left of him. He cursed as he checked his watch – just after one-o-clock, he realised he was heading east, back to where he'd started from.

Now he did not have a choice. He had to crest a hill to get back on his heading. He turned to his left and began the climb. He checked his watch again, and then dropped to a near crouched position, and began scrambling upwards. He'd been climbing for nearly five minutes when further hills appeared over the crest of the hill he was climbing. He lay on his belly, checked over his shoulder to the valley below, then, satisfied that no one was in visual distance, began to crawl forward to the brow.

After another three minutes, Sanjar raised his head and looked down on to the Jed Valley running diagonally across the land in front of him. He smiled. He remembered Jedburgh from a trip in his uni days, and he remembered the distinctive snack caravan parked up on the road that followed the line of the valley below. He calculated that the caravan would be sited about two miles ahead and, if he figured it correctly, seven miles beyond that was Jedburgh.

He wriggled across the brow of the hill, and then pivoted one hundred and eighty degrees, leaving his feet pointing down toward the road that lay in front of him. He shugged out of his jacket and T-shirt, then lay on his back.

The sun beat down on his chest. He pictured himself in Iran, lying back against a palm tree on the banks of a river. He'd be a teacher, and he'd talk about life in the west… and… no, no he would not. He'd give himself up to the police, explain how he was blackmailed, how his father's life was put in danger, how the cleric pulled him into the web… He wanted to stay in England, but, it was too late now… after what he'd done… if the police found out…

Sanjar saw the chopper before he heard it. Not unreasonably, he determined it was looking for him. It was flying too low to be on a simple journey from A to B.

He looked around, quickly. He spotted the clutch of Scots pines one hundred yards to his right. He weighed the odds. If the helicopter kept on its present bearing, it would pass from his left to his right, following the trunk road below. He thought they might not spot him; it wasn't as though he was a snow coloured white man. He would blend in to a certain degree. He guessed the civilian pilot would be looking ahead, following the road, and maybe there would be a police officer watching the ground below.

And then doubt set in. He could not lie still, he was too exposed. Keeping below the skyline he made a bolt for the pine trees. He reached the cover of the trees as the helicopter slowed, hovered, and then turned toward him.

"Shit, shit, shit!" Sanjar cursed as he frantically tried to scramble beneath dead branches lying on the ground. Only partially covered and lying flat on his stomach, with his jacket and T-shirt beneath him, he gripped the soil. He looked ahead, between the trees, and watched as the helicopter hurtled toward him. He saw the police identification on the body of the chopper.

The high-pitched scream of the engine grew louder as the machine steadily rose in Sanjar's vision. He closed his eyes and held his breath, waiting for the police helicopter to slow and then hover in front of him. He gritted his teeth as the chopper screamed overhead, shook the branches of the trees like dandelion seeds with its thundering engine and whirling blades, then hurtled past and on towards the horizon.

He lay still, listening to the noise die, until it was a faint rumble from afar. Sanjar stood, the branches falling from his back to the ground. He turned, saw that the dark blue helicopter was now a speck in the distance, and thought for a moment. Were they after him? Of course they were. How many prisoners had escaped en route to incarceration?

He squatted for a moment, staring into the distance to where the chopper had disappeared. He thought of Balvindar and of the cleric, and he knew that they'd be waiting.

He looked to the ground, thinking back on events that had driven him to where he was. He growled, angry with himself for going on the run. He nodded, acknowledging his inner voice telling him that he should have simply hid until the hijackers had disappeared, and then hotfooted it back to the prison van. Sanjar looked up, sighing, remembering the timeline.

After taking the charity jar from a corner shop en route and emptying it of its contents, he'd jumped a bus to Newcastle. From the city centre, he'd jogged through the back streets to the office of his brother-in-law, Ali.

Ali owned a taxi firm in Walker, a district in the east end of the city. Ali had flapped and panicked, and tried to persuade Sanjar to give himself up.

"It's only a burglary charge," he'd said. "You'll be out in months. What the bloody hell are you doing, man?"

Sanjar had checked the cash draw as Ali ranted behind him.

"Forget it, Ali," Sanjar had said, "I'm not going to jail. Give me money; I'll pay you back when I sort out what I'm going to do."

"When you sort out what you're going to do? You can't do anything, you silly man. You have no future until you serve your time. You need to give yourself up, or run forever, which is stupid. Have you contacted you father?"

Sanjar had turned, holding a bundle of notes.

"There's nearly three hundred pounds here; I owe you. I'll make arrangements to get money to you to pay you back. Now, can I have a taxi, please? I need to get at least to the Rothbury turn-off on the A1. No, no more discussion. Do I get a lift or not?"

Ali had closed his eyes, and slowly nodded his head.

Sanjar walked to the edge of the copse. He stood slightly to the left and behind the trunk of a large pine. He silently surveyed the land to the north, slipped his T-shirt back on, and tied his jacket around his waist by the sleeves. As he did so, he felt the knife that he'd stolen from the farm, He pulled it out from where it was tucked into the belt holding his denim jeans up. He studied it for a moment, deciding, then crouched and dug a small depression; he buried the knife and stamped the loose soil back down. Down on his haunches again, he began to frog hop until he was below the skyline. Satisfied that he was not outlined against the clear blue sky, he stood and began to jog, keeping as close to the shrubbery as was possible without stumbling.

*

Alex Taylor squeezed his eyes shut, then opened them exaggeratingly wide. He sat more upright, behind the sun visor, but still his eyes hurt.

"Knackered, sir?" asked his driver.

Alex nodded. "Just a bit, Tommo. I've been awake since four."

95

Tommy 'Tommo' Thompson, checked his watch as he drove the car out of the car park at Newcastle airport.

"Yeah, I know, I know," Alex said. "It's nearly, what, eight hours travelling? I could have done it quicker in a bloody car."

"No company plane, sir?"

"This situation to all intents and purposes has a cap on it, therefore it's less urgent."

Tommo frowned. "We're chasing a fledgling terrorist group and it's less urgent, sir?"

Alex shrugged. He shook his head.

"Christ, I can't believe I said that," he said.

He pondered for a moment, and then carried on.

"We know they're going to plant a bomb, we know all the people involved and everyone of them has a tail. The only one without a tail is the bloody bomb maker. But, he's on the run, without his chemicals and friends. However, we know where both those items are – but that job is less... urgent"

He held up two fingers of each hand.

Tommo said, "He's gonna stick out like a sore thumb, sir. Geordie or not, he's still got his father's colour and in the wilds of Northumberland, if that's where he is, he's gonna be spotted very quickly. Unless he travels at night, of course."

"Maybe. How far now?" Alex asked.

Tommo pointed ahead.

"Couple o' lefts, rights, one or two roundabouts, and we'll be there in, what, ten minutes." He glanced at Alex. "It's a factory, sir. What they call a starter unit, for new business. Our cover locally is that we're a team of surveyors for Ordnance Survey, checking out the possibility of upgrading the old A1 between Morpeth and Edinburgh. Once out in the field, we're birdwatchers."

Alex nodded, and again rubbed his eyes.

"Hell, I'm tired."

He rolled his neck.

"How long have you been on the case?" he said.

Tommo grinned, ignoring the question. "Why don't you just put your head back for ten minutes, sir? Just relax, and I'll de-brief when we dock?"

Alex shuffled in his seat. "Good idea. Just rest my bloody eyes." Within sixty seconds he was breathing deeply and evenly.

Tommo tensed the upper half of his six-feet, two-inch frame, and then relaxed. He pushed back against the seat and stiffened his arms against the steering wheel. Then, driving relaxed with one hand on the wheel, he ran a hand across his fair hair - number two cut - and then settled down to a slow, steady drive. He unwound slowly. It had been a long day.

*

Lynn Gibson repeated the words. "I'm sorry, but if you don't speak within the next ten seconds, I'll hang up and then I'll report nuisance phone calls to both B.T. and the police."

She paused a second, then began counting. "One… two… three…"

"I'm sorry… I… where do I…?" the voice stuttered on.

Lynn heard an angry, frustrated, growl on the other end of the line. She waited. The voice came again. "I'm sorry…"

"Look," said Lynn. "Why don't you stop being sorry, and start by telling me your name, then just get on with whatever it is you rang me for. I understand, you're nervous, but just spit it out, please."

The caller inhaled deeply, noisily.

"Okay, okay. My name is Sue Donnelly. Your husband called me yesterday, his name is John, isn't it, John Gordon?"

Lynn frowned, and said, "Nearly right. It's John Gibson, but that's the only information you're getting out of me until you tell me why you rang. Now, please, get on with it."

"Yes. Sorry. John told me that my husband was in a hospital in Newcastle, and that he'd been mugged."

Sue stopped, waiting for confirmation.

"Go on," said Lynn, tersely.

"Well, he's not there, he walked out, and I'm really worried. I'm worried sick. John said that …"

Once again, Sue paused.

"Look," said Lynn, "Tell me the bloody story or hang up. I'm a copper's wife, I know all about the shit end of life; so please, if you're considering my feelings, don't. I've heard it all before.

Again, Lynn heard the sound of an intake of breath.

"My husband, Stephen Donnelly, the man in hospital, he thought that he'd killed me. We had an argument, a fight, he hurt me, thought I was dead. He panicked and ran. And now, according to a message from your husband on my answer-phone, he's on the run again. He took off before your husband had a chance to tell him that I'm fine. I'm okay." Sue hesitated for a moment, and then said, "And that's it – in a nutshell. But now I need to find him, he's got a problem, a… a problem, he may hurt himself. Please, I really am worried. I need to speak to your husband."

Lynn thought for a moment.

"If you're fine, why didn't you contact your husband? Ring him. Doesn't he have a mobile?"

"He has, or did have. I hated him after what he did to me. And, on top of what he did, he's an alcoholic. I… look, for days afterwards I hated him, I was glad he'd ran off. I thought that's it, I'm rid of him. But… you can't help your feelings, can you?"

She paused for a moment. Lynn waited. This wasn't going to be easy.

"Anyway," said Sue. "He's not answering his phone, or he doesn't have it any more."

Lynn sighed, long and loud. "Jesus!" she exclaimed. "Why the hell does he do it? This is all going to come to no good."

"What? What do you mean? I don't understand?" said Sue.

"Helping the bloody sick and injured. If I had a penny for every… oh, never mind. Give me your mobile number, and I'll ring him. Then, if he wants to speak to you, he can ring you back. Right, I'm ready. Gimme the number."

Sue gushed, "Yes, yes, oh thank you, thank you. It's …"

Lynn took down the number, forced a pleasant goodbye, and then rang John.

Nearly thirty miles away, sitting comfortably on a hilltop commanding a view over a circular area of nearly twelve square miles, John patted his pockets. He found his ringing phone, pulled it out, and smiled.

"Hello love."

"Don't flamin' well 'hello love' me. You've done it again haven't you? Why don't you just set up a home for waifs and strays?"

John put his hand to his brow, hung his head and waited for the tongue-lashing. He groaned, and began to speak. "Ah, love, I-"

"No, no," interjected Lynn. "Don't bother, I know what you're like. I know you mean well… but, John, it really is time you gave it a rest. If you keep going on like this…"

Lynn paused, took a deep breath, and thought for a moment.

"Oh hell," she said. "Why oh why do I now feel like a real heel?"

Another pause.

"Lynn?"

"*Yeesss,* I'm still here." She sighed. "Look have you got a pen handy? Jot this number down, will you?"

John scrambled for his backpack, fumbled inside and brought out a pencil and sandwich wrapper. Lynn recited the number, John wrote it down, and then he read it back to Lynn.

"Yeah, that's it," Lynn said, "the mobile number of your mystery man's wife. She needs to speak to you urgently."

She paused, paying only skant attention to John mumbling..

"Are you all right?" she said. "Managing okay?"

John laughed. "It's a... I don't know. I honestly haven't a clue where to start. I'm just guessing. At the minute I'm on top of a hill with a pair of binoculars, just looking. Any ideas?"

"You need a local, someone who covers the area daily, you know, like a travelling shop, or a mobile library."

John's eyes lit up. "You know, I've just had an idea. Thanks love, I'll call you later, okay?"

Lynn stabbed at the 'off' button, and pitched the roamer phone onto the sofa.

Chapter Eleven

The imam listened intently to Hameed. He cocked his head to one side, and forward, looking at the floor, seeing nothing, but analyzing every word Hameed said.

"No one has seen him, no one has heard from him."

"And Balvindar?" said the imam.

"No. No contact."

The imam wore black; black loose fitting trousers with elasticised bottoms, black Oxford brogue shoes, a black morning suit jacket on top of a white shirt, and a black v-neck jumper. The only contrast in the black visage he projected to the world, were the flecks of white whiskers scattered around his black, full set of facial hair, and a black turban.

The room, in which he and Hameed stood, was a dusty, windowless box-room at the back of the mosque. It was a storeroom for religious ornaments and books. There were no chairs or tables in the room.

The imam walked back and forth, brow furrowed in concentration. Hameed waited patiently, head bowed slightly. The imam stopped. He spoke as once again he looked to the floor, focusing.

"He is not coming back. His attempt at burglary was not for gain. No, I believe he wanted to be taken away from us. He has changed, he has lost his nerve."

He began pacing again, still talking.

"Where do we start? Who would help him? He is not white, he is a criminal, he is on the run. He will not get help from the English, so…" He turned to Hameed and asked again, " I repeat, where do we start?"

Hameed was dressed in blue denim jeans, black trainers, a black crew neck sweat-shirt with a Nike logo, and a blue nylon blouson. He stood just under six-feet tall. The only visible remnant of his Iranian Muslim upbringing was his full facial hair set.

He took a deep breath, his chest expanding massively. The man was a rock solid mass of muscle, aged mid-thirties, and, with his unshakeable belief in the fact that paradise and seventy virgins waited for him on his death, he feared nothing on earth. His full name was Hameed Ahad Malik.

Hameed shook his head, slowly.

"Wherever he his," he said, "he needs help of some sort. He will not escape the police without help from someone."

"Who are we watching, following?" asked the imam.

"Up until today, only Balvindar, but, as I'm sure you're thinking, we must at least begin to watch his family.

The imam steepled his fingers under his chin - still pacing.

"We have lost a day. Yesterday spent waiting, gave Sanjar a head start."

The cleric's thoughts were uttered, and then a pause, more thought, then another voiced observation. He threw up his hands as he spoke.

103

"He could be anywhere – that is the truth of the matter," said the imam

Malik's suggestion was not original.

"I'll visit all the family, ask a few questions. They don't know me. I can be a… anyone." He paused, then shook his head. "I will get information from someone." The imam said nothing. He stared at the floor again. After a few seconds, he said, "Find him, before the police do."

Finally he looked up and turned to Hameed.

"And when you do, kill him. Do not hesitate. Do not speak to him, do not let him speak, simply kill him and leave him where he falls. May Allah go with you."

Hameed nodded, then bowed his head, and left the room. The imam gave his aide time to leave the building, and then followed.

*

Billy smiled, as Stephen blinked and jerked his head sideways a spark exploded, took flight, and missed his eyes by inches. The sun was down beyond the hills, with the last of the daylight chasing it and darkness filling the void. Both men sat on logs, opposite each other. The campfire lit up the space between the two men, as dusk encircled them. Stephen poked the fire again, lifting small twigs and heavier, stumpier branches, to let the oxygen rich air feed the flames from below.

"That was bloody lovely. I thought the lunchtime salad was tasty, but that stew was… "

He touched his lips, and then threw a kiss into the air.

He pushed his wooden poker onto the fire, letting it burn, and then silence hung for a few moments - each man deep in his own thoughts.

"So, are you going to tell me then?" Stephen said it softly, kindly.

Billy stared into the fire, eyes narrowing, lips sealed, and his mouth down-turned. Stephen let him continue thinking for a while. Billy closed his eyes for a moment, tight, as if enduring pain.

"I wasn't on holiday in America," said Billy. "I was recovering, recovering from the effects of anything that would fit into a syringe, a spoon, or a glass, and give me a high."

He looked up at Stephen.

"And you think you've got it hard giving up the booze."

He shook his head, just the barest of movements.

"No, forget I said that," he said.

He looked into the flames again, as they flicked shadows across his face.

"I had a wife once - she betrayed me. I remember it clearly, the night we got married. We swore on the bible we found in the hotel. We swore that we'd never lie to each other, no matter what, infidelity included, we swore, no lies."

Billy paused again, shaking his head. He took a deep breath, and sighed.

"But she did, she fucking lied big time. Two years into our marriage, and she held back the truth from me."

Stephen watched the tears begin to form in Billy's eyes, and reflect the colours of the flames before him.

"It's called Lymphatic Cancer." Billy sniffed. "Ever heard of it?"

Stephen grunted.

"And she never told me, all the months, the pain, pumping the painkillers in… until it was too late."

He stood, turned his back to the fire and looked toward the hills.

"She died within nine months, and soft, weak, cowardly, me couldn't even respect her by acting with dignity after her death."

He was silent for a while, then turned back to face Stephen.

"Well, you can guess the rest, can't you. A few drinks to drown my sorrow, and then more and more. Then, to try and get out of the depression, I injected…"

He sat down again.

"Well, anyway, it's all in the past now, isn't it?"

Once again, both men pondered. Billy picked up a fallen piece of smouldering stick, and pitched it back onto the fire.

"And you?" he said.

Stephen sat grim faced, his swollen face casting shadow valleys between the swellings and bruises. Billy broke the silence.

"Embarrassed? That bad is it?"

Stephen thought for a moment. "I remember," he said, "at one of the A.A. meetings.

This lad in the corner, he came out with all the standard cop-outs for turning to drink. You know, to forget his mother's death, then his father's death, then after nearly two months, he finally came out with the truth; his mother had caught him… you know… it makes you go blind. Fuck me! Can you imagine that? His mother? He was what, twenty-three, when she caught him. Sad, isn't it. You know, not him, just, you know, his mother would have forgiven, or just ignored it anyway, like mother's do."

Stephen paused for a second, his face solemn.

"Anyway, he topped himself," he said, "a fortnight later. Hung himself. Well, we think he topped himself. Either that or just another sexual… anyway…" Stephen put his head in his hands. "I wish… I wish my case was as simple as that."

He looked directly at Billy.

"Can't tell you mate, but, I reckon you'll find out sooner or later."

Billy stared back at Stephen, stone faced.

"No kids involved, are there? Nothing of a… sexual nature?"

Stephen stood, quickly.

"No, no. Jesus! What do you think I am?"

He gave Billy a challenging look, and then cocked his head to the side, trying to see around him.

"What?" said Billy.

Billy turned to look in the direction of Stephen's stare. Through the maze of high-level branches, and dense low-level shrubbery, Stephen

107

strained to see. He saw nothing. The two men remained motionless and silent. Billy squatted slowly, and the fire crackled and spit as he dropped another few twigs on to it; more sparks shot off and died within two feet of the fire, yet still Stephen looked out into the night

"I thought I saw something," said Stephen. He thought, 'Maybe a policeman.'

Billy spoke softly, "Aye, he's out there. There's a small ditch, just beyond the silver birch. He went into it, but he hasn't come out yet; and it's only about ten feet long. So, I reckon he's in there watching us."

Stephen thought 'Police' again, but said, "What do you mean? Who is he? A nutter or what?"

Billy smiled, "Stephen. How the fuck should I know? I saw a shape, that's all. A man's shape."

He stood, and stretched.

"Tidy up a bit, will you?" said Billy. "You know, scatter the food scraps in the bushes by the stream, and put the non-food stuff in the bin-liner. Just pile up the dishes ready for cleaning tomorrow morning, that sort of thing."

Stephen made an effort at shrugging nonchalantly and began tidying up. Billy brushed past him, still visible in the glow of the fire, pulled the flap back on the tepee, and entered.

For the next two minutes, Stephen looked around the camp and planned for quick exit routes should the stranger, possibly strangers, be the police hunting him. As he strolled around the clearing, he gathered non-organic rubbish and dumped it into a black plastic bin-liner. The food scraps, as per

Billy's instructions, were then taken down to the stream, and scattered along the banks. He formed a ridge of loose soil around the still burning fire, and pulled the dry kindling away from the flames. He stood, and surveyed his efforts.

He walked to the tepee, pulled back the flap. He shouted as he walked in.

"All done and…"

The tepee was empty. He turned and looked to the fire. He heard noises, twigs snapping underfoot. He exited the tepee, released the flap and looked toward the ditch.

Stephen watched as Sanjar walked out of the darkness.

Chapter Twelve

Tommo dragged the wooden pointer across the Ordnance Survey map that was laid out on the table in front of him. The small factory unit was well lit from fluorescent tubes and the white emulsioned, cinderblock walls reflected light in all directions. Token pieces of apparatus lay randomly around the unit - just enough to create an illusion of enterprise. An empty trailer stood on end against the rear wall, and down the length of the factory lay coils of rope of varying thicknesses. Near the roller shutter at the entrance to the premises, surveying instruments stood along with drums of oil, empty petrol cans, and measuring rods. On the adjacent walls, on bent nails, overalls hung alongside weather-proof jackets and hi-viz vests.

"And we're not even sure if he's in the bloody area, are we? What is it, about three thousand square miles?" asked Alex.

Tommo stopped the pointer just south of Jedburgh. The six men around the table stood grim-faced.

Alex looked at the faces in the group.

"Where the hell do we start?" he said.

Tommo grinned, "Not the words we wanted to hear, sir."

Alex smiled. "Thinking aloud, thinking aloud."

He studied the map.

"Okay, he's been on the run for two days now. He's fit, he's young, he's slim, fast as a racing greyhound and his adrenalin is pumping. What, twenty miles a day?

"Easy, maybe more."

Tommo looked to the men, the squad, for affirming nods.

Alex moved alongside Tommo, and indicated on the map with his right index finger.

"So, he started here two days ago, at what, ten-fifteen in the morning?"

Tommo shrugged, and looked around to see if anyone else was about to speak. He saw faces locked on studying the map.

"Yeah, give or take a minute or two," he said. "Anyway, that's the time the recorder stopped in the prison van.

Alex studied the map again. He pivoted side to side as he looked around.

"Paper, anyone?" he said.

Tommo picked up a journalist's notepad from a chair behind him, and handed it to Alex. Alex tore a small piece of paper from the corner of a page, and placed it on the map. He performed the same action another six times, placing the pieces of paper at what looked like random spots on the map, then looked at Tommo.

"Get the idea?"

Tommo expression was grim. "I see seven bits of paper, and I guess we have seven foot soldiers here if you include me, but... ah, aye, I see. Yes, it may work, but how much time do we spend at each position?"

Alex saw the other men frowning. He beckoned them in towards the table.

"Come closer," he said.

Alex picked up the pointer again, and tapped on the pieces of paper.

"High points. All north of the small town of Glendale, which is just ahead of where I estimate our target to be. A man sited on any of those points would have a full three-sixty degree view of the surrounding area. Where it's not full three-sixty, the hidden area eventually leads into an area we can see. Okay?"

Again, nods and grunts of agreement all around.

"So, the boys in blue are looking for Sanjar in the usual places, nation-wide. The local boys are doing their bit, choppers are up at night, and we're doing our bit during the day."

Alex summarized, still scanning the map.

"He has to eat, he has to sleep, and he has to drink. The choppers have a chance when he's sleeping; the rest is up to God, and our good eye-sight."

Tommo said, "He'll make a mistake, sir. They always do. On top of that he's young, inexperienced…"

Alex snapped, "Yes, but he's also a zealot. He'll be driven by anger, indignation, and determination to prove him and his mates correct."

Alex betrayed his frustration in the tone of his reply.

One of the squad, Robbie, from Glasgow, who had found his true vocation in the service of Her Majesty, chipped in.

"Why the hell did he do a stupid burglary, sir? What the hell was he after? It doesn't make sense. Even the way he carried it out, he was just asking to be caught."

Alex nodded. He looked to Robbie.

"You're the second person to voice that opinion in two days and, the truth is, a lot of senior personnel are trying to figure that one out. Anyway, that's it. Relax now. Tommo will brief you in a few minutes"

*

Alex moved away from the table to the factory office. Tommo followed him and watched as Alex sat at a desk and took a laptop computer from his briefcase.

"Orders, sir?"

Alex looked up from under the desk where he was plugging in the power lead of the laptop.

"We sit and wait until daylight, I'm afraid. It's pointless dropping men off at this time of day, so let the lads relax and put their feet up for a few hours. Unless the choppers spot something tonight, it'll be a case of all quiet on the western front until tomorrow morning."

"And tomorrow, sir?"

"I've been in touch with relevant parties. We're to meet the police chopper and the air-sea rescue chopper, tomorrow morning at Newcastle Airport – cargo side. We'll be lifted just before dawn, and, all going to plan, we should be in position within thirty minutes. Vehicles have already been sited for us, and you will receive keys when we land."

113

Alex switched on the laptop.

"After what we've decided tonight, I'll contact both parties now and confirm our intended positions. Do me a favour, Tommo, scribble down the co-ordinates, please."

Tommo said, 'Sir,' and left Alex to his computer.

*

John Gibson punched in the number on his mobile. The mobile was sited in a hands-free unit on the dashboard of his car. Once the number began ringing, he set his car in motion and headed south. After two rings Sue Donnelly answered John's call.

"Sue. It's John Gibson. You rang my wife."

"Oh, yes, yes. Thank you for ringing. It's just... I..." Sue stumbled again and again, before saying, "I'm going crazy, Mr Gibson. I'm worried sick. I can't sleep, I can't eat, I... I need to be there, I should be out there looking for him."

John sighed, silently taking a deep breath. He let it out slowly, silently.

"First of all, just call me John, Sue. Secondly, I honestly doubt if you being here will do anyone any good. In truth, you'd maybe be a hindrance. You need to remember, Sue, what I'm doing is unofficial. Unless you want to take out a charge against Stephen, as far as the police are concerned, he's just a man who's walked out on his wife."

In the kitchen of her tiny semi-detached house on the east side of Higham's Park, Sue lit the final third of her allowance of three cigarettes a day, dragged long and deep, and exhaled noisily. She placed the cigarette in a shiny clean ashtray, then stood and switched on the extractor fan of her cooker. John waited.

"Can't you just let me tag along, John?"

John peered ahead, around an articulated vehicle that was loaded with tree-trunks, then, seeing a clear road, accelerated past the vehicle, touching seventy. As he steered back into the left, he slowed to the national speed limit.

"What have you in mind, Sue? Today I sat on a few hilltops, and watched the world go by. I don't even know if I'm in the right area. Christ, he could have headed west, for all I know."

"You don't believe that. You know he's heading in a straight line for Scotland. Just look where he's come from. At least if I'm up there, I'm roughly in the right area, and I'm closer to him."

Sue paused for a moment, then continued.

"Would you give me a second, please?" she said.

Sue put the phone down, sat down at the table again and put her head in her hands. She sat for a moment with tears in her eyes. She gulped, reached for a tea towel hanging on the door of the oven, and wiped her face. She dropped the towel on the table, and then picked up the phone. She spoke matter-of-factly.

"I was having an affair, we argued, he… well, you know what he did. I've driven him to this, John. I love him… it was his drinking… I wanted comfort, a shoulder to cry on. He… I… I couldn't live with myself, if something happened to him."

John groaned. "A shoulder to cry on? What the hell drove him to drink in the first place? Jesus!" John shook his head. "Do you have any kids? Do you not talk to each other as a family?" Then, "No, no. Wait, I'm sorry. None of that is my business."

He dropped a gear, and then roared past another skeletal framed wagon loaded with tree trunks.

"Okay, okay. But look, you need to know I'm only gonna spend another day up there anyway, so be aware that after tomorrow, you're on your own," said John.

Sue gulped back the tears.

"Yes, yes, that's okay," she said. "All I need to do is spend a few hours with you, you know, see what you've been doing, what path you think he might take…"

"Okay. Look, I'm going to lose the signal shortly, so how about we meet tomorrow morning at, what, say five-o-clock, on the Newcastle Western-by-pass? Can you make that in time? There's a Nova Hotel on the left, about a mile past the Metro Centre, on the Kingston Park turn off. I'll meet you there. Okay? And don't be late. I hate waiting for people."

Sue repeated, "Western-by-pass, Nova Hotel, five-o-clock. No problem."

John said his goodbyes, had another groan, and continued his journey southeast.

Chapter Thirteen

Billy loped in behind Sanjar, his bow in his left hand, his hair falling over his face. He brushed it back and grinned at Stephen.

"Stephen, meet Sanjar - another addition to the family. You're like the bloody buses. Don't see a soul for days, then…"

Billy edged around Stephen and Sanjar as they shook hands, avoiding the fire. "What's happening out there in the civilized world - everyone on the run?"

Stephen frowned. Sanjar smiled.

"No, no, relax," said Sanjar. "A forced marriage, dishonouring the family and all that."

"Hey, hey, that's your business. Keep it to yourself if you don't want to talk about it," said Billy. "There's a little rabbit stew left in the pot if you want it. Or do you not eat rabbit? I get mixed up with which religions don't eat what."

Sanjar smiled, "I'm Muslim…

Billy leapt back in mock alarm; he held his arms up.

"Whoa, fuck! Where's the bomb, where's the bomb?"

Stephen groaned inside; he looked at Sanjar. Sanjar smiled.

"Aye, we need a good P.R. man at the minute, don't we?" said Sanjar

"And you're not putting the accent on, are you? What are you, second, third generation?" asked Billy

117

Sanjar shook his head, but still held a pleasant expression.

"I'm a Geordie, man. My dad's from Iran, so's my mother, but I was born here, in Gosforth, Newcastle."

"I'm joking, mate, I'm joking," said Billy. "Go on, sit down. Here, take my log, park your arse, and get stuck in."

Billy handed Sanjar a metal plate from the stack underneath the picnic table at the side of the tepee.

Sanjar sat, leaned forward, and began ladling stew from the pot.

"So, do you live here then?" he said. "It looks a bit too permanent for you to be just here for a holiday."

"It's my home," said Billy. "But Stephen, like yourself, is just passing through. He'll be on his way tomorrow."

Sanjar looked at Stephen and said, "Forced marriage?"

Billy laughed heartily, and Stephen smiled uncomfortably. Stephen shrugged.

"I've got a problem. I need to be… err… isolated, yeah, isolated from it for a while. Try and beat it." He thought for a second. "Alcohol. I'm an alcoholic."

Billy laughed out loud again, as he spoke to Sanjar.

"And I was, once. And isn't it funny that you lot sell it, but your religion says you shouldn't drink it? In other words, you can sell drugs, but you can't indulge. That's hypocrisy, that is."

Stephen groaned, then forced a smile.

"Bad choice of words, Billy," said Stephen

Sanjar stared stonily at Billy.

"I don't sell it," said Sanjar

"Aye, but you know what I mean. Most of the off-licenses are owned by Pakis, aren't they? And they are Muslims, yeah?"

Stephen winced silently, and turned away. He closed his eyes momentarily, afraid for what could happen next.

Sanjar's expression soured.

"Billy, I'm not a Paki, I'm English. I'm not Iranian, I'm English, out of Iranian parents; not English by choice, by place of birth."

Billy pitched another few sticks on the fire, blissfully unaware of the tension he'd created.

"Aye, well, but you know what I mean. Anyway, enjoy you meal, mate. I'm off to bed. Stephen will show you where to kip, and keep the noise down, will you?

"And my dad's not a shopkeeper, he's an architect. He helped design the Metro Centre."

Sanjar's tone was challenging.

Billy laughed out loud again, genuine hearty laughter. He squatted down beside Sanjar and put his left arm around him.

"Come on, yuh bugger. I'm winding you up. Take a joke, eh?"

Sanjar turned and stared hard at Billy. Then slowly, visibly, he softened. Now he understood Billy. His grin split his face.

"Yeah, sorry, I'm so fucking sensitive. It's gonna be my downfall."

Billy pointed at Sanjar, accusing.

"You swore, you fucking swore. Now you'll have to say ten Hail Marys, or whatever Muslims do when they swear."

Sanjar shrugged, grinning, and then pushed Billy away. "You're a fool, man, but I'm beginning to like you."

*

Matty banged on the door again. "Come on, for fuck's sake. Talk to me." He paused, and listened. "Is anyone there?" He looked around the office again, nothing of any use leapt into view. He picked up a small stapler; the door opened as he raised his arm. Gurp Sahid levelled the gun, a pistol, at him.

"Get back against the window!"

Gurp did the ordering as he indicated with the gun.

"Yeah, yeah. No problem, mate," said Matty. "But at least tell me what's going on, eh? Why the fuck did you snatch me? I'm a friggin' burglar, and not a good 'un at that. What use am I to you?"

After two days, Gurp and Jamal were tiring. Guard duty shifts were not relished at the best of times; constant guard duty was a pisser. A request to release Matty in the middle of nowhere had been rejected.

Gurp backed Matty up against the window. On the tenth floor, the black of the night was total. Only moonlight from the other side of the building pervaded the gloom.

Gurp snarled. "Do you want the truth, *mate*! Yeah? You want to know what's going on?" He prodded Matty again. "Well I'll tell you, *mate*. You, my noisy friend, were a…"

Sanity settled on Gurp. He ceased his rant.

"You're no use to us whatsoever," he said.

He backed away from Matty, the gun still level with Matty's chest.

"Now, silence! Do not annoy me, friend. I'm tired, my mate's tired, and none of us want to be here, do we? So, let's just relax, and I'm sure you'll be on your way to prison, with a clean slate, within twenty four-hours." Gurp edged back toward the door.

"So why the gun, if you ain't gonna shoot me?"

Gurp stopped. "You're big, you're fit. I'm big, I'm fit. Who's to say who would come off best in a rumble? I can't take a chance with you."

Matty gulped. "I'm hungry, mate. Fucking starving. It's nearly two days. All I've had is a meat pie. Anything. A fucking hamburger, chips, crisps, anything. And a drink. That bottle of tap water you gave me yesterday is warm, stagnant."

Gurp nodded. "Yeah. I'll sort something out. But, no noise, understand?"

Matty nodded, said, "Yeah," and watched as Gurp locked the door behind him. Matty closed his eyes and groaned. He looked around. He got down on his hands and knees, squinting in the dark. He felt around on the floor for five minutes; nothing. He stood up and checked the desk drawers again, nothing. Turning toward the window, he spoke to his dim reflection in the glass.

"Well here's hoping I last until tomorrow."

He looked to the clock tower over the rooftops to his right; it was just after eleven-thirty. He pulled his jacket around him, and once again, lay down on the office chairs and waited for sleep to come.

*

Nearly one hundred and fifty miles to the north, Billy looked over the edge of his blanket to the opposite side of the tepee. He saw Sanjar staring up to where the support poles met in the middle, and out on to the stars beyond. He rolled over and stared into the wide-open eyes of Stephen. Billy winked, shut his eyes and pulled the blanket around him.

*

In the temporary command post in Newcastle, Alex gave up trying to go to sleep. He felt for the zip-pull on the inside of his sleeping bag, gripped it and pulled it down to his waist. Immediately, the other seven men stirred, looking towards Tommo. Tommo sat up. He made a settle down motion with his hands.

Tommo slid out of his bag and walked towards the basic kitchen sited at the far end of the industrial unit. He stuck his head into Alex's temporary office.

"Hot drink, sir? The usual?"

Alex nodded and grunted as he stepped out of his sleeping bag. He reached for papers in a file. Tommo returned two minutes later with two cups of tea.

"Not quite as much caffeine, sir."

Alex thanked him and smiled.

Tommo sat for a while, watching, then offered, "Doesn't make sense, does it, sir?"

Alex took a sip from his cup, and then shuffled the papers back into a brown paper folder.

"Go on, then," he said, "you tell me."

"Well, a bomb-maker one minute, and a burglar the next. And what was he doing? A corner shop, in the middle of a middle-class housing estate. No place to run, no place to hide, didn't isolate the alarms, didn't run, on a Monday night, when all the weekend banking's already been done. It stinks."

"Say it."

Tommo pondered for a moment. He nodded, confirming his thoughts.

"I reckon he's diverting us, sir? Like a lame duck leading us away from the nest? Maybe letting his mates get on the real job, the killing and the maiming?"

Alex put the folder back into his briefcase. He turned to Tommo.

"Who's looking after the shop tomorrow?" said Alex.

Tommo pointed to the end of the row of sleeping men.

"Jameson, sir. Six months away from retirement."

Tommo weighed up his commanding officer.

"What do you think, sir?"

Alex smiled. "It's true what they say, isn't it? When you get something on your mind you're like a bloody dog with raw meat." He nodded. "I agree with you - partly. I reckon he wanted to go to jail. Why?" Alex shrugged. "He's upset his bosses, and he needs to be in a secure place? He's come to his senses, wants out of the organisation, but is afraid of the revenge of his bosses for letting them down? Or, as you say, he is a diversion, but I don't think so. Far too convoluted, and time consuming. If a diversion was the true reason, then that would indicate that his group know of us, which isn't true. My money is on the option that he's turned, but does not want to be seen as a refuse-nik. Now, the question is, has he turned out of conscience, or fear of being captured and the consequences?"

Alex raised his hands in a 'who knows' gesture.

"Anyway, let's just catch him and leave the rest to London, eh?"

Tommo said, "Sure," then checked his watch. "Pointless even trying to sleep now. Transport should be here in an hour, sir."

Chapter Fourteen

John Gibson swung off the single carriageway and into the car park of the Nova Hotel. It was five minutes to five-o-clock, and another brilliant hot day was forecast. He spotted who he guessed to be Sue Donnelly resting against a sunlit wall, catching the early morning rays. John saw that her face was uplifted, presenting her neck and face to the rising sun, and her eyes were closed. Her left leg was locked, stiff, at an angle to the wall. Her right leg was bent at the knee, with the foot pushed against the wall. She was dressed in tight, dark blue running bottoms. Her matching top was unzipped to the waist. Her blue Nike running shoes completed the fashion style. John thought, ' Leisure, or working gear? Was she a runner? And how the hell did she look so fresh after driving for most of the night?'

He pulled his car in front of her and lowered the passenger front window.

"Sue?" he enquired. "Sue Donnelly?"

Sue smiled, a beautiful smile, and immediately John could see why any man could fall for her, whether she needed a shoulder to cry on or not. She used her shoulders to push herself away from the wall, and stood upright. John saw that she would be about five feet-nine, with a curvy figure that bounded an exquisitely slim waist. Her brunette hair was tied back in a ponytail, showing her peaches and cream complexion beautifully, and emphasising her wonderful hazel eyes. In essence, Sue Donnelly would stop any man in his tracks.

"That's me."

As she leaned forward, she reached out her left arm to rest on the passenger door; she winced, and then smiled again. She reached up with her right arm and gently caressed her shoulder.

"I guess that's where the knife went in," John said. "And the hospital believed you did it yourself, even at that height?"

Sue stopped smiling.

"Are you in a bad mood?" she said. "Is it because you don't want to do this? Or because it's early, and you're not an early riser?"

John studied Sue for a second, and then looked at his wristwatch.

"Okay. McDonald's opens any minute now," he said. "I'll park the car, and then we can have a coffee, and maybe get to know each other. Fifteen minutes won't make a difference one way or another."

Sue did not reply. She stood back from the car and watched as John drove into a parking bay below the famous McDonald yellow arches

The McDonald's franchise was sited twenty feet to the left of the shady side of the Nova. As they entered, John played the gentleman, took Sue's order, then repeated it to the young man behind the counter, Three minutes later, John placed two coffees on the table Sue had chosen.

"You start," he said. "Begin with the argument."

Sue reflected for a moment, nodded, then more reflecting before she spoke.

"Okay. He didn't find out, I told him – there was another man. We were in the kitchen. He was stunned, I told him why. I couldn't handle his drinking on my own anymore. The A.A. wasn't working, the doctor wasn't working, my pleading, reasoning, aloofness, loving, contradictory behaviour wasn't working; but, I still loved him - still do."

She stirred her semi-skimmed milk into the coffee, speaking as she looked at the whirling liquid.

"I began confiding in a work colleague, and, well, you know where that led. So…"

Sue took a deep breath.

"I told Stephen. He went ballistic, smashed the kitchen to pieces, calmed down, asked me why, I told him, and he smashed the kitchen into even smaller pieces. Then he punched me, then…" She paused. "You know, I honestly can't remember the sequence of events after that, but I do remember him pulling the knife out of my shoulder… chest, whatever. I don't remember it going in, but I remember looking up, I was on my back on the floor, and seeing him pulling the knife out. I remember the blood on the blade, running down the serrated edge to the tip. He was crying, sobbing, pleading; then I passed out. When I woke up, he was gone. The knife was on lying on my stomach. I picked it up, threw it in the sink, and then phoned an ambulance. The police questioned me in hospital, but… I couldn't tell the truth. For all he'd done, I still felt protective toward him. Like a mother with a murderous son, I suppose." She shrugged, and looked to John. "I didn't phone him because, in truth, at that stage I was hating him. Pure hate. Anyway, you know the rest. Now it's your turn."

John held his palms out wide.

"You know it all," he said. "We found him beaten up, took him to hospital, he discharged himself, well, walked out the next day. And, I think that he's still in the Borders region following a route parallel with the A68 toward Jedburgh, and then onward to Edinburgh. Why? One, he always been heading north since he left you. Two, he's not going to stick to the main roads if he thinks he's being hunted for murder"

"I checked an atlas last night," said Sue. "What if he's taking the coastal route?"

"I doubt it. Too busy, more police cars and, if he thinks we're looking for him, I figure he'll want to be away from civilisation, so to speak."

"And you reckon you have a plan which might help you, us, to spot him?"

John leaned his head to one side, thinking on his response to Sue's question.

"Look, I don't want to build up false hope. What I'm doing is far from scientific, but it's the best I can think of Sue. I am, or I was, one man trying to find someone who doesn't want to be found, in an area the size of Christ knows how many football pitches. That's what they say, isn't it?"

Her sunny smile dissolved.

"Do you think we stand a chance?" she said.

"Listen, bonny lass, I'm possibly the worst person you could direct that question to. I really am the eternal optimist. I see good in all, deserts sprouting water, and science beating all diseases."

John shrugged. "I honestly don't know. We can try, but I have to tell you, this is my last day."

Sue's face showed her disappointment.

"Lynn needs me, business this weekend, a little venture of hers, and I must be there. Sorry."

Sue raised her right wrist and John saw the Casio sports watch. It all tied in with her dress; the Nike Air trainers, the blue, skin-tight Adidas running bottoms, and the yellow, armless running vest. Initially, John had thought it was necessary dress for the day ahead – the terrain, and the heat. Now he was satisfied that Sue was possibly earnest about her inner health, as well as her figure.

Sue pushed her coffee to one side.

"Okay, in that case, we need to spend every minute usefully. Can we leave now?"

She levelled her eyes on John, and raised her eyebrows. He smiled, took a last sip of the scalding black liquid, and stood.

"Right. I'll explain as we go."

*

Seventy-five minutes later, John took his left hand off the steering wheel and pointed to a hilltop a quarter of mile beyond where Sue sat. The fields between the road they travelled, and the hilltop, were filled with golden corn just about ready for harvesting. In the corner of each field, clumps of trees marked ancient boundaries, and provided a haven for wildlife. Where the fields butted up against the road, thick hawthorn hedges offered protection from the wind, and two-feet deep ditches provided field run-offs.

"You can see the problem. For all the good viewpoint I had, even if he had been in the area, if he'd been on the wrong side of the hedgerow, or even in a ditch, I'd have had a heck of a job to see him."

Sue scanned the fields, nodding.

"Not easy, I can see that."

She turned back to John.

"But I do have my own plan of sorts," she said.

She reached between her legs and rummaged in her backpack lying in the passenger foot well. Her hand came out holding an inch thick bundle of A5 black and white copies of a portrait photograph. John saw the grainy image of Stephen Donnelly.

"Which is?" asked John. "And by the way, how long do you intend to stay in the Borders? It doesn't look as though you have much in the way of clothing. And what about your car, back at the hotel? You should have driven it here."

Sue smiled. "Yeah, first mistake. Anyway, I've paid for three days parking at the hotel, and I'll find digs somewhere around here. I have three sets of underwear, three running vests and a change of leggings, simply because I reckon that if I haven't found him within three days, Stephen will be long clear of this area by then. And, more importantly, my mum will be pulling her hair out looking after my two teenagers. If I haven't found him in three days, I'll go back, pick up my car, make apologies to Mum, then make base further north. Though where, I don't know. " The smile faded from her face.

"Once he gets to Edinburgh, well, he could take any direction, couldn't he?"

John checked his rear-view mirror, and then pulled out to overtake a tractor. As he pulled in again, he said, "Nil desperandum…"

"Auspice Deo."

Sue grinned at John's surprised look.

"It was my old school motto, 'Never Despair, Trust in God'."

John accelerated the car as the road straightened out and opened up for a good mile ahead. He pointed over to his left, in the distance.

"Okay the new area is beyond that ridge. If you look at the map, you'll see a circle around a hilltop and today's date. My plan was to site myself there today, but it would get me off the hook with Lynn if you take the hilltop view, and I'll hand out a few leaflets. You know garages, pubs, shops, that sort of thing? It just means that I'll get back to Lynn sooner rather than later. Oh, and I had a word with a mate of mine – he drives a county car in the region. Unofficially, he's passed the word on. They'll keep an eye out for Stephen if he's travelling the main roads"

"Thanks, but you and I know that's not going to happen is it? But yeah, I'll take the hilltop. Are you going to head back when you've dished out the leaflets?"

John shrugged, and gave a 'sorry' look.

"'Fraid so," he said. "But don't worry, I'm always at the end of a phone."

John crested the ridge and the Jed Valley lay spread out in front of him. The river ran across his

131

view from left to right. He looked down into the valley, and then concentrated on the road as it began to wind down the side of the hill. Sue took in the beauty of the view, all the different shades of green, trees in full bloom, lush rich grass with sheep grazing, and fields of corn on south facing slopes with vegetable fields along the bottom of the valley.

Within another fifteen minutes, John pulled his car into a stoned area in front of a weathered, wooden gate leading into a field. He hurried around to Sue's side of the car, and took the backpack from her as she swung around in her seat.

"Jesus, I thought you were travelling light," he said.

He swung the pack over his shoulder.

Sue laughed. "Like I said, clothes, trainers, binoculars, maps, torch, compass, bottled water, enough sandwiches for all day, and a flask of hot coffee, courtesy of the Nova Hotel."

She was talking to John's back as he climbed the gate and headed for a clump of trees. She caught up with him as he laid her bag on the ground, next to a Scots pine.

"You haven't locked your car," she said.

John pointed to her bag.

"Can I use your field glasses a moment?"

He looked to an adjacent hill as he spoke. Sue shrugged, and pulled a small set of binoculars out. John put them to his eyes, and spun the focus wheel.

"You've got company."

He spoke with the field glasses still held to his eyes.

"He's dressed in… well, could be camouflage gear, you know, army surplus. Bird watcher, maybe. Must be bloody keen. I was gonna site myself there, but couldn't get near enough with the car. See where he's standing, the sheer drop in front of him? Well, believe it or not, that's the only way up – there's a bloody great overhang on the south side. That must be his car, half a mile down the slope. Anyway, don't worry about him, I doubt if he'll bother you. Seems too interested in whatever he's looking for. And he's only six feet above you, according to the contour map. So, you're gonna see as much as him, apart from where his hill blocks your view"

He gave the binoculars back to Sue.

"That's it then. I'll get your leaflets dished out, and head off home. Sorry, I can't stay, but Lynn really does need me today. Woman's thing. Hospital."

He turned to go, and then stopped.

"Hang on a minute," said John. "Have you got a bed for the night? Have you booked in anywhere? The pubs and hotels are pretty busy this time of the year."

Sue slapped her forehead, and held her hand there.

"Shit!"

John grinned. "Don't worry. I've got your mobile number. I'll try to get you in somewhere. I'll ring you either way."

Sue smiled, sheepishly. "Sorry."

John flapped a hand. "Forget it. Anyway, keep in touch, Sue. Anything I can do, just give me a ring."

Sue shouted her goodbyes, and watched as John got into his car, did a four-point turn in the narrow country road, and drove off.

Chapter Fifteen

Stephen watched as Billy got the fire going. He shouted from the bank of the stream.

"Why don't you use matches?"

Billy grinned, and looked up from the crackling tinder.

"Cheaper, and more satisfying – in the summer," he said.

He put the flint and a piece of broken hand-file back into the tobacco tin.

"And flint's easier to keep dry."

Stephen kneeled, dipped his head in the moving water, and counted in his head. He got to twelve before the cold got to him. He stood, water dripping from his face and hair, and began to towel dry. He walked back over the lush green grass to where Billy was now building up the fire.

Billy said, "Your face is healing fine, and you're talking better. You're not spitting in my face as much." He grinned. "Two minutes, then I'll put the eggs on."

He made a great show of deciding on something that was troubling him.

"Does he eat eggs," he said, "the Paki?"

Stephen stared, stony faced.

"He's not a *Paki*, Billy. He's a fucking Geordie, and even if he was a *Paki*, what makes you think he wouldn't eat eggs. You're not racist, are you?"

Billy stepped back from the fire, raising his arms.

"Whoa, whoa, bit touchy ain't yuh? Fuck me, man, I was joking. Yuh know, a bit of daft carry-on."

Stephen turned back to drying his neck.

"Don't say behind his back what you wouldn't say in front of his face. Simple as that," he said.

Inside the tent, his head showing above the tightly wrapped army blanket, Sanjar listened to the lowered voices. After a moment, he made waking up noises, stretched, yawned, and stood. The conversation outside the tent continued.

"What are your plans for the day then, mate? Heading on, or spending another day with your Uncle Billy? I'll show you how to use the bow if yuh like?"

Stephen grinned, "Nothing definite, yet, but yeah, I'd like to have a go with your arrows, and at the same time maybe see if you're as good as you make out."

Billy settled the fire, and then stood.

"Right, we have heat. As soon as the flames calm, I'll put the frying pan on."

He walked to the nearest tree. His bow and quiver lay against the trunk. He spoke to Stephen as he hooked the quiver over his belt and then picked up the bow.

"Pick a spot within a hundred yards - anything. Anything that'll take an arrow."

Stephen looked around, and pointed.

"The second fork in that tree. The fork on the left. See it? Just below where the wood pigeon is sitting?"

Billy acted quickly. The arrow was in the bow, the bowstring was pulled taut, and the bow bent; within four seconds the arrow was released. The wood pigeon was knocked back eight feet before hitting the branch of another tree, and then falling to the ground. The arrow had hit the bird in the neck, and was protruding nearly half its length out the back. Before Stephen could turn to express his amazement, Billy loosed off another arrow which hit the fork in the tree that Stephen had indicated. Billy turned and smiled at Stephen's open mouth.

"Had to do it that way," said Billy. "Would have scared the bird off if I'd hit the fork first."

"Frightening, if you ask me," Sanjar spoke from the entrance to the tent. He was stripped to the waist, and holding his T-shirt in his right hand.

He continued. "Where did you learn to shoot like that, Billy?"

Billy grinned, and said, "Morning, mate. Good kip?"

Sanjar grunted, nodded, and then rubbed his eyes.

Billy continued. "Necessity is the mother, and all that. Couldn't get a gun licence, needed to eat cheaply and certain animal traps are illegal now, so, I bought this from a lad down near Rothbury, and practiced, then practiced some more, and practiced again. I spent as much time searching for my arrows as I did firing them."

Stephen asked, "Do you use it much? Could you hit something on the run, or on the wing?"

Billy cocked another arrow, took up the tension on the bowstring and indicated left with the primed bow. "Start running. I'll give you thirty yards start."

Stephen instinctively turned his back, protecting his heart.

"Fuck off, you idiot."

Billy laughed as Stephen performed a dance of ducking and dodging the bow. Billy let him squirm for a few moments, then lowered the weapon. Stephen settled down. He squatted beside the fire, then lifted the frying pan and waved it.

"Come on then, Billy the Bow, let's hear the eggs sizzling."

Billy smiled, and then nodded.

Sanjar watched the mild confrontation, and then walked to the stream. As he passed, Stephen handed him his hand towel.

"A bit damp, but it'll get the wet off you."

Sanjar nodded, took the towel from Stephen, and walked on.

*

Sue sat back against the tree. She laid her forearms on her raised knees and looked across to where the man still circled the near flat crest of the adjacent hill. She watched as he scanned three-sixty degrees, approximately every five minutes. On the one occasion that he'd caught Sue looking at him through her field glasses - as he looked at her through his - he'd smiled, and then waved to her. And, once, she'd spotted him tapping away at what looked like a laptop.

At his post on the hill, Tommo checked out Sue again. Yes, she was still there and still scanning, surveying a full circle around her position. Earlier, from behind a silver birch, he'd taken her photograph using a Canon D.S.R. fitted with telephoto lens. Tommo had then emailed it to Alex. Alex in turn had forwarded the snapshot to London. First indications were that Sue was not known, but matches were still being checked.

Tommo saw the man come up behind Sue before she did. He watched as Sue turned, startled, and spotted the man eight feet away. Tommo figured from the smile on Sue's face, that the man's explanation for his being there had been accepted. Tommo also knew that the man could have slit Sue's throat before she'd realised he was there – if that had been his mission.

Sue declined the man's offer of a cup of coffee from his flask, but instead opened her own and poured out black unsweetened Nova Hotel's best. She chatted for a while, exchanged information on names, and hometowns and jobs, then the man made his excuses and wandered back down the hill. Sue had accepted the man's explanation of looking for the recently released red kites in the area. He had not accepted Sue's story of her meandering the Cheviots as a relaxing break, but, as he reported to London, he was pretty sure she had, '… bugger all to do with Sanjar.'

Sue looked across to the other hill, and saw Tommo watching her.

*

Stephen and Sanjar held out their metal plates as Billy dished up the sausages, eggs, and beans. Stephen put one of his slices of unbuttered bread into the frying pan, and put the pan back on the hot embers; the bread was fried in seconds. Billy pointed to the left of the tent.

"There's a donation tin across there, if you feel like it."

Sanjar looked around him as they ate in silence. The sparkling stream to his right was flowing gently north, probably to River Jed. The sun had risen to just above the Scots pines in front of him, while deciduous trees circled them from his left to around behind him. It was a perfect campsite, but, he thought, once the deciduous trees had shed their leaves in winter, he imagined it could be pretty exposed. Directly across the stream a lark rose from a field, whistling its song. Downstream, behind him, sheep mooched, chewing grass to within a half-inch of the ground. Not a breath of wind blew; it was going to be yet another hot day.

"They're beef - the sausages - just in case you're wondering."

Billy spoke as he indicated Sanjar's plate with his fork.

Sanjar frowned, and then asked, "Why should I wonder, Billy?"

Stephen hid his grin with a double mouthful of fried bread. Billy looked to him, a puzzled look on his face, then turned back to Sanjar, and shrugged.

"Yuh know, in case yuh thought it was pork. You're all right to eat beef, aren't yuh? Yeah? It's just that yuh haven't touched them, you know. In case you think they're not clean, tainted as it were."

Stephen's grin spread across his face. He just managed to swallow his half chewed mouthful without choking.

"Jesus, Billy. You're a fucking nutter," he said.

"I'm just trying to be nice. Yuh know, put our guest at ease."

Stephen started to speak, but Sanjar got in first.

"Billy. I'm grateful for your hospitality, mate, but you need to relax. I'm a Geordie, man. I was bred and born in Newcastle. I eat chips, and hot pot, and Chinese take-a-ways, and pizzas, and Greggs' pasties, and… just chill, Billy, eh? See past my colour and you're home and dry. Then, if you can stretch your mind a bit further, just treat me as you would a Christian, or a Hindu, or a Scientologist, or whatever. You're making it hard work for yourself." He smiled, spread his arms, and shrugged. "Okay?"

"Aye, yes, no problem. I was just trying to be nice."

Embarrassed, Billy sliced his sausages and overfilled his mouth.

Stephen asked, "What's your story, Sanjar. How come a young lad like you is on the road?"

Sanjar gave the exact same reply that he'd given to the lady at the farm. Stephen looked surprised. He spoke between mouthfuls of food.

"Fuck me, as ugly as that, eh? Was she older than you?"

Sanjar held up his hand.

"Can we leave it at that? I'm not too keen on talking about it, if that's all right with you?"

Stephen laughed out loud, and winced. He raised both hands to his face and massaged his cheeks.

He said, "Course you can, you little liar."

Sanjar stopped eating, and stared at him.

"Well, what a load of old cobblers. How old are you? Early twenties? An intelligent lad? English bred and born you say. Your dad's an Iranian who is an architect in Newcastle, and you're trying to tell me he's trying to force you to marry someone from the old country maybe? A country that he couldn't get out of quick enough when the bother started?"

Stephen saw the anger rising in Sanjar. He held up his palm.

"Hey, it's your business, I honestly couldn't care less why you're on the road, but don't treat me like a fucking idiot and expect me to believe obvious lies."

He carried on eating, leaving Sanjar to glare.

Billy said, "Let's just calm down, eh? Enjoy our breakfast."

Sanjar continued eating in the painful silence for a while, and then said. "You're right. I am lying. But I've done nothing wrong. I just don't want to go home. Is that okay with you?"

Stephen turned to his right, and scraped dirt and ashes over his empty plate.

He said, "Listen, son. You can guarantee that whatever you've done, if it's wrong, sooner or later your god will find you out. But me, personally, I

142

couldn't give a fuck. Okay with you, Billy? Oh, and by the way, Billy the Bow, if you're living off the land, how come we're eating Walls sausages?"

With that, Stephen turned and walked to the stream. He dipped his plate into the water, and washed off the dirt and grease. He turned to see Sanjar and Billy staring at him.

Billy shouted, "Hurting today, is it?"

Chapter Sixteen

Sue leaned back against the tree, and then bent forward. She had one hand on her knee and one hand resting against the bark. She panted, noisily, inhaling in deep breaths. She looked to her right and squinted up at the sun. Her arms were beginning to burn; she moved around the tree into the shade. Tommo watched from fifty yards away. Sue looked up and flapped a hand. When she got her breath back she would shout a greeting.

Tommo, soldier to the last, did not leave his post, as much as he wanted to. Thirty seconds later Sue had regained her breath, her pulse rate had dropped, and the heat had gone out of her face. Tommo held out a fresh bottle of water as she walked towards him.

"Surprises you," he said, "doesn't it?"

He pointed downhill.

"You think, what, it's only about half a mile, but it sure as hell takes it out of you. Are you jogging for fitness? Or a runner who fancied a run?"

Sue gulped half the bottle of water down, replaced the cap, and wiped her mouth.

"Thanks. Fitness," she said.

She offered the bottle back to Tommo. He shook his head, "Keep it."

Sue crouched. "You're right. It doesn't look so steep from the bottom. And yes, I'm a jogger, as you've probably gathered, and not a runner."

Tommo smiled. "So, why did you exhaust yourself coming up here? I'm not that handsome."

Sue decided she would kill that one stone dead immediately. She held up her left hand, and flashed her rings.

"Happily married mate. Well, married, but short of a husband at the minute."

Tommo frowned, and Sue had a decision to make. She decided to tell; half the story anyway.

"Hurt my husband's feelings and he took off; simple as that."

She balanced herself, pulled her right leg up behind her, and looked to the ground as she spoke.

"You hurt his feelings! Sheesh! Now that *is* what I call sensitive."

Sue smiled, changed legs, and looked at Tommo.

"Yeah, well," she said.

She held out her hand.

"Anyway, hello. I'm Sue, Sue Donnelly."

Tommo took her hand, and shook it gently.

"And I'm Tommy, Tommy White, but everyone calls me Chalky," he lied.

Sue noticed that he released her grip without the trailing fingers that some men have.

"So, what are you doing here, Sue? Running away from your problems for a few days?"

Sue thought for a moment, and then decided.

"No, beautiful as the area is, this is business. I'm looking for said errant husband."

She saw Tommo's eyebrows rise.

"Okay, not errant, sensitive. We used to holiday around here a lot," she lied, "and I figured maybe he might get sentimental and, well, you know…"

Tommo wondered if Sue also was sensitive to a fault. She certainly avoided finishing sentences of that nature.

"And you, what are you doing here, Chalky?"

"Oh, boring stuff. Just doing a bit of bird watching. You probably wouldn't know, or care, but there's been-"

"Oh yeah. A couple of red kites released in the area. I've just been speaking to someone about that. You saw him, the man who climbed my hill?"

Tommo nodded, smiling. "Your hill, eh? Aye, I saw him."

Of course Tommo had seen him, he'd been relayed the information that the man was going to check out Sue, though why the group didn't stick to the surveying story was a puzzle. Surveying he knew a little of - red kites he didn't have a clue. But, he doubted very much whether Sue knew much about birds of any description either.

Sue said, "He gave me the creeps. I've never seen such a pasty-faced birdwatcher in my life."

Tommo cast a glance at his tanned arms; his fortnight on the Costas showed.

"Anyway," Sue continued, smiling, "my bird watching friend, the reason I climbed this bloody hill is to ask would you keep an eye out for my husband?"

Tommo grinned, embarrassed, at Sue's blunt question.

"What... how will I know him? You need to describe him. And I'll need a phone number." He shook his head. "No, no, hang on a sec. What the hell am I saying? I don't even know you. What if you're the evil one of the partnership? You could be-"

Sue's demeanour changed, instantly. "Okay, forget it. No problem." She turned, and began to trot downhill.

Tommo groaned, thought for a second, then shouted, "Wait, wait. Okay, let's talk about this. Yeah, I'll help if I can"

Sue stopped, turned, and waited. Tommo took a deep breath, and then exhaled in a loud sigh.

"Okay," he said. "Description please."

Sue described Stephen and the clothes that John said he'd stolen from the hospital.

"And your phone number?"

Sue recited the numbers, as Tommo keyed them into his handset. He put the phone into the back pocket of his combat trousers.

"Okay," he said, "all you'll get is the last seen location of anyone who I think may fit the description. Oh, and thanks for the conversation – as short as it was."

Sue nodded, smiled, turned, and began the descent down the steep hill.

*

Billy laughed and pointed at Stephen.

"Weakling."

Stephen pouted, and simpered.

"Not fair. I haven't been well."

Sanjar watched from the shade of an elm tree. The tree was at the inner edge of the copse, protecting his back from being viewed from behind, but giving him a clear view over the stream and nearly a mile beyond. The dense tree canopy also afforded protection from prying helicopters.

Billy egged on Stephen.

"Come on, soft arse, you need to really bend the bow to give the arrow force and distance."

Stephen focused on the target. He remembered what Billy had told him; line up the arrow, point the arrow up slightly, allowing for drop over distance, or not, depending on how far the target was. The rabbit, the biggest of the bunch, lying on the outside of the group, suddenly sat up. Billy spoke softly, watching the rabbit.

"Okay, he's got the scent of something. If it's a fox he'll be off before you can loose the arrow, so you need to be quick."

Stephen pulled a little more, lowered the bow fractionally, and released the shaft. He missed, and hit the doe sitting two feet away from the target. The arrow connected just in front of a hind leg. The group scattered.

Billy shouted as he splashed, waded, across the stream.

"Jesus, are you lucky or what!"

Stephen watched as Billy retrieved the rabbit, necked it, and then pulled the arrow out. Stephen turned to Sanjar.

"Fancy a go?" he said.

Sanjar heaved himself away from the tree trunk, and walked to where Stephen stood proudly.

"How are you feeling?" said Sanjar

Stephen looked at him, waiting for him to expand on his words.

Sanjar continued. "You know. Are you…
thirsty?"

Stephen thought for a moment.

"Sanjar, it's not a thirst. If it was, I've got a
whole fucking river… stream, in front of me. It has
to be alcohol, beer, wine, spirits, anything, fucking
cider, whatever. But, if you mean is it on my mind,
the answer is yes – every minute… no, that's not
true, it's only every five minutes when I'm not
doing anything. If I can keep my mind occupied, I'm
fine, but Jesus, mate, it's tiring, continually thinking
of something to take my mind off the drink."

Sanjar listened, solemnly.

"Have you tried prayer?" he said.

"Ah, for fuck's sake! Gimme a break, mate.
It's hard enough without someone preaching to me."

Stephen turned towards the tepee.

"No, no, Stephen, here me out. Just listen a
second."

"What while you fucking yammer on about
your Koran? Is that what it's called? The Koran?"

"Listen, all I'm saying is anything that can
give you peace of mind, hope. You're saying it's
tiring, continually thinking. I'm saying you don't
have to think, just read, words, words of hope,
peace, vision… Try reading your Bible."

Stephen waved a dismissive hand.

"Forget it, forget it, I'm past redemption.
Way fucking past. Ain't no going back for me,
sunshine. I'm just trying to gain enough brownie
points for God to maybe turn down the heat of hell."

He stopped and looked up, listening. He
turned a half circle, his head cocked.

149

From across the stream, Billy watched as first Stephen, and then Sanjar, looked to the sky.

Billy knew what it was - the Air Sea Rescue chopper from R.A.F. Boulmer, probably on a maintenance test run. The only other helicopter that he'd ever heard in the area was the Northumberland Police Force Chopper, but that had a lighter high pitched whine from the engine, as opposed to the rumbling, whup-whup of the rescue ship.

From the level and direction of the engine noise, Billy estimated it to be about two miles to the east. He stepped into the stream and began to wade back to camp.

He stopped in mid-stream and watched as Stephen casually dropped the bow, and then ducked into the tepee. Sanjar walked to the shelter of the copse. Billy wondered for a moment. He stood still, listening to the sound of the water, watching it run around him at just above knee level. He watched fish pass, heading up stream, until the chopper roared in from over his camp and swept past him, heading toward the hills to the west. He waded to the bank of the stream, just as Stephen and Sanjar emerged.

He took off his homemade moccasins, lay them in a log in the sun, and spoke with his back to Sanjar and Stephen.

"So, will you have to kill me to keep me quiet, or do you think the police won't come here? Or, then again, maybe your crimes are really not that serious."

Billy turned and saw the others staring at him.

Chapter Seventeen

Alex swore again, and then pushed forward, one foot in front of the other, pushing off each one. Jesus, he'd have to do some sort of training - this was ridiculous. He could feel his heart thumping in his chest. What was it, half a mile at the most from where the road ended? He looked up and saw Tommo looking out over the valley to Alex's right. Tommo spoke without taking his eyes off whatever he was looking at.

"Come on, sir. Maybe only ten minutes to sunset. We need to be out of here before dark."

Although Alex couldn't see him grinning, he just knew Tommo was enjoying every second of his struggle. He battled on, reached Tommo in two minutes, and promptly sat his backside on the remains of a felled tree.

"Phew," he panted. "What, only a year out of uniform, and now totally out of condition?"

Tommo grinned. Alex breathed deeply, calmed, then looked out over the hills and valleys.

He said, "Absolutely beautiful, isn't it?"

"Aye, it certainly is. I used to come up here most weekends with me mam and dad when I was a kid. It seemed all the more beautiful when we got back to Scotswood Road. What a bloody contrast. From grassland to grime."

They admired the view for a few moments, and then Alex asked for a de-briefing.

"Absolutely nothing sir, apart from the usual traffic you'd expect on these roads and tracks at this time of year. Back-packers, walking groups, mountain-bikers; at least a hundred I'd estimate."

Alex sat tight-lipped, nodding in agreement. After a moment's thought, he spoke. "What do you reckon? Travelling at night?"

"If he's in the area, sir. But… I don't know, with his appearance I reckon he'd be a fool to come up here. Far better head for Bradford, or Southall, somewhere he wouldn't stick out like a strawberry in the snow."

Tommo took his eyes off the sunset and looked behind him. Darkness was heading their way from the east, fast.

He said, "May be better to move off now, sir. Just enough light left to see our way down."

Alex thought for a few moments, and then stood.

"Yes. I think it's going to be down to the helicopters," he said.

He paused, his eyes narrowed, and then he continued voicing his thoughts.

"Yes, definitely, three more days, with the choppers at night, then that's it; plan B, whatever that is." He moved off, trotting. "Come on then, Super Geordie. Race you down."

Tommo passed him within ten metres.

*

Two hours later and five miles to the south, Billy put another log on the fire. Sparks danced and flew upwards, and then the embers settled, gradually heating the bark of the log toward combustion. Small flames licked around the log, until it caught and burned steadily.

Another hot day with a cloudless sky had made for a starry night. Although not absolute darkness – the full moon afforded good vision – the reflected light of the fire strongly contrasted the uncovered arms and faces of the three men. They sat on blankets around the fire, against the background of the copse and the sparkling stream.

Billy stammered. "Sanjar, you know... you know... like Catholics have confession, do you lot have that? You know, can you sort of sin, not intentionally like, and get forgiveness by confessing to the priest, or whatever you call him?"

Stephen stifled his grin. Sanjar shook his head and smiled.

"Billy. Which lot do you refer to? Do you mean us lot north of the Tyne, or the lot in County Durham, south of the Tyne? Or maybe you mean the Sand Dancers, you know, the folk who live on the coast, in South Shields?"

"No, no," Billy said, laughing. "You know what I mean. Muslims, like."

Sanjar's face lit up as his soft smile became a huge grin. He looked at Stephen, hiding his face behind his hands, his body shaking. Sanjar waited until Stephen settled.

Stephen looked up, still smiling, and said, "Come on, Sanjar, you've got to give him ten out of ten for effort. And it is a healthy interest he's showing."

Sanjar pointed at Billy.

"If you insult me once more, my faith allows me to kill you."

"What? Fucking hell, I'm only asking. You know, just curious like."

Sanjar reached out to Billy.

"Billy, Billy, I'm kidding. Relax. All right?"

"Jesus, Sanjar, pack it in will you. You scared the shit out of me there. You know, with all the carry-on lately."

"And what 'carry-on' would that be, Billy the Bow?"

"Come on, Sanjar, you know what I mean. Nine-eleven, the London bombers and all that. We don't know how to take your fucking lot."

Stephen winced.

Sanjar sighed. "There you go again, Billy; which lot do you mean? Our Turkish Muslim lot, where you may go for your holidays? Or maybe you refer to our Mohammed Ali and his boxing lot or whoever? Or maybe the Muslim doctor who possibly attended the A&E unit at Newcastle R.V.I. today? Exactly which lot do you mean? Oh, and the London bombers you refer to. Would that be the I.R.A, or the factionist Al Qaeda?"

Stephen stood up, warming his hands over the fire.

"Okay, enough. It's getting complicated now, tetchy. Let's forget it, eh?"

Stephen saw Sanjar smile and nod. Billy shrugged. Stephen turned his back to the fire, resting his hands on his backside, palms towards the flame. A cloudless sky made for a cool evening.

Billy said, "Talking about confessions, anybody feel like having another go?"

*

154

In the empty office tower block in Leeds, Matty watched the red glow fade into the western horizon. The city was already lit up, a crossword pattern of lights on or off. Now he was pissed off. He'd convinced himself that no matter which way he looked at this situation, there was no way he was going to get out of this alive. He'd seen their faces. Simple. He could identify them, therefore they would kill him.

Matty mumbled to himself. "And as for releasing me, yeah, believe that if you like."

Matty's problem was not the walls that surrounded him; he figured he could be out of here in seconds. The problem was the noise he would make attempting to escape, and how far could he get before his captors arrived on the scene?

He looked through the window again; only the smallest window ledge showed below, and even then it was not concrete or stone, simply folded metal sheeting. There was nothing to cling on to even if he did manage to get out on to the face of the building. He studied for a moment, then, with a slow nod of the head, decided.

Matty figured that if the building diagonally across the way was built on the same level, he was ten floors up. Obviously he could not survive a jump, but… maybe…

As Matty unzipped his blouson jacket with his left hand, he dragged a chair over to the window with his right hand. Once again he looked out of the window; shit or bust, he decided.

Along the corridor from Matty, at the head of the emergency stairs, Gurp stood, stretched, and then rubbed the circulation back into his backside. He bent over, touched his toes, stood again, looking ahead, then said, "Fuck!" His face was now a permanent mask of misery.

He picked up the pistol from the table in front of him, along with a bunch of keys, ejected the magazine and then shot it back into the butt of the handgun. Gurp put the gun down his waistband in the small of his back. He entered the office to his left, three offices down from where Matty was imprisoned. He dropped the bunch of keys on the desk nearest to the door. He drifted to the window, idly scanning the empty desks around him. The moonlight showed nothing different to what was in the other offices; paper, elastic bands, paper clips, staples, all littered the floor, and defunct computer cables lay open-ended, leading out from electrical wall sockets.

Gurp looked out of the window. Two miles to his left, on the south end of the city, near the M62, his wife would be preparing for bed. He pictured her in the bathroom, combing her hair, her raised arms showing her full figure. She'd tried, but after four children, Gurp just couldn't see anyway at all that she'd get her pre-marriage, slim figure back. He smiled at her naivety, thinking of all the diets and slimming aids she'd used and tried. In essence there was nothing wrong with her appearance. She was still shapely, still active, pretty, and, combined with a lovely nature, she was a wife to be proud of.

When he heard the crash, he swung his head to the right, wide-eyed, and just in time to see a chair fly out of a window, followed by a male figure. Both tumbled to the ground below. He shouted for his friend, and then remembered, Jamal was not in the building. He was out there somewhere getting a carryout for both them and Matty.

Gurp snatched the bunch of keys from the table as he passed, and pulled the gun from the hollow of his back. He sprinted to the office that had held Matty. He fumbled with the keys, finally got the door open, and burst into the office. He saw the broken window directly in front of him. He dashed across to the broken pane, and looked out. In the glow of the street lighting around the base of the building he saw the figure splayed out, twisted, on the paving slabs. The chair used to break the window was lying nearly twenty feet to the right of the figure.

Gurp repeated himself. "Fuck, fuck, fuck!"

He turned, and walked straight into the steel drawer that was being swung by Matty with every ounce of strength that he possessed. Before the drawer hit him, Gurp registered that Matty was in his underwear and shoes. If he'd had time to continue his train of thought, he'd have maybe figured that the 'figure' lying on the ground below was in fact Matty's jacket, and trousers. The jacket had been taped to a waste paper bin, and a Yellow Pages directory, and scrap paper rolled into each trouser leg. All loose ends had again been taped.

Gurp was unconscious before he hit the floor.

Matty took the gun from Gurp's right hand and looked at it. He'd never handled a gun before now. He looked back and forth between the door and the gun that he held.

Matty knew what the trigger was for, and he figured that the little pivotal pointer was the safety catch. He guessed that Gurp would have had the safety off, so he moved the pointer to its alternative position, aimed the gun at the wall, and pulled the trigger to confirm or otherwise. Otherwise. The bang of the shot being fired scared him, and the recoil alarmed him. How the fuck were you supposed to shoot straight? He looked to the door again, as he fumbled with the catch on the gun. He put the safety switch back to the on position.

He dashed to the exterior wall and crouched, watching the door. He waited, breathing softly, heart pounding, and waited. No one came. Jamal must still be out there, doing the meals-on-wheels bit.

After what Matty judged to be a minute, he stood and tiptoed to the doorway. He looked both ways down the corridor – nothing, no one in sight. Matty darted out and set off to the staircase at the end.

The opposite wall to the line of offices consisted of floor to ceiling glass, in two metre wide panes. The view on the other side of the glass wall was a car park, come recreation area that consisted of a small fountain, set in a large circular area of grass, surrounded by wooden benches. Four street lamps lit the scene below. Matty stooped low as he hurried to the staircase. His bare arms and legs showed up vividly in the moonlight shining through the panoramic glazing. He reached the end of the corridor and stopped.

He listened for what he estimated to be nearly five minutes, then began his descent into the pitch blackness below. Matty kept to the wall, and made wide sweeping turns at each landing. He paused at each floor, listening, and making use of what light showed through the glass fire exit door leading onto the staircase.

Just about midway, Matty thought that he could hear a mobile phone ring above him. It rang out. Obviously his jailer was still unconscious. He had reached the fourth floor landing when he thought that he heard the sound of door hinges squeaking, somewhere below him. He realised that the door could have been on any of the landings down from where he stood, but rationalised that it was probably captor number two returning with food.

Again Matty waited, crouching against the wall, away from the metal banister that enclosed the stair well from top to bottom. It was now silent below. He waited five long fear-filled minutes, and swore to God that, if he got out of there alive, he would never ever commit another crime. The silence was convincing, and got the better of him. He stood, stooped, and began his descent again, very slowly.

As he drew nearer to the ground floor, the sounds of the city filtered through the building and up the stairs. He heard the hum of the traffic, and emergency service sirens. As he hit ground floor level, he heard a car skidding. It sounded a long way off. He paused, with his right hand on the panic pad of the fire exit door. He pressed it slowly until it would go no further.

Slower than he'd ever moved in his life, Matty eased open the door. It opened left to right, out-over. When it was wide enough to squeeze his body through, he edged forward and stretched his neck to see outside. He pushed a little more with his shoulder, his right hand on the handle, and his left hand holding the gun.

Matty led with his left hand. As he opened the door, he swept the area in his vision with the gun. It was when Matty turned his head to look behind the outside of the door that he saw Jamal. Jamal had takeaways in his left hand, and his gun in his right.

Jamal aimed his gun at Matty's head.

"Drop the gun, Matty. Drop the fucking gun! There's no need for this. It'll all be over peacefully tomorrow."

As Matty swung the gun to aim at Jamal, Jamal ducked. Matty fired his gun, and the bullet passed two feet over Jamal's head.

Jamal shouted again. "Drop the gun, Matty. Drop it."

As Matty aimed at Jamal, Jamal pulled the trigger on his gun. The force with which the bullet hit Matty knocked him backwards. Matty's gun arm flew skywards and his gun discharged again, aimlessly. Matty hit the concrete path with a thud. Blood pumped from his chest, covered his vest, and then ran onto the pavement.

Satisfied that Matty was immobilised, Jamal stood, slowly. He moved forward, gun arm outstretched and aimed at where Matty lay. He reached forward and eased the gun from Matty's hand; only then did he holster his own gun in the pocket of his NATO jacket.

Jamal looked around, a full three-sixty scan. He saw no one, and heard nothing suspicious. He opened the door that Jamal had exited, and held it open with one outstretched leg. He reached forward again, gripped Matty's feet, and dragged the body back into the building.

Quickly, Jamal stepped over Matty, and exited the building again. He stood the chair up, grabbed the jacket that was wrapped around the rough and ready dummy that Matty had constructed, and then dragged them both back into the building. He laid the dummy next to Matty, and then closed the exit door from the inside. A trail of blood now led from the outside of the building to where Matty lay at the foot of the stairs. Jamal began climbing the stairs, fast.

Four minutes later, Jamal crouched over Gurp, slapping him. Gurp's forehead was swollen, massively, and was rapidly changing colour to a bright purple. Jamal picked up the bottle of Evian water left by Matty and poured it over Gurp. Still Gurp did not move. Jamal shook him roughly. Gurp came around slowly, and in seconds, Jamal had Gurp on his feet and was helping him toward the stairs.

At the foot of the stairs, Gurp stood watch over Matty as Jamal went to retrieve their car from a street two-hundred yards away. Within another ten minutes, both men were heading back to Gurp's home, dreading having to make the phone call that should have been made the instant they'd exited the building for the final time.

Matty's body would be found soon enough. Three gunshots would not go unheard in this area.

Chapter Eighteen

Sue checked that no one could see her from the bar, and then lifted her feet onto the stool opposite. The public bar of the Black Bull was beginning to fill up, with a mix of regulars and tourists, all dressed in summer clothes, and all showing off the results of the day's sunshine. Sue was the only customer in the Snug.

John Gibson's efforts on her behalf had resulted in a room for two nights only. After the second night Sue would have to search out lodgings again, unless the owner of the pub had contacts further north.

She slouched against the high back of the bench seat that took up nearly eight-feet of the partition wall. She studied the contour map laid out on the square, wooden topped, wrought iron table in front of her. Sue hoped for some magic factor to jump out at her in an epiphany moment - it didn't. She checked the topographic scale again, and sighed. She sighed and looked at the area she intended to scan tomorrow. Halfway through her calculations she slapped the pencil down on the reporter's notepad she was using, and muttered.

"What's the bloody use?" she said.

"These any good to yuh?"

Sue looked up to where the voice had come from - beyond the partition that separated her from the public bar. Two hands with fingers splayed appeared. The hands disappeared and after a moment, the door between the two rooms opened and Tommo appeared, grinning.

"Stuck with your calculations?" he said. "I heard you cursing."

Sue smiled. A nice feeling washed over her.

"Well, hello there. You're not following me, are you?" said Sue.

Tommo laughed, as he sat down at the table.

"Maybe some other time. Too busy at the minute though."

They exchanged pleasantries, then Tommo pointed at the map.

"So why the swearing? Looking hopeless is it?"

Sue's eyes closed momentarily, and then she shook her head.

"No, I… arrghh."

She took a deep breath, and sighed.

"I just feel absolutely useless, lost. I mean, he really could be anywhere, couldn't he?"

Tommo nodded, grimfaced.

"Got to agree with you on that one, Sue. He could even be somewhere down south if the truth be known. What made you choose the Borders anyway? I know you said he liked the place, but, maybe he liked Cornwall just as much. If you've ever been there, that is."

Sue smiled, and she ran her hands down over her face, dragging her tired skin with her fingers.

"You're right, of course you're right. The only other factor is that the police found him in Newcastle a couple of nights ago, and…"

Sue told Tommo the whole story, including Stephen being a recovering alcoholic, and the fact that he thought he'd murdered her.

Tommo shook his head slowly at each revelation. He thought for a moment, as he looked at the circles and directional arrows that Sue had scribbled on her Ordnance Survey map. He pointed to the area on the map that Sue had circled.

"Look, a lot of the twitchers are moving into that area tomorrow. I'll pass on your info, except your phone number, of course, and, if it's all right with you, I'll ring you every hour. Just to keep you informed that is. Okay? If nothing else, it'll be a little company for you, albeit by telephone."

Sue's face lit up.

"Oh would you? That would be great. At least I wouldn't feel as if it's me against the world."

Tommo held up his palms.

"No problem. Right. What can I get you to drink? Hard days demand relaxing nights, so, you just sit there, and let me do the honours."

Sue saw the no-nonsense look in Tommo's eyes, and gave in. She indicated the bar with a sweep of her hand.

"As you wish, Mr Birdman. Mine's a pint of any local ale."

She sat back and smiled.

*

Stephen poked around the warm ashes, and then rolled the potatoes over. The mud had fully baked around them.

"Now?"

Billy smiled. "Patience, mate, patience. Give them another few minutes."

He turned to Sanjar.

"Come on then," he said. "You start. And mind we want the truth, none of that crap about arranged marriages."

Stephen looked to Sanjar. Sanjar had literally drawn the short blade of grass. Stephen wondered that if he'd drawn it, would he have told the whole truth? Would murder be accepted by his homeless camp colleague? He pondered. Would Sanjar tell the truth?

Sanjar looked to them both.

"First I want your word that whatever I say, you will not report me to the police."

Billy's eyes opened wide. The shadows across his face, and the light from the fire, made for an eerie look.

"Whoa, bonnie lad. Just how serious is this? I mean, are kids involved, is it … like… sex or something?"

Sanjar stood up sharply from the log he was sitting on.

"What do you think I am? It is-"

Billy raised his palms to Sanjar.

"Hey, whoa. Okay, okay, calm down. Just asking. I mean, the way yuh said that, it could have been anything, couldn't it?"

Stephen spoke as he raked over the ashes.

"We need to feed this fire. Potatoes or no potatoes."

Billy and Sanjar looked at him, stone faced. He turned from the fire.

"Okay, I agree to that," said Stephen. "Whatever you say, we do not report you to the police."

He turned to Billy.

"Agreed?"

Billy thought for a moment, his face grim.

"Look, I'm not sure about this. Your bloody confession might be really serious, and yuh could just be agreeing with him just to make sure you're safe. What if you've both done murder? I've got to report it, haven't I?"

Again Sanjar raised his voice.

"I have not done murder. What is wrong with you?"

Billy snapped back. "Well you two fuckers started it. Who the hell wants to confess anything anyway? Never mind me, what's wrong with you?"

Stephen rolled the potatoes away from the fire with a twig, and then prodded them away from the heat.

"You got nothing to confess, Billy? Nothing to be ashamed of? No reason to be here other than wanting to get away from it all?"

"Not me, honourable guest. I'm happy the way things are."

Stephen and Sanjar looked at him. He raised a hand.

"Hey, believe me or not. I couldn't care less. You'll be on your way in a few days anyway. Nobody has ever stayed any longer than three nights. "

Sanjar sat down again, as Stephen cracked the mud off the potatoes. Stephen picked them up, and quickly dropped them at the feet of Billy and Sanjar.

"Ow ow ow!"

Billy smiled. "Arsehole."

Stephen blew on his fingers. "You know… " he flapped his hands, "you're finely balanced between being a cheeky chappie, and a nasty bastard." He smiled.

"I'm on the run. The police are looking for me."

It wasn't what Sanjar said, as much as how he'd said it. Stephen looked at Sanjar, and then turned to see Billy also looking at Sanjar.

Billy grinned. "Weeeell now. The fun starts here, eh? Come on then, sunshine. What are they chasing yuh for?"

Sanjar was on a downhill slide and couldn't stop.

"They think I don't know – but I do. Terrorism. "

"What! You're fucking joking," said Billy.

"Wait, wait, Billy," said Sanjar, "calm down. I didn't realise what I was getting into. I thought it was a protest group. Then, all of a sudden, I was going to… a bomb maker. Some people wanted me to make bombs for them. I've got a degree in chemistry. Two days ago I escaped from a van taking me to Durham jail for something else I did. The people who attacked the van took another man. You know, to make the police think it was him they were after. I should have made my way back to the Leader who…

"Leader?" said Stephen.

168

"He means 'boss'," said Billy. "If yuh say 'Leader', it politicizes crime; makes the crime more socially acceptable."

"What! Where the fuck did that come from? You on something?" said Stephen.

"Nah. I started a social sciences course at Northumbria University a few years ago, but… the distance… too far to travel. Chucked it in after six months."

No one spoke. They looked at each other. An owl hooted in the darkness behind Sanjar. No one moved. Something splashed in the river. No one moved.

"Well! Do you want to hear the rest?" Sanjar's aggression snapped the others out of their stupor. Soft mumbles and grunts of approval, and then Sanjar continued.

"I was expected to make my way back to the Leader, and then I'd go underground."

He paused for a moment, thinking.

"But, I… I'm wrong," he said. "My head was fucked up. All the prejudice, the hate, the silence when I walk into a room, the dirty looks… it got to me. I wanted to hit back, hurt people like they'd hurt me. I… I've really fucked up." He sighed. "Then, I did a burglary, to get put in jail, just to get away from it all, but they planned the escape, just to get me back…"

"Do they know you did the burglary to get away from them?" said Stephen.

Sanjar shook his head. "I didn't think so, but I guess they're wondering now."

169

Once again, Billy and Stephen reflected silently on what Sanjar had said.

Stephen said, "Me murdering my wife pales into insignificance compared to that."

Billy jumped up and reached sideways for his bow. In a split second he loaded an arrow.

"Whoa, just fucking hang on a second," he said. "All bets are off. We need the fucking coppers here. You're connected to terrorists and you've murdered your wife. Get over there with him."

He looked at Stephen and gestured toward Sanjar.

Chapter Nineteen

Stephen raised his hands in a placating gesture. Billy pulled on the bow and pointed the arrow squarely at Stephen.

Stephen shook his hands towards Billy. "Wait, wait, for fuck's sake, wait. At least let me explain. It wasn't cold blooded; it was passion, man, passion. I loved her."

"I'm not kidding, mate. Get over there with him," said Billy

Billy kept the arrow fully cocked and aimed as he spoke.

Stephen sighed, and moved alongside Sanjar.

*

Tommo traced his finger along the contour line.

"Yeah, good idea. I suppose that's what I'm doing. Y'know, pick a high point and hope to spot a red kite."

He paused for a moment.

"To be honest, Sue, I think I've got more of a chance of spotting a kite then you have of spotting Stephen. Sorry, pet, but it's the truth."

Sue thought for a moment, then said, "What would you do?"

Tommo replied instantly.

"Contact the police in the first instance. Okay, he's a grown man, and he can go wherever he wants, and whenever he wants, but, point out his… state of mind. And then do all the charities that've been tracing missing people for years. You know, like the Salvation Army, Catholic Church … that sort of thing."

Sue studied the map, her face fixed in a grim expression. Tommo waited. Sue shook herself.

"Yes, you're right. I'll give it one more day, then… although…"

Tommo smiled. "Hey, don't make your mind up tonight. Give it a few days, follow your plan through, and, well, who knows, with our help…"

Sue stood. "Of course. Now, come on. My turn. What'll it be?"

*

Ali backed up in his office chair, trying to push it even further away from the giant of a man who held him. Hameed had Ali by the throat with his left hand, while he pushed the sharp edge of a dagger against Ali's cheek with his right. Ali's eyes darted right and left, desperately looking around for help in any shape of form. He saw the glass paperweight that held down the driver's worksheets each time they opened his office door and let the wind blow in. It was out of his reach. His struggles to get away from Hameed had taken him further away from his desk. Ali prayed silently for one of his drivers to return early.

But, Ali knew, no one would enter. All of his drivers were out on the roads in and around Newcastle. Tonight was busier than usual because a local boy-band were back home, playing at City Hall after a successful national tour. For all the business the band had drummed up for his taxi company, Ali would not be able to tell you the name of the band, even if his life depended on it.

Hameed pressed the blade harder against Ali's cheek.

"You need to tell me, my friend. Where is he? We know Sanjar came to see you," he lied. "And you should know, cutting your throat is a quick death, but you are aware of every drop of blood that pumps out of your body."

Hameed tilted Ali's head back and moved the dagger to just below where he cupped Ali's chin.

"Whether you are dead or alive, my friend, we will find him. And the sooner we find him the better, for you and for him."

Hameed pressed the blade against Ali's throat. He waited a second, before speaking.

"Ah well, my friend. Go to meet Allah, and may you be judged fairly."

He tensed his arm.

"No, no, please, please. I will tell. Let me speak."

The tears flowed down Ali's cheeks.

"He was taken to the Great North Road, the A1, and dropped off at the Rothbury turn-off. He would not let us take him any further. He did not want anyone to know where he was going."

Hameed tensed his arm.

"No, no," Ali screamed. "I tell you the truth, please, believe me. Two days ago, ask the driver, he will be back soon. Please, ask the driver."

Hameed looked deep into Ali's eyes. He had no intention of killing Ali. He had seen the camera high on the outside wall as he had entered Ali's office. He released Ali's chin, and pointed the dagger into Ali's right eye.

"If you lie, you will die like a rat in a sewer. Do you understand me?

Ali nodded and looked up to Hameed through tearful eyes. Hameed stood back, fastened his jacket and turned. As he opened the office door he turned back to Ali.

"If he calls you, tell him Balvindar dies within four days if he does not return. And no matter where she goes, we will find her."

*

Billy kept the bow angled down in front of his body. He knew that he did not need to level it at Sanjar and Stephen. They'd seen how fast he was on the draw. They weren't stupid, they would not try anything.

"I'm in a right old pickle. Two of yuh, one of me. Out in the woods, pitch black. One of yuh an apprentice terrorist, and the other one an accidental murderer. Fucking hell! What a plight."

He studied his two fellow campers. They didn't seem worried. Maybe they wanted him to kill them. He'd read about that on his social sciences course. In simple terms, the lengthy paragraphs of four and five syllable words simply condensed down to two words of one syllable each – death wish.

Billy figured that Stephen could not have cared less. Stephen was at the black end of a guilt complex. Death please, if you don't mind; and as quick as you like. Sanjar was a puzzle. Running away from terrorists? Why didn't he go to the police?

"Now what?" said Stephen

Billy pursed his lips and shook his head.

174

"Wish I knew, mate. Wish I knew," he said.

Stephen spread his arms.

"Come on, Billy. Use your head. If either one of us had murder in mind, we could have done you and the other one in last night, while we all slept."

Billy pondered for a moment, and then indicated Sanjar with the bow.

"Tie him up."

"Wh…"

"Just tie him up – tight. Tie each wrist separately, then both wrists together, behind his back."

Sanjar protested. "Hang on, Billy. I've bloody well killed no one, he said he has. Shouldn't it be the other way round?"

Billy levelled the arrow at Sanjar's chest.

"You've got a bit of muscle. A good gust of wind would blow him over."

He turned to Stephen.

"Go on. Tie him."

Stephen stared, hard, and cold.

"So, where did cold calculating Billy come from?" he said. "What happened to the amiable Geordie?

"I'm still here, mate. But, I'm a man for all seasons. Now stop fucking about and tie him up. Or, I can put an arrow in his left thigh, and then tie you up. I'm serious. I want to get to the bottom of this."

*

Hameed waited for the amim to speak. The amim in turn waited for the person on the other end of his

175

phone call to speak. They were in the office adjacent to the mosque.

Hameed looked around and wondered. The room was filled with the minimum of essentials. The desk in front of the window. The Leader's chair behind the desk, and one chair, in which Hameed sat, in front of the desk. Hameed was wondering where all the money went to… the money that he collected on four days a week from sympathetic Muslim shopkeepers throughout the northeast of England. He frowned for a moment. The collections of late were getting less and less. A sign of hard times, or a sign of a change of attitude to the cause? Second generation Muslims, like Sanjar, were contributing very little. His frown deepened.

The imam gave his salutations, and then said goodbye. He switched the cell-phone off completely, put it into his inside jacket pocket, and then turned to Hameed.

"A man will be here within thirty minutes. He will have a car for you, and he will have appropriate dress for you. In the boot of the car he will have a backpack and enough camping equipment for four days, and a map. "

He paused, letting his words sink in.

"We will study the map, decide on our course of action, and then you will leave tonight. My plan will be to put you ahead of Sanjar, and wait, or work backwards. We do not know where he is going, but we can safely assume he is intending to hide in the Borders, or head toward Scotland. I will send others tomorrow to assist you."

Again, he paused, and again Hameed did not speak.

The imam stood, and reached out his hands to Hameed. He placed them on Hameed's shoulders.

"You are a loyal friend, Hameed. May Allah go with you, and keep you safe."

Chapter Twenty

Sue shook hands with Tommo, as he opened the car door. The car park was beginning to empty, as last orders were called. Tommo had sat with one pint of a local small brewery ale for the whole of the evening, Sue had maybe had one more than she was comfortable with. She blinked, as tiredness began to take over her body. She looked up and saw a beautiful star filled sky. Still no clouds in the sky to keep the heat down, but still the heat of the day rose from the parched ground. There had been no warnings of drought yet, but she thought that maybe another week of this weather and hosepipe bans would be issued.

Tommo offered his hand. "Okay, Sue, maybe I'll see you tomorrow. And I've enjoyed your company. The night's flown over."

Sue nodded stifling a yawn. Tommo laughed.

"Sorry, sorry," she said. "Too long a day. I'll be fine tomorrow."

She flapped her hand.

"That's it. I'm whacked. See you tomorrow, Chalky."

She turned and walked, head down, back towards the pub, and her room above the public bar.

Tommo laughed, and got into the car. He watched Sue enter the pub, before he started the engine. He picked up a small hand set from a pocket in the car door, and checked in with Alex. He confirmed his position for the next day, and then ended the call. He slipped the car into first gear, and then exited the car park. He had a three-mile drive ahead of him, to the cottage that was the group's base.

Tommo frowned. Alex had seemed pre-occupied. He seemed down. He'd taken the details from Tommo mechanically; no banter. Alex had simply confirmed Tommo's position for the next day, and then ended the call.

*

Balvindar pressed down on her mother's shoulder. Her mother, Aalilah, tried to stand. She was not strong enough to overcome Balvindar's pressing down, but she could shout as loud as Balvindar.

"Look around you! Look at my house, my furniture," said Aalilah.

She tried to wrestle Balvindar's hands from her shoulders. Balvindar bore down with her full body weight.

"Listen to–" said Balvindar

"No, I will not listen to you. I am English. I am an English woman. I was born in Newcastle. I was brought up like other Geordie girls. I have my own voice."

Aalilah twisted her body with all her strength. She freed herself and stood. As she did so, Balvindar pulled back her arm and opened her palm.

"Don't! Don't you dare." Screamed Aalilah. "You do, and tonight will be the last time you see me… and your brothers and sisters."

Balvindar froze, her arm still raised. She stared at her mother for a few seconds through tear filled eyes, then slowly lowered her hand.

179

"I have to go. I must."

Aalilah stared, wide-eyed.

"Go where? Why? Why are you mixed up with this man? He is not one of us. He is violent. Tell him you want nothing more to do with him. Just leave."

Balvindar sat down slowly, wearily. She looked to her mother and shrugged.

"Sanjar is not violent. He's angry... I can't, we can't..."

"Why?"

Balvindar struggled to find the words.

"Because... look, you've seen films. They are worse than the mafia, how they go for the whole family. It's not just me, Mam. He... they, they'd go for you, my brothers, I..."

Aalilah dropped into a chair. She stared at her daughter.

"They? What have you done? It's not just a burglary, is it? Oh no, what has he done?"

*

Billy indicated the log on the opposite side of the fire.

"Just sit together. Slowly now, no sudden movements and everyone'll be all right."

"Billy. You're overreacting, mate. I didn't exactly murder my wife, it was just an expression."

Billy stared, tight-lipped. He looked from Stephen to Sanjar, then back to Stephen. The two fugitives sat.

"Talk. Just talk, Stephen. Tell me how killing someone is just an expression."

Stephen hung his head.

"It was passion, Billy. She'd been having an affair, we argued, she pushed... there was a knife... I... then she was on the floor, blood coming out... I ran." Stephen paused. "And that's it, believe it or not. And you know what? I couldn't give a fuck. Call the police, or whatever you do out here in an emergency."

Billy smiled. "I'm ready for any eventuality, mate. Flares inside the tepee. Got an arrangement with the local bobby. A nice game bird now and then works wonders."

He pointed his arrow at Sanjar.

"Your turn, bonny lad. When you're ready."

Sanjar sat stock still, staring ahead.

"No!" he said.

Billy studied him for a moment, thinking. He glanced at Stephen, and then looked back to Sanjar.

"Not bothered?" asked Billy.

Sanjar spoke as he stared into space.

"Not really. Why the hell should I tell you anything? Who are you to judge?"

He turned and faced Billy.

"What?" he said. "I please you with my story, or maybe you can identify with my story, and you let me go, or stay? No, forget that, you couldn't let any of us stay could you? No, you think we're both potential killers, don't you? Don't answer that. I'm not bothered anyway. Fire the fucking arrow. Who gives a shit?"

Billy studied both his prisoners, grim faced. Sanjar turned away again, and looked out across the stream to the outlines of the animals grazing. Stephen looked up from fire, gazing.

"Think about it, Billy," said Stephen. "We're both off the radar here, aren't we? And, as far as I know, no one is combing the hills looking for us, are they?"

The expected reply from Billy was not forthcoming.

Stephen continued. "What I'm saying is that first of all if we were dyed in the wool killers would we have told you what we have told you? 'Course not, we'd be bloody mental to do that. Secondly, if we were cold-blooded murderers and we butchered you, as soon as your was discovered the police would be crawling all over the Borders in hours. Something neither Sanjar nor me want, is it? And, also, I guess you get hikers passing here on a regular basis, don't you?"

Stephen paused in his pleading, and still Billy said nothing. Stephen reached forward, pitching another twig on the fire.

"I tell you what, Billy," said Stephen. "Fuck you! Go on; fire your fucking arrows, who gives a fuck? Look, I'll make it easy for you."

Stephen stood, and Billy jerked the taught bow and levelled it at him. Stephen turned his back and began to walk out of the camp.

"Hold it, Stephen. I mean it. I'll fucking fire."

Stephen carried on walking. He waved an arm in the air.

"Yeah, whatever. Loose your fucking arrow, Robin. Who gives a shit!"

The twang as the arrow was released froze Stephen to the spot momentarily - only

182

momentarily. Not feeling the sting of the tip, he began to walk again. He'd gone eight paces when the arrow zinged down from directly above him, and stuck in the ground beside him, two feet away to his right. He stopped and turned.

Billy smiled. "Bit close that. Didn't expect yuh to get as many steps in. Still, it did miss yuh."

They looked at each other. Stephen wondering, and Billy enjoying the puzzlement on Stephen's face. Billy laid his bow on the ground, and walked to behind Sanjar. He untied him, and coiled the twine around his fingers. Stephen watched, frowning. Billy turned to him.

"Yeah, I'm convinced, but I'd still like to hear Osama's apprentice's story."

Sanjar turned quickly. "You can't help it, can you? The little digs, you just can't stop yourself."

Billy reached forward quickly, grabbed Sanjar by the neck and stuck a kiss on his forehead.

"Come on, yuh fucker. Unwind. I'm joking." Billy grinned again.

"And that smile of yours is worse than anything Jack Nicholson ever produced," said Sanjar.

Stephen walked back to the fire, and sat on his log, as Billy sat opposite Sanjar.

Billy pointed to Sanjar. "Come on, then. Your turn."

Chapter Twenty-One

Sue opened the door of the pub and stepped out into the early morning sunshine. The car park in front of her was empty, and the main street to her right was quiet. She looked up to another cloudless blue sky.

She leaned forward, touched her toes, held the position for a count of five, then stood and reached for the sun. Again she held the stance for a count of five, and then relaxed. Sue continued her general stretching exercises for another five minutes, and then sat at a bench to the right of the pub door. She thought for a moment, and then looked up as a car turned off the main street and entered the car park. The car pulled alongside Sue and stopped, but the engine was not switched off. Sue stooped slightly to look into the car, as the front passenger window was being powered down. Tommo's face beamed from where he sat in the driver's seat. Sue smiled back.

"Hiya, Chalky. You're up bright and early."

"Yeah, the early spotter catches the bird."

Sue groaned. "That has to be a twitcher's joke."

Tommo nodded, still smiling.

"Not even a joke is it, really?"

Sue shook her head, smiling again.

"Need a lift anywhere?"

Sue held up a 'no-thanks' hand.

"I'm fine, fine. I'll have a good breakfast and then head for my spot for today. But, as I said last night, any help you can give…"

The pub landlord's head appeared around the door.

"Breakfast's on the table, Sue," he shouted.

"Lovely," she said, "I'll be there in a minute."

She turned back to Tommo.

"Sorry. Maybe see you later?"

Tommo nodded, "Of course. Bye. Enjoy your meal."

He slipped the car into gear, and accelerated toward the junction. After he'd completed the right-hand turn, heading north, he checked his rear-view mirror and spotted the lone traveller behind him. He took in instantly that the man was about five-ten, maybe one-fifty pounds, either blonde or grey hair... then stopped taking interest. As he'd calculated the physical aspect of the man he also noted that the man was in shirt sleeves, was not carrying a back-pack or any item of equipment necessary for a life on the road. Tommo slowed for a moment, twisted around in his seat, and checked the man again. He faced forward again, as he reached for his mobile. He looked to the rear as the man turned down a side street. He speed-dialled Sue, then put the phone into the hands-free unit attached to the dashboard. Sue answered, still chewing.

"You know," she said, "I really am happily married. Apart from my husband trying..."

Then she remembered, and the humour dissipated.

"Sorry, go ahead Chalky."

"I'm in Caller I.D. already, eh? You're a smart lady, Sue. Anyway, look, it may be nothing at

185

all, but a guy fitting your husband's description just turned down a side street, two streets before the turn-off to the pub. But, he wasn't dressed for the road. He was clean, old clothes, but smart. I don't know, maybe you want to check it out. Sorry I couldn't do it for you, but I've got to be where I'm going by eight-thirty. Sue? Sue?"

Sue was out of the door and running before Tommo had gotten to the dress description. Her still live phone was stuffed into the back pocket, the only pocket, on her black, skin-tight tracksuit bottoms.

She hit the street that Tommo had indicated in eleven seconds. She stopped, panting, thinking. Just after eight-o-clock, what would a person on the road be looking for? Provisions, water, milk, cigarettes; not cigarettes Stephen had never smoked. She looked up and down the street for a grocery store.

Sue spotted the Spar supermarket, on a corner, on the left, about a hundred yards along the street. As she jogged, she calculated the time that had past. Maybe ten seconds for 'Chalky' to pick up his phone from wherever it was in the car, another ten seconds to dial her, ten seconds for the call to connect, five seconds for her to hit the receive button, then fifteen seconds for her to answer it. Total fifty seconds, and then add her time to dash out of the pub, approximately a minute to get to where she was now.

Sue burst through the wood and glass door to the shop, and looked around. The shop was small, seven short aisles. She scanned the aisles again, then turned to the young girl on the check out.

"I'm sorry, but have you just had a customer in, a man, about this high, grey hair, a southern accent?"

The girl blinked, bewildered by Sue's dash into the shop and the rapid-fire question. She spoke with a soft Scottish burr.

"Oh, aye, yes. I didnae hear his accent, he just put the medicine on the counter, paid for it, then left. Just seconds ago."

"Medicine?"

"Well no medicine, ye ken. Oil of Cloves. For toothache, maybe?"

"Was he… never mind. Did you see which way he went?"

The girl looked apologetic.

"I didnae see, but there's only a field that way, and…"

Sue garbled her thanks, and then ran out of the shop. The man could not have come back along the street she'd just travelled. The field the shop assistant had mentioned was along the same street past the shop. The man could only have gone right or left, right… or left… right?

Sue sprinted to her left – as Stephen stepped out of the pub opposite the shop. He turned to the cleaner, smiling.

"Thanks very much, love. You can never find a toilet when you want one, can you. You'd better lock the door though," he grinned. "You never know who's walking the streets nowadays, do you?"

He walked back along the street, turned left at the junction, and headed back to Billy's camp, three miles to the south.

Travelling in the opposite direction, Tommo scanned the hills and fields.

"Bloody beautiful," he said to himself.

Everything ahead was bathed in warm sunshine. Predominately sheep country, the fields were indeed full of sheep grazing. Any lamb born in the spring would be indistinguishable from its mother now, if it hadn't already gone to an early market. Tommo took his eyes off the road again, and admired the view to his left. Hedgerows interspersed with ancient trees stretched as far as he could see and, like so many soldiers lined up on a hillside ready to do battle, plantations of young pines stood to attention.

Traffic was light at this time of day, and the going was easy. Within two hours, it would be a shifting mass. Hikers, cyclists, families in cars - all nomadic holidaymakers enjoying a specific area for the day, and then moving on. The Borders was so vast, it had to be a centre-based holiday to fully appreciate the beauty of its towns and villages.

Tommo drove for nearly seven miles, and then took a right turn down a farm road. He approached the farm slowly and, after a quarter-mile, drove through the farm yard, past the farm house, waved to who he imagined to be the farmer's wife, and carried on up an incline to his post for the day.

He got the car a third of the way up the craggy hillside before the tyres began to slip. He took to foot for the last five-hundred yards. The view alone was worth the effort – three-sixty degrees with three miles clear vision. Where roads disappeared, either behind man-made structures or the natural form of the land, the road continuation could always be picked up on a few hundred yards to the right or the left.

*

Now ten miles to the south of Tommo and sixty-five minutes later, Stephen strolled into Billy's camp, rubbing his gum. Billy walked the other side of the stream, picking wild herbs, while Sanjar idly tidied up after the previous night's discussion; a discussion that had gone on long into the night.

"What did you get?" asked Sanjar.

"Oil of cloves, but it's not working. This is the second lot in twenty-minutes."

Sanjar shook his head.

"The tooth is slack, Stephen. The men who beat you up loosened your tooth. Every time you talk, or your tongue touches it, you jar the nerve. It's got to come out. Let me do it."

Stephen looked aghast.

"Are you nuts? What're you gonna use? Pliers?"

Sanjar smiled. "No, stupid. Tie a piece of thread around the tooth, then tie it to one of Billy's arrows. You won't feel a thing. Twang! Gone. Instantly."

Sanjar let his words sink in for a moment as he watched Stephen's astonishment, and then laughed.

"Only kidding, you clown, but definitely not pliers."

Sanjar walked to Stephen.

189

"Here. Just let me see, and then we'll decide what to do. Open you mouth."

Stephen opened his mouth.

"Now, when I touch it, you tell me."

"You're not gonna pull it out, are you?"

"Course not. Just tell me when I touch it. Sit on the log, please"

Sanjar put his index finger and thumb into Stephen's mouth.

"Now, tell me when."

Sanjar gently moved his finger along the right-hand side of Stephen's jaw.

"Ungh," Stephen twitched as Sanjar found the tooth.

Sanjar moved the tooth slightly, and Stephen groaned again.

"Yeah, it's slack," said Sanjar. "Okay now, Stephen. I'm just going to press down on it. Just to be doubly sure it's the correct one, then, as I say, we'll decide what to do."

Stephen's shout could possibly have been heard over the hills, but there was no doubt as to whether Billy heard it or not. He grabbed his bag of herbs, and dashed for the stream. He splashed through water that was now below knee level, and continued running until he hit the centre of camp. He saw Stephen holding his jar, and Sanjar laughing.

Billy stopped, and looked from one to the other. He spoke to Sanjar.

Billy said, "What?"

Sanjar held up the tooth between his bloody fingers.

Billy grinned. "Yuh fucking didn't. Tell me it fell out."

Stephen groaned, "Arrrgh. Ah, man, that bloody hurt."

He rubbed his jaw, and then spit out blood.

"But the pain's gone. Yes?" asked Sanjar.

Stephen nodded.

"So, all done," said Sanjar. "Now, Stephen. What would you like for breakfast? Nettle soup?"

Billy laughed, as Stephen turned away, waving a dismissive hand.

"Gonna get some sleep," he blubbered. "Just leave me until I wake up.

Sanjar and Billy watched, grinning, as Stephen made his way to the tent, then Sanjar turned to Billy.

"We okay after last night? Apprentice terrorist, and all that?"

"Sanjar, bonny lad, I should be the last of your worries. I'd like to bet it's not only the police that are hunting you."

Sanjar's grin faded, and his mouth down-turned, as he looked to the ground.

Chapter Twenty-Two

Sue made contact with the milkman on a small estate of council houses, just on the edge of town. She had already mail-shot three roads on the estate and was halfway down the last road when she spotted the milk delivery truck. It was small, flat back, silver coloured, and parked on the drive of a semi-detached. The empty milk crates holding a few empty bottles were the big clue.

Sue deliberated over knocking on the front door. She shrugged, and knocked. If the man was in bed after his early shift, maybe his wife could help. A young man aged about twenty-four answered. He was wearing brown slippers, blue and white striped pyjama bottoms and a plain white vest. He looked friendly enough.

"Aye? Canna help you? I'm just away to ma bed."

Sue held up the photocopy of Stephen's photograph.

"Sorry to bother you, and I know it's a long shot, but I was wondering if you've maybe seen this man on your rounds. You are a milkman, aren't you?"

The man rubbed his eyes.

"Well, no really, it's ma da's business, but he's on holiday for a fortnight, Spain. I'm looking after his round while he's away. Gis the photo, hen, lemme see it."

Again, he rubbed his eyes, and then stared at the picture.

"Oh, aye, nae bother. I met him this morning, on my way back into toon. He bought a pint o' milk frae me."

The man laughed.

"He had toothache, could'na chew. He gulped the milk down, then gi' me back the bottle."

Sue's heart raced. She stared wide-eyed as the man studied the picture again.

"Aye, that's definitely him."

"Where did you see him? What was he wearing? Did he look all right? Did he look healthy enough?"

The man laughed again.

"Oh aye, hen. He had a few bumps and bruises on his face, but he looked fine. A wee bit of a tan, even. A bit thin, though. But, aye, he looked fine."

Sue un-shouldered her backpack, and then stuffed the rest of the photocopies in to it. She spoke as she fastened the straps again.

"Please. It's important. Where did you see him?"

Sue saw the man begin to speak, then stop and look her up and down. She implored.

"Please. He's my husband. He hasn't been well lately. His... mind. That's why he's so thin. Please, there's nothing wrong in what I'm doing. I just want to make sure he's okay, and can fend for himself. Please."

The man studied her face for a moment, before he spoke.

"Aye. I can see you're worked up about it."

He looked into Sue's eyes.

"I tell you what. Jump in the truck, and I'll run you to where I met him, it's about a mile south of town. Come on, bonny lass, move."

Sue couldn't find the words. She pointed to the man's pyjama bottoms.

"Oh dinnae fret about that. This is no London."

Sue waited at the truck, while the man retrieved his keys from inside the house. As he closed his front door, he hit the remote button on his key fob, and the alarm system beep-beeped. Sue was in the cab before the man had opened the driver's door.

The man switched on the engine, then, as he put the gear stick into reverse, he reached across with his right hand.

"Hiya, hen, I'm Willie. Now, just you relax. I'll have you there in nae time.

*

Tommo circled the peak of the hill once again. He wiped his brow, and then wiped his hands on his shin-length faux desert combat pants. He looked up to the sun in a cloudless sky, and uttered one word.

"Fuck!"

He pulled his mobile from his back pocket, and dialled Alex. The face on the phone showed 'connection', but after fifteen seconds no one had picked up. He dialled again, and Alex answered.

"Hello, Tommo. Anything of interest?"

" 'Fraid not, sir. Anything from the other lads?"

"Well, a couple of points of note. The cleric on Tyneside has had one of his thugs speaking to

Sanjar's friends and relatives, and the Boulmer Rescue chopper will be back up tonight, with the heat sensor fitted, and the thermal imaging camera, So, with a bit of luck…. Oh, and we thought we had movement early this morning, but it was just a… well, I was going to say rambler, but he was the least equipped rambler you've ever seen."

Tommo figured he knew what was coming, but asked anyway. "Where was that, sir?"

"Just south of you. A man strolling south of where you were last night. But, as I say, just a rambler. White man, dressed for an early morning stroll, so, no doubt he had a small camp around here somewhere. Stopped a milkman on his return journey, and bought a pint of milk."

Tommo laughed. "Yeah, well, it takes all sorts, sir. Would it be worth looking for his camp? You know, ask has he seen anyone maybe?"

"Umm, I'll bear that in mind, but I think we'll stick to the plan for today, and let the chopper scour the area tonight." Alex cleared his throat. "Anyway, back to work. Keep in touch, Tommo." Alex cut the connection.

Tommo thought for a moment, and then continued pacing the tor, slowly. He raised his cell-phone again, ready to dial. He decided against it. It would wait. He raised his binoculars and began to check the northern sector. His method was simple, but very effective. He scanned from his right to his left, then raised the field glasses slightly and scanned left to right, taking in half of what he'd previously scanned. After five minutes, Tommo saw nothing; he moved to his western sector and

195

repeated the process, always overlapping on his previous scan. Still nothing.

*

Sue finished waving Willie off, and then checked her map pad. She looked to her left and saw a high ridge that ran for a good three miles away from her to the south. She checked the map and discovered the ridge ran for at least ten miles; she then looked to her right. She saw rolling fields, then woodland. She compared what she saw, to the layout of the map. The map showed that just beyond the fields a 'C' road ran north to south. Would Stephen have travelled that one? Would he have a base in the woods? It was now nearly eleven-o-clock, and the sun was beginning to burn. Inside her running gear, Sue was beginning to sweat. She removed her tracksuit top and tied the sleeves around her waist. She studied the map again. Beyond the woods she'd seen, a watercourse showed up on the map as running in the general direction of the road. For all Sue figured it would make sense to follow 'C' roads, she decided on another plan. She placed the map in the backpack, and shouldered it. She checked her watch, and then began jogging. Sue would be six miles further south in forty-five minutes, if not sooner.

Sue covered the distance in forty-two minutes, then turned east and jogged up the ridge. After another fifteen minutes, she had made the top, and flopped on the grass next to some gorse bushes. It was now seven minutes to twelve, and she was hungry. Eat or continue? Satisfy her hunger, or satisfy her search? Hunger won the day. Sue poured

196

tea from a flask, then opened the sandwich pack the pub landlord had prepared for her. Boiled egg, cress and tomato between slices of wholemeal bread never tasted better.

Fifteen minutes later and Sue had her plan of action. She would walk and jog the ridge, concentrating on the area to the west, to the watercourse, with only cursory glances to the east. Her field glasses had a sensible range of three miles, which would allow her to see clearly across to the woodland at the very least.

Sue walked slowly, and jogged only slightly faster, while checking her view every five minutes. The narrow ridge determined that she did not have to move much from her central track in order to view both east and west.

After nearly an hour Sue had travelled just under five miles. She sat for a moment and poured another cup of tea from her flask. As she sat, she noticed black smoke rising in the west, far over the woodland.

Sue pulled the pad map from her backpack and checked. She looked up again, and viewed the smoke from her field glasses. What was black smoke was now fading into grey, then white smoke. She looked down on her map again, and traced her finger from right to left. It had to be close to the run of water. Could it be a fire that Stephen had just lit?

She sat for a few minutes deciding. If she headed for the smoke, and it was not Stephen, she would have messed up her plan. But if it was Stephen, and she carried on heading north, by the time she tracked south on that far route tomorrow, Stephen, if it was him, may have moved on.

She sat studying the smoke and growled to her self, "Stick to the plan."

She packed up, stood, and walked north again.

Over to the west, Billy picked up two large twigs. He held them in front of Stephen, smiling.

"Wet one. Dry one. Wet. Dry. Get it? Green is damp, black is damp, but any other colour is probably dry. Wet wood, black smoke. Dry wood, grey or no smoke. Get it?"

"What, this is a smoke-free zone, is it?" said Stephen.

Billy threw the dry twig on the fire, and patiently expanded on his explanation.

"Nooo, it just takes longer for a wet fire to start blazing, if ever."

He patted Stephen on the head.

"Never mind, son. You'll get it before the week's out. Better still, just don't collect wood from the banks of the river."

Stephen grinned, then turned away from Billy and looked to the stream, sombrely. He sat for a while as the others mooched around the camp.

Sanjar bent over and picked up a small piece of broken branch as he approached the others. He sat and began to peel off the bark idly. Billy handed him his hunting knife.

"See what you can carve," he said.

Stephen watched them, eyes narrowed, frowning. He said, "I think I'll move on tomorrow."

Billy looked at him, but carried on with what he was doing.

"Aye, no problem. Good luck to yuh, mate."

Sanjar spoke without looking up, still whittling.

"You know, Stephen, there's been nothing in the newspapers or on the telly about the stabbing of a woman. Well, not up to the time I was sentenced. And I was on bail for nearly four weeks. Maybe you need to rethink. Are you sure your wife is dead?"

Stephen spread his arms indicating the camp, and gave Sanjar an 'are you stupid' look.

"How the fuck would I know?" he said.

"Did you check her pulse or anything?" said Sanjar.

Stephen shrugged, grim faced. He paused a beat.

"I just ran," he said, "Saw the blood and ran."

He buried his face in his hands. Sanjar and Billy turned away and busied themselves.

Chapter Twenty-Three

Balvindar put her head around the door and smiled a watery smile at Ali. Ali nodded, as he indicated the phone in his left hand with his right hand. He chatted on the phone for a few moments as Balvindar let herself into the office and sat down on the only other chair. Ali entered the caller's details on the computer, then turned on his swivel chair and looked at Balvindar.

"Any news, Ali?"

Ali smiled softly, sympathetically, and reached out to take Balvindar's hand. He was determined not to tell her about Hameed's visit, his threats, but most of all, not to mention that he gave information to Hameed relating to Sanjar.

"Only what you already know. And Rothbury."

"What was he thinking?" said Balvindar. "What was he suggesting? And why Rothbury? What the hell's the attraction in Rothbury?"

Ali shrugged. "I thought maybe him saying Rothbury was some sort of code between you and him. Maybe he is not heading for Rothbury. Maybe he just asked to be dropped off at the Rothbury turn-off. Maybe it was a smoke screen, and he is heading up the old A1, up the coast road."

Balvindar looked down.

"He's never going to phone me, is he?"

"Don't you think your phone may be tapped?"

Balvindar didn't reply. Ali sat with his arms folded across his chest.

He sighed. "That is what he will be thinking. And, he'll be frightened to show his face in public. If the police are looking for him, what we need..." He paused.

"What? 'What we need...' what?"

Ali swivelled his seat back towards the desk and reached for his computer mouse. A couple of clicks, and he studied the screen.

"Have you seen Sanjar mentioned in any of the newspapers? Any photographs?"

Balvindar's brow furrowed. "No."

"Nor me. A prison van is attacked, and there's nothing on the net newspapers, or anything coming up on the search engines. Seems funny to me."

They looked at each other, silently, contemplating the possibilities.

"So why aren't they reporting Sanjar escaping? And what happened to the others in the van? Or was... I don't understand this," said Ali.

Balvindar moved to the window, looking out onto the street. "We know he escaped. I know..."

Balvindar had a sharp intake of breath. She stared, wide-eyed at Ali.

"We've been stupid, bloody stupid. The police are on to us. They're waiting for us..."

"Stop! I do not want to hear. I do not want to know about who 'we' are; I don't want to know what you do. Please, Balvindar, go. Take your anger with you. I am happy. I love England."

"I did it for Sanjar. I followed him."

"Stop! Stop. Go. Get out of here."

Balvindar opened her arms, pleading. "Ali. I love him."

Ali rose pointing to the door. "No! Go. Now."

*

Sue watched the police helicopter pass overhead as she descended the ridge. She stopped for a second, watching it head in the direction where she'd seen the smoke rising. Now sure of its destination, she sat where she'd been standing and shugged her bag off her back. She watched the helicopter dip towards the watercourse, then bank south, as she pulled out the map pad. She stood again, reading the map, and watching the chopper circling where she'd ringed the position of the smoke on her map.

Sue checked the time on her Casio. It was now nearly three-o-clock, and once she'd descended the ridge, walked the remaining two miles into town, it would be nearer four–o-clock. Again she thought, should she cross to the west, check out where she'd seen the smoke coming from, or stick to the plan and check out the west tomorrow?

As Sue put the map back into her backpack, she saw the remaining photocopies of Stephen's photograph.

She said out aloud, "Finish one job, before you start another".

She stood, slung her pack on one shoulder and headed off down the ridge. The rest of the day would be spent putting photocopies into shops, pubs, and the other properties in and around town.

Now to the southwest of Sue, the helicopter circled Billy's camp, and then descended. The civilian pilot, and the police officer on his right, scanned the camp from five hundred feet, still descending slowly to the far side of the stream from Billy.

Billy acknowledged the police presence with a wave and a smile, and walked to the stream's edge. The chopper continued its descent, scattering the sheep in the field, then settled. A slight spray was being whipped up by the whirling blades, and drifting toward Billy. He smiled, enjoying the cooling water on his skin.

The police officer stepped out of the chopper and walked to the stream's edge on his side of the water.

"You okay, Billy?" he shouted, smiling.

Billy shouted back, just as loud. "Champion, Tom, just champion. And how are you? Busy?"

"Well, yes and no. Just cruising, as they say." Tom cupped his mouth. "Looking for a missing person," he said. "A Black lad, a Geordie, from Newcastle. You haven't seen him, have you?

Billy emphasised his shaking of his head.

He shouted again. "Nah, been quiet lately. Most of the hikers are sticking to the ridge, and then dropping down into town, before carrying on north. But I'll keep an eye open. Okay?"

Tom waved and half turned.

"Fine. Thanks for your help," shouted the policeman.

He walked back to the chopper and stepped aboard. He buckled up, the aircraft lifted off and

203

slowly headed east, across the water, and over Billy's tepee. As it passed over the tepee, the pilot nudged Tom, and indicated the screen showing the thermal imaging.

"I thought he said he was on his own."

Tom looked at the screen and saw the two distinct radiant glows picked up inside the tepee. He studied the images for a moment, and then said, "I thought that stuff didn't work in daylight."

The pilot said, "A fallacy. It's not as good, but believe me, it works." He smiled. "Check it out on Google."

Tom frowned. "Can you turn, and drift back slowly? But don't make it obvious; head east again, after we've crossed the stream.

The pilot did as instructed. He slowed, hovered, did a one-eighty degree turn, and then drifted back across the water. As they passed over the tepee again, Tom nodded.

"Yep, human. Now, why would Billy lie?"

The helicopter turned again and headed east, as the pilot picked up the radio handset. Within three minutes, Alex had been informed, and within another five minutes, Tommo's emergency relief was heading toward him, at a speed way beyond the national limit for country roads.

At three-twenty, Tommo met his fellow squad member and exchanged details. Within another five minutes, the relief was in position on the peak of Tommo's hill, and Tommo was two miles from town, heading to a position seven miles to the south. At three thirty-two, Tommo passed Sue on a right-hand bend, as she walked north to town.

Tommo saw Sue, but all Sue saw was the blur of a car whiz past her.

*

Billy reeled the line in gently, as the trout flashed and splashed in the gently flowing water. Stephen watched from the right-hand side of Billy, grinning. As Billy got the fish to the water's edge, Stephen stepped forward with the net.

"Got him," he said.

Stephen held the net at eye level, and smiled at Billy. Billy dropped his rod, reached for the net, and emptied it onto the grass bank. He picked up the trout, and guess-weighed it in his hands.

"Maybe four, four and a half pounds. Enough for three of us anyway. Start shelling those pea-pods, Stephen, and tell Sanjar to level the ashes on the fire."

"He's fucked, Billy. I kept him awake all night with my toothache. I'm not the quietest of patients, am I? Let him sleep, eh? We can cook it, and then wake him. Okay?"

"Aye, no problem. You do it. But keep the ashes about two inches deep."

Billy laid the fish on the grass, held it down on its belly until it momentarily stopped flapping, and then thumped it with the side of his fist at the back of its head. He waited a further ten seconds, checking, then slipped the hunting knife from his belt, and slit the fish from its anus to just under the gills.

Back at the campfire, and gutted and beheaded, the fish was wrapped in wet herbs and foil, before being laid on a bed of ashes.

From fifty feet away, just beyond the edge of the deciduous trees, Tommo nodded approvingly.

He mumbled to himself. "Couldn't have done better myself, son. Would have been better if you'd let the fish cure for a day, but…"

He scanned the camp again – still no sign of the third person. Was the officer in the chopper mistaken? Tommo checked his watch, sat on the ground, then lay back against a tree trunk. He raised his field glasses again, surveyed around the tepee, and then back to the two figures near the fire. He focused on Stephen.

"Aye, you're him all right."

Forty-five minutes later, with his stomach juices beginning to rumble, Tommo watched as Billy and Stephen scrubbed their plates in the river. He sat up, crouched and turned away from his observation post, as Billy turned to Stephen.

"Better wake him, Stephen. That fish won't stay warm forever."

Chapter Twenty-Four

Alex watched Tommo enter the hotel bar, look around, and then head toward him. Tommo held out his right hand as Alex stood. As they shook hands, a waitress appeared at Tommo's side. Before the waitress had returned with Tommo's drink, Alex had debriefed him, and was planning a course of action. He checked his watch, waited until the waitress had placed their drinks on the table, then spoke.

"Okay. The local police are positive that there were two heat images in that tepee. So, when you scouted, the other person had either gone for good, was in the tent, or was out somewhere doing something else. Yes?"

Tommo nodded, and shrugged. "Makes sense, sir."

Alex thought for a moment. "Are you sure the other person is this woman's… what's her name?"

"Sue, sir."

"Are you sure the man is her husband?"

"No doubt about it, sir. I've seen a copy of a portrait photograph."

Alex sat back in his chair. He stroked his chin between forefinger and thumb, and stared at Tommo.

"Right. Depending on a phone call I have to make this afternoon, we stand down the police, and bring in some of our men from Catterick, by chopper. We surround the camp tonight, and do a pass with the chopper. If we still pick up three heat sources, we go in and simply inspect. Full masks. Got it?"

Tommo nodded. "If the third person is Sanjar, do we expect him to be armed, sir?"

"He has picked up a breadknife on his travels, but I don't see how he could have acquired arms of any description, unless he's picked up a farmer's shotgun. However, we've had no reports of stolen guns, but still we take no chances. Okay?"

"Fully understood, sir, but what if the third person is not Sanjar."

Alex nodded, grim-faced. "We apologise to the people concerned, stand upright and retain our dignity as we fly away."

Tommo grinned, "Again, fully understood, sir."

"Good. I'll leave you to finish your drink."

Tommo reached for his drink. Alex stood to leave, and then stopped.

"What's she like, Tommo? As a person I mean."

Tommo drained his small beer in one, and then wiped his lips.

"Level headed, feet on the ground; a no-nonsense person, sir. Anyway…" Tommo stood. "If it's all right with you, sir, I'll be on my way. I'll re-group with the others in the cottage at dusk, and await your further instructions. I'll also organise the equipment, transport, and cross country route."

Alex nodded gravely. "Full chest armour, Tommo, full chest armour. We take no chances."

*

208

Sue sat in the lounge of the pub. She studied her map. For all the heat of the day, she had wolfed down her meal; dumplings with mashed potatoes, steak and kidney, and peas, followed by apple pie and custard. The sandwiches and flask of tea simply had not put back the energy she had expanded on the miles covered that day. She slouched against the high back of the pew and massaged her tummy.

It was just after seven forty-five. Sue reflected on the day. She silently cursed herself for not investigating the smoke. And what was the helicopter doing flying in the area? Grass fire? Youngsters, boy scouts, or girl guides, where maybe a campfire had gotten out of control?

She pushed her bottom lip over her top lip absently, and looked on the map for roads leading to the watercourse. There were none. The closest route for a fire engine to take would be on the 'C' road which ran parallel to the river, and then across a few fields. She sighed and began to fold the map, when Tommo walked in.

"Oh, hi. Nice to see you again. Spotted your kites yet?"

Tommo was now feeling ashamed. Lying to a member of the public was never a problem in the course of duty, but this was different. Sue was putting on a good face, but he could see the strain behind the smiling eyes. He pointed to the bar counter.

"Same as last night?"

Sue shrugged. "Sure, but I'm paying."

Tommo flapped his hand, a dismissive gesture. He ordered the drinks, and handed a ten-pound note to the barman. He smiled at Sue, as he sat down beside her.

"You can pay next time," he said. "What about you? What about the man I saw this morning? Any further forward?"

Sue unfolded her map again. "Well, I don't know how significant it was, but a milkman positively identified him this morning. The time and the distance fitted in with you seeing that man. The milkman took me to where he'd last seen Stephen and then I took off in a sort of squaring of the area."

"Hey, good thinking. So, any good news?" Tommo was genuinely impressed.

Sue grimaced. "I think I squared the wrong area. I did the east side of the main road, looking west from the ridge. About halfway along the ridge, I saw a smoke, possibly from a fire, over to the west, just about here."

Tommo looked to where Sue indicated on the map. "Yeah, gotcha. Just beside the large stream, isn't it?"

Again he thought on the lies and the deceiving manner in which he was dealing with Sue. Lies told with the interests of his country at heart were fine, but, here he was, sitting next to a woman who was chewing herself up in what she thought was possibly a hopeless search for her troubled husband. He was deceiving her, lying through his teeth.

"Aye, it figures. If he was heading south when he left town, maybe he was heading back to that spot - if it is a campsite, and not just a wildfire."

Tommo turned at the sound of the barman's voice.

"Beer and juice, friend."

He rose, collected the drinks, and placed the beer in front Sue. She saw his drink, and raised her eyebrows.

"Thirsty. And I'm going to have an early night. I reckon I'll be moving on tomorrow." Tommo was pleased to see Sue show just the slightest trace of disappointment.

"Oh." She looked at him. "Why? I mean, have the kites moved on? No, that's stupid, of course they haven't."

Tommo smiled, pleased at her interest. "No, they haven't moved on, but our group will be. So, I have to stay with the club."

Sue stared at him for a moment. "You don't look like a bird-watcher, Chalky."

Tommo grinned again. "And what does a bird-watcher look like?"

Sue shook her head. She was serious. "Not lean, not whip-cord muscles. Not clear bright eyes, not… Are you ex-army… or navy?"

Tommo forced a smile again. "No fooling you, eh? Aye, Sue, I'm ex-army, finished about four years ago. But, the discipline stayed with me. You know, the fitness regime, the recommended food, the health and hygiene."

Sue nodded, disappointed. "Oh, I see. So, you're leaving." She took a sip from her beer, forced a smile, and said, "Okay. Tell me about birds. Start with your elusive kite. Why has it got a forked tail? I mean, what is the point of that? Does the tail help it

211

to turn in mid-air? You know, like a right tail to turn right, and a left tail to…?"

Tommo laughed. "The truth is I don't know, Sue. Maybe it's just a hangover from evolution. Maybe it is right tail for right, as you say. Anyway, forget the birds, let's talk about you. What do you like doing? What do you do when you want to enjoy yourself?"

Tommo checked his watch, and sat back as Sue began to talk about herself.

*

Four hours later, Billy put down his hunting knife and held up the carved branch. "There yuh are, not bad, eh?" He moved the carving so as to offer different views to Stephen and Sanjar. Sanjar hunched forward on his log, and took a closer look.

"And it's a what?"

Billy turned the carving around to face himself, puzzled. "Eh? It's a bloody horse's head. What the hell d'yuh think it is?"

Stephen laughed out loud. "A horse's head! A horse's head! It's more like a rabbit, or a hare. It looks nothing like a flamin' horse's head."

Billy looked closely at his handiwork. He held it against the light of the fire.

"Aye," he said, "yeah, you're probably right. But yuh get the idea, aye?"

Sanjar and Stephen looked at each other, grinning. Sanjar reached forward with his wooden poker and once more raked the ashes.

Billy smiled, and said, "Yuh enjoy that, don't you? The raking around in the ashes. It's productive, isn't it? Peaceful."

Sanjar nodded. "Yeah, peaceful."

He thought for a moment, and his next statement jarred his camp mates.

"I'm going to hand myself in," he said. "I'm going to tell them everything." He looked to the others. "I can't live like this for the rest of my life."

No one spoke. Sanjar, morose, went back to raking the ashes. Billy and Stephen looked at each other. Billy shrugged.

Stephen said, "Have you thought about this? Seems to me the British judiciary system is the last of your worries. I doubt if the lot you're mixed up with will forgive you just like that."

Sanjar rubbed his brow. "I'll take one thing at a time. I guess the info they get out of me will kill that ring I'm mixed up with. Any fallout from other groups... I don't know. Will the police protect me?"

Again quiet for a moment, then Billy spoke softly, "Twenty-four seven? Year in, year out? Can yuh see that happening, mate? I just can't."

"You've got a choice," said Stephen. "Run from both the police and your 'ring' as you call it, or give up, and hope the police can protect you. I don't know, maybe a new identity, a new home. You hear about it all the time."

Sanjar threw his poker into the fire. "Damned if I do, and damned if I don't"

He stood, turned, and walked into the tepee.

Chapter Twenty-Five

Brasher indicated for the driver to pull over and to wind the partition window up. The driver eased over to the left, and pulled up in the loading bay in front of a group of shops. Brasher settled in the right hand side of the rear seats, out of line of the rear-view mirror and the eye line of the driver. He looked to his right and saw the hustle and bustle that was Brixton High Street, then turned and looked ahead again. He tapped receive on his cell phone.

"Alex?"

"Yes, sir."

"A progress report?"

"Yes, sir, and a request."

"Go ahead, Alex, fire away."

Alex moved to the window of his room, and looked out on the red sky to the west. The last light of the day did not pervade the square of cobbles in front of the hotel. He looked at the hiker, and bikers, enjoying the sunset that showed above the housetops, as they ate and drank.

"I think we have a possible. We have two unidentifieds staying in the camp of a local eccentric. He's a back to nature guy who lives permanently in a tent, a tepee, about three miles south. Apparently he has two people using his facilities, one we can positively identify, and the other who we have not seen yet. They were both picked up on thermal imaging cameras on one of our choppers. We're ready to go in, but I'm wondering, sir, should we be using the police, or is this our job?"

"Why do you need to ask, Alex? Do you need extra men? Don't you have enough men and equipment?"

Alex cleared his throat. "Indeed, sir, we do. However, I'm aware that the police are the specific anti-terrorist squad in the U.K., and the use of army personnel on British soil is... well, a sensitive situation. I was originally going to stand down the police, and bring up a chopper from Catterick, but..." Alex paused for a moment. "What I'm saying, sir, is that I don't want to capture our target, if it is him, and then have some bloody European Human Rights character come marching in laying the law down, and then our damned capture walks free."

Silence.

"Are you still there, sir?"

"I am, Alex, I am. And I see where you're going with this. Give me a moment."

Brasher looked at the shopping parade, seeing nothing. He absently tapped his teeth with his cell phone. He ummed once or twice then put the phone to his ear.

"Right. Zero hour is when?" he said.

"O-Two-hundred, sir."

"Okay. First of all check your maps, and when you decide on a chopper pick-up point, contact me. In the meantime, I'll contact Catterick and arrange for an Apache helicopter to be on stand by for my call. I'll also arrange for the police chopper to be out of the area at the time you decide on. Do I make myself clear, Alex?"

"Perfectly, sir."

"Bugger his human rights. He forfeited them when he deemed to make bloody bombs. And Alex, remember. We need him alive."

"Yes, sir."

"Good man. And good luck."

Brasher hit the end button.

Alex ended his call, and then tapped in Tommo's number. Tommo answered on the third ring.

"Sir?"

"Group at base in thirty minutes. Okay?"

"Yes, sir. Thirty minutes."

Tommo switched off his phone, then turned to his colleague. "Group text. Back at base in thirty-minutes."

His colleague began predictive texting.

*

Forty-five minutes later, as the car carrying Brasher south down the A23 crossed the M25 just north of Horley, Surrey, his phone rang again. Brasher checked the caller I.D., and frowned. He looked up and saw the driver's raised eyebrows in the rear-view mirror. Brasher shook his head, and the driver continued on the road south.

Brasher spoke in a kindly voice. "Jonathan. Lovely to hear from you."

"And you too, Clive, you too. Bit of news for you old chap. We have recovered a parcel from our collection that went missing in County Durham. Do you remember? Three parcels in total?

216

"Yes, yes. Good news is it?"

"'Fraid not, Clive. Damaged beyond repair, old boy."

Brasher closed his eyes, tight lipped, then said, "Hope it wasn't the parcel wrapped in the black paper was it?"

"Actually, no. So, I suppose that is a bit of good news, eh?

Brasher nodded. "Ah, well, we must be thankful for small mercies. Nice to speak to you, Jonathan. Give my love to Margaret, will you. And maybe we'll see you at the weekend. Bye for now."

Brasher sat back. He thought of the innocent man, albeit a minor criminal, who was now dead through no fault of his own, and probably hadn't the faintest idea why he'd been abducted from a prison van.

*

At the foot of the emergency stairs in the office block in Leeds, the security man stood to one side as police forensics busied themselves around Matty's body. Portable spotlights were arranged in a square around the cadaver. A senior police officer moved into the square and spoke to one of the men in white coveralls. A few seconds later the officer walked to the waiting ambulance men, standing in the glow of the blue flashing light of their vehicle. He spoke to the taller of the two.

"When you're ready, and please watch where you're treading. Keep away from the chalk marks on the ground."

The ambulance man looked to his partner, and made a face which showed he was not happy at being told the obvious.

The officer reached out an arm, and placed his hand on the medic's chest.

"Don't twist your face at me my friend. I've been twenty-five years in this game, and I'm proud to say that I still feel compassion for innocent victims. And believe me, this man is an innocent victim. Understand me? So, be careful. Do not destroy evidence. I want the fucker who killed this poor bastard."

The medic hung his head, and spoke as he sidled past the officer, "Yeah, 'course. Sorry."

*

Brasher said, "Keep the engine running."

He slammed the door as he exited the car and walked toward the country pub, as he checked his loose change. It was a full moon overhead, and the night air was warm. One or two people were outside the pub enjoying their drinks. He wished them, 'Good evening,' and walked on into the public bar.

Brasher checked out the various information signs hanging around the room, and behind the bar itself. He spotted the 'telephone' sign and followed the arrow beneath the printed word. The sign led him to a small room to his left. There was no furniture in the room, just the wall phone with a directory hanging on a chain from a small shelf.

He picked up the phone and dialled a London number. He heard the change in ring tone as the phone was diverted. Obviously James was out of his office. The ringing ended.

"James speaking."

"Hello James, sorry to bother you at this time of night, but I'm afraid we must close the north-east branch."

"Oh dear, never mind. Costs and all that, eh?"

"Yes, of course. So, as quickly as you can please. And when you're talking to them, please talk to them as individuals, eh? No mass meetings."

"As you wish, Clive."

Brasher hung up, knowing that his instructions would be followed to the letter. All known individuals connected to the terrorist cell would be rounded up, separated, and held without questioning, or contact of any kind, for twenty-four hours – then the interrogation would begin. What resulted from Alex's action later that night would then determine how the cell was questioned and what form the questions would take.

Brasher exited the pub and walked towards the car. He placed his hand on the door handle as his phone rang. Again he checked the I.D., and then answered the call from Alex.

"Positions, sir."

"Go ahead, Alex."

Brasher closed his eyes, memorising the landing co-ordinates, as he paced the pub car park. Satisfied that he had understood the message clearly, he then rang his man in Catterick and gave the details of the mission, the co-ordinates, and the landing time.

He walked back to his car, let himself in, and placed himself to the left of the driver.

He sighed, "Arthur, on the day I was going off to university, my father said to me, 'Clive, if you remember nothing else I tell you, do try to retire to your bed in the same day that you got out of it.' And I did, and I always have where humanly possible. Of course, there were times when it was impossible to do so; parties, celebrations, travelling, but generally, I did follow his advice."

Brasher paused for a moment, then continued, "As I get older, I find it extremely difficult in this increasingly mad world to adhere to what my father said. And I must say, I do wish it were not so."

He paused again.

"Sir?"

Brasher shook himself, and pulled his coat around himself.

"Nothing, Arthur, nothing. Just musing."

Chapter Twenty-Six

Billy looked over his shoulder to where the sound of the hooting owl was coming from. He identified the tree, but could not see the owl. He looked beyond the stream, to the sheep grazing peacefully. The stream sparkled in the moonlight, on its way to the larger river that would take it to the east coast.

Billy turned back, and looked at his two guests. Sanjar sat staring into the fire, Stephen paced, between Sanjar and the tepee.

"Anybody want a cuppa?"

Sanjar shook his head, and grimaced. Stephen did not answer.

Billy puckered his lips, paused, and then said, "Do yuh really have a decision to make, Stephen? I mean, she might not be dead."

He waited for some response. Billy paced the camp.

"I mean, why don't yuh phone home?" said Billy. "Yuh needn't even speak, just see who answers. If it's not her, ask for her and…"

Stephen spun on his heels. "Billy, I'm not fucking stupid. Don't you think I haven't thought of that?" He paced again, looking to the ground. "She… I mean… she would have contacted me if she'd been all right, wouldn't she?"

"But you haven't got a phone, how could she?"

Stephen sighed melodramatically, exasperated. "I had a phone – for four days, after I left home. She could have contacted me then, couldn't she?"

"I fucking doubt it like. Howay, man, she was probably in hospital. Yuh know, knife in the chest, and all that? And maybe the police were hanging around."

Stephen stared at Billy. Billy shrugged. Sanjar turned around and looked at Stephen.

"He's got a point, mate," said Sanjar.

Stephen looked at them both, and then nodded.

"Tomorrow, tomorrow."

He walked back to the fire, and sat next to Sanjar.

"Yes, I'd like that cuppa now, Billy… if you're still in the mood."

Billy grinned, picked up the billycan, and walked to the river.

*

Tommo looked around at his squad. All six were kitted out for night-time action, and dressed in black from head to foot. Blackened faces, black Kevlar vest, black trousers, and dull black boots.

The cottage that was their base was blacked out with black felt at every window, and a curtain hung behind each of the two exit doors; one at the front, one at the side. The path from the front door, unlit, led to a lane, again unlit, which stretched for a mile and a half before it joined a C road. Only the outlines of trees and hills were visible.

Each man had his chosen beverage in front of him; nothing stronger than Red Bull. Tommo took a slurp from his coffee, and scanned the map again.

He said, "Okay, any problems, any queries, any second thoughts on anything?"

Grimaces and shakes of the head all round.

He pointed to a position on the map which lay three-quarters of a mile from the cottage.

"Good. Now, for the last time. Prior to our action, a police chopper will fly over the target and confirm or otherwise that there are three humans present. If all is as we would expect it to be, we will be collected at zero-one-thirty, from this point here. You know where that is. We will then be transported from there, south, past the town, and further south, to a point one mile south of the target. We will be dropped…" Tommo indicated with a pencil. "Here. We will then make our way to the target over generally flat terrain. One man will be on the west side of the stream, that's you, Hughes. The rest of us will surround the camp, in the normal alphabetic pattern, starting with you, Crabby, here, on the north side, and spaced out with you, Simpson, on the south side."

Tommo paused, and looked up at his men. Each member of the group was reading the map intently. He studied each face. Satisfied, he took another sip of his coffee.

"Okay. Our colleagues from Catterick will remain at our drop off point until zero-one-fifty eight. At that time, they will lift off, come north following the river. At the camp, and not until they are directly overhead, they will switch on full beams and flood the camp with light. We hold until we see all three figures out of the tepee. We do not move until I give the command. Is that clear? Our target is not believed to be armed in the true sense of the word. However, he is known to have collected a simple breadknife on his travels."

Tommo paused for a few moments, letting his words sink in. He then continued.

"No matter what action they take, we do not move until I give the command – *unless you're fired on directly!* Then, and only then, do you return fire, as and when, and to the source only."

Each man replied in the affirmative.

"Okay, final checks," said Tommo, "and then we move out to the pick-up point."

*

Balvindar rinsed the toothbrush under the tap, and then put it into a red beaker on a shelf above the washbasin. She leaned forward, scooped water into her mouth from the running tap, gargled, then spat out the debris.

She pulled on the light cord, and exited the bathroom. She moved toward her bed. As she pulled back the duvet, the front door to her flat flew back on its hinges, and the policeman with the battering ram stepped to one side. Armed police ran past him, automatic weapons at eye-level, scanning the room.

Their shouted commands, "Armed police. Get down on the floor!" and statements, "Clear!" terrified Balvindar long before the officers appeared in the bedroom.

When they did enter her bedroom, they found a young girl pushing herself back against the headboard, duvet pulled up around her neck, with tears streaming down her face. There were four armed, and armoured, officers, aiming their weapons at her.

The officer on point, the front man, shouted, "Get out of bed! Out of the fucking bed! Keep your hands in view. Move, move, move."

Balvindar was frozen to the spot. Staring. Sobbing.

The second officer edged forward, tentatively. Still holding his gun at shoulder level with his right hand, he reached out and snatched the duvet from Balvindar with his left hand. Still the point man screamed at her.

"Get out of bed! Get out of the fucking bed!"

And still Balvindar did not move.

A third officer entered the bedroom. He held a handgun, and his gun arm was extended and pointing at Balvindar. He took in the scene immediately.

He shouted, "I have control."

He moved towards Balvindar slowly. His eyes did not leave her hands. He got within reaching distance of her.

"Balvindar, please get out of bed. Do not make any sudden moves. If you do, these men will shoot you. Do you understand? They will *shoot* to kill"

Balvindar wailed, and looked to the heavens. Her sobbing increased.

"Balvindar, Balvindar. Did you hear me?"

She nodded, still crying.

The officer took another step towards her. Balvindar pulled her legs up to her chest. She

225

pushed the duvet away with her feet. It dropped past her knees and her Winnie the Pooh pyjamas slid down her backside as she shuffled sideways.

"That's it, Balvindar, well done. Come on now, swing your legs out."

She did as she was told, and stood facing the officer, head bowed, shoulders slumped and still crying hysterically.

"Turn around, Balvindar, and put your hands behind your back. Come on, good girl, nearly finished. Just do as you're told and you'll come to no harm."

The crying eased. She sniffled. She held her head up and looked at the nearest of the two officers holding their guns aimed at her. She turned, and offered her hands behind her to the commanding officer.

The officer moved quickly. He cuffed her in seconds, and then shouted to beyond the bedroom.

"Connelly. In here, now."

A female officer entered the bedroom, again in full chest armour. Her weapon was a pistol, which she held with both hands. Her arms were diagonal to her body, right to left. She scanned the room.

The officer in control jerked his head toward Balvindar.

"A full body search. Now."

Balvindar stiffened, "No…"

The officer raised his voice.

"Frisk her now, completely, then into the bathroom and a full body search."

Connelly moved quickly. She holstered her weapon, and moved to behind Balvindar. She dragged her hands down the sides of Balvindar's torso, outside of her legs, eased her legs apart, ran her hands up the inside of her legs, and then turned her.

Balvindar stared ahead as Officer Connelly dragged her hands down her body.

Connelly turned to her superior and nodded.

He said, "Okay, into the bathroom."

He turned to the other two policemen, as Connelly closed the bathroom door behind her.

"The spooks will be here shortly," he said. "As soon as they step foot over the premises, you identify yourselves for the record, answer any questions they may have and then leave. Jameson will be outside with the van. I'll leave Martin and Lloyd outside the flat. I'll go with Connelly and Balvindar. We'll use the Land Rover. Frenchy can drive."

He paused, giving time for questions. None came.

"A good job, professionally done. Thank you, gentlemen. It's a pleasure to work with you."

Chapter Twenty-Seven

Tommo wiped his brow. His inner voice repeated over and over again; Focus. Focus.

He looked up at the approaching helicopter and then around at his group. Were they concentrating? The atmosphere was too light. They were cracking jokes. Did they not realise what this kid, this youngster, was capable of? How tricky he was?

What he knew of Sanjar had been told to his men. 'Second generation Iranian immigrant. Intelligent. Well educated. Street wise. Potential bomb maker. At present on the run after being set free from a PTV on its way to Durham. His crime was burglary. He may have used it as a guise to get away from the group he belonged to. We do not know if he is armed or not, however, he may be in possession of a simple breadknife. Take him alive, if at all possible. I repeat, we need him alive.'

The slight drop in engine noise signalled a drop in height. Tommo watched it hover and then settle. He moved to the door of the Apache. He saw the face of the pilot in the glow of the dials.

*

Stephen pushed the flap back, slowly. He looked to Sanjar and Billy, watching for movement; neither stirred. He stepped outside, and gently laid the flap back against the surface of the tepee. He turned, and walked to the glowing ashes of the fire.

Stephen sat on the log, picked up the slate that was used as a fan, and wafted. He picked up a few sticks and laid them on the small flames he'd produced. He heard a helicopter pass above him, heading north to south, the noise fading then dying.

He sat for a few minutes thinking, and then turned at the sound of the soft footsteps behind him. Billy stood watching him, smiling.

"Still making yuh mind up?" said Billy.

Stephen snorted a short laugh. "I've made it up. Now I'm pondering the consequences. If Sue did die, I'm going to jail. For how long? Where?"

"So you're giving yourself up?"

Stephen nodded.

"Don't yuh think you should try again? To contact Sue. I mean, if you hand yourself into the police, and she isn't dead, maybe they will charge yuh with attempted murder; no matter what your wife says."

Billy sat in his usual spot, directly opposite Stephen on the other side of the growing flames with his back to the stream. Stephen frowned, thought for a moment, and then looked up from the now rekindled fire.

He said, "Look, I'm gonna take a walk, clear my head"

"D'yuh want company?"

"No, I'm fine. Catch you later."

*

The last of the group exited the Apache, and gathered around Tommo. He looked around at his command, waiting for the rotors to stop. Finally, the whooshing, and the beat of the blades ceased.

His men looked to him expectantly.

"Okay, again. After me, we go alphabetically. It's as silent as the grave, so we need ambient noise cover. As we move off, the chopper will power up. When we sight the camp, we hold and wait. The pilot and his gunman will remain grounded until one minute before we are to move in, and then he will lift off. He will then move toward the camp. You move on my command, which will be when I judge the noise to be enough to cover any noise that we may make. We circle the camp. As soon as our targets exit the tepee, we move in, again, on my command. And remember; only one man is considered dangerous – easily distinguishable, he's the only black guy in the camp. Hughes, you move off now. You should be there ahead of us, but the stream will cut out any noise you make."

Hughes grinned, "See ya later, alligator."

Tommo snapped back, "Hey, take this seriously. There are two civilians in there, innocents. I want no friendly fire fuck-ups."

Hughes made to reply, saw the look on Tommo's face and thought better of it. He nodded, and moved off.

Tommo checked his watch, looked up to the full moon, then moved to the chopper. He spoke to the gunman.

"We move off in two minutes. Give us eight minutes, then do your bit. Any questions?"

Both the pilot and the gunman checked their watches. The pilot said, "We're fine."

Tommo walked back to the men. "You've got less than two minutes if you want a smoke."
Four cigarettes were pulled from four pockets, and

one lighter sparked. Tommo move away from the still tempting smell of tobacco. It had been fourteen years since his last cigarette. He moved to the edge of the clearing, to the tree line, and pictured the possibilities. The target gave up without a struggle. The target made a dash for it. His men cornered him, he gave up. The target pulled a gun, and his men shot him. Doubtful, unless Sanjar had managed to collect a gun on his travels. A shoot out ensued and the innocents were caught in the crossfire. Whatever the outcome…

Tommo checked his watch. He turned to his men, as he shouldered his rifle.

"Lights out. Move off."

*

Sanjar stirred as Billy pulled back the flap. He looked up and saw Billy's outline, back lit in the moonlight.

Sanjar mumbled, "Problem?"

Billy spoke, resigned.

"Nah, just absorbing Stephen's… sadness."

He slipped into his sleeping bag. "Things always look worse in the middle of the night, especially when you're lying on your back, defenceless like. He went for a walk, about ten minutes ago." He gave a short laugh. "I doubt if he'll be gone long. It's bloody scary out there at night. The slightest noise and he'll crap himself. Anyway, g'night, Sanjar. Sleep tight."

Billy laid his head back on the battered punch bag that doubled up as a pillow. Then, just before slipping over into full sleep, he heard the rumbling. He opened his eyes, still motionless, still

231

listening. The noise grew louder. He lifted his head off the bag, just slightly. And the noise was now a roaring. He sat up, and lay back on his elbows. Sanjar stirred, then sat, then got out from under Billy's overcoat that served as a blanket. The thunderous roar was frightening, but the light was terrifying. Both men jumped up.

Billy shouted, "Fucking hell,"

Both men exited the tepee, and moved towards the dying camp fire, looking up.

Sanjar turned to Billy, and shouted. "No decision to make now, Billy. I reckon that's a police helicopter." He looked at the chopper, shielding his eyes. "I'm captured mate," he said

Billy shouted back, "That's not the police. I know their chopper, and that's not it."

Their fifteen-second conversation was ended by the tannoyed voice of the gunman in the chopper.

"We are officials of Her Majesty's Government on Her Majesty's business. You are surrounded. Both of you, raise your hands."

Billy squinted in the bright light as he raised his arms.

"Fucking awesome! Where's the music?" he shouted.

Sanjar turned to him, puzzled, his arms held upright. He shouted back to Billy, "Do you mean sirens?"

Billy closed his eyes, and faced the ground.

"Nah. *Ride of the Valkyries* and all that shite," he said.

Sanjar shook his head, and looked at the ground.

The tannoy blasted out again.

"Sanjar take six steps to your left. When he has done that, Billy, you move six steps to your right."

After the two men had completed the move, the gunman switched off the tannoy, and picked up his radio.

"Are you watching, Tommo?"

Tommo stood, and moved around the bush he'd used as an observation point. He held down the switch on his radio. He shouted into the mouthpiece.

"I'm watching, but where's the other one? The third man?"

"In the tepee, maybe? But he's not showing up on the thermal camera."

"What? He's sleeping through this racket?"

"Only one way to find out."

Tommo thought for a moment, his eyes scanning the camp. He spoke into the radio again.

"Okay. Hughes, stay on the other side of the water. Crabby, you and Simpson move around and in, and keep tabs on the two prisoners. Dawson and Edwards, you cover the tepee front and rear in that order. Johnson, move towards me."

Tommo moved forward another twenty feet, Johnson appeared at his side, and the rest of his group moved in, encircling Billy and Sanjar.

Tommo shouted, "On the ground, Khan, on your belly. Come on, fucking down, on the ground."

Sanjar fell to his knees, then, press-up style, lay on his belly.

233

Tommo used hand signals and indicated for Crabb to cable-tie Sanjar. Crabb moved forward and did the necessary.

"Same with you, Billy," shouted Tommo. "On the ground. Come on, move it. Fucking chop-chop."

Billy shrugged, and lay down. Tommo moved to Billy as he was being cuffed by Simpson. He crouched over Billy.

"Where is he, Billy? Where's Stephen? The other lad"

"Hang on, yuh cutting off me circulation," shouted Billy.

Tommo ignored Billy's plea.

"Where's fucking Stephen? Is he in the tent?"

Billy turned his head to look at Tommo.

"Probably halfway to Edinburgh now. Yuh'd have scared him shitless, mate."

Tommo indicated for the two men watching the tepee to go in, then reached down and pulled Billy's head up by pulling up on the back of his T-shirt.

"I'm not kidding, bonny lad. Where the fuck is he?"

Billy's □hirt-shirt cut into his windpipe.

"Walk, man... honest. He went... for a walk... He's got a... personal problem... nowt to do with us. Just personal."

He twisted his head; Tommo relaxed his grip a little, and Billy's head settled back on the ground.

"Fuck, I was choking there, man."

"How long has he been gone? Come on. How long?"

"I… maybe ten minutes at the most. I'm not sure."

Tommo's interior voice shouted. Shit shit shit! He turned toward the tent. One of his men was exiting, pushing the flap back. The man shook his head.

Tommo stood and spoke rapidly into his radio.

"All secure here, all secure. One man is on the loose. Can you do a search, this side of the river, a mile radius at the most?"

"Roger. Mile radius. Out."

Tommo and his men herded Sanjar and Billy together again, toward the fire.

"Sit. Back to back. You on that log, Billy. You on the other one, Sanjar."

Tommo looked south and saw the chopper flying, slowly, about thirty feet from the edge of the stream. He watched as it began the manoeuvres of searching for one man in an area of nearly two square miles.

He watched, and waited.

Chapter Twenty-Eight

Stephen watched as the chopper moved south. He'd stood entranced as the aircraft had hovered over the camp, and the tannoy had blasted out the commands to Billy and Sanjar.

Stephen was sad. Sanjar's mind had been made up for him. You don't get that amount of policemen, if they were policemen, and that amount of machinery, looking for an escaped burglar. Stephen just knew; Sanjar was being hunted, and captured, for what he was; or at least what he had nearly been.

Stephen listened as the noise of the chopper drifted north, towards him, from where he figured it to be, nearly a mile to the south. He strained his ears. He heard movement behind him. A loud crack. Not the sharp quick snap of a fox or badger, nosing around and treading on a twig. He'd heard that sound as he'd walked, and the same sound coming from the tree line during the previous night while he'd lain awake thinking. Tonight's sound wasn't the result of an animal nosing in the grass.

He crouched, amongst the gnarled roots of the oldest oak in the Jed Valley, and waited. The noise of the helicopter held, then began to grow. He looked to his left, to the source of the human noise, then to the south, the source of the noise from the chopper.

Within a minute, the sound of the engine on the aircraft drowned out all other sounds around Stephen. He watched the light of the chopper sweeping back and forth, east to west, as it came north.

He began to ease back, trying to anticipate each sweep in seconds. He would back off as the helicopter and its spread beam of light came towards him. Once the helicopter had tracked east or west, he would dart forward as the beam swept to the side, to the safety of the darkness of the area behind the flying machine. Easy – if the thermal imaging also missed him. He would lie low until the police, or whoever they were, did their business. Once they had completed their task, he would continue his journey north. He would phone Sue from the town. Any further action would depend on the result of the phone call.

The helicopter tracked towards him. He leaned forward, on his toes, like a sprinter. He watched. The whirring blades whipped up the grass, bent the branches of the trees, and blew his hair across his face. The noise grew yet louder.

Stephen saw the beam edge toward his left. He tensed, leaned forward a little more. The beam came back towards his right, the west. The helicopter held, hovered, to his left. Could he make it? Could he reach the darkness beyond before the machine continued its tracking? Leaves and debris stung his face, his hair whipped his brow. He squinted, looking ahead. Still the helicopter hovered.

Sod it! He charged forward into the darkness in front of him. Eight seconds and he reached the moonlit ground on the far side of the chopper; in the area already covered by the machine and its occupants. He continued for another five seconds, then eased, slowed, then stopped.

Stephen's heart pounded. He bent forward, his hands on his knees. He was out of the true force of the chopper's rotors, but still a soft breeze blew. He blinked, blinked again. What had happened to the light? He looked towards the noise of the engine, as the moon disappeared behind a clump of clouds. He watched for a moment, puzzled. Then, eyes widening, he realized the chopper was coming toward him.

*

The gunman radioed Tommo, as he peered at the screen in front of him.

He said matter-of-factly, "Our lights are off, Tommo. I've got heat. An image. Big man. Definitely hiding. He's crouching, scuttling from tree to tree."

Tommo frowned. Big man? Stephen hadn't looked big to him. Surely Sue would have mentioned that. A poacher, maybe?

Suddenly, the gunman's voice took on a sense of urgency. "He's up, Tommo. Up and running. We're tracking south."

Tommo shouted into his handset. "Just track him, he'll tire. We'll follow you. We're about half a mile behind you. I can see your lights. Just don't fucking lose him."

Tommo turned to the two men to his left, and pointed to Billy and Sanjar. "They're yours. Hold them."

He turned to the others, as he pointed to the helicopter.

"I will be directly behind him," he said. "Split up, half to the left of the chopper, the other half to the right." He shouted across the river. "Hughesy! Stay on that side. Follow the noise of the chopper." He turned to the others. "Spread out. Let's go."

The group set off at a measured dash.

*

Stephen looked back to his right. The chopper was following a track that would pass him by – with its lights off. He watched, only slightly relieved. Then, as if he'd been spotted, the chopper veered slowly towards him. He walked backwards. It came closer. He turned jogging, looking over his shoulder. It came closer. Now he was running. He heard crashing to his right, through the bushes and undergrowth. He concentrated on looking ahead, and running. His mouth hung slack, as he sucked in air. His healing face hurt with every thump of his feet on the ground.

Suddenly, he felt a presence, over his shoulder. It was running as fast as he was. He turned, as a hand reached out in the darkness and gripped his arm and pulled. Stephen stumbled, he fell and the person holding him fell on top of him. Stephen rolled and pushed up, trying to get the figure off him. He saw the figure was a man, and the man held a gun. The man stood, and then pulled Stephen up and stood behind him. The man held a gun against Stephen's spine. Both men faced the chopper.

The gunman shouted over the tannoy. "Lie down, we have men following you. Just lie down, face down. Do it!"

Stephen made as if to move forward and lie down on his belly. The man pulled him back and put his left arm around Stephen's throat. Stephen's arm reached up and grabbed the man's arm, as the stranger's right arm rested on Stephen's right shoulder. He held a gun in his hand.

Stephen's eyes darted right and left, trying to see the mystery man. The gun fired, the noise deafening Stephen. He stopped pulling the man's arm.

The gunman in the chopper hit the radio. "We are being fired on. Repeat. We are being fired on." The chopper swung right, to Stephen's left. The chopper pilot switched on the powerful light beam and Stephen and the man stood in full glare below as the chopper gained height.

The man fired again. The figures below separated. The gunman aimed and fired. One of the figures below fell, and lay prone. The other figure turned, and ran.

Again, the gunman grabbed the radio. "We have one target down, the other is up and running. I'm dropping a flare near the man down. We are chasing the runner."

Tommo ran, twisted, dodged and jumped his way towards the red flare. Two of them? What the fuck was happening? And Stephen didn't have a gun. He saw the chopper gaining height, and once again tracking south.

The wind was from the south, and the smell and the red mist of the flare was drifting toward him. He moved to his left, out of the direct path of the smoke. Thirty seconds later he stood at the side of the flare, picked it up and moved it away from the prone human form. He turned, moved to the figure and looked down. He closed his eyes, and shook his head slowly. His men came in from the left and right.

Tommo's men saw him looking down. His shoulders were slumped, his arms hung loosely at his side. He'd slung his automatic over his right shoulder.

Wilson said, "Tommo?"

Tommo opened his eyes, turned slowly, and stared at Wilson. "Dead."

"Tommo. What's wrong, mate? Do we continue? Who stays with the body?

Tommo shook his head, tight lipped, looking down on Stephen, then said, "A civilian. He's a fucking civilian. Fucking hell."

Tommo turned and looked to the helicopter. He said, resigned. "Follow it. Whoever they're chasing is either a terrorist, or a criminal of some sort. Catch the bastard. Let the chopper gunman be your guide. I'll relay my instructions to him."

Tommo was a professional through and through. Ice cool, a mechanic, a machine. In combat he was a fast thinking British soldier. The best of the best. A leader, but a team player. As he stood there, silently, his team wondered.

He snapped back to life. He pointed south. "Go. Get me that bastard." As his men took off, he spoke into the radio and did as he'd promised his men.

One minute later, he took his bearings, and ordered the two men holding Billy and Sanjar to bring the prisoners to him, and then he sat. He took out his cell phone from his swag bag, and dialled Alex.

Alex answered. "Tell me."

"We have the target, and we have the civilian Billy. Both are under armed guard. The second civilian, who you are aware of, sir, is dead. Shot by the chopper gunman, who was returning fire. At this moment, a group of my men are following the chopper, which is following a fourth man. End of report."

Alex responded immediately

"No, Tommo. That is not the end of your report. Expand on it, please."

Chapter Twenty-Nine

Alex picked up the receiver and dialled London. Brasher picked up on the second ring. Brasher ignored the bedside light, threw back the duvet, swung his legs out of bed, and walked out of the bedroom with the roamer phone. He heard his wife snuggling down behind where he'd lay.

"Yes?"

"Can you scramble this, sir?"

Brasher scratched the side of his head, looked around the landing, and said, "Hold on. Give me a minute." He switched on the stair headlight, gripped the banister, and took the stairs gingerly, easing each leg joint into reluctant action. He blinked, squinting at the light coming from the chandelier at the foot of the stairs. He crossed the wide reception area of his nineteen-thirties detached house, entered the sitting room, and pressed the 'secret' button on the base unit. He sat in the armchair next to it.

"Okay, Alex. Go ahead."

"Good news and problems, sir. We have the target, and we are on the trail of another person who may be included in this affair. We should have him within the next fifteen minutes."

Brasher said, "Problems?"

"I'm afraid a civilian was killed in our operation. A male, possibly late thirties."

Brasher paused a beat, and then sighed. "Oh dear. And how did a civilian come to be in the line of fire, in the woods, in the early hours of the

243

morning? And how is the man who shot the civilian."

"It was the gunman in the chopper, sir. The man he was chasing joined up with another man, shots were fired at the chopper from an automatic weapon, and the gunman returned the fire. The other man was in fact an innocent, a man with personal problems, hiding in the woods. Our man returned fire, the wrong man was hit."

"A minute, Alex."

Brasher wiped the tiredness from his eyes. He stood, opened the top button on his pyjama jacket and paced the room. He checked the clock on the mantle shelf, thought for a moment, and sighed again. He put the phone to his ear.

"Okay, Alex. Thank you for the speedy report. It's now, what…?" He looked to the clock again. "Two-thirty five. I want to know as soon as the runner is captured. Please God take him alive. As soon as you have him, get everyone out of the area, and I mean everyone, including you. Leave the base cottage, and forget the factory unit at Newcastle. I'll make sure they are cleansed immediately. I want everyone shipped to Catterick. And, it makes me sad to say this, but that includes the dead civilian."

He paused, rubbed his forehead, and then continued.

"The man we're trailing, him, if alive, I want separated from Sanjar in the Apache, along with the usual blindfolds. If he's dead, I want Sanjar to see the dead body. Understood?"

"Yes sir."

"Okay. Goodnight, Alex. And well done. My sympathies to you for the civilian. I can understand how you feel."

"Thank you, sir. And goodnight."

Brasher paced again, and thought again. He mumbled to himself, and then dialled an inner London number. He hit the 'secret' button again, as his call was answered.

"Simon, my friend," said Brasher.

"Ah, Clive, you have a problem. You called me your friend."

Brasher allowed himself the slightest of smiles.

"Simon, Simon. How good to have a friend who really knows me. How long now?"

Simon breathed deeply.

"Oh, what, forty years?"

"Yes, indeed. Forty-two to be exact."

Brasher reflected for a moment.

"However, we have work to do. I need to get to Catterick camp, ASAP. Can you assist with transport?"

Simon nodded to himself. "Which do you prefer, Clive? Outrider escort door to door, or an R.A.F. flight from Gatwick?"

"Which would be the quicker?"

"Outrider escort."

"Do it Simon, I'll be ready in thirty minutes."

"Then my chaps will be there in thirty minutes. Be ready Clive."

Brasher said his goodbyes, and then repeated the process of dialling and scrambling his call to another colleague in Norfolk. No names were exchanged, just simple greetings, and an order from Brasher.

"First the cottage, then the factory."

Brasher's colleague ended the call with, "Understood. On our way," and hung up.

*

Simpson tried again, shouting above the noise of the chopper. From his viewpoint of fifty-yards away, he could see the man centre stage, in the clearing, dazzled by the spotlight from the chopper. Even at a range now beyond the danger of the man's automatic weapon, the light from the chopper was brilliant.

"Put down your weapon. You are surrounded."

The man looked at his weapon again and again Simpson wondered. Is it jammed, is he out of ammo, or is he deciding whether to shoot it out or not?

Simpson turned to Johnson, six-feet away to his right.

"What's his fucking game? Whaddya reckon?"

Johnson grimaced as he stared ahead

"Suicide maybe?"

Simpson thought for one moment more, and then spoke into the radio strapped to his chest.

"Right. I believe he's thinking suicide. We move in on my command. I'm gonna take his legs away. When he goes down, we rush him. Any attempt to fire back and we fucking shoot to kill. Okay, now, advance, slowly."

246

Simpson watched as the man stood on the spot and circled, trying to figure out exactly where his tormentors were. As the man came to a spot facing where Simpson lay, Simpson fired, a short burst, at a target below the man's knees. The man went down screaming, the gun falling from his hand as he reached for his legs.

"Now! Now! Go, go."

Johnson reached the man first, bursting from the shrubbery, racing to him, and kicking the automatic to one side. He stood over the man, pointing his rifle at the man's chest. He spoke matter-of-factly.

"You were warned, you cunt. More than you gave our lads. What was the fucking point? And what's your name? What's your fucking name?"

The man grunted, groaned, "Hameed…"

Simpson stood next to Johnson and spoke into his radio, looking up to the chopper.

"Anytime you're ready, just say where, and we'll carry this fucker to you."

"Roger. Stand by."

"Did you get that, Tommo?"

Half a mile away, Tommo helped to load Stephen onto the makeshift stretcher. He spoke into his radio.

"Aye, got it. Every one's making for the tepee. E.T.A. fifteen minutes."

*

Thirty minutes later, Tommo stood in front of Alex, being de-briefed, as the group loaded up the necessary equipment into the Apache. At the rear of the helicopter, the body of Stephen lay strapped to

247

the floor, now in a body bag, and lashed with ratchet straps. Nearer the cockpit, Billy sat opposite Sanjar, with army personnel either side of both of them.

At the opposite end to where Stephen lay, against the bulkhead separating the crew from the cargo of personnel, Hameed lay strapped to the floor. He was also wrapped in ratchet straps, but, in addition, his wrists and ankles were cuffed behind him. He lay on his belly. His head was covered by a black bag.

Billy turned and spoke to Johnson on his left. He indicated the body bag with his head. "Anybody we know?"

Johnson looked to him, puzzled. "How the fuck should I know? And don't talk to me."

"Sorry."

"You will be."

Billy looked to the floor of the aircraft, and then shrugged. He spoke to the floor. "Am I supposed to be frightened?"

Johnson scowled at him.

"'Cos I'm not. I'm frightened of fuck all. And I never worry."

Billy looked to Johnson; Johnson stared straight ahead.

"You married?" said Billy. "Got anyone yuh love? Really love? You know, not a bit on the side, not just someone who's a good shag, but someone yuh love, admire, want to be with for the rest of yuh life?"

Billy nudged Johnson. "C'mon, you can talk to me."

Johnson turned to Billy, stone-faced, dead-eyed.

"Do that again, and I push your teeth down your throat with the butt of this fucking rifle."

Billy stared back, wide-eyed. "Aye? Yuh'd really do that? What for? What harm have I done to you?"

Silence.

Billy continued. "I had a love of my life. Beautiful woman, beautiful nature, too good for me, but we were together for a few years. I tried, did my best… but… anyway, she died. Still a young woman and she died."

Billy turned and stared at the side of the Johnson's face.

"And y'know what? I've been beaten to a pulp and left for dead in New York, kicked to fuck by football fans, rolled from top to bottom down a Northumberland fell, and I'll tell yuh, sunshine, nothing compares, even comes close, to the pain of losing a loved one."

Billy paused. Johnson blinked, shifted his eyes, took in Billy's closeness to his face, and continued staring ahead.

"So go ahead, fucking Action Man. Knock my teeth down my throat, and yuh know what, I'll spit the fuckers right back at yuh."

Johnson closed his eyes, thought for a moment, then nodded. He turned to Billy.

"I don't know if you know him. I don't know him, none of our men know him, so, I don't know. Now, please, shut the fuck up."

Billy sat back.

"Fine. Thank you."

Alex climbed aboard, and slid the hatch door along its tracks. He nodded to his man behind the bulkhead and, in turn, the man leaned into the cockpit and spoke to the pilot. Alex strapped himself in as the engine was switched on. The rotor began a slow rotation, and then picked up the beat until they hit maximum revs. Seconds later the chopper lifted, tilted forward, then after holding for a few moments roared off and up into the night sky.

Chapter Thirty

Tommo walked through the town centre as the rising sun shortened his shadow with each minute. He called at the Spar shop, bought a bottle of water, a cold sausage roll and a bar of dark chocolate. He wandered back along the street he'd just walked, turned right at the end, and followed the main road toward the pub where Sue was lodged.

Ten minutes later he finished the last of his sausage roll, drained the last of the water from the bottle, dropped the bottle in a waste bin, and walked into the pub. He'd had to force the food down. He'd lost his appetite, but acknowledged the necessity of food for the long day ahead.

It was just after seven. He'd checked out Billy's camp, after evacuating the cottage, and then sat by the river thinking until the sun had cleared the hills to the east. He'd rehearsed his speech to soften the only facts that had been cleared to be allowed to be passed on by Alex. The facts were, a body had been discovered in the woods, it had been discovered by the local Territorial Army unit, while on manoeuvres. The captain of the unit was an old friend of Tommo's from regular army days. He'd spoken to Tommo, this morning. The description fitted Stephen.

What a crock of shit.

She'd never believe that.

Tommo spoke to the pub landlord. "Look, I'm sorry, but I've got real bad news for one of your guests. Sue. Do you mind if I wait here until she comes down to breakfast?"

The landlord frowned; a questioning frown. Tommo nodded.

The landlord said, "Of course not, I've seen you together in the pub. And I'm sorry to hear that it's bad news. Anyway, have a seat."

At seven-thirty five, Sue entered the restaurant area of the pub and saw Tommo at the table in the far corner. She was dressed for another energetic day. Trainers, black skin-tight shorts that reached to her mid-thigh, and a tracksuit top over a running vest. She smiled, saw the expression on Tommo's face, and then stopped in the middle of the room.

"It's bad news, isn't it?"

"Do you want to sit down, Sue?"

Tommo's sympathetic tone more than gave the game away.

Sue whispered, more to herself than Tommo

"You've found him, haven't you? He's dead. He's dead, isn't he?"

"Please, Sue. Come and sit down."

Sue's shoulders slumped, her head flopped forward. She stared at the floor for a moment, and then walked to Tommo. Tommo got out of his seat, which backed up against an exterior wall, and stood aside, letting Sue sit where he'd been seated. He took a chair from another table and placed it on the opposite side of the table to her. Sue would barely be seen by the other diners when they arrived.

Sue looked Tommo in the eye. "Tell me. Just tell me."

Tommo's rehearsed speech went out of the window. He nodded.

"Stephen's dead, Sue. He is dead."

Sue blinked back tears, gulped, and nodded just once. "Where? What happened? How did you find out?"

Tommo looked down at the tablecloth, thought for a moment, then said, "Sue, I'm going to tell you the truth. I'm going to tell you everything. It will come out sooner or later..."

Sue frowned, her eyes narrowing.

"I'm not a birdwatcher, Sue. You were right, I'm military," Tommo looked up from the table, "and that's as much as I can say about me."

Sue shook her head, just slightly. "What's going on? How do you know about Stephen?"

"Sue, what I was told to tell you was a pack of lies, but I'll tell you as much of the truth as the government will let me. The whole truth will come out sooner or later."

Sue stared at him. Tommo continued.

"There was an incident in the woods just south of here last night. The incident resulted in a chase. The person being chased was armed, and somehow or other he managed to meet, or join, up with Stephen as our chopper was chasing him. The chopper was using thermal imaging, and, when it was fired on, our man in the chopper was not aware that Stephen was not with our target, a member of the... gang that we've been watching. Stephen was shot accidentally. Believe me, Sue, it was an accident. I'm really really sorry. Our man has been stood down. He's as devastated as the rest of us."

Sue put her head in her hands. She spoke –
her words muffled.

"You say in the woods. Was it anywhere
near where I saw the smoke… yesterday?"

Tommo breathed in deeply, tight lipped,
through his nose. He let it out in a rush.

"Yes, it's probable that he was sleeping in
a… tent, there. There were others there. One of them
was the man we wanted."

Tommo paused for a second. Sue looked up
from her hands.

Tommo said, "It was international, Sue.
Global. Our being there last night was part of
something bigger, something that is worldwide. And
that's it, as much as I can tell you."

Sue's eyes widened. Tears seeped over her
lower lids. She gulped. "Stephen's dead! And that's
as much as you can tell me!"

Tommo raised his palms to Sue.

"I've told you more than I should have, Sue.
Believe me, anyone else and I would have passed on
the lies they wanted me to say."

He hunched forward slightly, towards her.

"There are people coming to see you today.
They'll tell you the whole story, and they will offer
you assistance." Tommo looked at her, sadly. "He
was in the wrong place at the wrong time. It was an
accident, a terrible accident."

"Was it quick?"

"Couldn't have been any quicker, Sue.
Instant. He honestly wouldn't have known about it.
No pain."

Tommo watched her as she struggled with the news.

"Would you like some tea, Sue? You've had a shock"

She nodded. Tommo stood and walked to the kitchen.

*

At seven-o-clock that morning the Land Rover carrying Brasher had swung west off the A1, followed the slip road back over to the east side and carried on towards the Marne Barracks. Brasher saw the solitary Apache helicopter at the far end of the camp, and indicated to his driver to head towards it. As the front outrider slowed, he pointed left with a gloved hand, and the driver of the Land Rover took a looping turn in the indicated direction. Brasher spotted Alex, and one of his squad, outside the camp commander's office.

Alex walked toward Brasher's car as it slowed, then stopped. Brasher was out and greeting Alex as the car pulled away. He held out his hand, and shook with Alex.

"A bloody drink, Alex, please. Anything hot and sweet, with milk."

Alex turned to the Ranger beside him. "Tea for two, please. Sergeant Major's brew. In the Commander's office."

The ranger said, "Yes sir," saluted, then jogged off.

Alex spoke to Brasher.

"The Commander is waiting, sir. He knows nothing, but understands that we are part of a sensitive situation. He has no problem with vacating his office, sir. He is genuinely welcoming."

"And the latest from up north?"

"Two of our own counsellors and a P.R. person left this morning, about two hours ago, by road. They should be there by now. However, Tommo requested that we let the deceased's partner wake naturally, and that he be the one to give her the news; a censored version."

"Is he close to her?"

Alex paused for a moment.

"Difficult to ascertain, sir. He has spent a bit of time with her in the last few days. She spotted him under his guise as a birdwatcher, and asked him to keep an eye out for her husband."

"Is she intelligent? Sensible?"

"Apparently so, sir."

Brasher chewed on his bottom lip.

"Um. Don't be surprised if he is kind and tells her more than he should."

He clapped his hands, decisively.

"Right. Let's go. Grab a seat, and if you don't mind, I'll pace while you tell me all about our Geordie Iranian friend. My backside is rather stiff. Oh, first, I'd like to see the body of... Stephen."

Alex pointed to the far side of the camp. "In the camp hospital, sir. Do you mean now, or after your drink?"

"Yes, of course. After the drink. Do they have the facilities to deal with bodies? I mean, as in undertakers? Or do we farm out?"

"We have the facilities, sir. Just since modern terrorism became a part of everyday life."

Brasher shook his head, then walked off, ahead of Alex.

Chapter Thirty-One

Brasher smacked his lips and placed the hot tea on the desk in front of him. He nodded, checking the notes he'd taken. He stroked his chin, shook his head and grimaced.

"So, having said all that, Alex, what is your gut feeling? Is he genuinely a... a mixed up kid? Is he really trying to break away? Or is he just scared witless of what he could face if found guilty?"

"He's an angry young man; very angry. In his lifetime, contrary to what we have on file, he has been subject to racial abuse, quite a lot when he was a child – unknown to his father. However, I think he thought that the extent of his obligations to the group would be maybe organising protests, marches, and speeches – political stuff. All of a sudden, he's roped into the mechanics of bomb making, he's subject to threats, his girlfriend is putting pressure on, and his family is throwing him out of his home because of his connections to extremists. That burglary was him simply asking to be put beyond the organisation's reach - prison."

"Naïve, but it shows his character." Brasher took another sip of his tea, then said, "But can he be turned willingly? Would he be of any use to us, and could we trust him?"

"My opinion, yes, with the help of his family, and his girlfriend. But he needs to go to prison, otherwise all credibility would be lost. And we've got a heck of a lot of covering up to do. For instance, why are the military chasing a burglar?"

"Not a problem. I spoke with the Minister on my way here, and, thank God, he does have a mind of his own, and he is very principled, and morally upright. He will do whatever necessary to save lives, and that includes upsetting anyone in the U.K. or some bloody Eurocrat."

Alex smiled. Brasher looked at him and returned the smile.

"Yes, I did get carried away a little, didn't I," he said.

He stood and walked to the window. He looked towards the medical centre. He thought for a moment.

He turned to Alex, raised a clenched fist and stuck his thumb in the air.

"Summary," he said. "One. Every trace of our ever being in Newcastle and the Borders is being removed at present. Two. That poor man's wife is being attended to. If she is as you say, I think we can rely on her silence.

"Who handles the compensation, sir?" Us? The Ministry?"

Brasher shook his head. "Not our problem, the Minister will handle that. However, I would like you to arrange to keep an eye on the lady, make sure she is not subject to any hardship. Okay. Now. Three."

Each time Brasher numbered a summary item, he raised a finger.

"This Billy the Bow man," he said. "How do we control him?"

"Um, well, we may have a bit of leverage there, sir, in so much that we have discovered a small cannabis farm near where his tepee is located. We could, in fact I think we should, threaten him with all the possibilities of a result of the police discovering his little smallholding, but, in truth, all he is aware of is the fact that a man who was living with him has been arrested. He is not aware of Stephen's death. All he saw was a body bag in the chopper. We could plant the seed that Stephen got away and is back on the road again."

"Sounds good to me. I'll leave that with you, but I must have a report daily on that one. Understood."

Alex nodded. Brasher raised another finger.

"Okay, finally, Four. Our Geordie chemist friend. First of all he has to go to prison, but we need to give him hope for when he gets out, and we need to give him something to miss while he is in prison."

"His girlfriend."

"Precisely. And I have it in hand."

*

At precisely nine-o-clock, as Brasher and Alex made their way to the camp medical centre and Tommo sat with Sue in the pub courtyard watching the counsellors approach, an unmarked BMW saloon car swung into Marne Barracks. Once the vehicle had cleared security, it headed toward the camp guardhouse.

The military policemen on duty stood by and observed the handing over of a prisoner by the men in the BMW to two rangers. The rangers entered the guardhouse, under supervision of the military police as the BMW sped away.

Once in the guardhouse, the prisoner was slowly walked along the row of cells, on the west side of the block. Each cell faced the same blank wall on the east side. None of the cells had windows. A toughened glass roundel in the centre of the steel cell door, covered by a round-hinged plate on the outside, was any prisoner's view on the outside world.

Sanjar watched and waited, listening to the footsteps drawing nearer. He pressed the side of his face against the roundel, straining to see who else was being placed under guard. The footsteps drew nearer. The slowness of the approach worried him; tension increased. He held his breath, chest paining. He wondered. Which one of the group had been arrested?

The rangers were either side of the prisoner as they walked. As they approached the cell next to Sanjar's, they edged the prisoner to the right, just in view of Sanjar. Sanjar looked, and cried out involuntarily.

"Balvindar! Balvindar."

The rangers grabbed Balvindar as she cried out Sanjar's name. They threw her into the cell. She rushed back to the door, and screamed, "Sanjar. Sanjar. Can you hear me?"

*

The two counsellors and the P.R. lady introduced themselves with false names, then the taller, thinner, man of the two males said, "May we go to your room, Sue? Somewhere private?"

261

Sue said, "Are you afraid someone might hear you? Afraid something terrible may become public?"

The man looked at Tommo,

"Don't look at him," said Sue. "It's me you're talking to."

Suddenly the man's expression changed; from kindly to stern. He leaned forward, and spoke, softly, controlled.

"We can all be nice and understanding about this, or we can create a dangerous scenario. Your husband stabbed you. He ran away from home. You have not seen him for quite a while. Last night he was in the company of a very evil man, a killer, a fanatic, a member of a worldwide organisation. They were both in the woods, running from our men. Last night, your husband was shot while in the company of that man. So do we release this to the press and damn your husband's name to hell, or do we be understanding and reasonable about it? And you should know that one of our personnel, the man who was fired on, is now under sedation, suppressing the muddled mess his head is in, and trying to kill the terrible guilt feelings that he has because he shot an innocent man while *defending himself*. Soldiers are human beings."

Sue's lip quivered. She looked down. The chameleon that was the counsellor changed again. "Sue, we're on your side. If we weren't, Tommo would not be at your side now. He'd be cosied up in some army camp somewhere. So, why don't you give us a chance, and just listen to us?"

The tears ran down Sue's cheeks. She spoke, still looking down, gulping, her voice breaking, squeaking. "Can you get a message to him… that man, your… the man who fired the shot? Can you tell him I understand, I forgive him, and if… if there is anything I can do…"

Tommo reached out and held her hand. "Let's go in, Sue. Somewhere private."

*

Imam Nasr peered into the cul-de-sac. No one was evident, nothing unusual leapt out at him. Still, he was undecided. He turned away and walked back to the high street. At the junction of the cul-de-sac and the high street, he looked right and left. Again, there were no parked cars, no men loitering, no one idly reading a newspaper, no one looking into a shop window opposite.

He continued looking into the shop window. From where he stood, he considered his reflected image was acceptable. Of course, he could not disguise the fact that he was not European, but his dress was now… less radical, less challenging. He was fully suited, his beard was trimmed, his collar and tie were fresh on that morning, and his shoes were gleaming.

He turned, looked down the cul-de-sac again, paused for a while, just looking, then moved off again.

He entered the building through the door in the lobby, and checked the nameplates on the sectioned wall plaque screwed to the wall. He noted the flat number – three hyphen two; third floor, flat two. He walked to the stairs. He began his climb up the stairs.

On the third floor landing, Nasr reached for the handle on the door to the corridor. He paused, and then peered to the right, through the vision panel in the landing door. He saw what he took to be a carpenter, or joiner, working on the entrance door to a flat; he could not see which number.

He looked to the two flats to his left, and noted the door numbers – four and three, in descending order coming towards him. The next door in the corridor was to his right, the one being repaired. Flat number two, Balvindar's flat.

The imam turned and descended the stairs again.

Chapter Thirty-Two

The counsellor took in Sue's smalls hanging at various points around the room. Panties hung drying on a cold radiator, and what he took to be running socks, along with a sleeveless T-shirt hung on the back of a chair, opposite an open window through which sunlight streamed.

He turned to the P.R. lady.

"Would you like to go and have a word with the landlord, the proprietor?"

The lady squeezed Sue's hand, and said, "Anything you want, just ask."

She left the room.

The room was not small. The bed was a double, just; bigger than a single, but smaller than queen size. The floor was carpeted wall-to-wall - beige and the walls were painted a neutral colour. The double-glazed window to the right of the bed was fire standard, opening horizontally, and vertically. Beside the bed were two white bedside cabinets of the self-assembly type, and at the foot of the bed, against the wall, was a wardrobe - again white and again self-assembly. A small dressing table, yet again white and self-assembly stood to the left of the window. There were two chairs, one in front of the dressing table, and one beside the window. Sue sat beside the window, her back against the wall, and the counsellor sat at the dressing table.

The counsellor smiled kindly. "Okay to start, Sue?"

She nodded.

"I'll start at the beginning. Last night, an operation of great importance to the security of this country took place in the woods just south of here. Our target was identified as being in the company of two unknowns, and sleeping, living, in a tepee by the stream, in the woods. A plan was set up to capture that person. Everything went according to plan, and we captured all persons in the camp; unfortunately all persons in the camp at that time were not the full compliment as we knew it."

Counsellor paused, and asked, "You with me so far, Sue?"

"Yes, and I think I can see what's coming."

Counsellor nodded.

"Our helicopter took off," he said, "and, in a search of the surrounding area, discovered a man in the woods, who then proceeded to run from the helicopter. The men in the chopper gave chase, and, from their vantage point, they watched as the man teamed up with another person. All our man in the chopper knew was that one, or both, of the persons in the thermal image began to fire. Our man returned the fire, and… unfortunately, Stephen was shot… dead. The other man was captured later."

Sue sat for a moment, silent, rubbing and wringing her fingers. Counsellor let her take it all in. Sue looked at him, gave a slight nod, and said, "That's it then, isn't it? It was an accident. I understand. Let's all go our separate ways."

Sue looked at her hands in her lap. No one spoke for a few moments.

Sue broke the silence. "When can I see him? When can I have his body, bury him?"

There was the gentlest of knocks, and the P.R. lady entered. Counsellor stood, vacating his seat. He walked to Sue.

"Sue," he said, "you're taking it very well, but there are a few things that need to be discussed. Not nice things, but we want to do well by Stephen."

Sue buried her head in her hands, and dragged them down her face, stretching the skin below her eyes. "Yes, yes, whatever." She groaned, looking to the floor. "Oh, God. How am I going to tell the kids?" She thought for a moment then looked up. "Just let's get it over with... I've just thought; what will the death certificate show as cause of death?"

Counsellor looked to the P.R. lady, and raised his eyebrows.

The P.R. lady stepped further into the room. "That's my department, Sue. We'll let these gentlemen leave, and then we'll get down to what needs to be done, eh?"

Sue nodded. The counsellor and Tommo made to leave.

Sue raised her voice. "No. Wait. Can Tommo stay? I want someone with me, even though he's on your side. I want someone to talk to."

Tommo looked to the others.

Again, the Counsellor smiled kindly. "There are no sides, Sue. We're all with you, and yes, Tommo can stay."

*

267

Alex took the call, as Brasher studied the cadaver that was Stephen. Brasher shook his head and turned as Alex put the phone to his ear.

"Yes. Go ahead," said Alex.

"He's been to the flat, sir. The imam. He paced the cul-de-sac, double-checked everything, and then used the stairs to her flat. He got no further than the top of the landing. I guess the sight of the carpenter spoke volumes."

"Okay, that's fine. Just ensure no one shows their hand until I give the word. No interference. Just follow him, and all the others in the frame. No action, just reports. Thank you."

Alex turned to Brasher.

"All as normal, sir."

Brasher pointed to the body.

"An inch to the right, and we'd have been talking to him at this very minute. So sad."

He stared at Stephen's face, then shook himself, literally, starting with his shoulders, and finishing with his hips. He pointed in the direction of the guardhouse, clapped his hands, and then moved off.

"Right. Let's start with his girlfriend – after a coffee, and something to eat. I'm famished."

Over a late breakfast in the mess, Alex and Brasher spoke of their prisoners. Opinions were offered, suggestions made, tactics discussed, and then a decision made.

*

Ten minutes later, they stared though the glass roundel, Balvindar stared back from where she sat on her bunk. They were calm, detached, pondering.

Balvindar trembled, shook, and moist eyes held tears back.

Brasher signalled to the guard at the end of the corridor. He approached at the double.

"We'd like to go in, please," said Brasher.

The guard quickly, efficiently, smoothly, pulled out his keys attached to a key chain, and turned the lock. He opened the door, in-over, and Brasher and Alex entered. The door clanged shut behind them.

Balvindar sat facing them, still sitting on her bunk, still not moving, still in shock. Alex moved to her left, Brasher stood a metre in front of her. Balvindar was dressed in blue jeans, a dark jumper, and flat black shoes. Brasher stared at her for a full minute, not speaking, until the dam broke and the tears flowed. He waited a few moments, then handed her a folded handkerchief from his jacket pocket. She took it and dabbed her eyes.

"Balvindar. Be calm. We're the nice guys."

Balvindar's tears gradually dried up and Brasher began pacing. Balvindar looked up to Brasher, and her eyes followed him as he talked.

"You know what you're mixed up with Balvindar. We know who you're mixed up with. The imam, Sanjar, the others in Yorkshire, we know them all, and they live and breathe at our whim. And did you know that your... companions, have murdered a simple petty burglar, in Leeds. A first time offender. He was the man taken by your lot to disguise the fact that you wanted Sanjar back. An innocent man, shot in the head."

Balvindar looked up sharply.

"Oh yes, my dear. Believe that." Brasher paused a beat. "Look, Balvindar. I will be asking simple questions, just getting to know you. The people who come in after me are entirely different. They will want every bit of intelligence out of you, every last scrap of information, every last syllable, sentence and full stop, and they will get it. And your sex, or age, or physical build, will make no difference whatsoever to their interrogation. You are an object, a source that must be drained of everything we need to know to ensure the security of this country."

He paused, studied her, seeing the fear arise in her face.

"So, the more boxes you tick with me, the fewer boxes they have to fill in with them. Do I make myself clear, dear?"

Balvindar looked at him, soft folds, worry lines, on her forehead.

"Why did you join them, my girl? What was the attraction?"

She thought for a moment, and then nodded. "I felt the same way as Sanjar. I wanted to fight back, at the bigotry, the racism, the colour prejudice, the hurtful remarks, the… you know?"

"Oh no, I do not know. I've heard about it, I've seen it, but I've never suffered it. How I would react to it, I honestly could not say. But, one thing I would say is that I would not be of a mind to manufacture a bomb and indiscriminately kill innocent people. *That* I will not stand back and let happen, as an individual, and as a member of Her Majesty's Armed Forces. Is that what you believe in? Bombing, mass killings, of babies, and innocents?"

Balvindar cried again, and looked to the floor; Brasher waited. Again she dried her eyes, gulping. She sniffled as she said, "It was not supposed to be like that. We joined to march, to protest…"

"Who are 'we'?"

Balvindar looked at Brasher, and said, "You know. You have Sanjar in the next room."

"Is that all? None of your other friends from university? Family, colleagues? You need to tell me now, Balvindar."

"No, no. Sanjar was going to the meetings long before he told me. I went along out of interest. I thought it was political, a new party, but I never met anyone other than the imam and his… whatever he was… his bodyguard, and a cleaner. I thought it would be phone banks, leaflet drops, door to door canvassing. I dreamed of a Muslim Democratic Party… votes… a democratically elected M.P. then…" She pleaded with Brasher. "Please speak with Sanjar. Please. I'm sure he is not the man you think he is."

"What do we think he is?"

Balvindar spoke softly, resigned, as she looked at her intertwined fingers, "A bomber, a killer, a madman."

Brasher looked to Alex, and raised his eyebrows. Alex grimaced and made a barely discernable shrug. Brasher turned to Balvindar again.

271

"Okay, young lady, we'll leave you to think on. The people we spoke of will be with you tomorrow."

Brasher knocked on the cell door.

Chapter Thirty-Three

"Don't tell me. She's scared shitless."

Alex leaned across the table to Billy. "Can't tell you what she is or isn't, Billy. You do the telling, we do the asking."

Billy leaned back against the wall of his cell; the wall that his bunk was fixed to.

"Am I here to assist the police, or army, as they say, 'cos yuh can't believe I'm a terrorist? Or do yuh?"

Brasher observed as Alex stood, and paced the ten-feet by eight-foot cell, with a ceiling nine-feet above the floor. Alex leaned against the cell door, and looked directly at Billy.

"Who mentioned terrorist, Billy?"

"Ah, man, for fuck's sake. Apart from the fact that yuh stormed the camp with a fucking helicopter and armed men, I took Sanjar's confessional."

"Go on."

"No, not until yuh tell me who was in that body bag."

Alex shook his head. "Can't tell you who that was until we figure out where you fit in."

Billy stood, and pointed his finger. "Stop fucking about! Yuh know where I fit in. I've been in that tepee for years. People come and go. I've met doctors, lawyers, actors, dustbin men, bricklayers, Japanese, Yanks, and possibly every other breed and trade on this planet. Three days ago, I met an angry young lad who was being sucked into evil by others.

Yuh *know* Sanjar's just a fucking mixed up kid.
Now, if yuh can't tell me who was in that body bag,
could yuh tell who wasn't?"

Brasher's lips remained tight shut.

"A man called Stephen wasn't in the bag,
was he?"

Alex lowered his head.

Billy said, "Fuck!" and sat down

Alex let Billy sort his thoughts, then said,
"You'll be questioned tomorrow, Billy, by others. If
you give them cause to suspect that you are holding
something back, they will get it out of you, by
whatever means necessary."

"Like I give a fuck."

"You should Billy, you should."

"Why? 'Cos they're gonna hurt me? Well
they can't hurt me, anymore than I've been hurt.
People come…" he paused, reflecting, "people go. If
I go, who cares, who gives a shit? And if what I've
told yuh is not enough for them, they're gonna have
to kill me, 'cos there's no more to tell."

Alex nodded, "We'll see. We'll see."

He banged on the cell door.

*

Billy the Bow was released after six days. He
returned to his camp on a gloriously sunny day, and
found everything he'd left in apple-pie order. He
scoured the camp, but there was no trace of Sanjar
or Stephen ever being there. The ranger in the
bushes watched; Billy appeared to be at a loss,
disheartened, sad.

Billy walked to the stream. The previous
three days of constant rain had raised the water level

274

to nearly mid-thigh height, but, today, the summer sun was reaching its zenith. The heat was stifling and the stream tempting. The ranger knew that Billy had not suffered as Balvindar and Sanjar had, so, he wondered, what was troubling Billy. The ranger looked around him. He frowned. Where was the bird song? Where were the butterflies? No wood pigeons, no lark singing, no rooks, or crows flying. He looked across the stream. The field was empty. The sheep were God knows where, and not a rabbit showed its fluffy tail.

The ranger looked up. Not a vapour trail showed in the blue sky. He looked to Billy. He had waded to the centre of the rushing water. Billy stood for a moment. He looked around him, up stream, down stream. He looked to the sky, raised his arms out at his side, to shoulder level, and stood for a second.

The ranger's eyes narrowed. He stood from his crouched position. Suddenly, Billy pitched forward. The ranger tensed as Billy went under the water. The ranger watched, as the seconds ticked by. He waited a minute. Had Billy surfaced downstream? The ranger took one step forward. The explosion of water as Billy surfaced, arms reaching for the sky, surprised him. The ranger watched as Billy gasped for air, then shouted, roared, an angry shout. Billy let his arms drop. His shoulders slumped. He stood in the middle of the stream, head bowed,

The ranger crouched again as Billy turned, and waded to the bank of the stream. Billy walked to his tepee, and stood for a moment. Then he shook himself, took off his shirt, and hung it on the lower branch of a Scot's pine. He skirted the edge of the copse, and gathered kindling.

As Billy knelt, sparking the fire into life, a couple, a boy and girl, wandered into camp from the north. They were young, both blond, and both in shorts, walking boots, and T-shirts. The ranger saw Billy stand and exchange a few words. Billy smiled and indicated his tepee - the young couple shugged off their backpacks. The ranger turned to his left at the sound of a bush moving. A fox moseyed past, behind him. A bird startled at the sound of the fox and took flight, just as a lark rose from the field on the opposite side of the water.

The ranger turned back to Billy, just as he pulled back his bow and let the arrow fly. A wood pigeon fell from a branch, the arrow through its fat chest. Billy retrieved the pigeon, pulled the arrow through its chest, and indicated to the couple, to get water from the river. The ranger grinned, turned, and headed for the road.

*

Sanjar was kept in custody for three weeks, and he talked of what little he knew. He told of the imam, Hameed, and local gophers. He knew nothing of contacts in Leeds. It seemed to Sanjar that a lot of people were surprised when the so-called political group began talking of explosives and bombs. And everything Sanjar said was verified by what Brasher already knew. Brasher's men threw in names of people beyond Leeds, beyond Sanjar's line of knowledge, and Sanjar looked blank.

The men with no names were kind to Sanjar, and were cruel to Sanjar. They used drugs, sleep deprivation, white noise for minutes on end, had him stripped naked for days and holding a designated physical position for hours. Sexual humiliation was hinted at, but never used, and Sanjar gave the same answers and statements every time. He lost ten pounds in weight, and he rued the day he was born.

At the beginning of the third week, Sanjar was held outside the slightly open door of Balvindar's cell, and heard her going through the same interrogation that he had so far suffered. The cell door was closed just before mid-day, and Sanjar was pushed up to the glass roundel. He saw Balvindar being stripped of her clothing, until there was no more clothing to remove.

Balvindar stared through the roundel, and saw Sanjar, and the tears running down his face. She smiled kindly, shook her head, and mouthed, 'I'm fine.' If Balvindar had been in profile, Sanjar may have seen the slight swelling of her belly. He was dragged screaming and shouting back to his cell.

After three weeks, the people left, Sanjar was allowed to sleep uninterrupted, with the lights off. After twenty-three days, his mother and father visited, and he told them of Balvindar, and the fact that she was in the next cell. Sanjar's mother smiled, kindly, pleased, but pained, for her son. Sanjar's father told him to expect to go to prison, for a long time, and Sanjar's mother sobbed and sobbed.

*

As Sanjar's mother shed tears, Tommo checked the piece of paper again. He looked up and cursed

UPVC doors without numbers fitted to them. Finally, he spotted a house with the number screwed to the wall at the side of the front door.

The road was in an estate probably built in the seventies, at the beginning of the boom of the workingman and woman owning their own home. Working his way along the road, counting in his head from the house with the number, he eventually found the house he was looking for.

The house was a semi-detached, with a two-foot wall along its front, stopping at the drive which ran up the side. The front garden was a simple lawn, border, with a small apple tree set to the side of the front window. A Vauxhall Corsa was parked in the drive.

Tommo hesitated for a moment. He thought on the events of a month ago, then took a deep breath, and walked to the front door. The half glazed door was on the side of a storm porch built on to the house, probably an early improvement by the first owner of the house. He pressed the bell push. He didn't hear it ring, so he rattled the doorknocker.

He looked up and down the road as he waited. A noise coming from inside the porch turned him, and he saw Sue. The smiley surprise on her face pleased him.

Sue opened the door, and gushed.

"Tommo. Lovely to see you. Come in, come in."

Tommo returned the smile, as he entered the porch, and then moved past Sue as she stepped to one side. A flight of stairs rose directly in front of him, and a glass-panelled door into the front room was to his left. He entered the room, and stood, waiting.

Sue followed him in and shut the door behind her.

"Go on, sit down. Relax. What'll it be tea, coffee…?" she said, still smiling.

Tommo spoke, half embarrassed, "Err… coffee, please. White, weak and half a sugar."

Sue walked through to an adjoining room, and entered the kitchen by a door to her right. She shouted to Tommo.

"Come through if you like, don't stand on ceremony. What brings you around this way, anyhow?"

Tommo walked into the kitchen as Sue filled the kettle.

"Oh, just passing through as it were."

Sue laughed. "Passing through? There's not an army camp within fifty miles of here, and this place is on the road to nowhere."

She busied herself with cups and a jar of coffee.

Tommo smiled, "Aye, you're right. I… just wondered if you were all right, if you were managing. And… if the funeral went off okay."

Sue switched on the kettle, and turned to him. She frowned.

"It went off fine, I suppose. Stephen was given a Christian burial, he was lauded to the heavens in the eulogy, all lies of course, and… and it went off fine." She thought for a moment, "All according to plan."

279

Tommo watched her as she busied herself with cups.

"Are you happy?" he said. "I mean, do you see why it was handled the way it was?"

Sue sighed. "Yes, of course I do. For the better good of all, and all that. There are times when I get angry, but... it was an accident, wrong place, wrong time..."

She turned back to the now boiled kettle, and poured hot water into the cups. She handed a cup to Tommo.

"I'm sorry, Sue. For the lies, I'm sorry. Do you understand I had to do it, protect the operation? If I could have saved Stephen, if I could have done something..."

Sue held up her hand. "Tommo, I understand. If I'd been in your position, I would have done the same thing. That's what you signed up to do. I understand."

Tommo nodded, took a sip of his coffee. He looked to the floor.

"So, where are you really going? Another operation, anywhere interesting, exciting? Oh..." Sue laughed, "you can't say, can you?" Tommo smiled wryly.

"Aye, I can tell you. I'm on my way to be D'd. Debriefed, decommissioned, demobilised, call it what you like. In civvy street you'd say I'd given my notice in."

Sue raised her eyebrows. "Really? You can do that?" She frowned. "Anything to do with what happened... in the Borders?"

Tommo nodded. "Aye, I can do that. It's not straightforward, but basically the same. They'll help me get a job in civvy street." He put his cup on the table. "And yes, it has a lot to do with what happened in the Borders, and what I saw, but, anyway, I'm on my way out." He smiled.

"What you saw? Surely you've seen worse than that."

"Not the incident, the area. Billy the Bow, his lifestyle, his… I don't know."

He thought for a moment.

"There are times, Sue, when I think about what I've done and how it fits into the scheme of things, and how I can put right some of the… I want peace, Sue, I want peace, innocence, and I want to enjoy the natural world."

Sue stared at him, not speaking. Tommo shrugged and stared back.

Sue said, "Who's Billy the Bow?"

Tommo smiled again, sat down, and said, "Let me tell you about him, and the Borders."

Chapter Thirty-Four

One year later

Sanjar walked into the visitor's area, and looked around. He saw Alex at a table in the corner, his back against the wall. As always, Sanjar checked out the other prisoners and their visitors. If he'd seen anyone he vaguely recognised, or anyone who did not look quite right, he would have turned around and walked back to his cell; he did not.

Alex pushed the plastic cup toward Sanjar.

"Here you are, black sweet tea. And how are you? Any problems, anything of note?" asked Alex.

Sanjar hitched his chair nearer to the table.

"No, no problems."

He swirled the tea around, looking down into the cup, and thought for a moment.

"Come on, Sanjar," said Alex, "Spit it out. What is on your mind? Why did Balvindar ask me to come and see you?"

Sanjar nodded. "Okay. I'm suspicious. I've been here, what, over a year now, and not had one pick of bother. Now why is that, I wonder? There are gangs in here…"

"Get to the point, Sanjar. There are gangs in every prison; Durham is no different to any other."

"No, let me finish. There are gangs in here, Newcastle lads from the west-end, Newcastle lads from the east-end, a Yorkshire gang, a gang of Afros, the gays stick together, the body builders stick together…"

"Like I said, no different to any other prison."

Alex sat back in his chair, and folded his arms.

"Yes, but all those gangs, those groups, have... fall outs, spats, either with each other, or with other gangs or groups. Trouble touches everyone in here..."

"And?"

"Apart from me."

Alex frowned. They stared at each other silently. Sanjar shrugged, opened his arms, imploring an answer.

Alex pushed his bottom lip over his top lip, and then said, "Um. And your question is?"

"Do you have someone in here looking after me, putting the word about?"

Again Alex paused before answering. He said, "No. And now you're thinking what I'm thinking, aren't you?"

Sanjar cocked his head and raised an eyebrow. "Do you think that maybe they have someone in here watching me? It's possible."

Alex stared. "Has anyone approached you, do you have your suspicions about anyone?"

Sanjar shrugged, and grimaced. "Absolutely not. But what about the group I was with. Are they still active? I asked you to visit because the little niggles are beginning to sneak in. What is it like on the outside?"

Alex leaned forward again, and drummed his fingers on the table. "Are you still receiving your letters from Balvindar?"

Sanjar smiled, "You know I am. You check them before I get them."

Alex returned the smile.

"And her and the baby are doing fine, aren't they? Your father dotes on him. I think your father spends more time pushing a pram than he does over the drawing board. Or do architects not use drawing boards now?" Alex mused for a moment, then said, "Anyway, how long have you got left to do, Sanjar."

"After your lot had finished with me, I got another six months added to my sentence for running away from the prison van, didn't I? You should know."

"Yes, yes, but how long have you got left to serve? I don't keep track."

"With good behaviour, I may be out in six months. And you still haven't answered my question."

Alex looked around, studying the little visiting groups clustered around the tables.

"The group of people that you were connected with in the north-east no longer exists. That's as much as you need to know."

A silence hung for a minute, as they both looked around.

Exasperation crept into Sanjar's tone. "So? Does that let me off the hook?"

Alex frowned, his eyes narrowing, as he stared at Sanjar. "No, my friend, that does not let you off the hook. I'm surprised you can even think that."

Alex watched Sanjar for a reaction. Sanjar sat waiting for Alex to complete the answer to his question.

"It will be a long time before you are... off the hook," said Alex. "You sought out these people, you trained with these people, and then you got cold feet. You may not want to play with them any more, but they will not let you simply walk away. Do you understand that?"

Sanjar wiped his face with his right hand. He sighed.

"I... no one's even tried to contact me. It's got me worried. I can't understand the group just letting me go without threatening me, or instructing me in some way."

"As far as we can ascertain, there is no one in the north-east left to contact you. But, you can bet your next six months that someone will be in touch; even if it is only to find out how much you know about the organisation."

Sanjar rested his elbows on the table, leaned forward, and massaged his head with both arms. He looked up, his face a study in torment.

"Look," he said, "is it possible that the imam was just a... a wannabe? You know, a fanatic who his friends laughed at, would not listen to?"

"Sanjar, don't get political. You're in here because you tried to circumvent the system, tried to use a dangerous alternative method of getting your voice listened to. You can either accept that you made a mistake, accept what has happened, is happening, for the foreseeable future, and get on with your life, or you can worry. Believe me, your presence, your activity in this prison, and what you were connected with, is known to only three men in my organisation. What happened to you after the raid is not known to the men who captured you. Any leakage, should there be any, will not come from us."

Alex watched Sanjar's eyes blinking rapidly. Obviously, thoughts were racing through Sanjar's mind just as quickly.

"Sanjar. Do your time. Believe that you were caught by the police, and you're serving time for a burglary. That is what the criminal records show, that is what the police have on record, and that is what was published in the local newspapers. The happenings in the Borders never occurred."

Sanjar sat back in his chair, his chin on his chest. He thought for a moment.

"How is Billy, and where is Stephen buried."

Alex sighed. "Billy the Bow, as you call him, is doing fine. And, as far as I can gather, he is having a good summer as far as tourists are concerned.

Sanjar smiled. "He's a one off, a funny guy; innocent, but not as stupid as he's makes himself out to be. And Stephen?"

Alex shook his head, tight-lipped. He ruminated for a moment, then said, "Sorry, no information on Stephen. Whatever you find out we cannot prevent. But we will not assist you. Oh, and just in case you're wondering, his wife is fine, and has what appears to be a regular boyfriend."

"It would have been nice if Stephen had died knowing his wife was still alive," said Sanjar.

Alex nodded. "If, would have, should have, could have…. Believe me, Sanjar, I feel as sad as you with regard to Stephen, but…" He leaned into

Sanjar. "Okay, my friend. I need to leave now. If you have any other questions, or suddenly remember more information, let Balvindar know when she visits."

Alex stood, shook hands, and left. Sanjar sat, looking down at the table top. He thought for a while, staring at the same spot, then stood, turned, and headed off back to his cell.

A visitor at the far end of the room looked up and frowned as Sanjar came towards him. Sanjar returned the look. The visitor's face creased, deep in thought.

Chapter Thirty-Five

Gurp Sahid stiffened at the noise that came from beyond the back door. The door led onto his back yard, which opened out onto a back lane. He stood, and stepped away from the kitchen table, leaving his newspaper still open at the editorial comment page.

He stood against the sink, looking out of the window into the yard; he saw no one. He opened the back door and stood on the small step. He cocked his head, his right ear towards the bottom end of the lane. He walked across the yard, slowly, softly, still straining to hear. He opened the yard door, and looked out into the lane to his right. A white Ford Transit, engine purring, was crawling, slowly, steadily toward him. Gurp stepped back into the yard, closed the door, and shot the bolt. He placed his ear close to the door.

The van drew nearer. Gurp looked to the kitchen. He ran, dashed through the terraced house, and swung the front door open. He looked up and down the street. He dashed to the back yard again.

The van was nearly to his door. He stepped away from the door, staring at it. Then he heard the voice shouting.

"Iron! Scrap Iron. Iron."

Gurp let out his pent-up breath. His shoulders slumped. He shook his head. The voice from behind startled him.

"Was it worth it, Mr. Tough Guy?"

Gurp turned, and looked up to the window. His wife, Aadila, looked down on him, from the back bedroom.

"Well? Was it?"

He hung his head. "You don't understand," he said.

Aadila stared down on him. She watched him agonising.

"I understand. You weren't happy with your lot. But, I also understand you never tried to mix. You created your own ghetto, you joined the gangs, you clung to the old ways, and you listened to that dick-head of an imam. You…"

Gurp looked up again. Aadila stopped.

"I'm tired," said Gurp. "Tired of arguing, tired of fighting mentally, tired of the strain, of waiting for the knock on the door."

He lifted his arms, held them up toward Aadila, and then let them drop.

"I'm fucked," he said.

Aadila watched Gurp. Was he crying? Her eyes filled. She shouted as she slammed the window shut.

"Come in. We'll talk."

Gurp entered the front room, as Aadila stepped off the bottom stair. She moved to the television that no one was watching, and switched it off. Gurp sat in his armchair, and she sat on the sofa.

"Where are the kids?" asked Aadila.

"What?"

"There's bugger all wrong with your hearing so don't' start with the bloody 'Whats'."

"I don't know what you mean," said Gurp.

Aadila shouted, "Our kids, your children, your two sons, your daughters. Where are they?"

Gurp shook his head. "I… don't know. I…"

Aadila shouted louder. "You don't know? You don't bloody know! Well you should, shouldn't you! Do you know about guns, about bombs, about… *bloody killing?* Do you? Do you?"

Gurp made a pressing motion with his hands. "Sshh, calm down, calm down."

Aadila jumped to her feet.

"Calm down? Calm down? Can't you see what's happening? Where this is heading?"

She waited for a quick reply, none came.

"I don't know you, Gurp. What are you? Who are you? Do you want to go back to the old country? Our parent's country? Do you not like what we have in England?" Aadila paused a moment, then continued, her voice slowly rising " You do know that you're either going to prison or you're going to die, don't you?"

Her voice rose to screaming.

"*You are going to die!*"

Gurp stared at his wife; she stared wide-eyed at his silence.

Aadila calmed. She sighed. "You're treading water," she said.

She looked to Gurp for a response, none came.

"You have another option. Leave the country."

Gurp stood, and paced. "I don't want to. What would happen to you and the children?"

Aadila closed her eyes.

"Say what you mean," she said. "You want to leave, but you want me to agree to it. You want me to give you my blessing, so you can run away without a guilty conscience." She rubbed her eyes. "Well go. Leave. I'm not bothered."

"I'm not…" said Gurp

"Go! Leave! You'd be better off without us, and we'd be better off without you. Go."

Aadila intertwined her fingers, and wrung her hands. Neither spoke for a while, then Gurp stood and moved to the stairs. He stopped, and spoke without looking back.

"I love you, my Aadila. I love you more than life."

Aadila shook her head, and looked at the wall.

Gurp climbed the stairs. Aadila heard him close the bedroom doors. The base unit of the roamer phone lying on the small table next to her clicked. She looked to the ceiling and heard Gurp's muffled voice.

*

Two minutes later, Aadila stood, moved to the kitchen and filled the sink. She squirted washing-up liquid under the running tap, and then slid the breakfast dishes under the soapy water. Six minutes later she heard sirens, and the front door open, but not close. She turned, soap suds dripping from her arms, and looked to the door.

Gurp stood framed in the doorway, arms raised. Aadila frowned.

"Gurp?"

"Stay there."

291

"What are you doing? Gurp?"

Aadila heard the squeal of tyres, then the noises of a skid. Gurp stepped out onto the street. Aadila dashed after him.

"Gurp!"

"Stay there! Stay indoors!"

Aadila froze. She heard the loud speaker, the voice crackling.

"On the floor, Gurp Sahid. Lie down. Keep your arms outstretched."

Aadila watched through the frame of the door. The voice sounded again.

"Is there anyone else in the house? Answer me, Gurp."

"My wife. She's in the kitchen. Only my wife."

"Tell her to come out, Gurp. I repeat. Tell her to come out. Hands high."

Aadila moved to the front door and shouted, "I'm coming out. I'm coming out. It's only me. I'm coming out."

She exited the house, hands held high, soapsuds running down her arm, and walked to where Gurp lay. She stood next to his prone body.

"Lie down! The female. The woman. Lie down."

Aadila lay down next to her husband. She turned her head toward him.

"Look at me, my husband."

Gurp did not move.

"I'm Aadila. I'm your wife. Look at me."

She waited as Gurp slowly turned his head
He stared at the ground for a moment, and then
turned fully. The tears streamed down his face.

Gurp spoke through his crying.

"I'll be back. I promise. Please wait for me.
I'll come back. They cannot kill me. Don't leave
me. I'll do my time. I'll be back."

Aadila smiled through her tears, and nodded.

"I'll still be here. You'll find me here -
husband."

*

Alex knocked, waited for the command to enter, and
then pushed open the door. He saw Brasher behind
his desk. The window, as usual, was wide open
behind where his immediate superior sat.

Brasher said, "Have a seat, Alex. Get
yourself sorted and we'll start. Shouldn't take long."

Alex opened his briefcase as Brasher stood,
picked up a letter opener from his desk, and then
took his pipe from his pocket as he walked to the
raised sash. He used the letter opener to scrape loose
the stale tobacco in the pipe bowl. He wiped the
letter opener on a tissue, and then tipped the tobacco
scrapings into a flowerpot on the window sill.
Another sixty-seconds later, and Brasher was
puffing on his fresh bowl of best Virginian tobacco.

He turned to Alex.

"Ready?"

"At your convenience, sir."

Brasher sat on the window sill.

"Yorkshire?" he said.

"A man called Gurp Sahid, sir. A man we've
been watching. Just out of the blue, he simply rang

up, said he had been part of a terrorist group and that he wanted to hand himself in. However, bloody annoying thing is that we cannot tie him into any specific incident, apart from the north-east incident."

"How long did you have with him?"

Alex referred to a piece of A4 paper on his knee.

"Fifteen days, sir. What he admitted to was that he received orders from that idiot imam in Newcastle, and that it was him and Jamal Hakim who released Sanjar from the prison van. But, they were literally raw recruits. That whole prisoner hijack was mostly down to pure luck. They had only been in the group for about a month, and had met the imam four times. Up until then, neither of them had taken part in any incidents that we are aware of, and he has no idea who anyone else is in the group."

"Who killed the prisoner in the block of flats?"

"Gurp Sahid's statement, and the evidence, all point to Hakim. Apparently, the prisoner, Matty, actually knocked out Gurp and was trying to escape when he was shot by Hakim. Gurp still has scars on his face to back up what he said happened to him, and we checked DNA on the drawer that Matty used to knock him out. It matches Gurp's."

Brasher pushed off the window sill.

"And what are your plans now, for both of them?"

Alex once again reached to his briefcase, and searched his papers. He pulled out a bound document.

"A plan, sir. For your consideration."

" Any special… considerations to take into account?"

"Time, sir. Only time."

Chapter Thirty-Six

<u>Four months later</u>
The door to Sanjar's cell was open. He sat idly, reading a book on the table which stood against the wall separating him from the cell next door. To the right of Sanjar was his bunk and, behind him, on the adjoining wall of the other cell was a small bookshelf. To his left was the open cell door.

Sanjar turned the page, pressed against the spine of the book to flatten the page, and then became aware of someone in the doorway. He turned and looked at the figure. The figure, a female officer, Jennifer Farr, Jenny, smiled.

"Okay to come in, Sanjar?"

Sanjar returned the smile, nodded, and said, 'Yeah'.

He folded the corner of the page, closed the book and stood. He indicated his chair to the officer.

Jenny laughed.

"No chance. If anyone caught me sitting in your cell I'd be for the high jump. And that would be after someone had told the lie of seeing us having sex. No, no, I'll just stand in the doorway here where I'm in full view of every nosey bastard."

Sanjar still smiled. "Yeah, I understand. Is this official, or just passing the time?"

Jenny stood just under five-foot nine, with blonde hair, a figure that was slim, but not skinny and she was very pretty. Sanjar had often wondered what she was doing in the job of a prison officer. The odd times that he had spent with Jenny had shown him that she had intelligence in abundance - and street sense. The thought had crossed Sanjar's mind that Jenny was maybe undercover intelligence, purely there for his assessment.

"Oh, just a chat. You know, how's things, how are you, any plans for when you get out, and any problems?"

"I'm fine, and I've got plans, and no problems. Why do you ask? Can you fix me up with a job?"

"Sorry, Sanjar, I've no connections in the world of chemistry. Anyway, what do you do with a chemistry degree? Make things, or test things, or what?"

Sanjar scratched his head, pondering. He smiled.

"How does chemistry fit into the real world, eh? Have you got a spare couple of hours?"

Jenny smiled. "Howay, man. It must fit in somewhere with something that touches me directly."

Sanjar grinned. "Soap powder, toothpaste, petrol, cling film, face cream, medicines…"

"All right, all right, I get the picture. So it's not all mad scientists trying to blow the world up, eh?"

Sanjar's grin dropped from his face. He turned to the bookshelf and slipped his book in between two hardbacks on the top shelf.

He thought for a moment.

"Where do you put burglary on your C.V.? Is that under 'Other Skills'?" he said.

He sat down, a black mood settling on him.

Jenny studied him for a moment.

"What was it? A brainstorm, or were you drunk? What the hell drove you to burglary?"

Sanjar snapped out of his reverie.

"My business, Officer Farr, my business."

"Oh, aye. Sorry Sanjar, just… I don't know, astounded I suppose. I've seen your parents on visiting days and you seem to come from a respectable family. I wonder…"

Jenny saw the cold expression on Sanjar's face.

"Okay, enough. Anyway, just think on, whatever you decide, you can get help. There's people in here, and out there, who can help to smooth the way a little. So don't get disheartened."

Jenny turned to go.

"Any problems, Sanjar, just give me a nod."

"Officer Farr."

Jenny turned to Sanjar again.

"Thanks for your offer, and your kind thoughts. There's not many like you in here."

Jenny smiled. "And I could say the same about you, Sanjar. Anyway, you're welcome. Watch how you go."

She walked off, along the landing.

Sanjar stepped out on to the landing and watched her walk off. Most of the other inmates on the landing followed her progress. She had a cute natural swing of her behind as she walked.

Sanjar had less than one month left to serve. All he had to do was keep his nose clean, and walk the line. Most of the other prisoners were happy for him, and their continued cries of, "Not long now, professor," were coming at him on a regular basis. He'd gotten along fine with nearly everyone, although they laughed at his attempt to be a burglar.

He allowed Jenny to get far enough ahead of him before setting off in the same direction. He got as far as where the landing joined a small steel gantry bridge, which in turn was joined to the landing opposite, then stopped. He looked over to the other landing. A new prisoner on the block was being led to his cell from the other direction; the only other single occupation cell on that level.

The prisoner was Asian; maybe Pakistani, maybe Indian, too light skinned to be from Sri Lanka. Sanjar glanced at the prisoner, just as the prisoner looked at him. Sanjar turned away, and carried on walking. As they drew level with each other, Sanjar looked across again. The prisoner's eyes were locked on him. Sanjar stopped, stared back, as the prisoner continued forward, but continued to look back at Sanjar. Only when the officer pulled at the prisoner's shoulder did he stop, and take his eyes off Sanjar. Sanjar watched the new man enter his cell, and the officers lock the cell door behind him.

Sanjar shrugged, and carried on.

*

Alex knocked on the door, and paused, waiting for the command from beyond. In anticipation, he leaned forward, and gripped the handle. The command did not come. He heard the indistinct bass mumblings from beyond. He pressed his ear to the door, testing – nothing. Then silence.

Brasher's voice, boomed out seconds later.

"Enter."

As Alex entered, Brasher reached forward and then picked up his letter opener. He stood, and then pointed to his desk.

"Help yourself, Alex."

Brasher turned away, pulling his pipe from his pocket, as Alex laid his briefcase on the desk, and clicked it open. Alex wondered if Brasher used Alex's visits as a prompt to relax and have a smoke. And how the hell Brasher got away with smoking in his office was beyond Alex.

Brasher walked to the open window behind him. One minute later he puffed on his pipe, and watched as Alex sorted his papers.

Brasher pointed with his pipe as he said, "You seem concerned. Are we still winning?"

"Oh yes, sir. No problems whatsoever. Just this... paperwork seems to breed in my briefcase."

Brasher smiled. "I used to think that. Then, I finally admitted to myself that I found life in the field more enjoyable than office work, and that I was using every ruse in the book to avoid being in the office. Then I also admitted to myself that no matter how much I ignored it, the damn paperwork would not go away."

Alex sat down in the chair, and sighed.

"Yes, sir. You're absolutely right. That is my problem. But... anyway, yes, we are winning."

Brasher raised his eyebrows.

"Yorkshire?"

"Yes, sir. Gurp Sahid is inside, as you know."

"And the information he provided?"

Alex leaned one arm on Brasher's desk. "Actually, sir, he knew more than he thought he did. Initially, I was sceptical with regard to the information provided. It came over too easy. I mean, he didn't simply pour it all out, we did have to put pressure on, but, believe me, sir, very little leaning was necessary."

Brasher nodded. "Can we progress with the information provided?" he said.

Alex sighed, and held his arms open.

"I honestly think that Yorkshire was the end of the line. That imam simply stirred hatred amongst five or six characters in the north-east, and set about becoming a… a man to be feared. I honestly doubt whether he would have had the balls to implement a terror campaign, sir."

Brasher puffed on his pipe.

"Remind me, his sentence?"

"Minimum of fifteen years, sir."

"Umm. I think he would have had the balls. Sanjar Khan was running away from something that scared him. Or at least the prospect of something he was expected to do scared him. And, if that damned imam had given some information to Sanjar about an intended target… anyway, 'ifs and buts'."

Brasher ruffled his hair, half scratching.

"It was too bloody neat," he said, "too amateurish… I'm still uneasy about the whole affair. Are you sure we have not forgotten anyone?"

Alex shrugged.

"As much as anyone else is sure. I do feel it's over, sir. I firmly believe that is it. The imam was simply a nobody, a wannabe, a plastic terrorist who had the desire, but not the wherewithal. Just a man full of his own importance, but, yes, he could have been very dangerous."

"And Sahid?"

"Just the other half of the Yorkshire duo, sir. Both were promised money for what they did and, by God, they did it professionally for two first timers. Too professionally, I'm afraid, in the case of that poor burglar that was executed. But, like the imam, Matty's killer did receive a severe sentence."

"Has Sanjar been instructed with regard to what is expected from him?"

"Fully, sir. He is to make friends, and get as much info out of Sahid as possible. Anything that we may not have extracted. And, the same applies to Gurp Sahid. If Sanjar lets slip something that may be of interest to us, Gurp will also inform. "

Brasher drew on his pipe again, blew out the smoke, and thought for a moment.

"So, with regard to finality and closing the case," he said, "we're all in Sanjar's hands now, eh?"

Alex nodded, grimly. "If there is anyone Gurp feels he can take into his confidence, it has to be Sanjar, sir."

Chapter Thirty-Seven

Balvindar held up the baby boy, facing Sanjar, and smiled. Sanjar reached across and held the baby's fingers. He looked to the family group on the table next to his in the visiting room.

"What do you think," he said, "handsome or what?"

"Too handsome. I'd be having a D.N.A. test done."

The other prisoner had smiled as he spoke. Sanjar turned back to his family.

"How are you getting on with Mum and Dad?"

Balvindar grinned. "You ask the same questions every time I visit. They're fine with me. Honestly, they couldn't do any more than they do?"

"And your mum and dad? Have they accepted me yet?"

Sanjar saw Balvindar's smile falter, just for a split second.

"They've not even seen you yet, but they are happy with what I've told them about you."

Sanjar watched her for a moment, and then nodded.

"You're not a good liar, Balvindar."

Balvindar's smile dropped, and she frowned.

"Forget it. And you?" she said. "Are you managing okay? Any problems? Any news?"

"News? Like who fought with who last night? Like which gang controls the cannabis at present? And who has the undiscovered mobile phone at present?" Sanjar smiled kindly. "You don't want to know. Some of the squabbling is below that of a child. But, I suppose, no natural light, no stimulation, same people every day, nothing of interest, has to anger people and it has to get vent somehow."

Balvindar joggled the baby in her arms and then looked around, as Sanjar gently played with the baby's fingers.

"Oh, yes…"

Sanjar dropped his voice to a whisper, and leaned into Balvindar.

"We have a new person on the landing opposite. I passed him on his way in, and his eyes followed me. That was a fortnight ago, but, since then, he's hardly bothered me."

Balvindar frowned, eyes narrowing.

"You should watch him. What nationality is he? What colour is he?" Her eyes widened, and she shrugged as she thought on. "Why should his eyes follow you?"

Sanjar gripped her arm, the arm that kept the baby upright as he danced on Balvindar's thighs.

"Relax. He's pleasant enough when we see each other, but he never speaks, just smiles. Rumours are that he's English, from Yorkshire, and he is second generation Pakistani. He is in for money laundering. Drugs and illegal gambling."

Forty-five minutes later, the bell sounded and visiting ended. Sanjar said his goodbyes, kissed Balvindar and the baby, and stood as they walked off. He turned, joined the line of other prisoners, and followed them into the corridor that led into the main prison.

As he entered the block, and made his way to his landing, Gurp Sahid came down the metal steps. Sanjar waited at the foot of the stairs until Gurp was close to him before he spoke.

"Fancy a chat, or a game of something?" he said.

Gurp stopped and stared. His mouth was shut tight, and his expression revealed nothing.

"Why?"

Sanjar made to brush past him.

"Forget it. Sorry I asked."

He got past Gurp and onto the third step.

"Wait, aye if you like, "said Gurp. "It'll pass some time."

Sanjar turned, shrugged, and said, "Dominoes?" He pointed to an empty table to the right of the tea urn that was bolted to the wall underneath the stairs.

"Aye, if you like."

Sanjar followed Gurp to the table. They made non-committal chatter and derogatory comments on the prison facilities as Sanjar tipped out the dominoes from the box and shuffled.

After five minutes, Gurp said, "So, whereabouts did they catch you?"

Sanjar looked up from his dominoes, a shaky smile on his face.

"Where? That's a funny old question, isn't it?"

Gurp spoke as he studied his dominoes.

"Aye, where? You had a good hour's head start. If you'd made your way back to the mosque, you'd have been as safe as houses."

Sanjar's heart pounded. He felt his cheeks flush. He forced himself to get angry.

"What the fuck are you on about?"

Gurp laid down a domino, and spoke without looking at Sanjar. He spoke matter-of-factly.

"You. I cut you loose. In the prison wagon. On your way to Durham."

Sanjar reacted instinctively.

"Keep your fucking voice down." He made a play of looking around him. "Who are you?" he said.

Gurp indicated Sanjar's dominoes with his head.

"Hurry up. You need to lay one down, or knock."

Sanjar growled a whisper, "Who are you?"

Gurp laid his hands on the table, still holding his dominoes. "I've told you who I am, and I know who you are. Now stop fucking about, and just act natural. No one can hear what we are saying."

Sanjar played out the act.

"No. First of all, if you are who you say you are, what are you doing in here?"

"They got me for money laundering – and drugs, amongst other things."

"What about your mate? The man who was with you when you freed me from the van."

"Fuck knows," lied Gurp.

"And the man who you took with you, from the van?"

Gurp sighed. "I think his name was Matt, or Matty. The fella that we took in place of you. The idiot I was with was trigger happy, and a fanatic. He shot him. Matty I mean."

Sanjar sat back, and laid his hands on the table, dominoes face down.

"A fucking innocent?" he said. "You shot a fucking innocent man, for no reason whatsoever?"

Gurp's eyes blazed. "Don't act the fucking nice guy with me. You were ready to blow women and kids to bits. And I didn't do the fucking shooting."

Sanjar looked around him again. "Keep it down! Watch your mouth," he said. He loosed his dominoes and let them fall onto the table. He stood. "C'mon, up to my cell. We need to talk."

Gurp laughed derisorily. "We? We? Who the fuck are you? Why the fuck should I want to talk with you?"

Sanjar leaned closer. "I'm in for burglary. I don't want a fucking suspected bomber charge hanging over me."

Gurp frowned. "So, what, you maybe want to kill me? To shut me up?"

"No, no. I... Look, you really need to watch your mouth."

Gurp looked at Sanjar in amazement.

"Are you fucking serious? *I* need to watch my mouth?" He stared at Sanjar, and whispered vehemently. "They're all inside! Every fucking last one of them."

"But you said you're in for money laundering. Look, I need to know what the fuck

307

happened. Can we go to your cell then, if you're not happy with mine?"

Gurp shook his head, and smiled. "If you need to, but believe me, just accept it. It's over."

He stood and Sanjar stepped aside to let him pass, and Gurp led them off to his cell.

Gurp's cell was a mirror image of Sanjar's, but his possessions were more playful than thoughtful. A radio set on the shelf, a thousand-piece jigsaw, and a scale model of Columbus' Santa Maria waiting to be constructed. On the wall facing where his head would lie on his bunk were photographs of his wife and children.

Gurp sat on his bunk, while Sanjar sat on the chair.

"So, what happened?"

Sanjar glanced at the open cell door as he spoke.

Gurp grimaced and shrugged.

"I've told you, and I couldn't be any plainer. They fell like ninepins. Hameed is dead – suicide. He was shot when they captured him; they took his legs away."

Sanjar raised his palms to Gurp.

"Hang on, hang on. How do you know all this? And how do the police not know that you're connected? Are you telling me that everyone was captured, and no one talked?"

"Seems that way."

"And you're in for money laundering? How? What did you do? How did you launder money?"

Gurp shook his head.

"You may have been clued up on bomb making, but you know fuck all about street life."

Sanjar made a pressing down motion with his hands.

"Ssh, keep it down will you? Can you stop using those words, please?"

Gurp smirked.

"How do you launder money? Easy, but, before I tell you, we need to make some ground rules. You know, as we did with our friend the imam?"

Sanjar eased the cell door to within six inches of being closed.

Chapter Thirty-Eight

"You first."

Sanjar looked acceptably offended, then shrugged, and began lying.

"Nothing to tell, they captured me about four days later up at Eyemouth, on the coast. I suppose I was bloody stupid to even try. And…" Sanjar pointed a finger, "I'd rather you hadn't released me. It cost me another six months on my sentence."

Gurp smiled. Sanjar raised his eyebrows.

"You can smile?" said Sanjar

"Of course I can, it was fucking crazy from the off. He was a nutter, the imam." Gurp sneered. "Holy war my arse. He wasn't connected. He was just an idiot using us to give vent to his hatred. He was just a fucking coward."

"So if he wasn't connected, how come he got in touch with you and your mate?"

Gurp studied Sanjar for a meaningful moment.

"What's it to you? What difference does it make?"

Sanjar snapped back. "Hey, no particular reason."

Gurp stood, his posture defiant.

"That's as much as you need to know," he said. "And, by the way, you seem to ask a lot of questions. So I'll ask you one. Why the fuck would you want to commit a burglary when you're supposed to be laying low, waiting to be contacted?"

Sanjar shrugged, and then recited his oft-rehearsed reply.

"Planning for the worst. If I'd been caught planting a bomb, or captured afterwards, I wanted to make sure that my girl had a few bob."

"Why didn't you see the imam?"

Sanjar stared, amazed. "Are you serious! He hated women. They were a necessary evil. He'd have let her starve."

Sanjar turned, startled, as the cell door swung open, creaking on its hinges.

Jennifer Farr stood framed in the doorway. She surveyed Sanjar and Gurp for a moment, then said, "So? Do I have to ask?"

Sanjar held up his hands. "Sorry, Officer Farr. My fault. I closed the door." He pointed to Gurp. "A… err, personal problem." He pointed to Gurp's groin."

"You a doctor?"

"No, no. He was just asking my opinion. Chemist and all that."

Jenny looked back and forth, between the two prisoners.

"Utter shite! I don't believe a word you say. And you…" she indicated Sanjar with a nod of her head, "must be mental. You've only got two weeks to go, and you put yourself in a position where you could be up on a charge. What an arse."

Jenny looked at them both, deciding. She spoke to Gurp. "It's your cell. You keep the door open when another prisoner is in here with you. Savvy?"

Gurp nodded.

311

"I can't hear you."

"Yes, boss."

"'Yes, Ma'am', or 'Yes, Officer Farr'."

"Yes, Ma'am."

Jenny nodded.

She turned to Sanjar. "A word, Sanjar. Outside."

Jenny entered the cell to allow Sanjar to exit through the door; she followed after giving Gurp the studious eye.

Sanjar leaned against the handrail opposite the row of cells. Jenny put her face within six-inches of his. She stood with her arms behind her back, leaning toward him.

"Screw your bloody head on. You've got a lovely partner, a beautiful kid and, like I said in there, you've only got weeks to go. Take my advice, don't mix with arseholes, and don't get caught in suspicious situations. Make yourself visible to as many officers as possible. Remember, Sanjar, there are some evil bastards in here, and they would just love to spoil that feeling of impending freedom that you're experiencing now. Understood?"

Sanjar nodded emphatically. "Yeah, yes. Absolutely. It won't happen again."

Jenny studied him for a moment. "Okay, on your way."

Jenny watched Sanjar walk off, and then turned to Gurp's cell. Again, she stood on the landing side of the doorway.

"Did you hear that, Sahid?"

"I did, Ma'am. And I agree with you."

Jenny frowned, just for a moment.

312

"And you're not going to spoil his party, are you?" she said.

"Wouldn't dream of it, Ma'am. He's one of us."

Jenny's eyes narrowed.

"Us? You a racist? Object to Whiteys and Christians do you?"

Gurp stood. Jenny tensed. Gurp's face softened. He thought for a moment.

"I used to be," he said, "but, like Sanjar it seems, I have a very good wife who sees the world better than I do. I just want to do my time and go home. I've learned a hard lesson."

Jenny watched him for a moment, and then gave him a just perceptible nod.

"That's fine. That's just the way we like it. You help me, and I'll help you."

She turned and exited the cell.

*

Brasher sat opposite Alex and watched as he scanned his file again. Brasher smiled, shook his head, and sat back in his chair. Alex spread four A4 sheets on his desk.

"Got them, sir."

Brasher sat up again, and reached across the table towards the papers.

"May I?" he said.

Alex gathered them together, and said, "Certainly, sir."

As the papers were passed to him, Brasher said, "Still rather be in the field, Alex?"

Alex grinned. "I enjoy the responsibility, the commanding, decision making, but, if you'll excuse me, sir, I'm buggered if I can see the need for all this… triplicate… filing… reporting. Anyway…"

Brasher turned to the papers and scanned the four pages. He looked up at Alex.

"In essence, Alex, in essence."

Alex nodded, breathed deeply, and then said, "In essence, I've got them both trying to get as much information as they can out of each other. They will both question each other, and whatever information they divulge to each other, will be passed on to us on solicitor's visits."

Brasher sat tight-lipped.

"This bloody caper has got me…"

He left the sentence unfinished.

Alex waited.

Brasher laid the papers down, and said, "If this imam was acting on his own behest, that's it, it's over, and everyone concerned is out of action. However, if that is true, I doubt very much that the imam was an original, he must have had a confidante, and someone very much like him is up and running somewhere else in the U.K."

Alex watched his boss, tight-lipped.

Brasher continued. "If his group was not an isolated organisation, we need…" he reached into his pocket and pulled out his pipe, " more intelligence."

He looked to Alex.

"Do you really think they will confide in each other? Tell each other more than they've told us?" said Brasher.

Alex raised his eyebrows. "If they do, sir, we're losing our grip on interrogation. However, I

314

really do feel that we have as much information as we are going to get on this particular group."

Brasher looked up from scraping the pipe bowl.

"I hope so, Alex. I bloody hope so."

Chapter Thirty-Nine

Sanjar stood on the gantry and looked across the landing. He leaned on the handrail of the gantry, with his head close to the net. The net stretched from underneath the walkway up to a centre point of the ceiling above the gap between his landing, and the landing opposite. The same net arrangement reached to the ceiling from the landing opposite, so creating a tent like feature when viewed from the floor below.

Sanjar watched Gurp as he chewed the fat with Benny Yardley. Sanjar mentally added simple, petty thief Benny, to the list of people that Gurp had befriended since arriving in Durham prison.

Satisfied that he'd seen as much as was going to be of interest to him, Sanjar walked back to his cell, picked up his towel, and headed to the showers. As he did so, another man banged up on the landing opposite, also exited his cell, also carrying his towel. He let Sanjar get ahead of him, then timed his arrival at the showerheads to be when Sanjar was undressed and washing himself down.

*

Balvindar held her baby's head close to her face, as she smiled and pointed at the camera. The camera on the tripod was a gift from Sanjar's mother, to Sanjar's father, Asad.

Balvindar sat in the sitting room of her in-laws' home; a home that was more English traditional than most other houses in the road where Sanjar's parents lived. She sat posed on the sofa,

316

which was at right-angles to the front window that looked out onto the front garden. Sunlight flooded the room, and the photographs about to be taken would light from the right, leaving the left side of Balvindar and her baby in slight shade. A Beatle shot, Asad called it.

After taking five shots, Asad uploaded the photographs to his computer, and then emailed them to Balvindar. She downloaded the images onto her iPhone. As she playfully pointed out their faces to her baby, Asad watched with interest.

He said, softly, "Your son is the son of an English boy born to Persian parents. Your son is English of English parents. He is an English boy name Khan."

Balvindar looked up at Asad. She nodded, smiling, silently acknowledging Asad's pride. Asad looked on at the baby, also with a smile on his face. He broke the spell.

"Will you be allowed to take the phone into prison, to show Sanjar the photographs?" said Asad.

"I doubt it. Maybe I should send him a print by mail. I think he will be allowed to have it. He has other photos of us."

"How long is it now, before he comes home?"

Balvindar stood and moved to a chair next to a table that contained the necessary items required to change a baby's diaper. She undid the buttons of the baby's all-in-one and began the changing process. She looked up and smiled.

"How many times have I told you, dad? Five days, five days, five days…"

317

She checked her wristwatch.

"And eighteen hours."

Asad raised his arms in a defeated gesture. "
I know, I know… my memory…

Balvindar loosened the culprit diaper
expertly and folded it, sealing the contents, before
laying it on a disinfectant sheet she pulled from a
box.

Asad returned the smile. "I know, I know.
And it's nice that you call me 'dad'. Anyway, will
you visit before then?" he said.

Balvindar talked as she carried on with the
day-to-day care of her baby. She cleaned the baby's
bottom, then laid him on the diaper, pressed the
sticky side tapes of the fresh diaper against the
diaper itself. She held the baby up in front of her,
smiling as she gently wiggled him side to side.

"That's it, my bonny baby. All fresh and
clean again."

The baby burped, and Balvindar lowered him
to her chest again. She turned to Asad.

"I'd love to visit before then, but my visiting
order is late. But, anyway, he will be home on
Friday, so, not long to wait now."

Asad stood and reached out his arms toward
Balvindar.

"Here let me hold him. You have a break,
put your feet up."

Balvindar handed over her baby to the proud
grandfather.

"And while you're doing that, if you don't
mind, I'm going to phone the prison and see if my

V.O. will come in time for a visit before Sanjar is released."

Balvindar left Asad laughing and gently stroking the baby's face and head. She went to the phone in the hall, a small six-foot by six-foot tiled area just inside the front door. She picked up the receiver, dialled the number, and pulled the telephone cable to its full extent to allow her to sit on the stairs. It took longer than normal for her call to be answered.

"Good morning. Durham Prison. May I help you?"

Balvindar stated her name, the reason for her call, and asked about her V.O., her visiting order. The receptionist, a man, asked who the V.O. related to.

"Sanjar Khan."

There was a slight pause, a beat, then Balvindar was asked to hold the line a moment. Balvindar frowned.

After a minute, another male voice came on the line. He asked Balvindar a couple of identity security questions, then told her to hold the line, again.

He returned within seconds. He was calm, measured, and extremely kind with his intonation.

"Balvindar, there has been an incident, and it may be best if you could come to the prison today, now. Would that be a problem? Are you at home, your home address?"

The request stunned Balvindar. She hesitated, frowning, thinking.

"Err... I... no. I'm at my in-laws' home... Sanjar's home... I can... err. Sorry, I'm confused... what...?"

"A police car will pick you up, Balvindar. It should be there within twenty minutes. Can you be ready for then?"

Balvindar stood, her hand on her forehead. She turned to her left, and the phone cradle crashed from the table it lay on. It fell to the floor. Asad came out of the sitting room, holding the baby, and looked at her.

"Is there something wrong?"

She still spoke into the phone. "Yes, yes, I'm ready now... anytime. What... why do I need to come to the prison?"

"I'm sorry, but that's as much as I can tell you at present. Twenty minutes. Is that okay?"

"Yes."

She let her arm drop. The phone hung loosely in her hand. She looked at Asad.

"There's something wrong. I have to go to the prison."

She stared blankly.

Asad frowned. "What did they say? What has happened?"

Balvindar closed her eyes, and shook her head. She snapped out of her lethargy.

"You'll have to come with me, Asad. There's something wrong. They're sending a police car for me. I have to go to the prison... there's been an incident."

Asad's eyes widened. He thrust the baby into Balvindar's arms.

"Hold him," he said. "I'll get Manjida. She can look after him while I come with you. Hurry. Take him."

Balvindar took the baby and hugged him to her, as Asad dashed out of the front door.

*

Alex took the phone call, as he walked away from the restaurant. He was reviewing a situation in Nottingham and had taken the opportunity to grab a small midday meal, when the man he was trailing had holed up in a mid-terrace house in the poorer part of the city. The ranger he'd left on surveillance would be fighting boredom.

Alex's meal had been an egg salad, a mediocre snack with wholemeal bread, and a cup of tea. The restaurant had been clean enough, the ambiance pleasant enough, and the staff more than willing, but the meal had been tasteless. He would not revisit the restaurant under any circumstances.

He hit the receive button on his Samsung. It was a traditional cell phone. His opinion was that iPhones and tablets were okay for youngsters, who had the time to play around. His phone was for phone calls and text messages. His company issue phone lay on the dash of his car.

He looked around him as he spoke.

"Yes, sir."

"Alex. Trouble in the north. You need to go and see our rebellious chemist."

Alex hesitated for a moment, taking in his new instructions and wondering why.

"No time for discussions, Alex. Just get there, now. Assess the situation, and contact me on my secure line. Just do it. I'll arrange cover for you in Nottingham. And thank you."

Alex tapped the 'end' button. He puzzled for a moment. Had Sanjar upset the system? Had he queered his release? Or had he remembered something of significance?

Alex calculated as he walked to his car. A journey to Durham would be at the most two to three hours. Any delays and he could command a police escort. He took out his phone again, and dialled his base office. He was brusque and brief.

"Is Tommo's time up?"

"No, sir. Two weeks left."

"Where is he now?"

"Catterick. Training recruits."

"Okay, contact him. Have him shipped to Scotch Corner service station, on the A1, for…"Alex checked his watch, "fourteen-forty five. Any problems tell him to ring me in thirty minutes. And he's to keep the call civil. Do I make myself clear?"

"Understood, sir. Thank you."

Again Alex clicked the phone off. He frowned, then, remembering what his son had said, deliberately widened his eyes. He mumbled his son's words, "Dad. Your face is beginning to look like a contour map of the Himalayas."

Alex hurried to his car.

Chapter Forty

The police car passed through the first gateway at Durham prison and drove into the secluded inner yard. A guard in the side room leaned out of the sliding window and took the details from the passenger cop. The guard waited until the exterior gate was closed, then hit the button to open the inner steel doors. Once the car had cleared, the doors were closed again, and the yard was sealed

The police were met by the deputy governor, and Balvindar and Asad exited the rear door of the car on the driver's side. Balvindar was asked to follow the D.G. to his office, while Asad was asked to have a seat in a waiting room for the moment. The police exited the prison in a reverse sequence to the one they'd used to get in.

The D.G. introduced Balvindar to the governor, and left the office. The governor leaned forward across his desk, and introduced himself as Donald Evans. He told Balvindar that she could address him as Mr. Evans; prison protocol forbad any other form of address from visitors. He wore a charcoal grey suit, a white shirt, and a red tie. His dyed black hair was beginning to thin, so, Balvindar figured, he could be approaching retirement. After offering tea or coffee - both declined, he cut to the chase.

"Balvindar, there was a disturbance today in the men's showers. We're not sure who or what started it, but at present we have your partner, Sanjar, and the other man in the prison hospital. A weapon was used, in essence a plastic toothbrush which had been formed, and sharpened, into a makeshift knife. Both Sanjar and the other man have suffered multiple stab and slash wounds, and both men have lost a lot of blood. I would emphasise, a lot of blood."

He paused, allowing Balvindar time to ask any questions.

"Will I be able to see him? Sanjar?"

Evans' eyes closed for a split second, and then he nodded.

"The reason you were brought in, Balvindar, is that on examining Sanjar, the prison doctor recommended that you be informed immediately, and, if possible, be allowed to see him."

Again, Evans paused. Balvindar remained silent.

"Do you understand… what I'm saying, Balvindar?

Still Balvindar did not speak.

"Balvindar, Sanjar has lost quite a bit of blood."

Balvindar stared at him. Evans stood, and walked around to her side of the desk. He put his hand on her shoulder.

"Come on. Let me take you to him."

Balvindar remained seated. "Why isn't he in hospital?" she said. "He… you need to get him…"

Evans removed his hand. He thought for a moment, and then said, "Balvindar, Sanjar's wounds, injuries, did not require major surgery. We have all his medical records on file, his blood group etcetera. Now, for whatever reason, every out of the ordinary occurrence with Sanjar must be reported to a government department in London. Those same people in London decided, after speaking with the prison doctor, that we had more than enough of what was needed for his injuries, here in the prison. We have had a visit from a specialist, and he was quite happy with Sanjar's treatment. Now, are you happy with the reasoning?"

Balvindar nodded, and then stood.

Balvindar was taken on a route which avoided prisoners, and cells, eventually arriving at the medical ward, via the back door. Sanjar was in a room just big enough for the bed he lay in, the chair next to his bed and the drip rack holding up the life sustaining liquid dripping from it. Balvindar, Evans, and a prison guard, entered quietly. Evans pulled up the chair for Balvindar. She stared at Sanjar. A female nurse entered. Balvindar turned to her.

"Can he hear me?" said Balvindar.

The nurse smiled kindly.

"He's sleeping. He was conscious when we received him, but he'd lost a lot of blood. He's very weak."

Balvindar turned defiantly to Evans.

"I'm not leaving until he wakes up"

He nodded.

"You can stay as long is necessary, Balvindar. Don't worry yourself on that account."

Balvindar repeated herself unnecessarily. "I mean it, I'm not."

She turned to Sanjar. She watched as his chest rose and flattened. She looked to the slow drip of the liquid. She saw wounds in his shoulder, and turned back to Evans.

"How much blood did he loose?

Evans looked to the nurse, and she raised her eyebrows. He nodded.

"It sounds a lot, but we've had worse..." the nurse began to say.

"How much?" demanded Balvindar

The nurse paused for a moment, and then checked the notes on the clipboard hanging from the end of the bed by a broad elastic bank. She looked kindly, smiling, at Balvindar as she spoke.

"We estimate early four pints, but like I say-"

Balvindar gasped, her left hand going to her mouth. She held up her right hand, halting the nurse. The nurse stopped, paused a moment, then let the clipboard swing back on its elastic band. She waited a moment, and then left the room.

Balvindar turned back to Sanjar, tears flowing down her cheeks.

*

Ninety minutes later, Alex pulled up in front of the car park at the Scotch Corner service station. He cruised the alleys, and then spotted Tommo in his car. He pulled alongside as Tommo, stepped out of the car. Tommo was dressed casually; polo shirt, jeans, and highly polished black leather shoes. He slung a small rucksack on his back and walked over to Alex. Alex reached across and opened the front passenger door. Tommo stooped to look in the car as he spoke.

"Would you like a break, sir? I drive, you brief me?"

Alex nodded, as he applied the hand brake, but left the engine running.

"Yes, of course - makes sense."

The two men swopped positions, and Tommo slung his bag onto the back seat, as he sat behind the wheel. Thirty seconds later he was back on the A1M, and speeding to Durham Prison. He covered the distance in twenty-two minutes, and ten minutes after entering the prison, they approached the room where Sanjar lay.

Balvindar turned to look as they entered the room. She stood, startled. Her mouth opened, then she remembered. She did not speak. Alex showed his Home Office badge to Evans. Evans frowned, and then Alex watched anger show on his face.

"Is this necessary?" asked Evans

"I'm afraid so, Governor Evans…"

"Donald, please. We both work for the same company."

"I'm afraid so, Donald. And we need some privacy; first of all with you, then with Balvindar and Sanjar. Can we find somewhere private?"

Donald grimaced, shrugged, and indicated the door with his open hand.

"Of course. There's an empty hospital bedroom along the corridor. Just turn right."

Alex turned to Balvindar. He smiled kindly as he spoke.

"He's a fighter, Balvindar. Remember that. He's a fighter."

She returned the smile, and looked to Sanjar.

327

Alex and Tommo followed Governor Evans to the room indicated. Evans offered the chair to Alex, while he sat on the freshly made up bed. Tommo leaned against the closed door.

"Who did the knife… toothbrush, belong to, Donald?" asked Alex.

"The other man, Victor Lewis. Well, we're checking that but Khan does have a toothbrush in his mug in his cell, Lewis doesn't."

"Tell us about Lewis, please."

Evans grimaced, and opened his arms to Alex.

"Nothing out of the ordinary. He's a career criminal. He's aged thirty-five, and doing his third stretch, not counting his time in correction centres as a youth. Up until his last sentence, he'd never used violence. He stuck to petty crime, shoplifting, burglary, but his last conviction was for robbery with violence. However, since he arrived, he's been a model prisoner."

"Religion?" asked Tommo.

"Well, none that I know of. But, he's Welsh, white, so, he'll have had some religious education at school. If he went to school, that is."

"Do you have a Muslim group in the prison?"

"We do, but not a gang. It's just that minorities, or like-minded people, tend to group up. Men from Newcastle stick with others from Newcastle, just as Londoners stick together."

"So, do you have a Welsh mob? Or was he just a loner?"

"A drifter, according to the officers. He simply mixed with anyone who would allow him into their company."

Alex scribbled on a note pad for a few moments, and then looked up to Tommo.

"Any questions, Tommo?"

"Was Khan close to any of the prison officers? Did he take anyone into his confidence? And ditto Lewis."

Evans nodded, and leaned his forearms on his thighs.

"Yes, Khan was close to Officer Farr. She tends to keep an eye on most prisoners due for release. She tries to prevent them from cocking it up in the last few days. You know, minor infringements which could delay their release. It's part kindness, and part efficiency on her part. We don't want anyone here longer than necessary."

"And Lewis?" said Tommo.

Evans' eyebrows rose. "Well, his original sentence was five years; he's served two, so he could have been out in six months, more or less... If he pulls through this, he's looking at a lot longer-"

Alex interrupted. He stood as he spoke. "You're basing that on the assumption that Sanjar didn't start the fight."

Tommo turned to Alex, frowning.

Evans was quick to respond.

"Oh, we know he didn't. Another prisoner walked into the showers, just as Lewis, quote, 'launched himself at Sanjar', unquote."

"Who was the other prisoner?" asked Tommo.

"The other one of our, your, special prisoners."

Alex and Tommo all but spoke in unison as they said, "Gurp Sahid?"

Evans nodded.

"Was he alone?" asked Tommo.

Chapter Forty-One

Sanjar's eyes opened, barely – a slit. He looked straight ahead, down the bed – nothing. He lazily looked out of the corner of his eyes, to his right, and saw Balvindar – she was sleeping. He knew why she was there. He was even surprised himself that he'd regained conscious. He stared at the ceiling.

Sanjar thought on what had happened, and then he checked his body. First, a slight movement of his neck, then a more pronounced slight rotation in one plane – no problem. He moved his shoulders, and felt a twinge where his left shoulder joined his arm. That would be where he had raised his arm to protect himself from the first stab. He squirmed, the muscles in his back moving - no pain. He tensed his stomach muscles, and the pain shot through him. White lightning pain that clenched the muscles of his arse, and shut his eyes. His mouth opened involuntarily, to scream, he stifled it, growling deep in his throat.

He used his right arm to raise the loose linen bed sheet, and looked down his torso. He saw seven large white pads, held down by medical tape. He estimated the pads to be maybe four inches square. The pads were stained with blood.

Sanjar closed his eyes for a moment, then opened them blinking. What time was it? What day was it? There was a window to his left, but that looked out on to a corridor. He listened. The prison was quiet, he thought; well, quieter than it would be if it was daytime. Was it evening, or the middle of the night, or early morning?

He licked his lips and tried to sit up. The pain in his stomach gripped him again. He lay back, thinking.

He remembered Lewis walking into the showers and greeting him. He also remembered Lewis returning the greeting; a normal day in the showers. He thought on. Then a shout, 'Sanjar!' He'd thought it was a shout from Lewis and he'd turned to him, just in time to raise his left arm to block the stabbing movement. Lewis was quick, almost frenzied. Sanjar remembered the stabbing movements to his unprotected stomach as he grabbed his injured arm.

Balvindar stirred, and Sanjar rolled his head on the pillow. He watched her, a loving smile forming on his face. Her mouth was open; she was dribbling, her head resting on her chest. Her arms were folded across her breasts.

He rolled his head again, again staring at the ceiling, thinking, and remembering again.

He remembered going down onto the tiled floor of the shower room, and his shower raining water down on him. He remembered seeing his blood being washed down the drain. But, where was Lewis in the picture in his mind?

Sanjar hadn't struck a blow. He had not pushed Lewis away, but he did remember Lewis shouting at someone, and he did remember blood flowing toward him from where Lewis had stood. He licked his lips again, and the voice cut through his thoughts.

"Thirsty? Would you like some water?"

Sanjar turned and saw Balvindar smiling at him. She pulled her chair nearer and stroked his arm

"How are you feeling?" she said.

He closed his eyes for a moment, as he said, "Thankful. I seem to remember a lot of blood." He licked his lips again. "What day is it? How long have I been out? Do Mum and Dad know about this?"

Sanjar paused for a moment, as he looked at Balvindar, waiting.

"Are you going to tell me?" he asked. "What did the doctor say? What are my injuries, and how much blood did I lose?"

"No, I'm not going to tell you. You'll find out soon enough when you're up on your feet." She grinned. "By the looks of it you're alive, and you're gonna live. That's all that matters. You've been out for nearly…" she checked her watch, "eighteen hours. And your dad was here, in the waiting room, until five last night. He's home now, so, yes, you can take it that your mum knows"

They looked at each other, happy for a moment, then Balvindar dropped the smile. "Why did he do it, Sanjar? Has it anything to do with the… group, and what you did, or didn't do?"

Sanjar rolled his head. He spoke languidly, softly. "Never spoke to him before. Well, nodded a greeting as we've passed each other, but that was it. I know he is called Lewis, and he's Welsh."

"Is he one of us?"

"What?"

"A Muslim. Is he a Muslim?"

333

Sanjar chuckled. "One of us lot."

"Us lot? What do you mean by that?"

"Where I was, where I was hiding. Remember? Billy the Bow? He once referred to us as 'your lot' and I pulled him for it."

Sanjar's eyes closed for a moment. He raised his right arm, limply. "Give me a second, will you?" he said. He turned to look out of the window, into the corridor. He stared for a while, frowning, thinking. He turned back to Balvindar.

"You need to contact Alex. Tell-"

"They're here... well, they were, up till about four-o-clock yesterday."

Sanjar lay back, suddenly drained.

"Sorry, love," he said, quietly. "I've got to sleep again. I'm whacked. Get yourself away home, I'm all right now."

He shut his eyes, and Balvindar stood by the side of the bed. She leaned over and kissed him on the forehead. She stroked Sanjar's hair, and waited until his breathing was regular and even. She backed out of the room on her tiptoes.

Balvindar closed the door behind her, and looked to her right, along the corridor to where a nurse sat writing on a desk in the glow of night light. She reported Sanjar being awake for a few moments, before drifting back off to sleep. The nurse frowned, a cleft forming between her eyes.

"You should have told me, contacted me immediately. There are signs we need to look for and tests that should be done immediately when he is conscious."

She reached for the phone. Balvindar listened.

"Good morning, sir. Khan has just regained consciousness while his partner was at his bedside. Unfortunately she didn't inform me." Pause. "I'm going to do that now, sir. Yes, and then I'll give him an hour then try to wake him again. No, no, sir. Yes. Thank you.

"I don't know who you are, or what connections your husband has, but you're to be given a bed, in a separate room, if you'd like to have a few hours shut-eye. Or you can doze by his bedside. Apparently people are being notified that your... that Khan is conscious, and they will probably be here to see him later."

Balvindar nodded, and flicked her hands up in a 'that's to be expected' gesture. She looked around.

"Is the other man in this area? The man who... did the damage... to Sanjar."

The nurse gathered up her paperwork, shook them and tapped them on the desk. Satisfied with the neatness of the pile she had created, she placed it in a folder, and then stood.

"Sorry, even if I could tell you – I wouldn't."

Balvindar breathed deeply, sighed heavily, and said, "Well, how is he? Can you tell me that?"

The nurse frowned again. "How is he? Hasn't anyone..." She studied Balvindar for a moment, deciding. "Sorry. You need to talk to someone else about that."

"Well can I use the phone, to phone Sanjar's parents? Tell them he's pulled through."

The nurse lifted the handset, handed it to Balvindar, and said, "Nine for a line then dial your number."

She brushed past Balvindar.

Chapter Forty-Two

Alex watched from the corridor as the prison doctor checked out Sanjar. Sanjar was sitting up, backing against two pillows propped on end to the bed-head. His eyes opened wide in mock alarm as the doctor inserted a needle then took a blood sample.

"Can I afford that, doctor?" he asked

The doctor grinned, "Don't ask me, I only work here."

Sanjar beckoned to Alex. He raised his voice.

"Come in. I haven't got anything contagious, and you've seen everything I've got."

Alex stood back from the bed as the doctor finished his work, chatted with Sanjar, filled in the forms on the clipboard which hung on the bottom of the bed, and then left.

Alex sat, and dropped the good humour. "Problems," he said. "He's dead. The man who attacked you, he's dead."

Sanjar's head flopped back against the pillows, his eyes closed, and he groaned.

"For all he did to me, I'm sorry. I can't hate him. I'm angry, but I would not wish him to die."

Sanjar reflected for a moment.

Alex grimaced, paused for a moment for Sanjar's benefit, and then opened his brief case. He shuffled papers, peeked into folders, and then took out a notepad and pen.

"The problem is - who killed Lewis?"

Sanjar's eyes snapped open. He frowned.

"Who? Well as far as I remember, there was only one other person in the showers when he attacked me."

"Yep, true. But our friend Gurp does not have a mark on him. Not a bump, bruise, nick, cut or slash."

"And? So what?"

Alex sat forward in his chair.

"You're obviously not getting this. Lewis is dead, stabbed repeatedly. Now, he sure as hell didn't stab himself. And you, by all accounts, were out of it, trying to plug the holes in your stomach. That was verified by Gurp Sahid."

Sanjar shuffled, trying to sit more upright. He winced, and touched his stomach, gently.

"Yes, but surely... self defence. You can't charge the man with murder. He was saving me, protecting me."

Alex sat back, his mouth downturned, as he studied Sanjar.

"There were two men in the showers along with you. Luke Thompson, three along to your left, and then Sahid, when he entered."

Alex paused, Sanjar shrugged. Alex leaned forward again.

"Thompson's statement says he shouted, you reacted by raising your arm, then before he could get to you, Lewis had done the damage. Thompson apparently got one on Lewis, a good punch, took the knife off him, and then defended himself by threatening Lewis with the knife. He said that it was then, and then only, that Sahid came to life. Sahid apparently ran over to Thompson, told him to get help, while he, Sahid, attended to you. Thompson says he gave Sahid the knife and that he, Thompson, never touched Lewis with the knife, merely threatened him."

Sanjar turned away from Alex. His mouth opened as if he was about to speak, then he turned back to Alex.

"I can see why you're here, and where you're going with this," said Sanjar

Alex paused, leaving Sanjar time to think on.

"Sahid says Lewis started to come at him," said Alex. "But, how tall is Gurp Sahid? Six-feet? Six-feet two? And how tall was Lewis? Five-eight, if that. And the weight advantage? Gurp by what? Twenty pounds?"

Sanjar nodded slowly.

"Facts," said Alex. "Gurp had the blade. Thompson says so, and Gurp does not deny it. Now, put yourself in Lewis' shoes. What would you do if faced with someone who had the height and weight advantage, and was also holding a knife?"

Sanjar remained silent, lips tight shut. He waited for Alex to go on.

"Would you rush onto his blade – five times?" said Alex.

"Well, if Lewis was having a go, Gurp was maybe just jabbing, trying to keep him at bay? Lewis had nothing to lose. He didn't know if I was going to live or die."

"Umm. You really think so? I doubt it very much."

Sanjar shuffled again, trying to sit more upright. His face reddened with the effort. Alex held out his palm to Sanjar.

"Don't bother. Relax; I'm finished for the moment."

Sanjar's eyes near closed as he struggled to remember. He remembered... he remembered the figure spinning Lewis around and one punch being thrown – at Lewis's jar, but.... He turned to Alex again.

"Look, don't go. You must trust me," said Sanjar. "I'm bloody working for you. Tell me... what you're thinking? What are you not telling me?"

Alex sat back again, crossed his right leg over his left, and then crossed his arms. He still held the pad and pen in his right hand.

"Gurp slashed at Lewis' throat. He said he did. He said it was instinct. He said that the little training he'd had from that imam... came to the fore. He was frightened; he just wanted to stop Lewis."

"Oh Fuck!" Sanjar stared, eyes narrowed. "Basic instinct, maybe. Fight or flight."

"Fuck off, Sanjar. You don't believe that. Maybe it was to make sure the failed assassin couldn't talk," said Alex.

"That's stupid. Why save me to kill the assassin? Why not just let the assassin complete the job?"

"But he didn't save you, did he. Thompson said Sahid didn't react until he'd floored Lewis."

Sanjar lay back against the pillow again. He rubbed his face with his right hand.

"Conclusions?" he said.

Alex lifted his briefcase, flicked it open, and put in his notepad. He put his pen into his inside jacket pocket, then stood, looking down on Sanjar.

"It isn't over, Sanjar. It isn't over. They got to Sahid somehow, and he recruited that lone Welsh man."

Sanjar rolled his head to look at Alex.

"Great." he said.

He shuffled for a moment, irritated, then growled. He turned to Alex.

"Can you help me? Prop me up?"

Alex laid his briefcase on the floor. Moved toward Sanjar, and then stopped. "On second thoughts, maybe not. I'll get the nurse for you. She knows what she's doing. Don't want to damage you, do we?"

He reached to the wall and pulled the cord. Sanjar lay back.

"What was Gurp's reaction to your accusation?" said Sanjar.

"Oh no. That intelligence, opinion, call it what you will, is for certain person's ears only. You're not included – at present."

Both men thought for a moment, as Alex paced the floor. The nurse arrived and Alex stood to one side as she got Sanjar upright and comfortable. Once Sanjar was happy, and, after offering Alex a drink of tea or coffee, which he declined, she left.

Sanjar groaned. "It's a mess, isn't it? This will never be over. You've underestimated the group, and its connections."

Alex thought for a moment, and then said, "Give me a moment, will you?

He picked up his briefcase, laid it on the bed, and clicked it open. He took out his pad, retrieved his pen from his inside pocket, and then began to scribble.

"I think you may be wrong in your assessment... of Gurp," said Sanjar.

Alex made an absentminded sound, and Sanjar continued.

"I've been with him for nearly a week now, and I honestly don't think he's turned back to the cause. Something's going on; someone's putting the pressure on him, or his family. It's got to be his family... under threat. I know the bloke, and I don't think he wants to get mixed up with terrorism ever again."

Alex looked up.

"Would you stake your life on it?" he asked.

"I would not stake my life on anything."

Alex nodded.

"Of course you wouldn't. But the fact is someone is after you... wants revenge. Who is it? Who have we missed? Who do we not know about? Or who have we forgotten?"

Sanjar shook his head, slowly.

"I don't even know who was in the group," he said. "I had limited contact. All they wanted out of me was explosive devices. I met the Imam, and the men close to him, in the mosque. Outside the mosque I met no one."

Alex spoke as he turned toward the door.

"You need rest, Sanjar. Don't rush things. We're still hunting, so you just concentrate on getting better."

"Am I still being released on Friday?"

"As soon as you feel well enough, you will be released. So, get your rest, let your body heal."

"And after that? When I'm home? Will I be safe there?"

Alex turned back to him.

"In the business you got yourself involved in, is anyone ever safe?"

He stared at Sanjar. Sanjar closed his eyes, and lay back.

Chapter Forty-Three

Three days later

Kenny McDonald watched as the visitor sat opposite the prisoner. He had not seen the visitor before, but he looked harmless enough. Kenny looked around the visitor's room and saw the usual faces. Wives, girlfriends, mothers, fathers, brothers, sisters, and friends.

He watched as the same visitor looked to his left to two tables away, and locked eyes with Gurp for a moment. Both men turned away, which in itself was unusual. With men in prison, either both men would stare, defying the other, or one man would immediately back away from eye contact.

Kenny checked the visitor's log. He noted in the comments column that an Abdul Badour appeared to make minor eye contact with Gurp Sahid. A simple comment, but Gurp was under constant surveillance and anything, but anything, out of the common place was to be recorded.

Gurp's visitor was his wife.

"You look tired," she said.

Gurp give her a 'what do you expect?' look.

She bowed her head and looked to her intermingled fingers on the table.

"I'm sorry," she said

Gurp sighed, resigned, closed his eyes and shook his head.

"It's not your fault. You did not bring these people to our door."

Silence reigned for a few moments.

"Is there any way out for you, us? How can they still get to you in prison?"

Gurp gave her another withering look.

"They will not give up until he is dead. They still believe he is to blame for the capture of all the other men," he said

"And you?"

Gurp thought for a moment.

"You need to know something," he said.

He studied his wife, as if deciding, and then a slight nod of his head. He looked around, again at Badour, watching him deep in conversation with another Asian man from Leeds. And, from his viewpoint, again Kenny McDonald made another note in his comments book. Gurp leaned over the table toward his wife.

"I've been helping the government," he whispered.

His wife had a sharp intake of breath, and her hand went to her mouth. Gurp waited a moment, before continuing.

"They got the confession out of me, and then I turned. I did it for me, and for you. Me for a shorter sentence, and you, I thought, to make your life safer. I knew evil bastards would come after me, but I didn't expect the threats they've made. I lied to you. It is not your life that they threatened me with. It is the lives of our children."

His wife covered her mouth again, but she did not stifle the cry. People around looked at her, and Abdul Badour frowned. Something was up.

345

Gurp reached across and lowered his wife's hand to the table. He gripped both her hands, and smiled.

"Don't worry. I have a plan. They won't harm you. Trust me," said Gurp.

His wife stared at him, alarmed.

"What are you going to do? How the hell can you fight these people on your own?"

"Don't worry; it'll all be sorted shortly. They won't harm the children, I promise you."

His wife smiled weakly.

*

Brasher watched the tourists in the Mall from his office viewpoint. He peered under the half-down blackout blind. Alex waited for Brasher's opinion and questions. Brasher turned, and smiled.

"They say that not even one percent of the Chinese have visited Britain, and yet you look out there… anyway, who is tailing him, this Badour. And why did it take so long for someone to figure out that he was the driver of the vehicle which blocked the motorway, causing the prison van to divert? That was the start of this whole damned escapade."

Alex thought for a moment. "Yes, sir. That part of the investigation is being gone over as we talk."

"And who is tailing him now?"

"Tommo, and four others," said Alex.

"Tommo?

"He still has four days left to serve, sir."

"Getting your money's worth, eh. He's a bloody good man, we'll miss him. Has anyone talked to him, tried to change his mind?" said Brasher.

"Indeed, sir, including me, but, he's adamant. However, he's also sad. He'll miss his mates of course, but I think the woman, Sue, outweighs his mates."

Brasher took out his pipe, and then sat at his desk. For all the heat of the day, Alex noted that Brasher still had his suit jacket on. One of the old school.

"So, Alex, are you still content to let Sahid have free rein, bearing in mind the fact that he's of no use to us now, is he?"

"He's not, sir, but I've left him going through the motions of being a prisoner while we track Badour."

"Has anyone tried to contact Sahid, or his wife?" said Brasher

"The day after the prison visit, when Badour was identified, Badour telephoned Sahid's wife from a mobile. He threatened her. I believe it was a repeat of what he'd been threatening Gurp with before we realised what was happening. She broke down, sobbed… anyway, as Sanjar is now free, I feel they are simply keeping Gurp on tenterhooks until he is released. But, in the meantime, I also feel that Sanjar is in great danger."

As Alex had talked, Brasher had scraped and cleaned his pipe. He'd ummed at the appropriate places as Alex talked, and then looked up when his pipe was freshly loaded. He stood again, walked to the window, raised the lower sash, and then lit his pipe. As he puffed and held the pipe in his left hand, he rolled the blind up by the continuous looped pull-cord with his right hand.

He spoke as he looked down on the Mall again.

"He'll be in danger for the rest of his life, unless those who matter can be convinced he hasn't turned. Do you think he is aware of that?"

Alex cocked his head, and raised an eyebrow.

"I would say so, sir. He's an intelligent lad. And you can bet that the thought has also crossed Balvindar's mind."

Brasher turned and leaned against the wall to the right of the window. He had his arms crossed with the stem of the pipe toward the gap created by the raised sash.

"There's an old saying," said Brasher. "'Ex-thieves make the best coppers.' What do you think?"

Alex raised his right palm to his forehead. He sighed, and then placed his elbow on the arm of the chair. He cupped his chin, thought for a moment, and then looked to Brasher.

"Fact, sir. Sanjar wanted out of the organisation, hence the childish robbery. I don't think he was scared of the consequences of being caught, I think he really did develop a conscience, a sense of justice and right and wrong"

He lifted his head from his cupped palm.

"Fact, sir. They did not know that Sanjar was responsible for the breakdown of the group, they've guessed, presuming. We need to convince them otherwise."

Before Alex could expand any further, the telephone on Brasher's desk rang. Brasher moved to the desk, placed his pipe on a coaster, and picked up the phone.

"Brasher."

He frowned at Alex.

"Yes, put him through."

He pressed the scramble button on the receiver.

"Hello, James. Yes, of course. Oh dear, oh dear. Yes, yes, of course... err on second thoughts James, could we make it later this evening. I may have some good news for you by then. Thank you, yes, of course. Goodbye."

Brasher lay the phone down on its unit, kept his hand on it for a moment, as he stared at the desk pad, then looked up to Alex.

"Problems, old chum," said Brasher. "You need to visit Durham Prison again, as soon as possible. Now."

Alex shrugged.

"Of course, sir. A one man job, or do I need assistance?"

Brasher smiled, briefly, then frowned.

"Take your sidekick with you. Give him something interesting to do in his last few days," he said.

Chapter Forty-Four

Tommo looked around the cell. Nothing looked out of place, no signs of a struggle. No splashes of blood. He turned to Officer Farr.

"Who found him, Jenny?"

"Yours truly,"

"How did it come about, how did you discover the body?" asked Alex.

"This morning, at wake-up. Looked though the glass, there he was, hanging"

Alex moved around the small cell, looking for anything out of the ordinary. Nothing showed. He was happy with his preliminary investigation, and the prison's reports; it was suicide. In his opinion Gurp Sahid had taken his own life, however, the police investigation would confirm or otherwise.

Once again, Alex studied the photos of Gurp's wife and family hanging on the wall. The largest photograph was an ordinary family group shot, with the eldest boy, aged about fifteen, holding up a two fingered V, palm facing, behind who looked like his younger brother. Everyone in the photograph looked happy enough.

"The letter he left, who has it now? I was promised it on arrival," said Alex

"Locked up in the governor's office, sir. And the local police are none too happy about it," said Tommo.

Alex thought for a moment, frowning. "Yes, and I think I would be slightly pissed if I was in their shoes."

Alex then spoke to Jenny as he continued to look around Gurp's cell.

"I think we've seen enough, Jenny. Can we go now? I really need to see this letter. You seen enough, Tommo?"

Tommo grimaced, and then nodded. Jenny stood to one side as the two men exited the cell. She followed, locking the steel door behind her.

The landing was deserted; lock-down was the rule after a suicide. Other prison officers could be seen making rudimentary checks of other cells, as Jenny, Alex and Tommo passed by.

In the governor's office, Jenny reported briefly, and then left Alex and Tommo to their business with Evans. They relaxed into their respective chairs as Evans all but cleared his desk.

"I'm yours, gentlemen. And forgive me if I say that I'm glad to be free of those two gentlemen... your special charges. I'm sorry about Sahid's problems, and the family he left behind, but... we choose the path we take."

"I understand what you're saying," said Alex, "but most definitely do not agree with the sentiment" He studied Evans for a moment, then continued. "Anyway, the letter. We need it in our possession when we leave... today. Who has it at this precise moment?"

Evans reached into a drawer at the right hand side of his desk. He pulled out a small folder, opened it, and showed the letter in point; Gurp's last words. He handed it to Alex

Alex read the letter, shook his head, and turned to Tommo.

"I don't know if I feel sorry for him or not." Tommo shrugged.

Alex stood, and held out his hand to Evans.

"Okay, fine," he said. "Unless there's anything you need from us, we'll be on our way."

Evans stood, shook hands with Alex, and said, "Have a safe journey."

*

As Tommo negotiated the narrow streets of Durham City, Alex repeatedly tapped his pen on his briefcase and looked around him at nothing in particular. Tommo cursed the narrow streets as pedestrians squeezed between the car and the buildings either side of him. Minutes later, Tommo exited the old part of the city centre, and headed toward the A1.

As they neared the top of the hill on the west side of the city, Alex indicated for Tommo to pull over at a public phone box. Tommo slowed to a stop as Alex scanned the road. Satisfied, he reached for the handle of the passenger door.

"Sorry, Tommo, Private call."

" 'Course, sir. And please pass on my good wishes to Commander Brasher."

Alex smiled, turned to Tommo, and said, "You're gonna be a bloody big miss. You know that, don't you?"

Tommo grinned. "There's always consultancy work, sir. As and when."

Alex, still smiling, exited the car.

He got through to Brasher in one minute. He waited until Brasher cleared the call to go ahead, and then reported his findings.

"No doubt about it, sir. Suicide. I have the letter."

"Excellent. Right, you have one more call before you head back. I want you to see Sahid's wife. I want you to give her the letter, to read, but emphasise we need it for security purposes for two days only. Do not let her take any copies whatsoever. None. No scanning, no copying, no photographing."

"Sir, I-"

"And I apologise if you think I'm treating you like an idiot, Alex, but I can't emphasise enough how important that letter is to us at present. Can you see the woman, and still make it back before nine tonight?"

Alex checked his wrist watch, and said, "Yes, sir. Without doubt."

"Good man. I'll explain everything when we meet. Good luck."

Alex heard the click ending the conversation, before he had time to say 'Goodbye'.

He slid back into the car, and Tommo twisted on his seat, waiting for instructions. Alex lifted his briefcase off the back seat and took out a file. Tommo watched in silence.

"What I'm after is Sahid's address. We have to show his wife his letter, then get to London as quickly as possible."

"Shit! My car, sir. It's still at Scotch Corner."

"Pool car?"

Tommo nodded, reaching for his mobile phone under the dashboard. As Alex searched for

Sahid's address, Tommo issued instructions to have his car collected from the Scotch Corner Service Station car park.

His reply to the question of where were the keys, was, "Fuck off. You're army."

*

Seventy-five minutes later, Tommo pulled up at what was Gurp's home. He secured the car by the hand brake and left it in gear, as Alex once again retrieved Gurp Sahid's folder from his briefcase.

Alex stepped out of the car and took in the surroundings, as Tommo exited and locked the car with the remote fob. It was a street of terraced houses. Here and there groups of people stood around front doors, and spilled out onto the pavement. More than a few of what he took to be elderly residents were dressed in traditional sub-continent dress, the young ones wore typical western style – jeans, T-shirt, and trainers.

He knocked on the door to Gurp's house. The door was opened by an elderly lady, again in traditional eastern dress, who had obviously been crying, and still looked distressed. Alex introduced himself and asked to see Aadilah. The door was opened wider to allow access and Alex and Tommo stepped in, into the front room. The front room was furnished in a typical British style. A grey cord-covered three-piece suite to the side and, in front of a faux granite fireplace, a forty-two inch television complete with the Sky plus box, and the DVD player set under the T.V. stand, near the window onto the street, and a standard lamp set between one of the armchairs and the sofa. Photographs and cheap prints hung around the wall, and the floor was covered with a light-blue fitted carpet.

Aadilah sat with her youngest child on the sofa. She was dressed in a summer frock, just below knee length, scoop neck and sleeveless. She looked up as Alex entered. Behind Alex and Tommo the elderly lady shouted to Aadilah in Urdu.

Aadilah sighed. "In English, Mum. They're guests."

She turned to Alex. "She says you're from the prison."

"Not exactly, Mrs Sahid, but we are government officials."

Aadilah looked at Tommo. "He's not an office worker."

Alex said, "May we sit, Mrs Sahid?"

"Sure, and my name is Aadilah, but you'll already know that, won't you."

Alex sat.

Tommo smiled kindly, and said, "I'll stand, if you don't mind. I've been driving for over an hour."

Aadilah turned to her mother. "Sit down Mother, please. You make the room look untidy."

She looked at Alex, weighing him up. "So, why are you here? You haven't come all this way to offer your condolences, and you're not here to take me to the prison. The man who rang said a taxi would collect me at four–o–clock."

Alex shrugged. "Your right, Aadilah, but I will say for all his crimes, I am sad that Gurp's life ended in the manner that it did."

Aadilah nodded, barely perceptible.

355

Alex held up the folder containing the file on Gurp.

"You seem a strong person, Aadilah, but…"

Alex indicated with his head to the child sitting next to Aadilah. Aadilah turned to her mother.

"Mother, take Abeer up to her room for a few minutes, will you?"

Abeer began to protest, but the grandmother guided the child by her shoulders out of the room. Aadilah looked to Alex again.

"I'll say it as it is, Aadilah. Gurp left a letter. It's very emotional, it is truthful, and I'm delivering it to you. However, as you know, the crime that Gurp was involved in was a threat to National Security. The letter that he left you has to go with me to London today. It will be returned to you within a few days, possibly tomorrow. I'm to let you read it, but in my presence, However, it will be your property and in your hands for good, as I say, within a couple of days."

Alex opened the folder, took out the original letter, and handed it over to Aadilah. He noticed that she set her jaw as she unfolded the single lined A4 page.

Alex and Tommo looked around the room, and then at each other in turn as she read. There were no tears, just moist eyes.

"Have you read it?" she said.

Alex nodded. "Of course."

"I won't have it," she said, emphatically. "He's not transferring the guilt to me. He says he did it to take the pressure off me, the threats. Well it's not that easy. He brought the trouble to our door the minute he got mixed up with that… I don't want the letter returned. You can keep it."

Alex hung his head. He thought for a moment then looked up to Aadilah again.

"We have a problem. They will be in touch again, Aadilah. It will be someone you've never seen before. It could be a door-to-door salesman. It could be someone you bump into at the shops, on the school run. It… well, do you get the picture?"

She nodded. "I figured that much."

"Good. However, when they do get in touch with you, we'd like you to hand over Gurp's letter to them. As simple as that. Can you do that, Aadilah? Once you do, I believe that you'll never see them, or us, again. Do you understand?"

She nodded. "Yeah. Now, can you leave me? I'm trying to figure out how to bring up four kids without a father and an income."

"I'll have someone come to see you, if that's okay with you. She's a good girl. I think she'll be able to help you."

Aadilah held up a 'thank you' hand. Alex stood and Tommo shouldered himself from the wall he was leaning against.

Twenty minutes later, they were driving south on the M1.

Chapter Forty-Five

Tommo sat with the engine running. He watched as tourists sauntered along the Mall, towards Cleveland Row and St. James' Street. He studied the interior rear-view mirror as the traffic warden slowly edged towards him, checking the cars behind him.

He did not give the warden time to speak. He simply flashed his identity card, and smiled. The warden nodded, and moved on.

At the top of the stairs, beyond the door in front of which Tommo parked, Alex turned right and entered the outer office of Brasher's department. Alice greeted him courteously, smiled politely, and used the intercom to inform Brasher of Alex's arrival. Alex was ushered through to Brasher immediately.

As Alex entered his superior's office, Brasher was puffing rapidly on a freshly lit pipe. Brasher grunted a greeting to Alex, as he sucked the pipe into life. He then moved to the window, and performed the last of his five times daily ritual. The sash window was lifted to three quarters open, and the blackout blind lowered halfway. He turned back to Alex, as he checked his watch.

"Well done, Alex. Excellent timing. You must be gasping for a drink."

Brasher walked to his desk, and then pressed his public intercom.

"Alice. Tea for two, please. And biscuits, chocolate digestives, if you will. Thank you."

As Brasher talked, Alex half sorted his briefcase. He looked up as Brasher sat at his desk, "Tommo's outside, sir. Could something be sent down to him? He's driven all the way without a stop."

Brasher replied in the affirmative, and passed on Tommo's request. He held out his hand to Alex, and indicated with his head.

"And now, Alex, if you would? The letter please."

Alex handed it over. He then put his briefcase on the floor to his side. He sat patiently as Brasher read it, making sounds at the back of his throat as he did so. Brasher took a magnifying glass from a drawer in the right-hand side of his desk. He scanned the paper. He scanned the writing, and he scanned the blank reverse side of the lined A4 sheet. He mumbled as he studied the letter.

Brasher continued examining the letter for a few moments then looked up to Alex, smiling. He placed the spyglass back into the open draw, and then closed it.

"Cold blooded bastard, wasn't he? You've read the letter of course?" said Brasher.

"Of course, sir."

"Factual, cold, trying to justify his unforgivable actions," said Brasher.

He studied Alex for a moment, and then threw up his hands.

"So, here's the plan. We shoot this letter over to the chaps on the south side of the river, along with a second page that I'll compose. They'll get a handwriting person onto it, match up the paper, and the ink, and we should have it ready for you to deliver by tomorrow morning. Have you got somewhere to stay tonight?"

"We'll book in somewhere, sir. It won't be a problem."

Brasher reached for the intercom and spoke as he pressed the button.

"I'm sure you could, but we need you somewhere local. I want that letter back in Yorkshire as soon as the ink dries."

Alice's voice came through the intercom. "Sir?"

"Two rooms, Alice, for Alex and Tommo. Within a quarter mile radius. Five star if possible, for one night only. Got that?"

"Yes, sir."

Two minutes later, Brasher clapped his hands as Alice entered with the food and drink on a large tray. She placed the tray in a space that Brasher was clearing on his desk.

Brasher stood, and said, "Help yourself, Alex. Alice, next door with me please," Alex reached for the teapot. He performed the necessary and a minute later sat with tea and biscuits.

Thirty minutes passed before Brasher returned. Alex dozed in the chair, and startled awake on the office door opening. Brasher moved to the window, stood silent for a moment, then said. "Shan't be much longer, Alex, just waiting for a courier."

Alex watched as Brasher scanned the Mall in both directions. Less than a minute later, Brasher stiffened, as a motorbike pulled up behind Tommo, revving his engine.

Ignoring the intercom, Brasher shouted, "Alice, our friend is here."

Thirty seconds later, Brasher watched from his window, as Alice handed over the A4 padded envelope to the motorbike rider. The rider stuffed the envelope inside his leather jacket, checked over his shoulder, then pulled out around Tommo's vehicle, and headed west along the Mall before turning right towards Piccadilly.

The return journey to Leeds was uneventful. The letter destined for Aadilah had been completed overnight, and was back in Alex's possession by nine-fifteen the following morning. Brasher had been explicit in his instructions, and left no doubt as to what Alex should do, and no more. Alex was on the road to Leeds by nine-forty.

The slip road off the M1 took Alex and Tommo in the direction of the Leeds city centre. At the first major roundabout, they exited the first turn-off and headed west. They arrived at Aadilah's home at one-forty-five in the afternoon. The blue light had only been used once – in a three-mile tailback just north of Luton.

In Aadilah's sitting room, Alex and Tommo watched as she sat reading the letter. Her face was expressionless. She finished reading then turned both pages over, examining them, then looked at the handwritten sides again.

She said, "Well I couldn't spot the join, and I've been married to... how did you transfer the signature to the second page?"

Alex smiled, and shook his head.

Aadilah stopped, hung her head and closed her eyes. She waited a moment then looked up to Alex.

"So, if and when they do approach me, I play reluctant, but eventually hand over the letter. You sure they'll ask for it?"

"They won't leave without it, Aadilah. Once they get wind of a suicide letter, they'll be onto you. They need to ensure that Gurp has not revealed any secrets. Okay?"

Aadilah faced the letter, but her mind was elsewhere. Alex left her in her thoughts, waiting. She turned to him.

"Will this be the end of it... them? I mean, how can you be sure? Even if you do this everyday, how can you know how they think? It's not possible."

Alex nodded. "You're right, of course. I can't *know* how they think, but, I can make judgement on their past activities, responses, planned actions, on how they will think and react in the future. The... office... has historical records, I have experience."

Aadilah rubbed her brow, and sighed.

"Okay, yeah, fine," she said.

She thought for a moment. "Am I being watched now? Do you know? Is there anyone in this street I should be aware of?"

"I can't say whether there is or not, Aadilah. All I would say is just go about your life as normal as possible from now on. And look on the whole of that letter as being the work of Gurp."

Alex gripped his briefcase at his side, and stood. Tommo made for the door, and turned.

"We'll leave you with it, Aadilah," he said.

Outside the house, Tommo closed the driver's door, and switched on the engine, as Alex once again went through this briefcase. Tommo grinned, and then sat back with his arms folded.

"How are you enjoying the office, sir?"

Alex took a long, slow breath, through his nose – his mouth tight shut.

"Permission to swear, Tommo?"

"Permission granted, sir," said Tommo, still grinning.

"I – fucking - hate – it. Do I make myself clear? No, cancel that. I do not hate it. I hate this… this item, this symbol of… of being desk bound, being sat on my arse all day, being starved of fresh air, of a filing cabinet crammed into a portable box… I…"

Alex calmed. He thought for a moment.

"I didn't say that, Tommo. That was not me speaking. We won't speak of this again."

Tommo grinned, then said. "Yes, sir. Are we ready, sir?"

Alex sighed. "We are ready, Tommo. Please, let's hit the road, eh?"

Chapter Forty-Six

<u>Nine days later</u>
Aadilah swopped over. The heavy plastic bag containing the potatoes and other vegetables was switched to her left side, and the bag holding the bread, teabags, and biscuits to her right. She stood straight, leaning back slightly, stretching her spine. She closed her eyes and groaned. Only feeling better slightly, she reached down and picked up the shopping bags again.

She'd gone nearly one hundred yards when the black Mercedes pulled alongside her. She ignored it as she walked the pavement, and it crawled alongside her, in the gutter. The car eased ahead of her, and the rear onside passenger door was swung open from the inside, partially blocking her path. She stopped, and sighed. The voice came from inside the car.

"Get in, Aadilah. Please. Get in. You look tired."

Aadilah turned, and saw the man in the back of the car. He smiled, and beckoned with a hand moving lazily. The man in the driving seat looked straight ahead.

"What if I say 'no'?" said Aadilah.

The man's expression changed. The smile dropped from his face.

"Then I will make sure you are visited in the night," growled the man.

Aadilah looked hopelessly at the bags she carried.

The man in the back said, "Chaz, see to her bags, please."

The driver was out of the car in seconds. He took the bags from Aadilah, and put them in the front passenger well, as she slid onto the back seat.

Aadilah looked to the man, he simply stared back, a half smile on his face. He held out his right hand.

"The letter. Gurp's letter, please."

Aadilah continued staring at him, as if deciding, then slipped her small, shoulder bag into her lap. She opened the bag and took out the opened envelope containing the letter.

She played the part well. "Please," she said, "don't take it from me. Read it, but please do not take my husband's last words."

The man held up a palm to her. He lifted the flap on the envelope and took out the letter. He read it, frowning, then turned over the pages and checked out the reverse sides. He told the driver to drive, and then read the letter again. For ten minutes, the driver cruised the area, while the man referred to the letter again and again.

At the man's command the driver then drove to Aadilah's house. The man returned the letter to Aadilah, and then instructed the driver to drop her shopping outside of her front door. Aadilah put the key into the front door lock, as the Mercedes was driven away.

She remembered snatches from Gurp's letter.

'... *I'm sorry... look after the children... not harm you now... I did it because... I am not a bad man... stay away from a man called Sanjar... he is evil... have nothing to do with him...he is not what he seems... he is more than a burglar... he is bad... I cannot say more... I will see you in paradise.'*

Aadilah put her groceries onto the kitchen table, and went to the sugar tin in the cupboard above the kitchen bench. She dug deep into the tin, and retrieved the cell phone. She switched it on, went into 'Drafts', retrieved the message, then pressed 'Send'. She waited for the 'Message Sent' display.

Aadilah crossed the backyard, and opened the door to an outhouse. After taking out the sim card Aadilah laid the phone on the ground. She reached up to a shelf in the outhouse, and took a hammer and a wood chisel out of a toolbox that Gurp had bought five years previously. The tools were unused.

Aadilah smashed the phone into pieces, Satisfied with her work on the phone itself, she then chopped the sim card into two pieces. She returned to the kitchen, and then switched on her gas oven. She placed the sim card pieces onto a baking tray, placed the tray in the oven, and set the oven to 220. The card cooked for sixty minutes, and melted into a mass of plastic and twisted circuitry. She then placed the sim card into the non-recyclable bin in her back yard.

*

Alex felt the vibration in his inside pocket, but left his phone where it was. He waited two minutes, allowed the minister to finish his speech, then, along with the other delegates, politely applauded, before stooping and exiting the large hall by a side door.

He pulled the phone from his pocket, along with his wallet. The wallet spread open as it fell to the ground. Alex stood on the wallet, left his foot there, and retrieved the message from the cell phone. He read – *The phone is broken.*

He deleted the message, picked up his wallet, and then paced the courtyard. He tapped his chin with the phone as he walked, and did the calculations. Time, against cost, against experience, against many lives for one life. He weighed up the possibilities, and the odds of success.

Alex had had the discussion with Brasher and, as expected, Brasher had agreed, along with the tentative sounding out of Sanjar.

The company had been set up and now two offices operated in England; one in Newcastle upon Tyne, the other in Essex.

Alex shook himself and growled, angry at his procrastination. He was acting as if a decision had to be made, when he knew fine well that there was no decision to make. The plan had been laid, and the participants were ready. He held his phone out in front of him and scrolled his contacts for T.R.I. – Thompson Research Industries. He hit the green phone symbol, and waited.

"Alex," said Tommo.

"It's on, my friend. How soon can you be in Newcastle?"

"I'm here now."

"Good. I'm on my way. I'll see you at the office."

"Yes, s... Alex." Tommo paused a beat, then said, "This new form of address is going to take some getting used to."

Alex smiled. "Get over it. See you in about four hours."

*

Balvindar watched as the baby toddled from her to Sanjar. She laughed, and the baby giggled. Sanjar held open his arms and scooped up his son. He could not keep the grin from his face. He turned to the right of where he sat and switched off the television. Balvindar looked at him, still laughing.

"I was enjoying that," she said

"No you weren't, you were enjoying our baby, the 'bairn'."

"Are you still happy with the names we chose?"

"Of course," he said. "Stephen Matthew Asad Khan sounds good."

Balvindar studied Sanjar for a moment.

"Isn't it a constant reminder for you, every time you say either name? Matty, Stephen, it must evoke memories."

Sanjar released his son, and watched as he wobble-walked back to Balvindar. He rested his forearms on his knees and interlocked his fingers. He looked into nowhere, thinking.

"I don't need names to remind me of them, or what happened to them; two innocent people, dead, because of me."

"No!" Balvindar snapped back. She scowled. "Matty was used by others, and Stephen was where he was because of what he'd done."

Sanjar bowed his head, and looked to the floor. Balvindar watched him closely. She smiled.

"Stephen Matthew Asad Khan sounds good," she said. "A bit of English, and a bit of Iranian or Persian, or whatever you want to call it. But we need to agree on which one we use. You call him Stephen, and your dad calls him Asad"

Sanjar looked up, nodding toward his son, and a smile returning to his face. "My mam and dad are okay with any name. What about yours?"

"You know, Sanjar, Things are still a bit strained with them at present."

Sanjar raised his eyebrows, shrugged, and opened his arms in a 'what can we do' manner.

"But," said Balvindar, "forget them, they'll come round eventually. What matters most is that we as a family are happy." She paused a beat. "But, baby must never know."

Sanjar nodded again, more emphatically. "Of course," he said.

The phone in the hall rang, and Sanjar stood.

"I'll get it," he said

Balvindar held out the soiled nappy wrapped in a sanitised bag.

"Here. Get rid of your son's donation to the world, while you're at it."

In the hall, Sanjar held the bag away from him, as he picked up the phone in his free hand.

"Sanjar Khan," he said.

The voice at the other end of the line was smooth, soft and friendly, with a Home Counties accent.

"Sanjar, my name is Forster, with an 'r'. I was given your name by a mutual friend who said you may well be looking for work, armed only with a degree in chemistry; no other work experience as it were."

Sanjar thought quickly. 'Who would put my name forward? Me, a near-terrorist. Tommo? Alex?'

Sanjar spoke hesitantly, suspicious. "That's true, but I am very willing, and would love the opportunity to speak to you if you think I may fit in to whatever it is you do?"

"Yes, exactly, Sanjar. Well, look, rather than waste time on the telephone, how about we meet up and have a chat. I'll tell you about my company, what we do, and you can tell me about yourself, and we'll see if we like each other. What do you say to that?"

"Yes, fine, of course. I can bring a C.V. of sorts, and…"

"Oh no need for that, old chap, my friend speaks highly of you. Look, are you free tomorrow? Say about ten-thirty?"

"Yes, certain-"

"Good. We're in Grey Street, Newcastle. In the city centre. You know what? I'm blowed if I can remember the number on the building. Anyway, halfway down on the right hand side. Do you know the street?"

"Yes, yes, I-"

"Jolly good, I'll see you then. Pleasure to talk to you, Sanjar."

"Wait, wait, what's the name of the company?"

"Ah, yes, of course. We are T.R.I. You'll see the name plate, as I say, halfway down, right hand side."

"Hang on. Who put my name forward?"

Silence.

Sanjar held the receiver away from his face and stared at it.

Chapter Forty-Seven

Tommo hit the button that was connected to the front entrance security intercom, as he looked out of his office window, down onto Grey Street. His eyes narrowed as he checked the reflection of his caller in the window of the premises on the opposite side of the street.

All he could determine was that the figure was male, and stood about five-feet ten. Yeah, the doorway was six-feet six, and judging by the gap above the caller's head, he would be about five-ten. It had to be Sanjar. The size was right, and the clock on the wall opposite Tommo's desk showed ten-thirty.

He spoke into the intercom. "Yes?"

"My name is Sanjar Khan. I have an appointment for ten-thirty – with Mr. Forster."

Tommo looked to both Alex and Nigel Forster. He smiled at Nigel.

"Ah, yes, he's expecting you," said Tommo. "If you come up to the second floor, Mr. Khan, and take the second door on your left, Mr. Forster is expecting you."

Tommo released the button, and then pressed another button that would release the magnetic door catch. He watched Sanjar on the CCTV screens as he entered the building. Tommo turned to Nigel.

"Do you need me in on this, Nigel? I'm available."

Nigel returned the smile. "Not for a while, but I would ask you, and you, Alex, to be close at hand. Let me have Sanjar to myself for a while, and then I'll bring you in, or otherwise, depending on his decision." Nigel stood. "Now, if you'll kindly show me to my room, I'll get down to business."

As Tommo and Nigel exited the office, Alex wondered. He wondered how the hell Nigel did the travelling part of his job without the need for a bloody cumbersome briefcase. He smiled to himself.

He turned to his left as Alice entered. Brasher's secretary had been released from the Pall Mall office for two days to allow her to complete the assessment of the remaining two applicants for the job of secretary and personal assistant to Tommo. Alex grinned, remembering how easy it had been to persuade Tommo to give up the natural life in the Borders. Sue was now hunting for a house on the edge of Kielder Forest.

Alex smiled. "Are you winning, Alice?"

Alice returned the smile. "Well, as far as competence and skills are concerned, I believe I've found Tommo's right hand person, but, you, and him, may want to have a chat with her. You know, give her the once over. She's in my office now. So, whenever you're ready."

Alex looked to his right, as Tommo entered. Alice repeated what she'd said to Alex, and Tommo, shrugged.

"She has already signed the Official Secrets Act in her previous position," said Tommo, "and she is experienced in… in the game we're playing, so, if you're happy Alice…"

Tommo studied them both for a moment. He could read their thoughts. Was he taking his new venture seriously enough? Was he comfortable being treat as an equal by previously senior officers?

"Aye, you're right, Alice," he said. "How about now? Let me meet my new wingman… woman." He turned to Alex. "Look, Alex, Nigel is going to be busy for quite a while, How about you sit in on this?"

Alex raised his arms. "No problem. Come on, the sooner we get this show on the road, the better."

The two men followed Alice back to her office.

Along the corridor, Sanjar waited while Nigel poured coffee. Nigel sat, smiled, and stared at Sanjar. Sanjar stared back, also smiling. After a while, Sanjar felt uncomfortable. He shuffled in his seat, dropped the smile, and stared back defiantly. Nigel nodded.

"Sanjar, I think that I can safely presume that you're expecting me to either ask you to tell me about yourself, or me to tell you about the grand new position we have for you with this company."

Sanjar nodded, slowly, still staring, lips tight together. He frowned.

"Well, in fact, Sanjar, I know more about you, than you probably know about yourself. My name is not Nigel Forster, and you will probably never know my real name, but, all being well, we will come across each other quite a lot in the future, and you will always refer to me as Nigel Forster."

Nigel paused, allowing Sanjar any questions or protestations. Still Sanjar did not move.

"At present," said Nigel, "you are in limbo. You do not know what is happening with a certain situation that is beyond your control – yes, beyond your control. You do not know whether certain people are still chasing you, whether these people exist any longer – or not, and if you will ever be able to lead a normal life."

Sanjar licked his lips. Nigel pushed a coffee cup towards him. Sanjar blinked, raised the cup to his lips and drank. He replaced the cup on the saucer, and returned to staring at Nigel. Nigel nodded.

"Let me bring you up to date. The story that was leaked is that Gurp Sahid discovered you were still an angry, radical, young man - and he said so in a suicide letter that he left to his wife. Said wife was… accosted by certain people, who then read that letter and formed an opinion of you. We firmly believe that they now feel you to still be sincere to their cause."

Sanjar shrugged. "So? That means they're not likely to kill me, and seeing as how you bust up the local crew, I would say that they expect me to be watched by you – which makes me safe again. An untouchable, if you like."

Nigel sat back in his chair, steepled his hands, and flicked his right index finger at Sanjar.

"A good deduction, Sanjar. Now, could you please tell me the one fact, or situation, that has not changed in the whole sorry escapade that you were mixed up in?"

Sanjar grimaced, frowned, and thought for a few moments. He then shrugged.

"I give up," he said.

"You, Sanjar, you. You're still a chemist, still capable of making an explosive device, and, as far as they are concerned, have never been thought of as being connected to terrorism by the British police. The British police arrested you for burglary, and re-captured you, still on the burglary charge."

Sanjar shuffled on his seat, and then leaned forward.

"Can you get to the bottom line? Tell me why you wanted to meet me here?"

Nigel stood, picked up the coffee percolator and refreshed his cup. He offered the percolator to Sanjar and raised his eyebrows; Sanjar nodded.

Nigel replaced the percolator on its stand, and turned to Sanjar.

"How would you like to work for the British Government?"

Sanjar froze. His hand taking the coffee cup to his mouth stopped, two inches from his lips. His eyes locked on Nigel for a moment, then down in front of him, to the floor, then to his left. He put the coffee cup back onto its saucer without taking a drink.

"A happy ending, Sanjar," said Nigel. "You already have... respect... from the crowd you were mixed up with, now you can earn the respect of your father's adopted country. Even help to pay a little back of what Great Britain has given to your father's family, and, it must be said, your family."

Sanjar shook his head. He stood. He moved to the window, staring down on Grey Street, seeing nothing. He spoke without turning.

"What would be my job title, and number? I gather 007 has already been allocated to someone."

Nigel smiled. "Research Consultant. And indeed you will be a research consultant. This will be your office, and you will be given a thorough grounding in the legitimate business that will operate out of this office. You will meet clients, you will attend training courses, management courses, and you will represent this company at trade fairs and exhibitions." Nigel paused for a moment, and then said, "Do you see where this is going? Are you with me, Sanjar?"

"But?"

Nigel leaned forward, and drummed his fingers on the desk. He looked at Sanjar, looking out of the window

"But nothing. That is it." Nigel sighed. "Do you honestly think they will leave you alone, Sanjar?"

Sanjar did not reply.

"The north-east area was being run by an amateur. However, that amateur had connections, and those connections are aware of you, and will contact you. Of that have no doubt." Again, Nigel paused, and then said, "You can be very valuable to this country, Sanjar."

Sanjar turned. "And if I say no?"

Nigel's response was immediate. "You will receive no help whatsoever. To any potential employer you will be an ex-criminal, a burglar, a thief. Add that to your colour, and I'm sure you can imagine the difficulties you would come up against

377

with some potential employers – qualified or not. And, be aware, you will be monitored by us."

Nigel saw Sanjar's shoulders slump. He stood and moved to alongside Sanjar at the window.

"Respect or rejection. Loved or loathed. Honoured or hated. Where's the decision to make?"

Sanjar turned to Nigel, and looked him in the eye.

"And my wife? What do I say to my wife?"

Nigel grimaced and shook his head.

Chapter Forty-Eight

Tommo shook hands with Avril Anderson, and indicated the office with a sweep of his hand.

"Welcome," he said. "Welcome to T.R.I. And I hope you enjoy working with us."

Alice watched Avril, as she looked around. "It looks… new."

Tommo laughed, and spoke as he pulled out the chair from the desk that was at right angles to the window that looked down on the street.

"It's new. Brand new. And this is your desk, Avril. The command centre as it were."

Alice said, "Start as you mean to go on, Avril. Ask Tommo to make you a cup of tea. Get the first one in."

Avril looked at Tommo, embarrassed. Tommo laughed.

"Ignore her, Avril," he said. "You'll get used to her sense of humour. C'mon, get used to your new position." He patted the chair.

As Avril sat, the intercom buzzed. She looked up, and raised her eyebrows. Tommo looked to Alice. Alice grinned.

"You as well, Tommo. You need to get used to your new position."

He returned the grin, and said to Avril, "Aye, go on. Take it."

Avril pressed the intercom button. "Avril, speaking."

Nigel's tone was kind. "Ah, good to have you aboard, Avril. Please ask Tommo if he could come along to his office, please."

And, like the professional she was, Avril slipped into action. "Certainly, sir."

She looked up to Tommo. "That was Mr. Forster, sir…

"Tommo," said Tommo. "That's one thing that will never change. I'll always be Tommo."

Avril smiled. "Tommo. He'd like to see you in your office."

Sanjar sat with his back to the door, as Tommo entered. He half turned, then turned back to face Nigel. Nigel stood.

"No, no, sir. Please, have the seat, I'll stand."

"Oh no, it's your office, and-"

"I'm in charge," said Tommo. "Please, sir. Have the seat."

Nigel grinned, and sat again. He indicated Sanjar, as Tommo moved to the right of Sanjar, and leaned his arm on the top of a filing cabinet.

"Tommo, I believe you already know Sanjar."

Sanjar turned and faced Tommo. He smiled, only half embarrassed. They nodded to each other.

"We've met," said Tommo.

Nigel watched as the two men acknowledged each other.

"Sanjar is joining the company, Tommo," said Nigel. "So, I felt it right that we should meet for a few moments, and discuss Sanjar's … induction process."

"Which will be?" asked Tommo.

380

"Not in any specific order, a trip to London, a month at Catterick, arms training, fitness assessments, parachute training, speed driving courses, you know, the usual. Then, back here in Newcastle, and the U.K. in general, a few exhibitions, trade fairs, then time in this office meeting suppliers, customers…"

"Just the usual, sir, but a bit of a crash course, eh?"

Tommo looked to Sanjar.

"You happy, Sanjar?" he asked.

Sanjar thought for a moment, nodded. "Happy, lucky, and proud to be of service." He looked to the window. "I suppose in a crazy way, Britain has proved to be what my father said it was; for all the bigotry I endured as a kid."

"Aye, well kids are cruel anyway, aren't they?"

"Not just kids, Tommo," said Sanjar. "What about you, Tommo? Are you happy with me being on board?"

"What? Because of what you were? A frightened kid who got mixed up with the wrong crowd? Listen, mate. I could tell you a few tales, believe me."

Nigel stood. "Enough, before you start crying on each other's shoulder. Time for me to go."

*

Sanjar took his key out of the front door, and pushed it open. He found Balvindar, holding his son, facing the door, sitting on the third stair up. His father stood in the doorway to the side of the staircase. They both smiled at him, expectantly. He held the

381

suspense for a moment, then laughed and held out his arms.

"I am now a salaried staff man."

Balvindar leapt off the stairs, and rushed into his arms. Sanjar cuddled her gently, looking down on their son. His father joined them, patting his son on the shoulder. Balvindar reached up and kissed Sanjar.

The phone rang, and Asad turned away from the group hug. He picked up the receiver.

"Asad Khan speaking."

Asad listened, a smile on his face.

"That is correct," he said.

Asad's eyes widened.

"Of course, of course. That is not a problem. One moment, please."

Asad put the receiver to his chest.

"Sanjar," he said, "it is for you. Your new employer. Quick. Don't make him wait."

Sanjar held on to the smile as he released Balvindar. He crossed the hall, and took the receiver from his father.

"Sanjar speaking,"

The voice at the other end of the line was female, but new to Sanjar.

"A car will collect you tomorrow, Sanjar. You will be taken to London where you will meet your directors. You will stay overnight, and return the day after. Two days after that, you will be based at the Yorkshire branch for a month. The first three days will be intensive product training with early starts and very late finishes. Do not expect to be home for those days. However, after that period of introduction to the company, you can travel daily from home, if you wish. " The voice paused for a moment, then said, "It is looking extremely possible, Sanjar, that your first customer will be in Birmingham. Do you understand?"

Sanjar nodded, and said, "Yes."

"Time to go to work, Sanjar. Time to go to work. And welcome aboard."

Sanjar looked to Balvindar. He said, "Understood," and put the phone down.

Balvindar, still smiling, said, "Everything okay?"

Sanjar nodded, smiled, and reached for his son.

Author's Comment.

The Border Region between England and Scotland is one of the most beautiful areas of the United Kingdom; thousands of square miles of rolling hills, meandering rivers, rushing rivers and gentle streams, with woodland, moorland, and meadows galore. It surely must be one of the greatest freshwater fishing spots in the world. And the castles must be seen to be believed.

And I have taken liberties with the area.

I have altered the geography of the Borders, only slightly, to suit the plot of my story. I have added a river – the Reiver River, in deference to the raiders, from both Scotland and England, who roamed the area from the thirteenth century to the beginning of the seventeenth century.

The reader would do well to visit the area, and enjoy, in particular, the region's greatest asset – the folk who live in the Borders.

Revell Cornell
February 2015

Printed in Great Britain
by Amazon